SUSPICIOUS ORIGIN

An unputdownable psychological thriller with a breathtaking twist

PATRICIA MACDONALD

JOFFE BOOKS

Revised edition 2023
Joffe Books, London
www.joffebooks.com

First published in the USA
in 2003 by Atria Books

This paperback edition was first published
in Great Britain in 2023

Cover art by Nick Castle

ISBN: 978-1-80405-732-2

To Ann, Mike and Barbara Chomko

"In thy face I see the map of honor, truth and loyalty"
William Shakespeare

ACKNOWLEDGEMENTS

For patiently answering my questions, special thanks to Jay Bethel, fire chief and bluesman, and to the winter-worldly wise Janet Miller. For their efforts on my behalf: France des-Roches, Michelle LaPautre, Jane Berkey, Meg Ruley, Peggy Gurdjin, Judith Curr, and that editorial angel on my shoulder, Maggie Crawford.

Most of all, always, to my severest, dearest critic, Art Bourgeau.

ACKNOWLEDGEMENTS

For patiently answering my questions, special thanks to Jay Bethel, fire chief and bluesman, and to the winter-worldly wise Janet Miller. For their efforts on my behalf: France desRoches, Michelle LaPautre, Jane Berkey, Meg Ruley, Peggy Gurdjin, Judith Curr, and that editorial angel on my shoulder, Maggie Crawford.

Most of all, always, to my severest, dearest critic, Art Bourgeau.

PART I

CHAPTER 1

Kevin Carmichael awoke with a start in his darkened bedroom and waited for the thudding of his heartbeat to subside. He couldn't remember the nightmare that awakened him. It vanished when he opened his eyes. But from his years of prepping psychiatrists for court testimony he knew enough to trust the lingering feeling. The affect, they called it. An anxiety dream. He'd had so many lately. Over and over he dreamed he was trapped in a maze, meeting one dead end after another, hounded by a sense of futility.

He glanced over at Caroline. She slept peacefully on her side, her abundant, caramel-colored hair spread in a thick tangle of curls across the pillow. He propped himself up on one elbow, reached over and gently brushed a few strands away from her forehead, so that he could see her face. In the dim moonlight, the vibrant peach and honey tones of her skin were faded to gray, but the hollow in her cheek was more pronounced than ever. With one finger he traced the taut, sinuous line of her back. She was an athlete, a lightning bolt on skis, religious with her workouts so that her body had the ideal proportion of muscle to curves. Gazing at the arch of her dark eyebrow, the sculpted curve of her lips, he was suffused with a familiar combination of tenderness and desire.

She looked so serene, as if she didn't have a care in the world. She never looked that way when she was awake anymore.

Kevin sighed and glanced at the clock. Twelve-fifteen. There was no way he was going to turn over and go back to sleep. He was as alert as if someone had thrown a bucket of water on his head. He could lie there, shifting positions until he either fell back to sleep, or he awoke his wife with his rustlings. Perhaps she would make a sleepy offer of a massage to help him get back to sleep. Perhaps the massage might lead to caresses and more. He'd never known a woman who stirred him the way Caroline did. Nor had he ever met a woman who could match him, need for need. From the moment they'd set eyes on one another, it had been chemistry, combustion. It was ironic, he thought, and maddening, that all their great sex was unable to satisfy her heart's greatest desire. Specialist after specialist had confirmed that she could never bear a child.

He sighed, and let her sleep. It would be selfish to disturb her.

Carefully, Kevin swung his legs out from under the duvet, stuffed his feet into slippers and reached for his robe which hung over the end of their brass bed frame. He shivered as he pulled it on, and tied the belt. It was only early December, but the Vermont winter had definitely arrived, he thought.

He tiptoed out of the room, and pulled the door closed behind him. He walked down the hall, passing Vicki's room. There was a bar of light under her door. Someone else who was not sleeping. *Serves her right*, he thought. She was the one who had stolen their peace of mind.

He went downstairs in the darkness and opened the kitchen door. Something dark and low to the ground rushed by him. "Good God," he exclaimed and then, immediately, he remembered. Of course. Vicki's eat, Kirby. Nothing would do but that she bring that flea-bitten furball with her when she moved in. And they had readily agreed to it. So far, they had agreed to quite a few things they would otherwise never have tolerated. Anything to keep her happy with them until she had the baby. Their baby. The baby she was going to let them adopt.

Kevin flipped on the kitchen light and looked around for the plate of brownies Caroline had made this morning. She didn't usually make sweets, because she was careful about their diet. But she'd wanted to make something she could give to their neighbors, the Lynches, to thank them for watching the house and the cat last week, and she'd baked an extra batch for home. Kevin began to rummage in the cupboards, wondering where she might have put the brownies after dinner. He walked over and opened the refrigerator door. There was the brownie plate all right, the plastic wrap crumpled up at the halfway point across the plate. And nothing left but crumbs. Vicki, he thought furiously. That was typical. She'd polished off the food and left the empty plate right there in the refrigerator. Sometimes, he wished he could just throw her out, bag and baggage.

Only a week ago, they'd returned from a wearying trip to Disney World. It had been no vacation for him and Caroline. Their idea of paradise was a hot tub after a day on the slopes. Not traipsing around in the heat from one silly ride to another with a pregnant teenager. But Vicki had never been to Disney World, and she wanted to go. That's ridiculous, Kevin had protested when Caroline had told him what Vicki wanted. But Caroline had pleaded with him, that stricken, anxious look in her huge brown eyes which Kevin had seen so often since Vicki had answered their personals ad. "Loving couple can offer your baby a good home, and a comfortable, happy life."

He slammed the refrigerator door, and put the kettle on for a cup of tea. It would be better for him than brownies anyway. It would all be worth it when they got the baby, he thought, as he waited for the kettle to boil. And it wouldn't be much longer until he'd be filing those adoption papers. Vicki was close to term. She'd moved in with them two months ago. *Seems like a lifetime*, he thought with a sigh.

Kevin carried his steaming cup into his study down the hall and put his feet up on the desk, tilting back in his chair. He flipped his desk lamp on, but the first place his gaze rested was on the pattern of water stains on the walls, behind his framed university and law school degrees. His curmudgeonly mood returned. *The Vicki effect,* he thought ruefully. She had left the water running in her private bathroom when they departed for Florida. Zoe Lynch, the eleven-year-old girl who lived in the next house down the road, had been coming in to feed Kirby, and noticed the flood that had already seeped through the ceiling, down the walls and all through his books and papers. Luckily, she'd called her mother, and Greta Lynch had come over, turned off the faucet, and spent an entire day cleaning up the mess as best she could. If not for Greta, they might have returned to a house ankle-deep in water.

Kevin caught a movement behind him out of the corner of his eye. He turned his head to see Kirby poised in the doorway, his yellow eyes glittering. *I suppose I ought to be glad you're here,* Kevin thought. *If it weren't for Zoe feeding you, the whole house would have floated away.* Kevin shook his head, and sipped his tea. *Relax,* he told himself. *Try to relax. It won't last forever. Once the baby comes, you and Caroline will have your life back. And your child. Vicki will have the money she wants, and she'll be gone from here. You only have to be patient a little bit longer.*

But it was hard. Caroline had quit her job as a physical therapist so that she could ferry Vicki to and from the doctor's, and the childbirth classes, and wait on her hand and foot. Kevin's income had diminished since they moved up here to Vermont, even though they had both agreed on the move. They had wanted to get away from his high-profile law practice in the city, with its attendant press coverage. Here they were anonymous. They could ski all they liked, and raise a baby in a healthier atmosphere. The practice would grow in time, but money was more of an issue than it used to be. *Keep your eyes on the prize,* he scolded himself. *For Caroline's sake.* It would all be worth it when he saw her holding that infant in her arms.

Kevin snapped off the desk lamp and returned to the kitchen, where he emptied his teacup and put it into the dishwasher. As he was about to turn and go back upstairs, he heard Kirby, mewing plaintively at the door off the enclosed back porch to be let out.

"Oh, all right," he said irritably. "But it's cold out there." Yawning, he stepped down and went to the door. The moment he pushed the door open, an acrid smell assailed him. Smoke, he thought. His first thought was of his own fireplace. They'd had a fire tonight. He had banked it before they went to bed. Could it have flamed up again? He closed the door and walked back through the house into the living room. A few embers sputtered in the hearth but that was all. *Uh-oh*, he thought. He opened the front door and stepped outside, shivering, to check around his house. The smell was stronger now, more pronounced, and as he looked out across the snow-coated field beside his house, through the border of bare trees he saw a brilliant red-and-orange glow in the spot where he normally could see the Lynches' farmhouse. "Oh my God," he said aloud. He leaned across his porch rail, trying to get a better look. All he knew for sure was that something that appeared to be a fiery ball was blazing, visible between the bare branches of the trees that separated their properties.

"Jesus Christ," he said. He rushed back into the house, dialed 911 and blurted out "fire" when the operator answered. He gave the address, and slammed down the phone.

Then he ran to the foot of the stairs. "Caroline," he screamed. "Wake up. There's a fire."

"What's . . . whatsit . . . Kevin," she mumbled, calling back to him.

"It's a fire," he cried. "It looks like the Lynches' house is on fire. I'm going over there." Not waiting for a reply, he doffed his slippers and robe and jammed his feet into some boots by the door. Then, grabbing his parka off the coatrack in the foyer, he burst out the door and began to run across the field, stumbling on the patches of icy grass in the dark, pulling on his coat as he went.

CHAPTER 2

Ray Stern and his wife, Annabel, walked out of the Coleville Public Library, stretching and rubbing their backs. "They ought to replace those folding chairs if they're going to show double features," Ray grumbled. They were part of a very small audience that had come to watch a double feature of Eric Rohmer movies, *Pauline at the Beach* and *The Green Ray*.

"But it was wonderful," said Annabel, her eyes shining. "I haven't seen those films since I was a student. Rohmer is just brilliant. A man who truly understands women."

"Well, I'm glad you enjoyed it," said Ray, even though his eyes were weary from reading the subtitles and the films of the venerable French director were altogether too talky and slow moving for his taste. It was their twenty-third wedding anniversary, and Annabel had chosen a hamburger and foreign films at the local library over an expensive dinner at some fancy inn. Ray always liked to oblige her wishes for celebrations.

"It wasn't too much Eric Rohmer for you was it?" Annabel asked.

"No, no, not at all," said Ray. After a long marriage, Ray understood enough about women to know when to keep his opinion to himself. Years ago, when Ray had met Annabel, she was an art student at NYU, here in Coleville on a ski vacation. She'd fallen in love with Ray, and the Vermont landscape. After twenty-three years here, Annabel did fairly well selling her landscape paintings, while Ray was the local chief of police. Meanwhile, their only child, Natalie, was back in New York City, studying in a premed program at Columbia.

Annabel tied a scarf over her copper-rinsed curls. "Brrr . . . It feels like snow. Did you hear the weather report?"

Ray gazed ruefully at the ring around the moon. He'd grown up here and he loved the sight of Mt. Glace and its neighboring range towering over the main street of their tourist town. He loved all the little shops and cafés on Main Street that catered to the skiers through the long winter season. It was great to live in such a scenic place, with its brief but gloriously green summer, and its breathtaking fall foliage. But sometimes, he had to admit, he got weary of the constant snow. Here it was, not yet Christmas, and they'd already had several snowfalls. Business depended on it. The season required it. But for his part, Ray always found he'd had enough of the white stuff by January. He secretly dreamed of retiring to Florida, at least for part of the winter. "Who needs a weather report?" he said. "It's always predicted."

"Come on now, Ray, don't be like that," Annabel chided him. "Everything looks so beautiful in the snow." Annabel, a city girl, never tired of the harsh Vermont winter. She scoffed at the "snowbirds" who fled to Florida at the first sign of snow, which was why Ray kept his "warmer climate" yearning a secret.

They arrived at their car and Ray opened the door for his wife. Annabel slid into the front seat and looked at the dashboard clock. "It's after midnight," she exclaimed. "I had no idea it was so late."

"You and I are getting wild in our old age," he said, climbing into the driver's seat and turning on the ignition. He winked at his wife. "Maybe we ought to go home and get even wilder." Almost the moment the words were out of his mouth, there was a squawk from the police scanner on top of the dash.

Annabel shook her head and sighed. "I don't think so . . ."

Ray listened to the scanner with a frown. "Fire," he said to Annabel, who was looking at him inquiringly. "Brightwater Road," Ray said. "There's some mighty expensive property out there. I'd better go." After all these years, they took such spontaneous changes in plan in stride. While Coleville was peaceful, and relatively free of serious crime, there was always some emergency for the police chief to attend to. "Shall I drop you at home?" he asked.

"That's the other direction. I'll go with you," she said.

"Okay," said Ray, backing out of his parking space and turning the car in the direction of Brightwater Road.

"You know, I think the Lynches live on Brightwater," said Annabel thoughtfully.

Ray frowned. "Alec Lynch? The snowmobile dealer?" he asked. "I guess he could afford it."

Annabel rolled her eyes. "That's for sure. Why is it that everything that ruins the countryside is so profitable?"

Ray shrugged. Annabel was more passionate about ecology and her adopted state than Ray, a native, was. "He's a good businessman."

"I don't know him. I do know his wife," said Annabel.

"Who's his wife?" Ray asked. "I don't think I know her."

"Yes you do. Greta. She works in Dr. Farrar's office."

"Ah," said Ray. Dr. Farrar had been their daughter's pediatrician and her role model. Now in her fifties, Dr. Farrar was a married woman who managed to raise two children, while keeping a thriving medical practice. She'd even been kind enough to write Natalie a recommendation for Columbia. Of course it had been the rare occasion when he'd been the one to take Natalie to the doctor. That had always been Annabel's department. "I'd probably know her if I saw her," Ray said.

"Greta's a blond. A real beauty. One of those women who always looks great, even without makeup."

"You know I never look at other women," Ray said solemnly.

"Right," Annabel said, and then a worried frown replaced her smile. "She's a lovely person. They've got a little girl, too. I hope it's not their house."

* * *

As Ray pulled up to the address, Annabel looked up and let out a cry of horror. This was no small kitchen fire. The rambling, wood-frame farmhouse was being consumed on one side by the raging blaze. Sirens were wailing as ambulances and fire companies from neighboring towns arrived on the scene. Two of Ray's patrolmen were already there. The Coleville Fire Department's two pumpers were rigged up and pouring water onto the flames as trucks from other towns pulled up and dumped their loads of water into a drafting tank. The WGLC newsvan was already parked there and Dean Webster, the station's irritatingly eager young reporter was in the midst of the emergency personnel, while Jeff Herrick, his seasoned cameraman, dutifully shot video.

"Stay here," Ray ordered his wife as he jumped from his car and ran closer. He looked around for Jim Shepard, the fire chief. Like all the other firefighters in Coleville, Jim was a volunteer. In his everyday life he was a pharmacist, who worked at the local Thrift Drug. Ray hoped he wasn't inside that blazing house.

"Chief," called out Sam Boudreau, one of his rookie officers.

Ray approached the uniformed man, gesturing toward the fire. "Make sure you and Porter keep all these people out of the firemen's way. And don't let anybody near that house."

"We're doing it," said Sam. "We're telling everybody to back up."

"Good. I hope there's nobody inside," said Ray.

"They went in to search," said Sam.

"Do we know who lives here?"

"The snowmobile guy. Alec Lynch. And his wife and kid."

"Jesus," said Ray, "is that somebody screaming?"

"Look," Sam cried.

The windows were ablaze and black smoke poured out the front door of the house. The intensity of the blaze seemed to be much greater on one side. A fireman, wearing a yellow helmet and a gas mask that made him look as if he had an insect's eyes, materialized in the doorway, backlit by flames, holding the limp, pajama-clad body of a young girl in his arms. EMTs rushed forward and lifted the girl out of the firefighter's arms, wrapped her in a blanket, and started to run with her toward the open doors of a nearby ambulance.

Smoke billowed out the door of the house, and then, another firefighter came trudging out, his arms locked in a bent position as if he were pulling a wheelbarrow. Several feet behind him, a second fireman was visible in the same hunched stance. Suddenly, Ray realized that there were legs hooked over the forearms of the fireman in the lead. The second fireman had his arms under the same person's shoulders. The figure of a soot-covered man in parka, boots and pajama bottoms hung hammocklike between them, his head lolling to one side. EMTs surged forward. The fireman who had been carrying the girl tore off his mask and cried out, "Get a backboard. He fell down the stairs, trying to carry the girl out."

"Is that Alec?" Ray cried.

"I don't know," said Sam.

A backboard was quickly produced. One of the EMTs was already examining the stricken man as the others strapped him to the board. "Was he conscious when you found him?" the EMT asked.

The fireman who had come out with the child tried in vain to wipe soot off his face with his glove. "Probably overcome by the smoke. You can't see your hand in front of your face in there." The fireman sighed. "I hope he's not paralyzed or something."

The EMT frowned. "Is he secured? Let's get him to the hospital." Ray and Sam edged closer as they lifted the man on the board and carried him to the ambulance. "Who is that?" Ray asked, as they passed in front of him. "That's not Alec Lynch."

Sam shook his head. "Maybe it's the neighbor. I heard he ran in to try and save the people inside."

Ray grabbed the yellow rubber sleeve of one of the passing fireman's jackets. "Did you see anyone else in there? Alec Lynch, or his wife?"

The fireman was about to answer when suddenly there was a crack and a roar and he let out a yelp. Ray turned around just in time to see the right side of the roof, where the fire was worst, cave in, sending up a star shower of embers followed by flames as the fire vented itself through the roof. The fireman began to run toward the blaze.

"Kevin," screamed a woman's voice behind Ray. He turned and saw a slender young woman wearing slippers and a parka pulled on over a nightgown. Her mass of tumbling, amber curls framed a cameolike face now contorted by fear. "My husband," she cried.

Ray took her arm and tried to calm her. "I'm Chief Stern," he said. "You're looking for your husband?"

"Yes," she said, shivering, tears running down her face. "We live over there." She gestured toward lights in the distance, holding her coat closed with the other hand. "My husband saw the fire. He ran over here to try to help. Is he still in there?"

Dean Webster approached, wielding the mike. "Chief Stern," he called out. "I need a word."

Ray angrily waved him off. "Not now," he snapped. He turned back to the distraught woman. "I think they just brought your husband out. Let's go see."

"His name is Carmichael. Kevin Carmichael," she said miserably.

"Okay, Mrs. Carmichael. You hang on to me." Propelling her toward the ambulance, Ray was able to part the crowd, exchanging brief nods with the men who were dragging hoses toward the towering blaze. Their boots crunched on the slushy, icy ground and there were shouts in the darkness, the sound of slamming doors, the screech of tires and the wail of a siren as one ambulance revved up and sped off from the scene.

"Is he in there?" Caroline cried.

"I don't think so," said Ray. "I think they took him into the van over there." They arrived at a second ambulance, as the EMTs were hooking up IVs to the man strapped to the backboard. Kevin Carmichael had regained consciousness, but his eyes were only half open as the painkillers the workers administered raced through his veins. Despite the oxygen mask and the soot on his face, Ray suddenly recognized the man. He was an attorney, new to Coleville. Ray had seen him in court a couple of times, sleekly groomed and wearing expensive suits the likes of which they rarely saw in Glace Mountain County Courthouse. Ray wished he could ask the man if he'd seen Alec Lynch or his wife in the house, but the man's nose and mouth were covered with an oxygen mask.

"Kevin, oh my God," Caroline cried and rushed to try to embrace him.

An EMT roughly blocked her way. "No, ma'am, don't touch him. He may have a back injury. We're not sure how bad it is, yet."

"I need to be with him," she pleaded.

"You can stay with him," the EMT said. "You can ride in the ambulance with him. Just don't jostle him."

Caroline nodded obediently and approached her husband, looking him in the eye and gently taking his hand. "I'm here, darling," she said.

"He's groggy," said the EMT. "He was in a lot of pain so we gave him something."

Kevin gazed at his wife. He mumbled something, but it was incomprehensible through the mask.

"Don't try to talk," Caroline murmured. "You're gonna be okay."

Ray leaned over Caroline's shoulder and looked the man in the eye. "I'm Ray Stern, the police chief. That was a very brave thing you did, Mr. Carmichael."

The man's gaze shifted slowly to Ray's face.

"The little girl's on her way to the hospital," the EMT said in a loud voice. "I think she'll be fine. We need to get you there, now, Mr. Carmichael."

Taking the hint, Ray stepped back out of the way as one EMT helped Caroline climb into the ambulance, while another slammed the bay doors closed.

As Ray turned away from the departing ambulance he saw Annabel, standing at the edge of the crowd, staring at the burning house as blackened sections of the walls began to crack and implode. He strode over to her.

Annabel looked up at him. "That must have been Greta's daughter. Was that man her husband?"

Ray shook his head grimly. "A neighbor. He went in to try and help. Brought the little girl out but he fell on the stairs and got banged up. I don't know how bad."

"God bless him." Annabel shook her head and looked back at the house. "What about Greta and her husband? Tell me they're not still in there," she said fearfully.

"I've been trying to find out. They had an oxygen mask on the neighbor, so I couldn't ask him," said Ray. "I'm going to go talk to Chief Shepard. He'll know. Are you okay here?"

"Good Lord, don't worry about me," she said.

Ray nodded and pushed his way through the crowd of emergency workers until he reached the fire chief. Jim Shepard was shouting and gesturing to the men around him. Ray waited until he paused.

"Jim . . ." he said. "What can we do?"

The fire chief shook his head and sighed. "You're doing it. All we can do now is keep people away. I just ordered all my men out of there. We've lost it. It's a surround-and-drown situation now."

"Was there anyone else . . .?"

The fire chief nodded. "Apparently the child's mother was on the second floor. It looks like the fire started in her bedroom. By the time we got here, that half of the second floor was fully involved. They could see her but there was no way to reach her. We tried going through the windows, but we couldn't get to her."

"Oh God, no." Ray glanced over at his wife who was watching him worriedly.

"No sign of the father," Jim continued. "I'll tell you. It's horrible to have to leave someone in there."

Ray shook his head. "You did all you could."

The fire chief stared at the inferno. "It went up so damn fast."

Suddenly, a midnight blue Mercedes roared up and screeched to a stop, narrowly missing a cluster of onlookers in the darkness. A dark-haired man in a leather jacket jumped from the car and ran toward the burning house. Ray recognized Alec Lynch.

"Stop him," Ray yelled, as Sam Boudreau and his partner, Randy Porter, seized the man and pulled him back to where the chief stood.

"Greta," Alec Lynch cried. "My daughter is in there. My wife . . ."

Ray grabbed the man by the upper arms.

"Alec," he shouted. "Listen to me. They got your daughter out of there."

The man peered at Ray as if he did not comprehend the words. "Zoe is safe?"

Sam Boudreau nodded. "She's in the ambulance already."

"She's gonna be all right," Ray assured him. "One of the neighbors pulled her out. She's already on her way to the hospital." Ray could hardly bear to see the panic, the disbelief in Alec's eyes as he stared at the hellish glow of the fire. "Your little girl is all right," he repeated. "She's in the ambulance. They're taking care of her."

"Are you sure?" Alec whispered.

Ray nodded. "I saw them taking her myself."

Alec stared at the blaze. Then he looked at Ray. "Greta?" he asked.

"Well, it doesn't look like . . ." Ray said, feeling like a coward for not wanting to repeat what he'd heard. "Alec, I'm afraid . . . I don't think she made it out of there."

Alec's knees buckled, and Sam and Randy Porter rushed to prop him up. Alec began to shake his head. "No. No. It can't be."

Ray pressed his lips together. This was the worst duty in the world, he thought. Having to tell people that their loved one was gone. It was always so sudden. So horribly unexpected. It was the kind of news you never got used to delivering.

"It's possible it wasn't Greta," Ray said. "But the firefighters saw a woman . . ."

Alec's eyes widened. "No," he pleaded. Then he tried to pull away from Ray. "Greta," he started to yell at the burning house.

Alec Lynch was shorter than Ray, but heavier, and very strong. Ray was glad when Sam Boudreau rushed to help restrain him. Ray couldn't have held him back by himself. Randy Porter joined them and together, they encircled the grieving man who was striving to break free and enter the inferno.

Ray felt a hand on his elbow. He turned and saw Annabel's pale face in the dark.

"Is it Greta?" she whispered fearfully.

"It looks like it," he said. Ray looked back at the fire. There were half a dozen hoses trained on it now, smoke belching from every window and door, and stubborn flames continuing to spring up in defiance of the wall of water.

"It's not her. I'd know it if it were her," Alec was insisting.

Ray nodded, recognizing the illogical reasoning of love. "I know."

"Let me go. I want to go in there," Alec cried.

"No one can go in there now," said Ray, gripping him firmly.

Annabel's lip trembled, and he could see that her eyes were bright with tears. "Mr. Lynch, I'm so sorry," she said. She tried to put a comforting hand on Alec's forearm but he recoiled and glowered at her.

"No," Alec Lynch insisted. He looked back at the burning house in disbelief. He began to shake his head furiously as if he could shake off the terrible news.

"Such a tragedy," Annabel said.

"Noooo . . . it can't be." Alec Lynch's cries rent the smoke-filled air. He covered his face with his hands, and his shoulders began to shake. The police officers released him, as he crumpled under the realization of his loss.

Ray gazed sorrowfully at the stricken man. Sam Boudreau looked questioningly at Ray. "Should I take him to the hospital, Chief? His little girl probably wants to see him."

Ray nodded his approval. "That's a good idea," he said. He spoke softly into Alec's ear. "Alec," he said. "There's nothing you can do here. Officer Boudreau will take you to see your daughter at the hospital. Come on now," he said. "You have to be strong for your little girl. She needs you."

Alec nodded slightly, staring at the ground. He did not try to shake off Ray's comforting hand. Sam stepped forward and took his arm. "Come on, Mr. Lynch. I'll drive you." Alec Lynch allowed himself to be led away, still hunched over from the shock. The TV newsmen hovered at a discreet distance from the distraught husband.

Ray watched Alec, his own heart filled with a sympathetic anguish. He pulled Annabel's arm through his and held her hand tightly. "That poor soul," Ray whispered to his wife. "He'll spend the rest of his life torturing himself . . . wondering if he could have saved her, if only he had come home sooner."

CHAPTER 3

Checking her watch and her clipboard, Britt Andersen hurried into the office across from Studio Three, Nancy Lonergan, a trim grandmother of three with frosted hair and carefully applied makeup, was gazing over the top of her tortoiseshell half glasses at a computer screen. On the monitor behind her, Donovan Smith was introducing a commercial, and mentioning the name of his next guest, a Massachusetts congressman, who would be the last guest of the night on his live talk show. "Nancy," said Britt, handing her a note off her clipboard. "Can you search this? Donovan wants to know how this guy voted on the gun control bill."

Nancy sighed and studied the note. She was used to these rush queries while the show was in progress. If a question occurred to Donovan during an interview, he expected the information right away. "Give me a minute," Nancy said, and began to rattle the keys on her computer, her fingers a blur.

Britt was always amazed at the lightning speed with which this widowed Boston matron could surf the Net. Nancy had worked as a researcher for Donovan when he was a columnist at the *Boston Globe*, and had joined him when he moved to network television. "It was a godsend," she had once told Britt. "It happened just after my husband died, so I could work nights rather than sit home in an empty house."

While Nancy impatiently urged her computer on, Britt stood beside her desk, and gazed absently at the framed photos of Nancy's late husband, Milt, her daughters and granddaughters. Britt had seen the photos a thousand times, but had never met any of the people in them. She and Nancy often stepped out for a glass of wine or a bite to eat, but Britt resisted any effort Nancy made to include her in family events and holidays. Just last week she had begged out of Thanksgiving dinner, saying she had to work. Britt preferred to think of her friend as just another single woman. Shaking her head, Nancy drew in a noisy breath. "Here we go. I'll print it out for you."

"Thanks," said Britt.

The laser printer spat out the sheet and Nancy quickly highlighted the sought-after information.

Britt lifted the page from Nancy's fingertips, ready to rush to the set when one of Donovan's assistants, an exotic, dark-haired beauty in a midriff-baring top, opened the door to the office and whispered, "Donovan really needs that voting record."

Britt handed her the page. "Why don't you run it out to him," she said coolly. Britt watched on the monitor as Donovan thanked the girl, with a lazy smile, and then, at a signal from the floor assistant, began his introduction of the congressman, smoothly incorporating the information into his remarks.

"Phew, I'm getting too old for this," Nancy said.

"Not you," Britt said. "Never."

"Really," Nancy insisted. "I've been with him for seventeen years and it never fails. At the last minute, he needs something more. I don't know why I even poured this." She indicated a mug on her desk with a tea bag string and label drooping over the side of the cup.

"Really," said Britt. She opened a bottle of water and took a swig. "Luckily, that wraps it up for the night."

Nancy picked up her mug of cold tea and lifted out the depleted tea bag. "I shouldn't complain," she said. "So many widows my age sit home at night, wishing the phone would ring. Me? I'm grateful for peace and quiet when I get home."

"Oh, I know," said Britt wryly. "This job is perfect if you have no social life."

"Well, you," Nancy chided her. "You're young. You should be out there having fun and meeting nice, *available* men."

"When would I fit it in?" Britt asked airily.

"Now Britt, you know what I think. You should get out of here. Get away from him."

"Wouldn't you miss me?" Britt asked.

"No," said Nancy firmly. "Because we would still be friends. But this job isn't good for you, Britt."

Britt glanced at her reflection in the mirrored wall. She was wearing the black turtleneck and khaki pants that were her work uniform. She had not combed her honey-blond hair since this morning, although a good haircut kept it in place fairly well. There were bluish circles under her large brown eyes. She had a wide jaw and features that looked great with makeup. She just never had time to apply any. "You're probably right," she conceded with a sigh. "I just don't have time to look for another job."

"Oh fiddlesticks," said Nancy. "You're making excuses. Taking care of Donovan has become a bad habit with you."

"You, too," Britt countered, trying to deflect her friend's advice.

"I'm not young and pretty and keeping myself out of circulation," Nancy reminded her. "I want to see you happy."

Britt sighed. "I am happy," she said firmly, wanting to change the subject. She had met Donovan Smith when she was seated next to him at a luncheon in San Francisco about three years ago. At the time, she was running the news department of a local TV station. Donovan was dazzling, and before the luncheon was over he had convinced her to move to Boston and take the producer's job for his TV talk show, a favorite with night-owl intellectuals in Boston. Their affair had started her second week on the job. Of course he was married, but at first she didn't care. It was heady and exciting. By the end of the year it was disillusioning. During her second year on the job, Donovan had started another affair with Britt's student intern. She should have quit then, but she didn't. She told herself it was a good job and she wasn't going to give it up over a failed romance. She could still work with him, and forget the personal stuff. At least that was what she told herself.

"You need to think about yourself," said Nancy.

"I do," Britt insisted. "But this is a great job." Sometimes, she thought, Nancy could overdo the motherly concern. Britt knew it was genuine, but all the same . . . She glanced at the monitor and saw the guest shaking hands with Donovan. "I'd better get out there," she said.

* * *

An hour later, Britt unlocked the door to her apartment and gratefully closed it behind her. She tossed her briefcase on a table in the hallway and picked up her mail. She carried it through to the living room and sank down into the cushions of the sofa. Among the usual bills and catalogs, a powder-blue envelope caught her eye. Britt recognized her sister's handwriting. She tore the envelope open and pulled out the sheet of notepaper. A photograph fell from the fold and fluttered to the floor. Britt bent over and picked it up. It was a school photo of a young girl with long, lank blond hair and braces, smiling shyly. On the back it said, "Zoe, grade 6." Britt held onto the photo and unfolded the note. "Dear Aunt Britt," it read. "Thank you for the check for Halloween. Sorry I took so long to write. My costume was a female vampire. I am putting the check into the bank to save it for college. I'm sending you my school picture from this year. I hope I will see you one of these days. Your niece, Zoe."

Britt sighed, studying the picture. It was hard to believe Zoe would be twelve soon and Britt had never even met her. She and Zoe's mother, her older sister, Greta, had been estranged for years. Ever since their father died. What started as a feud was now little more than a bad habit. They exchanged the occasional note or phone call, but they seemed to have little to say to one another. Britt never failed to send Zoe something on her birthday and holidays. Greta had thanked her stiffly for that during one of their rare exchanges. Still, the only way their relationship was ever going to change was if one of them broke down and went to visit the other. When Britt had lived in San Francisco, it had seemed impossible. Now that she lived back in New England, she thought about it from time to time. But every time she thought of it, she felt defeated by the prospect.

On the trunk Britt used for a coffee table sat the Christmas card that Greta had sent two years ago. Britt had framed it, and kept it there, as if to remind herself of why she didn't want to go to visit. The card was a photo surrounded by a holly-and-ivy border. In the picture, Greta, her good-looking husband and daughter were posed, smiling, around a snowman in front of their huge, pristine white farmhouse with green shutters and a lighted Christmas tree glowing on the front porch. Greta was a nurse, and her husband was a successful businessman who sold mopeds or snowmobiles or some such thing. Zoe was healthy and beautiful, and everything you could ever want in a child. The house looked like something out of a fairy tale. Britt could just picture spending a weekend there, being reminded in ways, subtle and not so subtle, of how Greta had managed to be successful in her relationships, while Britt, of course, had not.

Stuffing Zoe's note back into the envelope, Britt suddenly noticed that she was hungry. Donovan's eager young assistant had gone out to get him dinner tonight, and hadn't bothered to ask Britt if she wanted anything. Typical. Still clutching Zoe's picture, Britt went into the kitchen, and added the photo to the gallery of Zoe portraits on her refrigerator door with a magnet. Then she rummaged through her cabinets until she found some crackers and a can of Cheez

Whiz. It was better than nothing, she thought. She drank some milk out of the carton and ate her snack standing up, leaning against the cabinets while a row of Zoes, each one slightly older than the last, smiled innocently at her from the refrigerator door. How had she done it, Britt wondered? Somehow Greta had managed to get through all the heartache of their childhood relatively unscathed. After their mother's desertion, and their father's death, she had still had the will to love and to be happy. Britt, on the other hand, never seemed to be able to relax enough to trust anyone. Not that Britt would ever be interested in that provincial, small-town family life. But she knew exactly how Greta would see her choices. Interesting maybe, but empty. Proof of the selfishness Greta had always accused her of. Britt didn't need that. She liked her life. She didn't need the perfect home and all that family togetherness crammed down her throat or held up as an example of how life should be.

Britt cleaned up the crumbs, and then went into her bedroom, where a pile of books written by would-be talk show guests sat on the window seat, awaiting her perusal. *Not tonight*, she thought. *I just don't care. I'm going to watch an old movie and go to bed.* She undressed and pulled on her bathrobe. *Maybe a nice, hot bath*, she thought.

Just as she turned on the water, she was startled by the sound of the phone ringing. For a minute, her heart leaped. It was Donovan. It had to be. He was the only one who would call her at this hour. He often used to call her late at night, when he was sitting up and his wife was already in bed. That was marriage for you. His wife in the next room while he whispered that he was crazy about Britt. These days, they had hurried meetings at the studio before airtime that were all business. Maybe he was thinking about those times and missing them, she thought. And then, almost immediately, she felt disgusted by her own hopefulness. *Why would you even want him anymore? He's a career philanderer. If you had any sense at all, you'd call him and tell him to stuff his job.* She turned off the faucet and walked toward the phone.

She snatched up the receiver and growled, "Hello."

There was a hesitation at the other end. Then, a gravelly, unfamiliar male voice said, "Is this Britt Andersen?"

Britt was instantly on her guard. A single woman in a high-profile business had to be careful about callers. Especially male callers late at night. "Who is this?" she said coldly. "What do you want?"

"Sorry to call so late. I didn't know . . . My name is Alec Lynch. I'm . . . Greta's husband."

Immediately, Britt's heart started to pound. Greta's husband? Britt had never even exchanged so much as a hello with this man. And at this hour, it was something bad. Something terrible. "What?"

His words were halting. "I know you and Greta aren't . . . weren't . . . I thought I should let you know . . ."

"Something's happened," she said.

"Yes. I'm afraid . . ." He stopped and Britt heard the catch of a sob in his voice. Oh no, she thought. The room seemed to be suddenly airless. Britt could hardly breathe.

"There was a fire tonight. Your sister . . . was trapped in the house. She . . . she's been killed . . ."

Britt sat down heavily on the edge of the bed. "Oh God," she gasped.

"I'm sorry," he said in a clipped tone.

"Greta is dead?"

"That's right," he said. And then he added, perfunctorily, "I'm sure it's a shock."

A shock? Britt felt as if the man had reached through the phone and grabbed her by the throat. *No, it's not fair*, she thought. She stared out the window into the blackness of the night. A feeling of shame crept through her, making her flush hotly all over. Here she had been thinking some nonsense about Donovan Smith, while her sister . . . her only sister . . . was dying. Images of Greta flooded her mind.

Usually, when she thought of Greta, the habit of bitterness made her remember the scoldings she'd endured from her sister, the bossiness. Greta was eight years older than

Britt, and had virtually taken over raising her when their mother left. But now, Britt had a sudden, vivid memory of watching in awe as Greta got dressed for dates. Combing her shining blond hair, brushing mascara on the black fringe around her pale blue eyes. Turning to Britt for final approval. Britt's memories tumbled over one another. How Greta tried to fill the void left by their mother's desertion. Greta taught her to drive. And baked valentine cookies for Britt's class party. Tears began to seep out of Britt's eyes. She wiped them away, but new tears instantly replaced them.

Why did I blame her for everything? Britt thought. *Why didn't I make that visit and apologize to her while I had the chance? I was so concerned about what she would think of me. Now, it's too late . . .* Another thought suddenly jolted her. "Zoe?"

"Zoe's in the hospital . . . She's going to be okay, though." His voice was shaking.

"Thank God," said Britt.

After a moment's silence, the man on the other end said abruptly, "Well, I thought I should tell you."

"Yes," Britt said. His tone of voice was flat, but she didn't want him to hang up. She needed to know more. "Yes. I'm just so . . . stunned. And I'm so sorry. I know how much . . . how happy you all were. I was just looking at the Christmas card before . . ." She felt as if she was babbling. There was silence from the other end of the line but she thought she heard a muffled sob. "What happened? How did it happen? Tell me about Zoe. Are you sure she's going to be all right?"

Alec Lynch cleared his throat. "The house caught fire. We don't know how. . . . I wasn't home when it happened. Apparently it started upstairs, in our bedroom. The fire spread very rapidly. Engulfed the place. A neighbor went in and found Zoe. The firemen were able to bring Zoe and the neighbor out. But Greta was still in our room and they couldn't get to her."

Britt realized, with a desolate feeling in her heart, that she had never seen the house where they lived. She'd only seen the picture on the Christmas card. The tree, glowing on the front porch. "I still can't believe it. How did the fire start?" Britt asked.

"I don't know. I heard them say it might have been started by a candle, setting the curtains on fire or something," he said brusquely. "Anyway, the doctors tell me that Zoe will be fine, thank God. We won't have the services for Greta until Zoe is out of the hospital, of course."

Services, Britt thought. A funeral. The last time Britt had seen Greta was at their father's funeral. Where they had fought so bitterly and severed their relationship. With no parents to reunite them, it had been easy to drift apart and stay that way. She'd always thought that someday, somehow they would meet again. Now, Greta's life was over. There would be no more chances.

"Don't feel you have to come," Alec continued coldly. "If you want to send flowers. She loved flowers. . . ."

"I know," said Britt, her voice breaking. "I remember. Oh, why didn't I . . . I feel so badly. About everything. It was all so long ago. So foolish. Please, if you would, tell Zoe . . . I just got her note today. Tell her . . . I'm thinking of her."

"Sure," said the man on the phone. "I'll tell her. Okay, well, that's all. As I said, I thought I should let you know."

"Yes, I'm . . . I'm grateful that you did." Britt said. There was another silence between them. Hang up now, she thought. Instead, she said, "Where . . . is the funeral going to be there? In Coleville?"

"Yes," he said.

"I've never been there," said Britt. She looked around her familiar bedroom. She thought about her job. And Donovan, and this week's guests. Her work calendar was cluttered. Obviously this man did not expect Britt to show up for the funeral. No one did. Not even Zoe. She thought about the gallery of Zoes on her refrigerator. Greta's only child. The awkward little thank-you note on blue paper which Greta probably insisted that she write. The oversize, curliqued way her niece signed her name. Zoe. Britt took a deep breath. "I'd like to come," she said.

There was a silence from the other end.

"If that's all right," she said.

Her caller remained silent.

"You probably think its kind of . . . too little, too late, but . . ."

"Do whatever you want," he said in a clipped tone.

What she wanted to do was hang up the phone and forget he had ever called. But that would not be possible. Instead, she said, "Just a minute . . . Alec. Can you wait a minute? I need to get a pencil. I'm going to need directions."

CHAPTER 4

Britt drove toward Mt. Glace, glancing occasionally at the directions she had scrawled out while she was talking to Alec Lynch. Britt had rented a car at the airport and now she was navigating the mountainous landscape. Around every curve was a breathtaking vista. Gray December clouds hung low over evergreens which appeared black in the gloom. The ground was dappled white, gray and dun-colored. Mt. Glace loomed ahead, its snow-covered face freckled with antlike figures descending the barely visible trails. A stream ran alongside the road, rushing over piles of rocks, glinting like molten silver. Britt passed the first sign for Coleville and realized that she had almost reached her destination. It was a beautiful but melancholy place that Greta had called home, she thought.

Britt's face reddened when she thought about her call to Donovan to tell him about Greta's death and her intention to attend the funeral. She realized that she had been hoping for some expression of concern or sympathy from him. But when she said that she was going to Vermont he replied, "I didn't even know you had a sister."

Recalling Donovan's remark made her face burn with shame. She had told him about her family. He just hadn't remembered.

Yes, I had a sister, she had wanted to yell at him. A sister who once meant everything to me. But that would have only been more embarrassing. Instead, she'd said, "I thought I told you," and ended the conversation. As a child, Britt had been both coddled and disciplined by her older sister. Greta had always helped her with her homework, made sure she had clean clothes for school. On Britt's birthday, Greta had always baked her a carrot cake. It wasn't until the teenage years that Britt had rebelled. She had criticized Greta's homemaking skills, and scorned her ambitions to be a nurse. Britt's face burned as she drove along, remembering how condescending and obnoxious she had been toward her sister. *Why didn't I appreciate what she tried to do for me? Oh, Greta, I'm sorry*, she thought, and the tears rose again to her eyes and made it difficult to see the road.

Luckily, a sign for the route number which signaled the turnoff for the town of Coleville appeared in front of her. Britt made the turn and was able to drive more slowly for a few miles until she reached the center of town.

The main street in Coleville was charming, filled with quaint shops, and restaurants with smoke curling from the chimneys. People dressed in parkas and jeans came and went in pickup trucks. Others in sleek skiwear browsed the shop windows, although it was clearly not yet the height of the season. There were a number of parking spaces available, and people moved at an unhurried pace. The houses on the main street were a mixture of chalet-type buildings as well as green-shuttered, white colonial houses that appeared to be very old but extremely well kept. Britt consulted her directions again and peered at the street signs until she found a cross street called Medford Road which led away from town. She turned down it and drove, noticing that the homes quickly thinned out as she drove away from the center of town. Number 67 was a small, cedar-shingle cottage, gray with age. Alec had explained to her on the phone that it was the house of a friend, who spent the winter in Florida. Someone had called him with news of the fire, and he immediately offered Alec and Zoe his empty house as a temporary place to stay.

Britt parked in front of the house, got out of her car and stretched. Her stomach felt queasy and her teeth were chattering, both from the cold, for it was noticeably colder here than it had been in Boston, and from anxiety for the encounter that was ahead of her. On the other side of that door was a brother-in-law who was clearly resenting her arrival as an intrusion, and a niece whose growing up she had missed entirely. *Coward*, she said to herself. *They have it much worse than you. They have lost a wife and mother. Stop feeling sorry for yourself.* She left her duffel bag in the car, walked up to the front door and rang the bell.

After a few moments the door opened and the man she recognized from the Christmas card photo stood in the doorway in front of her. He was fortyish, his thick, dark hair shot with gray. He had deep-set, hooded gray eyes and sensual features in a face etched with grief. His chest, neck and shoulders were broad for a man of medium height. An unshaven stubble gave his complexion a gray tone and there were dark circles under his red-rimmed eyes.

"Alec?" she asked warily. "I'm Britt."

He made no effort to smile or look welcoming. "Come in," he said gruffly, moving to one side, to make room for her to pass. "Pardon the mess. People have been bringing us all kinds of stuff."

Britt saw what he meant as she squeezed by him into the dimly lit hallway. There were cartons everywhere full of clothing and food, forming haphazard towers, gloves, socks and shirtsleeves visible in the tops of the boxes.

"We're used to a lot more space. We had a very big house."

Instantly, Britt felt critical of him. As if a big house mattered, she thought. *You're lucky to have a roof over your head after that fire.*

"This house is cute," she said.

"Nowhere to put anything," he muttered. "Hang your coat there," he said, pointing to a hallway closet beside the staircase, "if you can find room."

His complaint irritated her. Britt had to wend her way carefully to the closet. He waited while she awkwardly jammed her full-length tweed coat onto a hanger and stuffed it in among the ballooning parkas. Then he pointed to a doorway on the right.

"This is the living room," he said. "Such as it is."

Britt entered the room. Like the hallway, the room had worn wood floors and parchment-colored walls. It was a simple, comfortably furnished room with armchairs and a sofa grouped around a brick fireplace with a white mantel and built-in bookcases covering up much of the wall space. This room also had boxes and shopping bags shoved against one wall. Curled in one of the armchairs was a somber-looking young woman with long, black hair and creamy skin. She was dressed in a tight, raspberry knit shirt and faded jeans.

The young woman looked up gravely at Britt as Alec said, "Lauren, this is my sister-in-law, Britt Andersen. Britt, Lauren Rossi. She works for me at the dealership."

Lauren gave Britt a fleeting smile and stood up to shake her hand. As Lauren rose from the chair, Britt noticed that her feet were clad only in woolly socks. A pair of hiking boots lay beside the chair on the jewel-tone oriental rug. "Sorry about your loss," said Lauren.

"Thanks," said Britt, although she couldn't help wondering what this girl was doing here, looking so at home at this moment of crisis.

Alec switched on a couple of lamps against the fading light of the afternoon. "Have a seat," he said, gesturing toward one of the armchairs. "Just move that box out of your way."

Britt set the box on the floor and sat down in the chair.

"I don't know what we're going to do with all this junk," Alec sighed. "Did you have any trouble finding the place?"

"No," Britt said. "Your directions were perfect."

"Good. I couldn't remember what I told you," he said.

"So, do I have this right? This is the first time you two have even met each other?" Lauren asked, sounding incredulous.

"I'm afraid so," said Britt.

"I'm going to get a drink," said Alec. "Anybody want something?"

"No, no thanks," said Britt.

"Lauren?" he asked.

"No thanks, Alec," she said.

Lauren watched him go, her head cocked to one side, her gaze pensive. Then she turned to Britt. "So, you live in Boston?" she asked. "I grew up there. My folks live there."

"Really," said Britt. "How did you end up here?"

"I love to ski. And I got a pretty good job working for Alec. What kind of work do you do? Alec mentioned something about television."

"My job?" said Britt. "I'm the producer of a talk show."

"Have I seen it?" Lauren asked.

"Donovan Smith Tonight?"

Lauren frowned. "Oh yeah. I think I've heard of it," she said doubtfully. She shook her wavy, dark hair. "So . . . Alec says you're not married."

"No," said Britt.

"Married to your career," said Lauren sympathetically.

Britt forced herself to smile back. She was wearing her customary wrinkled pants and turtleneck, and she hadn't even bothered to put on lipstick after the long drive. "I wouldn't go that far. I like my job," said Britt.

Alec returned to the living room with a long-necked bottle of beer and took a swig. Then he set it down on the mantel.

He turned to Britt. "Lauren brought over my suit. The one suit I have left. I'd picked it up from the dry cleaners and never brought it home from the office. Luckily."

Luckily? Britt thought.

"And the pictures. I brought the pictures," Lauren reminded him.

"Right. We lost all our pictures, all our albums . . . and we needed a photo to use . . ." He stopped in midsentence and swallowed hard, his eyes tearing up. There was an uncomfortable silence in the room. Alec took a deep breath. "For the services," he said.

"They're going to put the photo up in the church because there's no body," Lauren explained.

"No body?" Britt exclaimed.

"They had to take Greta's body to the Mid-State Medical Center to be autopsied," said Alec.

"Why are they doing an autopsy?" Britt asked.

Alec sighed. "Ray . . . Chief Stern said it's normal in any kind of violent or accidental death. Anyway, there's no telling when we'll get her back. I didn't want to wait on the funeral service. For Zoe's sake," he said.

"I understand," Britt murmured, ashamed now at her own pettiness, questioning Lauren's presence here. Judging from the generous outpouring of food, books and clothes in the scattered boxes, Greta and her family obviously had a lot of people who cared about them.

"It's such a tragedy," said Lauren. "I don't know how Alec and Zoe are coping."

"Where is Zoe?" Britt asked, looking around.

"She's asleep upstairs," Alec said. "I just got her home from the hospital this morning. She's worn out."

Instantly, Britt felt guilty. His tone made her feel as if her presence here would be putting an excessive burden on the already exhausted child. "I'm sure she is," Britt said.

Alec stood, fidgeting, and then his gaze fell on the fireplace. "Maybe I'll make a fire." He crouched down in front of the hearth and transferred logs from the basket to the hearth. "It's chilly in here," he said.

Britt wondered for a moment if Zoe might be upset at the sight of fire, after her ordeal, but she kept the thought to herself.

Alec struck a long match and held it out in front of him, staring at the flickering flame. He touched the flame to the newspapers he had wadded up in the hearth, and sat back on his heels as the flames raced up the paper to the kindling he had teepeed over it. All three of them watched the fire start, and the room was filled with an uncomfortable silence as if, after such a brief interlude, there was nothing left to say. Britt could feel a headache forming around her eyes. *What am I doing here?* she thought. *I don't belong here.* And then she reminded herself of her purpose. Zoe.

Alec jabbed at the wood in the hearth with a wrought iron poker. Then he replaced it abruptly with the other hanging tools.

"Would you mind checking to see if Zoe's awake? I'm so anxious to meet her," Britt said.

Alec frowned. "She's not going to be in much of a mood to meet anyone."

"She's the reason I came," Britt said stubbornly.

"Didn't you come because of your sister?" Lauren asked.

"Of course," Britt said.

"All right, all right," Alec said with a sigh, and walked out of the room.

"It's incredible. How long since you'd seen your sister?" Lauren asked.

Britt didn't really want to discuss it with this girl, but she knew exactly how long it had been. Their father had died while Britt was in college. She would never forget that. She was finishing her senior year internship in Sacramento, California, at the *Bee*, when Greta called to say he had passed away. He had been ill with cancer even before Britt left their childhood home in Pennsylvania. She hadn't wanted to go so far away, but it was a prestigious internship, and her father was proud of her and insisted she go. He didn't want her to miss the opportunity of a lifetime. So Britt had spent the year in California, while Greta, who had her nursing degree and her first job at a hospital, moved back home to Pennsylvania to care for their father as his condition worsened. "A long time," said Britt. "I was in college."

"You must have had quite a falling out . . ."

"It was so long ago," Britt said vaguely, avoiding the implicit question. After their father's funeral, Greta's bitterness erupted. How could you leave him, she had demanded, go thousands of miles away, never come to visit or help? Britt had tried to explain that their father had insisted she go, but Greta wasn't about to listen. Britt's face still stung at the memory of it. "You're selfish and coldhearted and you always have been," Greta had declared. "You don't care about anybody but yourself and what you want. He wanted to see you, he missed you. Didn't it ever cross your mind that he might want you to be with him at the end of his life? But no. Not you. You had more important things to do. As always."

"It's a shame you never made up," said Lauren.

"Yes, it is," Britt said. Twelve long years. In the beginning Britt had been so angry at her sister's attack that she didn't care about their estrangement. She had returned to California after the funeral and stayed on, accepting a job there after graduation. But, as time passed, the reality of their endless separation set in. Many holidays and birthdays Britt had been so lonely for Greta, for what remained of her family, that it was almost a physical agony, but her pride wouldn't let her beg for forgiveness. And Greta never offered it. As the years passed, the loneliness became a dull ache, and even when the sisters began to speak again, there was no real reconciliation between them. They were too far apart. It was too late. *It was my fault*, she thought. *My stubbornness and pride.*

"Aunt Britt?" said a soft voice.

Britt turned and saw a thin girl standing in the doorway, bony wrists poking out of an oversize hockey jersey. She wore navy-blue stretch pants and her narrow ankles were visible above fuzzy pink slippers. Her blond hair lay like lank, satin ribbons on her shoulders, and was held off her forehead by glittery butterfly barrettes. She was smiling, teeth encased in braces. Her blue eyes were the color of a spring sky, and the expression in them was eager, and innocent. She was at once Greta, as a girl, and a gallery of refrigerator-door photos come to shining life. Tears sprang to Britt's eyes. "Zoe!" she cried.

Her niece, whom she had never met, rushed toward her with open arms.

CHAPTER 5

Britt rose from the chair and took a step toward Zoe who hugged her around the waist, burying her face in Britt's sweater.

"I'm so glad you came," said Zoe in a muffled voice.

For a moment, as she embraced the girl, Britt could not speak. Tears flooded her eyes and constricted her throat. She wanted to hold her, and keep on holding her, inhaling Zoe's lemony scent, and feeling, for the first time, that she had done exactly the right thing in coming here. "Me, too," Britt finally replied awkwardly, wiping her tears away. "How are you doing? Are you all right?"

Zoe loosened her grip and leaned back, looking into Britt's eyes. "My throat's pretty sore. Not too bad."

"No, not too bad, considering what you went through."

"And what happened to Mom . . ." Zoe said, and then her voice broke.

Britt looked at her helplessly. "I'm sorry," she said.

"All right. Here you go," said Alec Lynch, taking a folded Indian blanket off the arm of the couch. "Go sit down." Reluctantly, Zoe released her aunt, and moved over to the sofa.

"Hi, Zoe," Lauren said. "How are you?"

"Better," said Zoe. She curled up in the corner nearest to the fireplace, leaving her fuzzy slippers side by side on the floor. Alec draped the throw over her lap. "You've got to keep warm."

Britt felt drawn to the girl, and had the urge to go sit beside her on the sofa, and put an arm around her, but she didn't want to invade Zoe's space. She sat back down in the armchair.

Zoe looked at her sadly. "Will you sit here with me?" she asked.

Britt's face reddened. "Sure," she said, "I'd like to." She crossed over to the sofa and sat down beside her niece. Zoe rearranged herself so that she could lean against Britt. Britt put her arm out behind Zoe, across the low back of the sofa. "Is that okay?" she asked.

Zoe nodded.

"Good," said Britt. And though, ordinarily, she was a little bit prickly about physical closeness, it did feel comfortable to have the shivering, coltish girl leaning on her. Surprisingly comfortable.

"So, how about that, Zoe?" Lauren asked in a friendly way. "Your aunt is here."

"It's cool," Zoe murmured, twisting her hands nervously. "Dad, can I have a drink?"

Alec, who was still standing, nodded. "Sure. What do you want?"

"Soda?" Zoe pleaded.

Alec rolled his eyes. "Soda again? All right. Lauren, soda?"

Lauren gazed wistfully at Alec. "No. I should get back to work," she said unconvincingly, as if she were hoping he would tell her to forget about work today.

Britt gazed down at her niece's gentle profile. "I'm lucky to be sitting here with you. That was a pretty close call," she said. "Do you remember what happened?"

Zoe frowned. "I don't remember anything. I went to bed, and I fell asleep and I woke up in an ambulance, on my way to the hospital with some mask over my face."

"They were giving you oxygen," said Lauren.

"The fire chief said it was a miracle Mr. Carmichael was able to get me out of there," said Zoe.

"Sounds like it," Britt said. "Who's Mr. Carmichael, anyway?"

"He's our neighbor. He saw it first and called the fire department. Then he came searching in the house. They told me he fell on the stairs while he was trying to get me out of there," said Zoe. "I don't even remember it. I tried to go see him in the hospital but he was in the X-ray room."

"Thank God he came after you," said Britt.

"Amen," said Alec fervently, returning to the room with Zoe's soda. "I'll never be able to repay him."

Zoe nodded thoughtfully. "I fed their cat when they were away. Now I wish I hadn't taken the money for it. The next time they need me I'm gonna do it for free."

Britt smiled. "Are they close friends of yours? The Carmichaels."

Zoe and her father exchanged a glance.

"Greta and Caroline were friendly, I guess," Alec said carefully. "They've only lived here for what . . ." He looked at Zoe, his hands gesturing widely.

Zoe shrugged. "I don't know. They were here last Christmas."

"Maybe they've been here a year or so," said Alec.

"And then Vicki came with the cat," said Zoe. "Around when school started. I love Vicki's cat. He's so cute. His name is Kirby."

"Oh, a cat lover," said Britt. "Do you have a cat?"

Zoe shook her head and tears came to her eyes. "Mom's allergic. Was allergic," she corrected herself.

Britt squeezed her shoulder. "That's right," she said. "I forgot."

Alec handed Zoe her glass. "Here you go, sweetheart. Seven-Up. Zoe loves all animals," he said proudly. "She's crazy about horses."

"Really?" said Britt.

Zoe nodded. "Dad's gonna get me one. Was gonna get me one. We were gonna fix up our barn. . . ." Her voice trailed away.

"Tell your aunt about the ranch," Alec prompted her as he sat on the edge of one of the armchairs.

"I went to a dude ranch this summer with 4-H."

"It cost an arm and a leg but you enjoyed it," said Alec.

"I never slept away anywhere for a week before," said Zoe. "Mom cried when I left." Zoe fumbled in the pocket of her pants for a Kleenex and then wiped her tears.

"That's a big step," Britt said.

"My mom told me you two had a big fight." said Zoe solemnly. "Were you still mad at her?"

Startled at the child's frank question, Britt shook her head. "No. Not really. I just wish . . . I wish I'd had a chance to say I was sorry. Now it's too late."

"You didn't know this was going to happen," said Zoe.

"Let that be a lesson to you, Zoe," said Lauren, who had pulled on her hiking boots and was slowly lacing them up. "Now, she'll never have the chance to make it right."

Britt blushed. Lauren's assessment was accurate but unwelcome.

Zoe assumed the role of comforter, patting her aunt's hand. "She wasn't mad at you anymore. She told me that, too."

"Enough about that. Your mother didn't think about it all that much," said Alec dismissively.

Britt recognized the unspoken implication that she wasn't really a part of their lives. "I'm sure she didn't," said Britt. "Well, I'm imposing. You're probably both exhausted. I need you to direct me to a hotel where I can stay while I'm here . . ."

"Oh no, stay here with us," said Zoe, clutching her hand.

"No, I can't stay here," said Britt, looking around at the piles of boxes, the general disorder, and the aversion in Alec's expression. "I'd just be in the way."

"You have to," Zoe cried. "Tell her that, Dad. She has to stay here with us. I want her to stay . . ."

"Look, Zoe, your aunt wouldn't be comfortable here . . ."

Zoe looked anxiously at Britt. "You wouldn't mind, would you? This is my only chance to see you . . ."

"Now, wait a second," said Britt. "We're going to have lots of chances after this. Believe me . . ."

"No, we won't," Zoe wailed. "We never will . . ."

A sudden knock at the door interrupted her. Alec disappeared into the hall. They could hear the murmur of voices.

"There's twin beds in the room," Zoe pleaded. "You can share with me. I don't have much stuff here. Most of my stuff got burned up, anyway. Please, Aunt Britt. . . ."

Alec reappeared in the living room, followed by a tall, trim middle-aged man with thinning hair. "This is our chief of police, Ray Stern," he said. "This is Lauren Rossi, who works for me at the dealership, and my wife's sister, Britt Andersen. Britt just arrived from Boston for the funeral. And you know Zoe," Alec said.

They shook hands all around. Alec indicated his armchair and Ray Stern sat down. "You're looking a lot better, Zoe," Ray said kindly.

"Thanks," Zoe said.

"I won't take up too much of your time. Tragic about your sister."

Britt was ashamed, feeling that she didn't deserve condolences. "Thank you."

Ray looked up at Alec. "Can we . . . uh . . . talk privately?" He cocked a warning glance in Zoe's direction.

"Oh, sure," said Alec, looking a little startled. "Lauren, will you take Zoe out to the kitchen? There's all kinds of food out there that people have brought over. Get her something to eat. Get yourself something, too."

Lauren nodded. "No problem. Come on, Zoe. Come with me." She extended a hand to the girl. Zoe got up, looking anxiously from her father to the police chief. She went along with Lauren, as she was supposed to, but avoided taking her hand.

Alec glanced at his sister-in-law. "Britt, weren't you getting ready to leave?"

Blushing, Britt started to get up, and then she hesitated. "I'd really like to know," she said stubbornly. "I'd like to hear what happened to my sister."

"You can stay, if it's all right with Alec," said Ray.

Alec scowled and avoided looking at Britt. "Fine. Do what you want."

Ray cleared his throat, and continued. "I've just . . . uh . . . just come from the house. The fire inspector, Todd Griswold, was there."

Alec was drumming his fingers on the mantel shelf. "Was he able to figure out how the fire started? Are they still thinking it was a candle? Because I had all the wiring in that house replaced. And if he says it was electrical, some heads are going to roll at Mountain Power . . ."

"It wasn't an electrical fire," Ray said. "They're pretty sure now that it was ignited by a candle."

Alec shook his head. "Greta was a great one for candles. Loved candlelight. And those aromatherapy, green tea candles. She loved that stuff. I always had to remind her to blow them out before we went to sleep."

Ray shifted uneasily in his chair. "Alec," he said, "were you doing any painting in the house? Anyone using paint thinner?"

"We probably had some in the basement," Alec said.

"I'm talking about upstairs," said Ray.

Alec frowned. "No," he said. "We had the whole place painted about two years ago . . . Well, actually, wait a minute. Now that you mention it. Greta was doing those stencil borders. You know, around the doors and windows . . ."

"In your bedroom?" Ray asked.

"No, not in our bedroom. In the guest room. She may have just left all the painting stuff out since nobody was staying there."

"The guest room?" Ray said, obviously surprised.

"Yeah," said Alec. "Why?"

"Well, that changes things," said Ray, frowning.

"Why? What do you mean?" said Alec.

Ray shook his head. "I hadn't thought . . . you caught me off guard. I have to ask—you and your wife, Alec. Everything was all right between you two?"

"Yes," Alec said quickly. "Of course. Why are you asking me that?"

"Well, there were paint cans and paint thinner in the room where Greta's body was found. As well as candles. We had assumed it was your bedroom. Now, from what you're telling me, the fire must have started in the guest room."

All the color drained from Alec's face.

"Any reason you can think of why she might have been sleeping in the guest room?" Ray asked.

Britt looked curiously at her brother-in-law.

"Maybe she was having trouble sleeping," Alec murmured. "Sometimes she got restless at night, and she didn't want to disturb me."

"But you weren't home at the time the fire started," Ray observed.

Alec frowned. "No, I was at the dealership, doing taxes. I came home to eat some dinner and then I went back. . . ."

"So, you weren't there when Greta went to bed," said Ray, frowning. "You don't know any other reason why she might have gone to bed in the guest room?"

"No," said Alec sharply.

"I'm sorry to put you through this, Alec. But I'm sure you understand. Until we can determine what happened . . . What about insurance?"

"What about it?" Alec bristled. "We had fire insurance, of course. A house that size? Who wouldn't?"

"What about life insurance?" Ray asked.

"We had life insurance," said Alec uneasily. "Don't you?"

"A lot of life insurance?" Ray asked.

"Hey, I was getting threats from these environmental nuts. They think I'm a menace to society. Including my wife's boss, Dr. Farrar," he said sarcastically.

"I'll need the name of your insurance agent," Ray said.

"I'll write it down," said Alec. Britt, studying him, thought she saw something evasive in his eyes.

"These are all routine inquiries, Alec," said Ray in a reassuring tone.

Lauren poked her head into the room. "All right to come back in?" she asked.

Ray stood up from his chair. "Come on in. We're just about done."

Zoe, who trailed Lauren into the room, piped up in a scratchy voice. "How come I had to leave?"

Ray looked kindly at the young girl. "Just police business. Grown-up stuff. We have to ask a lot of questions. Until we can figure out what happened. We can't rule out the possibility of. . . . We just have to ask a lot of questions."

Arson, Britt thought. *He was about to say "arson."*

"Here," said Alec, shoving a piece of paper at the chief on which he had been scribbling. "This is the insurance agent. It wasn't *that* long ago that I talked to him. It was Greta's idea actually, that we increase it."

"Really?" said Ray. "Okay. I'll speak to him." He glanced over at Lauren. "Miss Rossi, you work for Mr. Lynch at the dealership?"

"Miss Rossi is my assistant," Alec said.

"Mr. Lynch told me he was working late that night. Were you at work on the night of the fire as well?" Ray asked.

Lauren hesitated, her eyes wide. "Um . . . yeah," she said uncertainly.

"Lauren," Alec said in a warning voice.

Ray frowned at her. "Miss Rossi?"

"I was thinking back, trying to remember that particular night," said Lauren. "I work a lot of nights."

"So you can verify that Mr. Lynch was working at the dealership that night."

"Yes," Lauren said softly. "Absolutely."

"Kind of late to be at work, wasn't it?" Ray asked.

"We were behind in the paperwork," she said.

Ray nodded and replaced his hat carefully on his head. "Okay, good. That's what your boss told me. Well, I'll leave you all in peace now. You get to feeling better, Zoe."

"I will," Zoe said.

"Ladies."

Alec walked out with the chief while the others sat in stunned silence. When Alec returned to the room, Britt stood up and said, "I'd better be going, too. You don't need company at a time like this . . ."

"I thought you came here to see me," Zoe protested.

"That is what I came here for. I'll stay somewhere right nearby. Alec, can you tell me where I might get a room?"

Alec raked his fingers distractedly through his hair. "I don't know. I can't think. . . ."

Lauren said, "Well, there's the Glace Mountain Lodge. And there's a number of B & Bs that are nice . . ."

At this, Zoe's face crumpled and dissolved into tears. She buried her head in the crook of her elbow which rested on the arm of the sofa. Her thin little frame shook with sobs.

Britt looked helplessly at her niece.

"Honey," Alec pleaded, "what's the matter?"

"Why can't she stay here?" Zoe cried.

"She doesn't want to stay here," said Alec sharply.

"You and your dad need privacy," Britt tried to explain.

"No," Zoe insisted, stamping her foot like a toddler having a tantrum. "We don't need privacy. We need you."

"Zoe, that's enough," Alec said. "Please, I've got enough to deal with . . ."

"It's your fault she's leaving. You want her to leave. You're being mean."

Alec glowered at Zoe. "Zoe, stop it . . ."

The last thing Britt wanted was to stay in the house with them. But she was shaken by Zoe's fit of weeping. "Look . . .

All right," Britt said. "All right. Take it easy. I'll stay. I'll be glad to stay. If it's all right with your dad."

Zoe wiped her tears on the sleeve of her jersey and looked at her father.

"I guess so," he said grudgingly. "I don't care. Just stop crying."

Zoe beamed through her tears and then started coughing.

Alec grabbed the glass of soda and handed it to her. "Drink this," he said, "and settle down now."

Zoe took a sip.

Lauren stood up from her chair and shook out her dark, wavy hair. "Well, I'm gonna go. I've got to get this picture of Greta blown up for tomorrow." She held up a manila envelope. "I'll bring it to the church in the morning. Do you want me to get a frame at the photo place?"

Alec shook his head. "They've got some kind of easel rigged up."

"Do you need anything else?" Lauren asked Alec.

"We're okay," he said.

Lauren turned to Britt. "Nice to meet you. Despite the circumstances. I'll see you tomorrow at the services."

"Right," said Britt.

"Bye, Zoe," said Lauren, but didn't wait for a reply.

"Lauren, let me walk you to your car," Alec said quickly, starting to follow her out the door. Then, obviously as an afterthought, he turned in Britt's direction, although he avoided her gaze. "Make yourself at home," he said.

Zoe was watching her aunt hopefully. Britt forced herself to smile.

CHAPTER 6

Accompanied to the door by whirling snow flurries, the mourners hurried into the church and found seats in the wooden pews as an organ played hymns from the loft.

In the quiet vestry of the church, Britt lingered, staring at the large photograph of her sister, which had been mounted on cardboard and set on an easel. She gazed in amazement at the changes she saw in her sister. The picture that Alec and Zoe had chosen was of Greta kneeling in her garden, a blossoming begonia in one hand, a garden trowel in the other. Her long blond hair was in a French braid and she was looking over her shoulder at the camera in mild surprise, as if she had been interrupted in midmeditation, a pensive look in her eyes. She was still beautiful, as she had been when she was young, but her face had grown thinner, her eyes sadder with time. For Britt, it was a difficult photo to look at. When they were kids they'd had a similar photo of their mother in her garden which they always kept hidden from their dad. The difference lay in the expression in the eyes. Greta looked thoughtful and mild. Their mother's eyes had flashed with impatience and dissatisfaction.

Britt was glad to turn away from Greta's photo when she felt someone tap her on the shoulder. A tall, elegant gray-haired woman in a black suit, accompanied by an equally formidable-looking gentleman, regarded her quizzically.

"Are you Britt?" the woman asked in a quiet voice.

"Yes," Britt said in surprise. She had been introduced to a few people this morning, but this couple was unfamiliar to her.

"Oh, yes. You remind me of her," said the woman. "Not that you look alike, but the way you stand, gestures, that sort of thing. She told me all about you. She was so proud of your television career."

"She was?" Britt asked. "I didn't realize that. I'm sorry. I should know you . . ."

"Oh. I'm Olivia Farrar. This is my husband, Wallace. Your sister worked for me for a number of years."

"You're the doctor," said Britt vaguely, shaking Olivia's cool, dry hand. "It's nice to meet you." Britt was still taken aback by the information that Greta had boasted of her accomplishments.

"Unfortunately, we were running a little late because I had an emergency. This is my son, Derek, and my grandson, Pete," Olivia said as another tall man approached, carrying a child in a bow tie.

"It's so nice of you all to come," said Britt.

"I don't know how Mother's going to manage without Greta," said Derek. "Mother, I'm going to take Pete in. He's getting restless."

"You go ahead, dear," said Olivia. She turned back to Britt and joined her in gazing at Greta's picture. "This is a terrible tragedy. Someone so beautiful and good. I guess our only consolation is that Greta's suffering is over now."

"Her suffering?" Britt exclaimed. "What do you mean? Was she sick?"

Dr. Farrar frowned. "I thought you knew."

"Folks," whispered the undertaker in charge, "you'd better take a seat. They're about to start."

Olivia took her husband's arm. "We'd better sit, darling."

"Wait," said Britt. "What do you mean, 'her suffering'?"

"I'm sorry," said Dr. Farrar. "It's all over now, anyway. Nothing we can do for her. Come along, Wallace."

The Farrars hurried into the church. Numbly, Britt followed them, walking toward the front pew where Zoe was seated beside her father. Alec was wearing the tailored gray, pinstriped suit, which Lauren had brought over from the dealership, with a black shirt and a gray satin tie that made him look like a gangster. His arms were crossed over his broad chest and his hooded gray eyes stared blankly ahead. Beside him, Zoe slumped in the pew. She was wearing a pink parka, pulled this morning from the bags of donations, the sleeves of which were too short for her. Her blond head was bent low over her tightly folded hands.

Britt leaned down and whispered into Zoe's ear, "Can I get in here?"

"Sure," said Zoe dully. She squeezed up against her father and gave him a little shove. Alec looked startled, as if he had been asleep. Britt slid into the seat and looked around. The church was full. Most of the people she didn't recognize, of course, although she did see Lauren Rossi, dressed in fake fur and black lace, in the fourth row, and the police chief, Ray Stern, standing near the back. Britt swiveled around and faced forward as the minister led the gathering in prayer and a few hymns, and then he stepped up to the lectern and asked if there was anyone in the large gathering of mourners who wanted to say a few words about their departed friend, Greta.

Alec Lynch bent his head down and whispered something to Zoe, who was weeping softly. Zoe shook her head miserably. The room was silent and for a moment, Britt had a panicky feeling that no one would get up to speak. She knew she should do it, but she had not prepared anything to say. A pleasant-looking woman in a blouse and skirt printed with autumn leaves walked up to the lectern and smiled nervously.

"Mrs. Dietz," Zoe whispered, and tears trickled down her cheek.

"My name is Joyce Dietz. Greta and I met through our daughters. Kayley and Zoe have been friends for years. Greta and I were Brownie leaders together and she was somebody you could always count on. She loved her daughter more than anything and she just wanted to make a good difference in the world and, in my opinion, she did. She really did. She was the kind of person who, you could ask to do anything, any favor, and she would do it. She really cared about people and wanted to help. I'm really going to miss her . . ." said the woman, her voice trailing off at the end. She stepped down from the lectern and hurried to her seat, winking at Zoe through tears as she passed by the pew.

For a moment, there was silence again, and Britt knew she should get to her feet. Zoe was looking at her expectantly. Reluctantly, Britt started to rise, not knowing what she was going to say or how she could get through it without breaking down. Britt left the pew and walked to the lectern. She gripped the edges of the shelf with sweaty palms and looked out at the sea of faces.

"My name is Britt Andersen," she said. "I am . . . Greta's sister. Greta and I were very close once upon a time, but we've been estranged for years and it was all my fault." She paused, fighting back tears. "We . . . I let a stupid argument come between us. I kept thinking there would be time to make up . . ." Britt's voice cracked and she stopped for a moment, forcing herself to feel what the words meant. Then, she continued. "There's nothing I can do to make that up to her. Now she's gone and I'll just have to live with my regret. I just want to say today, in her memory, if there's someone in your family you think you don't want to talk to anymore, you should think again. Because, believe me, when you *can't* talk to them anymore . . . not ever . . . you may regret it someday." She saw Alec lift his head and stare at her. She didn't want to meet his unfriendly gaze. "I want to say that I'm very sorry to my niece, Zoe, for being absent all these years. I won't disappoint her again. I owe that to my sister. I owe her much more than that, but all I can do is . . . try to be more like Greta. Try to make this loss up to my niece, any way I can."

Britt hurriedly resumed her seat. Her blood was pounding in her ears, and she could barely hear the next tribute which came from an elderly man who leaned on a cane as he told how Greta did errands for him after his wife died and tried to help him out. The minister called for any last speakers. He looked over at Alec questioningly.

Alec sighed, staring at the floor, and then rose to his feet and approached the lectern. He stood there for a moment, the light from the chandelier above him haloing his dark head. "I'm not sure I can do this," he said. He took a deep breath. "I married Greta when I was a very young man. We were both young. We didn't know very much about what we were doing. But we did pretty well," he said, and then his voice broke. There was a hush in the church as he struggled to force the words out. "I wanted to take care of her. And I tried to . . ." he began again, and then he stopped, swallowing his tears, wiping his eyes.

There was a disturbing murmur and rustling from the rear of the church. Alec looked up, and Britt turned around in time to see a shadowy figure making its way out of the pew. Britt was startled to see someone interrupt such a poignant moment. Then, as the mourner reached the center aisle, Britt realized that it was Olivia Farrar gliding to the exit. It must be an emergency, Britt thought. Someone must have paged her. But she couldn't help remembering Alec's remark to the police chief. It sounded as if he and Dr. Farrar were at odds, and she wondered if perhaps that was why the doctor was leaving. She looked icy and composed, her silvery hair gleaming like sterling under the lights.

Alec waited until she was out of the church. Then he said abruptly, "Thank you all for your generosity, and for being here today to help us get through this," and stepped down. The minister resumed his place at the lectern and brought the service to a close with a few hymns and a homily.

The mourners in the pews began to don their coats, but the minister indicated that he had one more thing to say. "Before you go, Alec and Zoe invite anyone in need of some fellowship, or who wants to show their support to the family, to gather at the home of their neighbors, the Carmichaels. They live the next house over from where the Lynches . . . used to live and have offered their home today for fellowship. Thank you for attending this funeral service for our sister, Greta. May the Lord bless your coming in and your going out, now and forevermore . . ." He made the sign of the cross, and the congregants began looking toward the door.

As they got up and began to file out of the church, Britt felt Zoe's hand slip into hers. Britt squeezed it, and glanced down at her niece, whose face was pale and streaked with tears. "I wanted to talk about Mom, but I couldn't," said Zoe.

"Everyone understands," Britt assured her.

As they passed the fourth pew, Britt noticed Lauren waiting anxiously, and then easing herself out of the pew and into the line of mourners beside Alec Lynch.

"Ouch," said Zoe.

Britt realized she was crushing Zoe's hand in her own. She let go of the girl's hand and they were separated by the crowd as it surged out the front doors of the church. The snow flurries had stopped but the sky was still a blinding grayish white in color. As she stood at the top of the steps, Britt felt as if someone was staring at her. She scanned the crowd and then reddened as her gaze locked with that of a ruggedly handsome young man with a tanned face and wheat-colored hair that had been blown dry into a style of perfect, casual elegance. He was wearing a work shirt and a tweed jacket, and he looked as if he'd just stepped out of a Ralph Lauren ad. Britt looked away but she could still feel his gaze following her as she descended the steps.

Britt looked around and saw Zoe, at the foot of the steps beside her father. Alec, shadowed by Lauren, was standing to one side, accepting hugs and condolences. He rested one hand on Zoe's narrow shoulder as if to keep her planted there. Britt walked toward them, but before she reached them, she could see out of the corner of her eye that the good-looking guy in the tweed jacket was approaching her.

"Miss Andersen?" he said politely.

She turned and stared at him in surprise. Up close, he looked younger than he had from a distance. Young, virile and voracious. She hadn't had a man look at her like that in a long time—as if he wanted to devour her. It was undeniably flattering.

"Sorry to bother you. My name is Dean Webster," he said. "I work for WGLC-TV. Someone told me you're Donovan Smith's producer in Boston?"

Taken aback, Britt frowned at him. "Who told you that?"

"Oh, no secrets in this town," he said, grinning. His teeth were even and white against his tanned complexion. "Everybody knows it when there's a celebrity in town."

"I'm not a celebrity," she said severely.

"Well, I'm a big fan of the show. I wanted you to know."

"Thank you," said Britt.

"I know you're Mrs. Lynch's sister. I'd like a chance to sit down and do an interview with you."

A reporter on the make, she thought, a little embarrassed that she had mistaken his interest in her for attraction. "This is not the time," she said.

"Could I give you a call? Do you have a cell phone?"

"I'll call you," she said firmly.

"Be sure you do," he said, pulling a card out of his inside jacket pocket. "This is a big story. I'll really look forward to sitting down with you."

Alec walked up to Britt, and Dean Webster assumed a somber expression. "Mr. Lynch. Sorry about your wife. Can we sit down and talk . . .?"

"No," Alec barked. "You're like a vulture."

"Just doing my job," said Dean, and he withdrew, winking at Britt.

"I hope you're not going to talk to him," Alec said.

Britt ignored his warning. "What is it you wanted?" she asked.

Alec frowned at the departing reporter. Then he looked back at Britt. "Well, I guess you heard. Our neighbors invited everybody over to their house for a little while," he said.

"They've got a nice place. He's a big attorney. He's the one that saved Zoe . . ."

"I know. That is very nice of them," said Britt. "No trip to the cemetery, anyway. Where are you going to have Greta buried when the police release the body?"

Alec shook his head abruptly. "No burial. Cremation."

Britt couldn't conceal her surprise. It seemed redundant, even ghoulish, to cremate someone who had suffered and died in a fire. "Is that what Greta wanted?"

Alec shrugged. "It wasn't something we ever discussed. You know. We figured we had years before we would need to think about such things."

"But shouldn't Zoe have a . . . headstone? You know, somewhere she can got to . . ."

"Visit her mother?" he said sarcastically. "Her mother is dead. I don't see that she's going to find much comfort in visiting a headstone."

"How do you know? Did you ask Zoe what she wanted?" Britt demanded.

Lauren had come up and was standing a discreet distance from Alec. She was wearing a fake fur chubby over a black lace top, black pants and open-toe pumps. "Alec is only trying to do the right thing," she said protectively.

"It's okay, Lauren," said Alec. "She doesn't bother me." He turned to Britt. "Leave your car and you can ride with us to the Carmichaels'," he said.

"No, thanks," said Britt. "I'll drive myself."

"You don't know where it is," he said.

"I'll find my own way," she said.

"Fine," he said. "Zoe. Come on."

Britt turned around and saw Zoe surrounded by a group of reluctant, puffy-eyed preteens. They were gazing at Zoe with a mixture of pity and admiration, as they tried to imagine themselves in her shoes, their own lives derailed by such a terrible twist of fate.

CHAPTER 7

Following the black limousine from the church, Britt arrived at the Carmichaels' and entered the house close on the heels of Zoe and Alec. Inside the house, there were groups of people in dark clothes, talking quietly. Zoe and Alec were immediately surrounded by friends, offering kisses and condolences. Britt felt distinctly out of place. A beautiful woman with honey-colored hair approached her. She was wearing a sleeveless, navy-blue shift, and the muscles of her arms were smooth and sculpted. "Are you Britt? I'm Caroline Carmichael."

Britt smiled at her gratefully. "Yes. Nice to meet you. It was so nice of you to invite everyone," she said to Caroline. "Especially with your husband just home from the hospital himself."

"No trouble at all," Caroline said. "Your sister would have done the same for me." Caroline's smile was tight and fleeting. "I presume you know everybody here."

"Actually, no. I've only met a few of these people," said Britt. "I've never been to Coleville before."

"I heard what you said in church," said Caroline carefully. "You and your sister didn't . . . talk to each other often?"

"No, not at all," said Britt. "I'm sorry to admit."

Caroline's stiff posture seemed to relax a little bit. "She was a lovely person."

"I know," said Britt. She looked around the room, hoping to see Dr. Farrar. She was still curious about the comment she'd made in the church about Greta's suffering. She wanted to ask her about it, but apparently the Farrars had not come to the gathering. "Were you two good friends?" said Britt.

"We hadn't known each other that long," Caroline demurred.

Britt knew she should begin to wade into this crowd of people and introduce herself, but she was reluctant. "How is your husband doing?" she asked Caroline, stalling for time.

Caroline sighed. Despite her tumble of gleaming hair and her flawless, peachy complexion, she looked haggard. "Well, actually, it's not as serious as it could have been. He cracked a couple of ribs. But right now, he can hardly get around. I set up a bed in his office for him, for the time being. It's not very comfortable, but he can't climb the stairs yet so we have to make do. He's a terrible patient. He doesn't want to stay put."

"That's rough," said Britt.

"Especially with a baby on the way," said Caroline.

Britt glanced at Caroline's figure, trim in the navy-blue sheath, and frowned. If she was pregnant, she certainly wasn't very far along.

Just then, Zoe rushed up to them. "Aunt Britt," she said, smiling.

Britt felt as if she had been rescued. She put her arm around the girl. "How are you holding up?" she asked.

"Okay," said Zoe. She turned to Caroline. "Can I see Mr. Carmichael? I want to thank him. He did save my life."

"Sure," said Caroline. She led the way down the hall, through the dining room, where the table was set with a buffet of cold cuts, and a cluster of people were making sandwiches. Zoe politely greeted the people she passed, and then she edged away. Britt and Zoe followed Caroline into a sitting room. The television was blaring, and there, seated on the sofa, was a very pregnant girl, her slipper-clad feet up on an ottoman. She had a round face and large, blue eyes. Her bleached blond hair was pulled up into a bushy ponytail and she was wearing a maternity top with ducks and cows all over it. She was eating a chocolate bar as she stared at the program on the television.

"Hey, Vicki," said Zoe shyly.

"Vicki," said Caroline in a pleading tone. "Turn that TV down, we've got company here. Let me get you an apple. I've got some out there on the buffet. I'll cut it up in pieces the way you like it."

The girl on the sofa tore her attention away from the TV screen and looked up. "Hi, Zoe. It's too bad about your mom. I wanted to come but my ankles were swollen." Then, she looked at Caroline. "I don't really care for an apple," she said in a sweet, whispery voice. She brightened. "Can you get me something to drink?"

"Milk?" Caroline asked hopefully.

Vicki broke off another piece of candy and put it in her mouth. "Just a little cup of coffee would be good," she said. "Black. Do you want some, Zoe? She'll get it for you."

Zoe shook her head.

"Britt, this is Vicki Manfred. She's our . . . guest. Vicki, this is Zoe's aunt."

"Where's Mr. Carmichael?" Zoe asked.

"In his study," said Caroline.

"He's talking to the police chief," Vicki announced in her babyish voice.

Zoe walked over and perched on the sofa next to Vicki. Kirby, the cat, jumped up and nestled in between them. "I was knitting you a scarf," said Zoe. "But it got burned up in the fire."

"That's sweet of you," said Vicki.

"The lady at the knitting shop gave me more wool for free. So, I'm gonna start again."

Caroline studied Zoe as she petted the cat. "How is she doing?" she whispered to Britt.

Britt grimaced. "She seems . . . okay. But, I don't know . . . I don't really know that much about kids."

"Well, I'm no help. I don't either. This will be my first," she said, glancing at Vicki.

Britt frowned. "Your first?"

"Oh, I'm sorry. You don't know. We're adopting Vicki's baby when it's born."

"Ah," said Britt nodding.

The door to the study opened and Chief Stern emerged. He saw Britt and smiled, "Miss Andersen."

"How are you today, Chief?"

"Fine. Thanks for your hospitality, Mrs. Carmichael. I have to get back to work."

"You're welcome. Zoe, go on in," said Caroline. "I know Kevin wants to see you."

"Hey," said Vicki querulously. "What about my coffee?"

"Can't you wait?" Caroline snapped. Then she altered her tone. "I'm getting it."

"You go ahead, honey," Britt said to Zoe. "Chief, may I talk to you for a minute?"

Chief Stern turned and looked at Britt. "Miss Andersen?"

Britt thought again about Dr. Farrar's remark at the church. "Do you know if they found anything . . . I mean, any sign of illness in my sister when they were doing the autopsy?"

Ray shrugged. "I haven't seen the autopsy report yet. I'm supposed to get it tomorrow. You can come by my office if you'd like to hear the results."

"I would like to do that," said Britt. "If it's not a problem. Thanks."

"Glad to oblige." The chief shook her hand. "I'd better be getting back," he said. "I'll see you tomorrow." Britt watched him as he walked out to his car. She decided she would take the opportunity tomorrow to ask the chief some questions about this fire. Just as Britt reached for the doorknob on the study door, she heard a little wispy voice behind her.

"When you see him, tell him they were fighting that night," said Vicki, her eyes still glued to the television.

Britt felt the hair stand up on the back of her neck. She turned and looked at Vicki. "What?" she asked.

"Zoe's parents. They were having a big argument."

"The night of the fire?" said Britt. From where she was standing she could see Alec in the next room smiling and talking to people. "Really? You saw them arguing?"

Vicki shrugged, still gazing raptly at the television. "No. But I heard them."

"What were they saying?" Britt asked. "Are you sure it was them?"

"I'm sure. His Mercedes was there. I couldn't hear the actual words. Just that they were shouting," said Vicki.

"Who was shouting?" asked Caroline returning to the room, balancing a cup of coffee.

"Vicki says she overheard my sister and Alec arguing on the night of the fire."

"Really?" Caroline asked. "Vicki, what were you doing over there eavesdropping?"

"I wasn't eavesdropping. I went outside to get some air. I took a walk in that direction," said Vicki irritably. "Is that still allowed? Or am I an actual prisoner in this house?"

"Vicki, that's not fair," Caroline protested.

Britt frowned. "I thought they got along."

Caroline shrugged. "Well, I guess there are arguments in every marriage," she said diplomatically.

"Not like that," said Vicki, rolling her eyes.

Caroline noticed Britt standing with her hand on the study doorknob. "Go on in," she insisted.

Britt looked back at Vicki, who seemed to have forgotten her presence. Caroline excused herself and headed for a group of guests by the buffet table. This woman was a friend of Greta's, Britt reminded herself. Obviously, she doesn't think this argument was any big deal. Maybe it wasn't, she told herself. But why didn't Alec mention it to Chief Stern when he asked how they got along? Maybe that argument had something to do with why Greta was sleeping in the guest room.

Trying to put it out of her mind, Britt entered the spacious study which was lined with law books and framed diplomas. In the center of the room a bed had been set up. A ruddy-faced man in pale blue pajamas lay there, his lower extremities covered by a blanket. He was ordinary looking with buzz-cut, strawberry-blond hair, but, although his eyes were dull with pain, his gaze was unmistakably intelligent.

Zoe was clutching his fingers in her own. She turned and looked at Britt. "This is my aunt," she said. "She works on TV. This is Mr. Carmichael."

"Nice to meet you, Zoe's aunt."

Britt introduced herself, reaching out to shake Kevin's hand. "I want to thank you," she said, "for saving my niece's life. That was tremendously brave of you."

Kevin shook his head. "I wish I could have done something to save your sister . . ."

"I appreciate that you tried. Believe me . . ." said Britt.

There was a short, awkward silence. Then Britt said, "My brother-in-law tells me you're an attorney."

Kevin nodded. "Criminal defense. I used to practice in Boston," he said.

"Really? I live in Boston," Britt said.

He looked at her warily. "No kidding."

"I'm from the West Coast. I haven't lived there long. It must be very different for you, working in a small town like this," she said.

"I'm kind of taking what I can get," he admitted. "Most of the crime around here is of the misdemeanor variety."

"Can I sit down?" Zoe interrupted.

Britt turned and searched the girl's pale face. "Are you all right?"

"I don't feel too good," Zoe admitted.

"I'm sure you don't," said Kevin sympathetically.

"Maybe it's time I took you home," said Britt, putting an arm around her shoulders.

She expected Zoe to protest but Zoe just nodded sadly. "Maybe," she said.

"Stop telling me what to do," a shrill voice screamed from beyond the closed door. "I'm sick of you. I hate you." Britt sensed instantly that the harsh voice belonged to Vicki, although it bore no resemblance to her babyish speaking voice. There was the sound of one door slamming and then, after a moment, another fainter slam.

"Oh Lord," said Kevin with a sigh. "Here we go again."

The door to the study opened and Caroline stood there helplessly. "Kevin, she just stormed out. All I asked her to do was drink some milk."

"We ought to be going," said Britt firmly.

"But you haven't even eaten," Caroline protested.

"I know," said Britt. "But it's been a tough day for Zoe. It was so kind of you both to have this gathering."

"It probably won't last much longer," said Caroline. "Lots of people have already left." She walked to the study window and peered outside. "Where did Vicki go? God, I hope she's not smoking again. She can't expect me to just stand by and let her suffocate my baby."

"It was nice to meet you," Kevin said to Britt. "Zoe, you need to take everything slowly now. And remember that you have friends who care about you."

Zoe nodded shyly, and her lip trembled. "Okay," Zoe said faintly. "I hope you feel better."

"Thanks again," said Britt, guiding Zoe toward the study door.

"If you see Vicki out there smoking . . ." Caroline said, raising a finger.

Kevin turned to his wife. "Caro, sweetie. You need to ease up on her. The baby will be okay. A glass of milk, even a cigarette more or less isn't going to make any difference at this point."

Britt located their coats and together they approached Alec, who was listening intently to an old man wearing a hound's tooth cap.

"Excuse me, Alec," she said, "I think maybe I should take Zoe home. She says she doesn't feel well."

Alec squinted at Zoe worriedly, placing a hand on her forehead. "What's the matter, honey?"

"My stomach feels kind of bad," Zoe admitted.

"Poor kid. If you want to wait a few minutes I'll take you home," he said. "There are a few more people I need to thank."

Zoe shrugged. "Aunt Britt can take me."

"Is it all right with you?" Alec asked.

Britt smiled thinly. "Glad to be able to help," she said. "We'll see you later." As she turned away from him she saw Lauren, sitting alone in a chair in the corner, one shapely leg crossed over the other, wagging one open-toe pump impatiently.

CHAPTER 8

"Come on, Zoe," said Britt. To get out the door, Zoe had to run the gauntlet of sympathetic friends, which left her tearful and shaken. Britt tried to zipper up Zoe's pink parka but the zipper was off track, and Zoe pulled away from her impatiently.

The sky was gray and the day was chilly but both of them inhaled the bracing air gratefully. Vicki was sitting glumly on the picnic table behind the house, staring into the distance. She glowered at them as they came down the back steps.

"What happened, Vicki?" Zoe asked.

"'Don't smoke. Don't drink soda. Eat your vegetables,'" Vicki mimicked Caroline in a singsong voice. "She treats me like I'm five years old. Exercises and vitamins and her putting music speakers against my stomach playing some horrible songs . . . This baby is all she cares about. I'm sick of it. I can't wait until this whole thing is over and I can get away from here," she sighed, her voice soft and whispery again.

"I'll miss you so much," said Zoe earnestly. "You and Kirby."

"Thanks," said Vicki. "You're a good kid."

"Why don't you come over to our . . . place for a while?" Zoe offered.

Britt did not want to get into the middle of Vicki's problems with Caroline. She tried to think of a diplomatic way around it. "Zoe, you're not feeling well. You've had enough for one day. You just got out of the hospital . . ."

"That's true," Vicki agreed. "I'll come over another time."

"Oh, okay," said Zoe glumly.

Kirby, who had climbed up on the Carmichaels' woodpile, jumped down from the stacked wood and approached the picnic table. Vicki's angry expression softened, as the eat leaped up on the table and began sniffing the hem of her jacket. "C'mere," she said grudgingly.

"We'd better be going," said Britt, seeing a chance to escape. Zoe lingered to give the cat one last pat.

* * *

They pulled out of the Carmichaels' driveway and were rounding a curve, past a brown field patchy with snow, when Zoe suddenly cried out, "Stop."

Thinking Zoe might need to throw up, Britt quickly pulled over.

"What is it?"

"This is it," Zoe whispered, staring out the car window. Britt followed her gaze and saw, behind a bank of evergreens, the charred struts of the frame, jagged with pieces of lathe and plaster, and sooty clapboards tipping drunkenly, attached on only one side along the remaining wedge of what had been a house. Stairs rose up and ended where once there had been a second floor. Wisps of gray smoke rose from the heaps of ashes and rubble. The stench of the fire still hung in the air. There were a couple of men in hard hats and filthy coveralls shoveling the piles of debris on the lawn into a Dumpster. A man with a notebook, wearing a face mask and a hard hat, was stepping gingerly across the skeletal remnants of the first floor. Britt gazed out the car window at the sight with a feeling of disbelief. She could see, in her mind's eye, that framed Christmas card. The perfect family. The perfect house.

Before Britt could stop her, Zoe opened the car door and clambered out. She started up the low rise of the brown lawn toward the blackened frame of her childhood home. Britt got out of the car and followed her. Zoe stopped at the crisscross yellow tape which indicated a police barrier, a few feet from the smoldering ruins. When Britt reached her side she was trembling from head to toe.

Britt patted the child's back awkwardly and then looked around at the scorched debris. Greta had died here—trapped in her perfect house. Britt had a sudden memory of coming home from junior high school one day to find Greta on a ladder, painting the window trim on their childhood home. Why are you doing that? Britt had demanded. Greta had leaned back to admire her handiwork. In case Mother comes home, she had said. I want it to look nice for her.

"My whole life was in there," Zoe whispered, and then she began to sob. Zoe hid her face with her hands. Britt could see the tears running down the heel of Zoe's hand, streaking across her wrist.

"Zoe, maybe we'd better go," said Britt.

The child wept noiselessly, as if she had not heard.

"Let's go back to your dad's. Come on. We can come back here another day. It'll still be here."

"Can I help you?" The man in the gray jacket and the hard hat pulled down his mask, jumped off the low wall of the foundation and began to walk toward them.

"We just wanted to have a look," said Britt.

"Well, don't come any closer. We're working here."

Britt put a protective arm around Zoe's shoulders. "This little girl was in the fire. This used to be her house." She could see, from the consternation that rose to the man's eyes, that he understood this was the child who had escaped, but had lost her mother in the blaze. "We've just come from the funeral."

"I'm sorry, dear," he said kindly to Zoe. Then he removed a glove and reached across the tape to Britt. "My name is Todd Griswold. I'm the county fire inspector."

Britt shook his outstretched hand. "I'm Britt Andersen. It was my sister who was killed."

The man nodded and then looked back at the destruction. "It was a heck of a fire," he said.

Zoe sniffed, and tried to compose herself, wiping her eyes. "Is there anything left?" she asked in a small voice. "Any of our stuff?"

Griswold frowned. "Not from the house, honey. Between the fire, and the water from the hoses . . . There's a barn out back. I don't know if you might have had anything out there . . ."

Zoe shook her head sadly. "We were cleaning it out because Dad was gonna turn it into a stable. For a horse. For me. We took everything out of there. Maybe my old sled. My ice skates. They might be out there." She looked up at Britt. "Can I go and see if I can find them?"

"Is it safe?" Britt asked.

The fire inspector nodded. "Just steer clear of the house and the men who are cleaning up," he said.

Zoe began to trudge toward the back of the property, avoiding looking at the house and giving the cleanup crew a wide berth.

"What are you doing in there now?" Britt asked.

"I'm collecting some evidence," Griswold said. "For the investigation."

"Investigation?" said Britt. "What are you investigating? I thought you already knew how it started."

"Well, I can't say too much about it," he demurred.

Britt nodded, and then hesitated. Over the years she had found, somewhat to her dismay, that there was one sure way to get people to divulge almost anything. She played the ace that was always just above her cuff. "It's just that I'm trying to get a clear picture of things. I'm a producer for a television show. We're doing a program about fire safety. I thought I might give it a personal slant. You know, since I lost my sister in a fire."

"A television show?" he asked.

Britt nodded. "Probably part documentary, part discussion. I have a network show produced out of Boston."

"Will they show it up here?" he asked.

"Oh sure," she said. "Your local affiliate will carry it."

Griswold nodded, reconsidering. "Well, that sounds like a worthwhile program."

"It will be," she said. She hesitated. "Chief Stern said something about a candle starting the fire," said Britt.

Griswold, clearly seduced by the idea of being on television, was suddenly willing to share his expertise. "Well, we know a candle ignited it in the upstairs bedroom where your sister was sleeping. From the wax we can tell that the candle was on the floor. It seems to have set the long curtains on fire."

"I guess that could happen easily enough," Britt said. She looked around at the crumbling skeleton of the house. "It's hard to imagine how you can tell anything about the fire. There's not much left to go on."

"Oh, the fire leaves us lots of clues. I mean, look at the way the house was consumed. Fire has a pattern to the way it burns. It burns upward. It makes a kind of a V-shape, you see?" He pointed up at the scarred remains of the second floor. Britt looked up and nodded, trying to pretend that she saw what he was pointing to, although it just looked like a charred ruin to her.

"That bottom of the V should be it," he said.

"Should be what?" she asked.

"The point of origin," he said. "That should be the lowest point. Then it should move horizontally, across the second floor. But instead, as you can see, the fire moved right down to the first floor."

Britt frowned. "So why would it do that?"

"Accelerant," he said. "The fire followed the accelerant, across the floor, down the walls."

Britt felt the hair stand up on the back of her neck. "Accelerant," she breathed.

Griswold nodded. "I found a puddle of it in the basement. Dripped down through the spaces between the floorboards.

That happens in these old houses. It was paint thinner," he said. "We found the cans tipped over in the bedroom."

"Oh, right," said Britt, remembering Chief Stern's questions to Alec. "That's right. Apparently my sister was stenciling the walls up there. There were paint cans and thinner on the bedroom floor. I guess that's why the fire spread so quickly."

"Yep," he said. "That's what they used."

Britt turned and stared at him. "Excuse me?"

"Whoever set the fire," he said. He looked at her in surprise, as if he had just realized she didn't understand the language he was speaking.

"I'm sorry," said Britt. "Why does that mean somebody set the fire? Couldn't the cans just have been knocked over during the fire? It was dark. Maybe my sister got up, panicked by the smoke and the flames, and tried to put it out. Maybe she knocked the cans over by mistake. The accelerant could have dripped through the floorboards that way."

"Well that would have been possible except for two things. Judging by the burn patterns, the paint thinner had been hurled onto the walls and the furnishings in that room. That, and we found your sister's body still on the bed."

For a moment Britt felt dizzy, as if she was going to faint. She reached out, and Griswold grabbed her arm. "Are you okay?" he said.

"You're saying it was arson?" she asked. "You're saying it was done deliberately?"

"Oh yes," he said, looking at her in mild surprise. "No question."

"But . . . you can't be sure . . ." she breathed.

"Well, actually I can. That's my job. And furthermore, somebody was careful enough to take the batteries out of the smoke alarms. Whoever set it didn't want your sister to escape."

CHAPTER 9

"Good God," said Britt.

Griswold met her shocked gaze matter-of-factly. "I'm afraid so . . ."

"But, why . . ." breathed Britt. She tried to comprehend what it all meant. "Why would anyone want to kill her . . . kill them . . .?"

"Well, obviously I don't know the arsonist's intentions. But, clearly the fire was meant to kill your sister. She had to have been in the room when it was set. There was no accelerant in the other rooms, except for what leaked down to the basement," Griswold said. "Of course, once you set a fire like that, anyone in the house is in peril of their life."

Zoe suddenly appeared from around the back of the property, stumbling across the lawn cradling her white ice skates in her arms. "Aunt Britt, I found my skates," she called out.

"That's great," said Britt in a distracted voice as she gazed at her niece. Zoe was little more than a child, with her wrists extending inches past the cuffs of her jacket, and braces on her teeth. What reason could anyone have for wanting to kill her?

"Well, I'm going to get back to it," said Griswold.

"Thanks," Britt murmured. "Thanks for talking to me."

"No problem." He reached into his jacket pocket and pulled out a card. He handed it to Britt. "When you get your cameramen up here, just call me at this number."

"What?" Britt asked.

He frowned at her suspiciously. "For the TV show," he reminded her.

"Oh, right. Of course," said Britt. "I'm sorry . . . I was just . . . a little stunned by that news. Don't worry. I'll call you." She gazed at the card for a moment and then stuffed it into her pocketbook.

Zoe arrived at Britt's side and smiled sadly. "At least I have something left," she said.

Britt gently brushed Zoe's hair off her face. Her skin was pale, but still springy and unblemished. She was too young yet even for acne. How in the world could anyone want to take her life? It had scarcely begun.

She looked up innocently at Britt. "Do you skate?"

"No, honey, I'm afraid of breaking something."

"That's what my mom always said."

"She used to skate," said Britt. "We both did." She could remember their childish shouts of glee, as they skated on the pond near their house. She could see the roses in Greta's cheeks, her breath on the air.

"Mom liked to watch me skate. She said I was poetry in motion."

Britt gazed sadly at her niece. "You really did lose everything, didn't you?" she said.

Zoe took it literally. "Not everything. I've got these."

"Maybe I'll take you shopping," said Britt. "We can get you a whole bunch of new stuff. Would you like that?"

Zoe's shoulders sagged. "Maybe," she said. "I don't feel like it right now."

Britt studied her niece's face and noticed that there were dark smudges under her eyes. "No, of course not. Not right now," said Britt. "That was stupid of me. Let's go back and you can lie down for a while."

"Okay," said Zoe. She began to skip and run toward the car as if she couldn't get away fast enough. She opened the door and tossed the skates in the backseat, and then climbed in the front and slammed the door.

Britt meanwhile felt as if she was frozen in place, staring back at the charred remnants of the house. Todd Griswold was squatting down, sifting through ashes for evidence. Griswold's search was methodical, scientific. But Britt, accustomed to objectivity, felt overcome, as if a voice inside her head was screaming, "Why?" It was one thing to think about this fire as an accident. A sputtering candle. A floating curtain. It was horrible, but you could understand. But the idea of someone planning this catastrophe, setting out to kill them . . .

Britt began to shiver uncontrollably. Tearing her gaze away from the black reminder of Greta's fate, she hurried toward the car and slid into the driver's seat. Zoe was slumped in the passenger seat, her head back against the headrest, her eyes closed. Her eyelashes rested lightly on her pale, dewy skin.

Britt reached carefully around Zoe and pulled out the seat belt from above her shoulder. She tugged it down across the front of Zoe's pink parka and buckled it securely around her sleeping niece. Who could begrudge this child her existence? Who could look at that gentle face and see only a problem to be eliminated, an obstacle to be removed. Greta's only child. Someone had tried to kill them both, but Zoe was still alive.

Zoe started, and her eyelids fluttered, but then they closed again immediately.

"You just sleep," Britt said, pushing the button that locked the car doors. Then, using her index finger, she lifted a stray lock of hair off the child's forehead and patted it gently back into place. Zoe's face was softly rounded, perfect in repose. She was the image of innocence, unguarded and peaceful.

Britt felt something unfamiliar well up inside her as she gazed at the exhausted child. Normally, she was not given to maternal feelings. She looked on other people's children with disinterest. But this was different. This was Zoe, and there was no denying the fierce determination that rose in Britt's heart, in her throat, like tears. "Go ahead and sleep," Britt murmured. She lifted her wary gaze to the stark landscape that surrounded the car, the street and the smoldering remains of Greta's fiery grave. *You sleep*, she thought, *and I'll keep watch*.

* * *

That night, in the dark bedroom, Britt pushed the luminous button on her watch. Midnight. She lay in the narrow twin bed, the crown of her head brushing against the maple headboard, her feet nearly touching the footboard. This feels like a coffin, she thought. Irritably, she tore off the headset she was wearing and placed it on the night table beside her with the little Discman she had brought for the trip. She had been lying here for over two hours, listening to soothing music, trying to fall asleep, but she couldn't stop thinking about the fire inspector, telling her that the smoke alarms were disarmed, the fire set deliberately, to kill Greta.

No matter how many times she went over it in her mind, the shock was not diminished. Why in the world would anyone want to kill her sister? Her mind couldn't assimilate the horror of it. Britt glanced over at Zoe's bed. All she could see was a motionless mound of covers. At least her insomnia had not disturbed Zoe. She could hear the girl's even breathing across the space between their matching beds.

Selfishly, for a moment, Britt wished she had insisted on a hotel. At least in a hotel she could deal with sleeplessness by turning on the TV, making a phone call, turning on all the lights and reading for an hour or two. Britt sighed. If she were in a hotel, who would be here with Zoe? Not her father, who had never come back from the Carmichaels. He'd called, around dinnertime, to tell them he would be late. Zoe wanted to wait for him, but Britt had finally insisted on heating up casserole someone had sent over and eating dinner.

Britt seethed every time she thought about it. On this, the worst night of Zoe's life, Alec Lynch had left his daughter alone. What could have been more important than to be with Zoe? she thought. Zoe, who could still be in danger . . .

Britt swung her legs out of bed and pulled on a pair of socks, and a sweatshirt over the pajamas she wore. She'd go read, or watch TV in the living room. Quietly, she got out of bed and tiptoed out the door. The house was silent. She padded down the chilly staircase to the living room. The room was dark, except for some glowing embers that were left from the fire she'd made for them in the fireplace. Britt walked over to a table behind the sofa and fumbled in the dark for the switch on a ceramic lamp she'd noticed there earlier.

"Hey. What are you doing . . ." said a warning voice.

Startled, Britt cried out and swung around. She saw a tiny red ember floating in the dark in the moment before her fingers turned the switch and a dim light filled the room. Alec Lynch stood by the window, a cigarette burning in his hand. He was no longer wearing the suit he had worn to the funeral. He had on a sweater and heavy boots.

"Dammit," said Britt. "You scared me."

"Sorry. I live here," he said sarcastically.

"I didn't hear you come in," she muttered.

Alec sighed, and sat down in a chair, taking another drag on his cigarette. "Just sitting in the dark, having a smoke. I gave this up a few years ago," he said, gazing at the glowing cigarette between his fingers. "But my nerves are shot . . ."

He stood up and walked over to the fireplace, tossing the butt into the embers. It flared up for a moment and then seemed to vanish.

Britt thought about turning right around and going back upstairs, but she didn't want to give Alec the impression that she needed to avoid him. She walked around the sofa and sat down, pulling the blanket off the arm and arranging it over her pajamas. She reached over to the table and picked up a newsmagazine. She opened it and began to thumb through it, pretending to read.

Alec, still standing in front of the fire screen, cleared his throat, but Britt did not look up.

"How's Zoe feeling?" he asked.

His question made Britt's blood boil. "She's asleep," she said curtly.

"Was she feeling better by bedtime?" he asked.

Britt stared, unseeing, at the magazine page. "Physically?" she asked.

"Well, she said she felt sick to her stomach," he said.

"Physically, she was better," said Britt. "Emotionally . . . well, why would she be feeling better?"

"I don't know," he said, shaking his head. "My poor little girl. This is a day we'd all just as soon put behind us."

Britt was silent, fuming.

"Well, I know I've had enough. I'm going to go to bed," he said.

He was acting as if he wasn't expected to explain his disappearance today. Suddenly Britt felt as if she couldn't just let him off the hook. "I thought you might like to know. I spoke to the fire marshal after the funeral today," she said.

"Oh?"

"I don't know whether you've heard this or not. He told me the fire was deliberately set. It was arson."

They stared at one another in the dimly lit room. Alec began to shake his head as if he didn't understand.

"No, it . . . it was an accident," he said. "The candles . . ."

"It was set deliberately," said Britt, "so that Greta would be trapped in there. So that she would be killed. The batteries were removed from the smoke alarms."

Alec's face turned white, and he began to shake.

Britt's icy demeanor thawed somewhat at the sight of his obvious distress.

"Oh my God," he whispered. He swayed as if this news had struck him like a blow, and staggered to the nearest armchair, landing with a thud. "That's not possible," he said. He looked up at Britt. "The paint thinner. I thought . . ."

Britt smoothed the folds of the blanket over her lap. "The paint thinner was used as an accelerant. Whoever set the fire threw it all over the walls and the curtains and the floor."

Alec shook his head. "I can't believe it. Ray Stern said nothing . . ."

Britt felt a little bit guilty, because he looked like he was going to collapse at this news. "I didn't mention it to Zoe," she said.

"No," he said absently, shaking his head. "No, don't . . . How long have they known this?"

"I didn't ask. I didn't want to talk about it in front of Zoe. I figured she had enough on her plate," Britt continued. "It was a terrible day for her as it was. Her mother's funeral and then you . . . not coming home."

It didn't seem to register. He seemed totally absorbed in her news about the fire.

"She wanted to wait up for you," Britt persisted. "She was watching at the window."

"I lost track of time," he muttered.

"I'm sure you did," she said, disapproval ringing in her voice.

He looked up at her angrily. "I didn't mean to make her day worse. I would never hurt Zoe on purpose. She knows that."

"Well, somebody wanted to hurt her," said Britt. "Who would want to kill them? Do you have any idea . . .?"

"No," he snapped. "No, of course not."

"Aren't you . . . curious?" she asked.

"Curious? Am I curious? What do you think? What kind of a stupid question is that?"

"Don't shout at me," she said, stiffening.

"Sorry," he muttered. "I'm feeling very . . . edgy." Alec sat tensely in the armchair, glaring at the embers in the fireplace. Then, as Britt watched him, the anger and indignation seemed to drain away and he suddenly looked almost . . . frightened. "I can't believe it. It's hard to take it all in. You know something? In the last few days, my whole life has been turned upside down. My whole world. Everything that was important . . . except for Zoe . . . gone up in smoke. Today I had to get away and just be alone. I mean, when the person you love dies suddenly like that . . . your wife. And you've never had a chance to say all the things you wanted to say . . ."

You were arguing with her that night, Britt thought, as she listened to him. *She was sleeping in the guest room.* And then she reminded herself that she had let *her* argument with Greta come between them for years. People argued. It was a fact of life. If they were lucky, they had a chance to make up.

"I had to get away today. I took one of the snowmobiles up on the mountain, to a place where Greta used to love to go for picnics when we were first married. There's a lake. It's got a layer of ice on it now but in the springtime there are wildflowers all around it. And there's a little shelter up there. I'm thinking of scattering Greta's ashes up there. With Zoe, of course. In the spring. I sat there in that shelter and I tried to figure out . . . a lot of things." He shook his head slowly. "But I don't understand. I don't understand . . ."

From the moment they'd met, Britt had had difficulty imagining what it was that her sister had found to love about this overbearing man. But now, as he tried to absorb the news she had delivered, she felt some compassion for his helpless bewilderment.

As if to deflect her sympathy, Alec rose abruptly from the chair, walked over to the fire screen and jiggled it, making sure all the embers were well inside the hearth. "The funeral is over," he said. "You've done your bit. You don't have to stay any longer."

His words struck her like a bucket of cold water, but she refused to flinch.

"I'm not quite ready to leave," she said. "But, obviously we're crowded here. If you prefer, I'll go to a hotel."

Alec shook his head. Then he sighed. "You may as well forget the hotel. Zoe wouldn't stand for it."

Britt did not reply.

"Look," said Alec, and his tone was suddenly conciliatory. "Everybody's on edge. About today. I know I should have come back earlier, but I was . . . a zombie, I guess you'd say. I wouldn't have been any good to Zoe. Besides, I thought she might like to be with you today. To remind her of her mother. There are ways you are like her, you know."

"Dr. Farrar said that today," Britt admitted with a wry smile. And then she remembered the rest of what Dr. Farrar had said. She hesitated to ask. He was looking at her curiously.

"What?" he asked.

"Alec, was Greta sick or something?"

Alec frowned. "No," he said angrily. "She was fine. Why would you say that?"

"Dr. Farrar said she had been suffering," said Britt.

"Dr. Farrar," he snorted. "Dr. Farrar thought Greta was suffering from being married to me. Because I have a snowmobile dealership and Dr. Farrar is one of those bleeding-heart, do-gooder preservationists."

"Never mind," said Britt crossly. "Sorry I mentioned it." She thought about the autopsy results. Surely they would reveal any illness, even if Greta had kept it from her husband. *I'll know tomorrow*, she thought. *I can wait until then.*

"Look, Zoe wants to go to school tomorrow, and I said she could," Alec said abruptly.

"Do you think that's wise?" Britt asked, alarmed. "She's kind of weak."

"It's what she wants to do," he said. "I talked to Peg Slavin, the counselor at the school. She told me to let Zoe set her own pace with this. Mrs. Slavin is going to meet with her during the school day."

"The school counselor? Don't you think you should take her to a real professional? Someone with a psychiatric practice?" said Britt.

"She is a professional," Alec bristled. "Besides, she cares about Zoe and she's right there on the spot. Zoe likes her. I trusted her. You know, sometimes how many degrees you have doesn't say a damn thing about how smart you are."

Britt shrugged and gave him a withering glance. "She's your daughter."

"That's right. She is. And she needs to keep busy. Besides, she sort of has celebrity status as a result of this. She might enjoy the attention."

Britt wrinkled her nose, "Celebrity status? That's disgusting. You make it sound like she won a beauty contest."

"It's reality," he said bluntly. "Kids are like that. If it makes her feel better, it's all right with me."

"If you say so," Britt replied coldly.

"Since you're planning to stay around, could you go get her when she's done? It would help me out. I'm backed up at work. I'll let them know you're coming to pick her up. You have to have permission," he said.

"Yes," said Britt. *Wouldn't want you to lose any customers*, she thought irritably. "I'll pick her up."

"Great," he said in a flat tone. "Thanks." He walked past her without looking at her. "Good night," he said abruptly.

"Good night," said Britt. She sat up for a while after he went to bed, shivering, even under the blanket. She gazed out the window at the moon, visible behind the bare branches of the trees. *Oh Greta*, she thought. *What was your life really like? If you weren't sick, then why were you suffering?* Britt certainly didn't intend to ask Zoe. Children were rarely aware of their parents' feelings, anyway.

Greta always told Britt, when they were young, how she'd never realized their own mother was unhappy until the day she disappeared, leaving only a note behind. Greta had thought of it a million times, wondering if she might have prevented her mother leaving, if she'd only been aware . . . Britt never really understood what she meant. She didn't even remember that day. She was only four when their mother left. But now she understood. It was pointless to ask Zoe about her mother's state of mind. Zoe wouldn't know.

A spark in the fireplace popped, sounding like a shot, and Britt jumped. Take it easy, she thought. Part of her wanted to pack up her things and go back to Boston with the morning light. But she wasn't going to leave yet, and she knew it. Greta had been murdered. She couldn't just walk away from that fact. She needed some answers for her own peace of mind. And for Zoe's sake she had to stay around for a little while. It was all there was left that she could do.

CHAPTER 10

The gray light of dawn was filtering through the blinds when Britt finally dropped off to sleep. Later, she was dimly aware of Zoe getting up, getting ready for school, and tiptoeing out of the room. It seemed only moments later when Britt looked at her watch and saw that it was nearly eight-thirty. *Oh damn*, she thought. She'd wanted to get up early. She sat up on the edge of the bed and tried to shake out the cobwebs as she pulled on a pair of socks. *I'll take a quick shower*, she thought, *just to wake me up*. But when she opened the door to the room, she heard the water running in the bathroom sink and she could see the bar of light under the door.

Damn, she thought. *He's still here*. She was about to disappear back inside the room, like a turtle withdrawing into a shell, when she heard a knock at the front door.

It's not for me, Britt thought, hesitating in the hallway. *I'm not answering it*. But the knock persisted as did the water, running in the bathroom. *Maybe it's the police*, she thought. *All right. I'm coming*. She pulled on a sweater over her pajamas, and stumbled down the stairs to the front door of the house.

The knocking had ceased and, when Britt opened the door, the mailman was heading back down the walkway.

"Yes?" Britt called after him.

The mailman turned around and looked at Britt, and then at the bunch of mail in his hand. "I've got a registered letter for Mrs. Greta Lynch," he said. "You'll have to sign for it."

"Okay," said Britt. "I'll sign for it."

The postman remounted the front step and held out the letter and a pen. "This has been forwarded here," he said.

"The family had to move suddenly," said Britt. "A fire."

"Oh, that's a shame," said the postman, looking at Britt's illegible scrawl on the green postcard she had signed. "Okay, well, have a good day," he said.

Britt thanked him and closed the door behind him, looking curiously at the envelope. The return address read: GARDNER INVESTIGATIONS, MATRIMONIAL SURVEILLANCE, SECURITY SERVICE AND ASSET TRACING. Britt stared at the return address. *Matrimonial Surveillance?* That was a fancy way of saying that this detective spied on cheating husbands.

"Hey. What's this?"

Britt jumped as Alec walked up to her, adjusting his tie at his collar.

Britt looked at him guiltily. "Registered letter."

"Let me see that," he said, extending his hand.

Britt glanced back at the letter, wanting the address, but before she could see any more than the town and state, he snatched the letter out of her hand.

"Do you mind?" he said. "It's my mail."

"It's Greta's mail," she said.

"That makes it mine, now." He glanced at the return address and stuffed it into the inside pocket of his leather jacket.

Britt stared at him.

"So, I'm gonna go," he said. "What are you gonna do all day?"

Britt blushed, thinking about her planned visit to Chief Stern. *I'm going to look into the facts surrounding my sister's murder*, she thought. Strange, that her husband wouldn't be obsessed with doing that same thing, the very day after he found out that his wife was killed. "Not much," she said. "Nothing."

"Why don't you stop at the dealership? I'll take you out on a snowmobile. Have you ever been on one?"

"No," said Britt.

"It's beautiful on the mountain. You really should see it. Do you know where my place is?" he asked.

"I can find it," she said. *But don't hold your breath*, she thought.

* * *

The main street of Coleville was decorated for Christmas. White fairy lights were hung on every tree and wound around the gaslights that lined the street. Wreaths adorned the doors of every prosperous-looking shop and each window display revolved around a snowy theme, even though the day was gray and icy.

Britt's leather ankle hoots were the wrong footgear for the slick, sloping sidewalk, and, when she caught sight of her reflection in a gourmet food shop window, she couldn't help noticing how out of place she looked, her fists jammed in the pockets of her long tweed coat. Everyone else on the street was wearing some sort of parka or ski jacket and heavy boots with treads on the soles. Conversations burbled cheerfully among window shoppers she passed. There was a holiday feeling in the air which only served to make Britt feel cranky.

Making her way down the sidewalk, she noticed a white TV newsvan parked near the town hall. The doors were open and an overweight, middle-aged man with a videocam on his lap sat eating an overstuffed bagel. She smiled at him but he stared back at her blankly.

The town hall and the police station were side by side, in two severe-looking, old clapboard-side buildings. At some point before preservationists had come to the fore, the original door of the police station's building had been replaced with a swinging glass door that looked distinctly anachronistic. The words "Coleville Police" had been stenciled on it in gold capital letters. Britt pushed the door open and entered the old building. Inside, the building had been similarly compromised, with walls knocked down and replaced by wide fluorescent-lit areas with desks and files on either side of the room. The only remaining traces of the meeting house this must once have been was a loft balcony, and the wide wooden planks of the floorboards, which had not been carpeted or tiled over in the renovation. The atmosphere in the station was relaxed. A uniformed patrolman was chatting with a female sergeant at a desk near the front. Britt approached the desk, her boots squeaking on the shiny wooden floor. "Excuse me," she said. "I'm looking for Chief Stern."

"He's talking to someone," said the sergeant. "Do you want to wait?"

"I don't know," said Britt. "Do you know how long he'll be?"

"It's just a reporter from WGLC," said the patrolman helpfully.

Immediately, Britt thought of the guy from the funeral. Dean Webster. The guy who looked like he ought to be on a poster for the Winter Olympics, with that tan and the gold-tipped hair.

"I think he's expecting me," said Britt.

"I'll ring him," said the sergeant. She spoke quietly into the phone and then looked up at Britt. "Okay, you can go back."

"I'll show you where," said the patrolman, who led Britt past a neat row of desks to a partitioned-off room with a frosted-glass door.

"Thanks," said Britt as she rapped on the door frame.

"Come on in."

Britt entered the room and saw Chief Stern sitting behind a messy desk piled with disorderly stacks of papers. Dean Webster, who was seated in a swivel chair in front of the desk, spotted Britt and his face lit up. "Hey, you found me," he said.

"I'm here to see Chief Stern," she said.

"Not my day," said Dean as Ray stood up politely to shake her hand.

"Miss Andersen," Ray said.

"Chief, I hope I'm not interrupting."

"Oh, we're not that formal around here," said Ray. "I see you know our local TV reporter."

"We met yesterday, at my sister's funeral," said Britt.

"Miss Andersen here is in the TV business, too, Dean," said Ray.

"I know," said Dean. "I'm a fan."

The scanner on Chief Stern's desk began to squawk and Dean immediately looked interested. *This guy is a competitor*, Britt thought. She'd seen plenty of young guys, and women, too, with that kind of drive. Dean had plans for his future, obviously. He was already reporting on camera. Of course it was a small local station. But, obviously, he didn't plan to spend his career here.

Ray picked up his phone, punched in a number and asked a few questions. "Okay," he said. "Keep me posted," and hung up. He turned to the newsman. "Mountain rescue."

"How many?" Dean asked.

"Two guys," said Ray.

Dean stood up. "I hope Jeff's still in the van," he said.

"He was eating a bagel when I went by," said Britt wryly.

"We're on it. Ray, I'll have to catch you later. Hey, before I go, Miss Andersen," said Dean with a brash smile. "What about our date?"

"Do we have a date?" said Britt.

"I don't think I can trust you to call me. Give me your cell phone number." He leaned over to whisper in her ear. He had a masculine, sweaty scent that made her feel slightly dizzy. "I've got some ideas that might interest you," he murmured.

"I doubt it," Britt said, but she was curious in spite of herself. She scribbled down the number.

Dean touched her fingers as he took the pad from her. "Thanks," he said. "See ya, Ray."

Chief Stern shook his head and indicated the vacant seat. "Miss Andersen. Thanks for coming in."

"Britt," she said.

"Britt, some new questions have arisen since we spoke yesterday."

"I know," said Britt, taking a deep breath. "I spoke to the fire marshal at the scene. He said this fire was arson."

Ray looked taken aback. "He's not supposed to be giving out that information."

Britt ignored his dismay. "My sister was deliberately murdered."

Chief Stern hesitated, but seemed to realize that it was futile to deny it. Besides, Dean Webster had just informed him that he knew about it and was putting it on the news at noon. The bell could not be unrung. "Well, it looks that way," he admitted.

"Have you got the autopsy report?" Britt asked.

Ray nodded, and tapped a stapled form on his desk. "Would you like to see it?"

Britt started to reach for the paper and then she grimaced. She wasn't sure she wanted to read all the details about the examination of Greta's corpse. "Could you . . . maybe summarize it for me?"

"Certainly," said Ray. "Greta Lynch was badly burned, although she died from smoke inhalation. We found no evidence of any other injury on her. Slightly elevated blood alcohol. She'd had a glass of wine. And a significant quantity of a prescription tranquilizer as well. All that would explain why she slept through the setting of the fire. We presume that Zoe didn't awaken, but then kids, teenagers, can sleep through anything."

Britt nodded, as if she knew this. She took a deep breath and avoided the chief's gaze. "Do you have any suspects?" she asked.

"We're still trying to piece the events together," he said carefully.

Britt could feel her heart pounding. "Look, Chief Stern, I don't know if this matters or not, but I was there when you asked my brother-in-law about his marriage. He said everything was fine, but Vicki, the girl who is living at the Carmichaels'? She told me that she heard them arguing that night."

Chief Stern frowned. "This girl, Vicki, saw Alec and your sister arguing," said the chief.

"Right," said Britt. "Well, heard them."

"I don't know that that matters," said Ray.

Britt stared at him, though he did not meet her gaze. She hadn't been certain she was going to bring this up but now she couldn't help herself. All she wanted, she told herself, was to be sure that the police had all the information they needed. "Well, there's something else you'd better know. My sister . . . hired a private investigator."

Ray sat upright in his chair. "You know that for a fact?"

"She received a registered letter today from a private investigator named Gardner. The return address said something about matrimonial surveillance."

Chief Stern frowned. "Where is this detective located?"

"I don't know. Alec grabbed the envelope away from me before I could see any more. But I think you should find out."

"Oh, I will," he said.

"Do you think it's possible . . ." she asked.

"Alec, you mean? Well, naturally the prime suspect is always the spouse. But in this case, aside from the fact that he has an alibi, the problem is Zoe. He obviously adores her. I can't imagine a father doing such a thing."

"Apparently the accelerant was only in the guest room. The room where Greta was sleeping. Maybe he . . . the arsonist thought Zoe would escape."

"But that would be taking such a chance with her life. And leaving her to awaken in the middle of that inferno, knowing her mother was in the fire. That would make him a monster. I just can't picture him doing anything so . . . brutal and vicious."

"Still, it happens," Britt insisted.

Ray looked up at her. "You don't have any children, do you, Miss Andersen?"

Britt was irritated, but tried not to show it. She hated it when people lorded their parenthood over her, treating her as if she were some self-absorbed adolescent. She understood that most parents loved their children. But her own mother had walked away from her without a backward glance. Who could have predicted that? Who was to say that every display of parental love was real? For some people, those demonstrations of parental love were just part of a disguise, a socially acceptable illusion. But she didn't intend to sit here and try to convince Ray Stern of that. "I'm going to stay around town a little longer," she said. "Will you keep me informed?"

"Yes," he said gravely. "We'll be in touch."

There didn't seem to be anything more to say. Britt shouldered her bag and left him sitting there. She walked out of the police station and turned up her collar against the chill. Trudging up the street, thinking about their conversation, she hoped she had done the right thing. She didn't want to jump to any hasty conclusions. The private detective . . . it didn't necessarily prove anything. If Alec wasn't guilty then he had nothing to hide. None of this would matter. It wasn't as if she was going to announce her every suspicion to the newspapers or something. She had to think of Zoe, and how she would feel if Britt made such a thought public.

"Hey," said a voice behind her.

Britt jumped and turned around.

Alec Lynch was emerging from a coffee shop called Henry's. He walked up to where she was standing. Britt froze, wondering if he had seen her coming out of the police station, and if he was going to ask her what she was doing in there.

Alec gestured to the car that was parked next to where she was standing. Britt looked around and saw the blue Mercedes. "Must be fate," he said, unsmiling. "Come on back to the dealership with me. I'll take you for that ride."

CHAPTER 11

"Lauren," said Alec. "Give Britt your jacket. I'm gonna take her up on the mountain. She can't wear that bulky wool coat. Britt, take that thing off."

Alec, who had changed his own leather jacket for a dark green parka, searched for a particular set of keys from a Peg-Board on the wall. He had insisted on showing Britt the countryside on one of his vehicles and Britt had not been able to think of a polite way to refuse. She reluctantly removed her coat and donned Lauren's raspberry-colored jacket.

"Wear these, too," Alec commanded, as he reached into a closet and tossed a pair of hiking boots at her feet.

"These are too big for me," said Britt. "I can tell just by looking at them."

"It doesn't matter. Wear these heavy socks. You'll be fine. We're not going to be hiking." He handed her a pair of thick socks made out of some kind of marled wool.

"You've got a regular clothing outlet in there," she said.

Alec ignored the remark. "I'm going to bring the pickup around. It's got a machine in the back. Lauren, we'll be back in an hour or two."

An hour or two, Britt thought, alarmed. She dreaded the idea of spending that much time alone with him, out in the cold. "I'm not much for outdoor sports," she said, hoping he might recognize her reluctance and think better of this excursion.

"This isn't a sport," he said. "The skiers are right about that. But don't tell my customers I said so. You need to see some of our scenery though, since you're here. This is a very efficient way to do it. I'll meet you outside."

Britt tied the bootlaces and stood up, stamping her feet in the oversize boots.

"Have fun," said Lauren.

Britt gave her a feeble smile, and walked out through the showroom. She assumed that Alec wanted to impress her with the size of his dealership, and she couldn't fail to notice the number and range of vehicles that he had for sale. There were motorcycles, four-wheel all-terrain vehicles, and a dazzling array of snowmobiles. Judging from the number of people who were gazing at them in the showroom, and the three salesmen on the floor, it seemed to Britt that Alec did indeed do a booming business. There were several young men in a cluster, admiring a particular silver-and-black snowmobile by the door. She edged past them, feeling slightly self-conscious in the clown-size boots, and opened the tinted glass door.

As Britt stepped outside, Alec pulled up in a white pickup that had a snowmobile secured in the bed of the truck. "Get in," he said.

Britt sighed, and got in on the passenger side. She dreaded this drive, and didn't know what she was going to talk about with him. She knew she had better not mention the letter from the private detective, or her conversation with Chief Stern about Greta. She glanced surreptitiously at Alec's dark, gloomy profile. *Shouldn't you be thinking about who killed your wife*? she thought. *Rather than about showing off your business or giving a tour of the local scenery?*

As if he could read her mind, Alec said, "I find that going up into the mountains is the best way to clear my head. It's magnificent up there. It doesn't allow you to think about anything else."

Britt nodded, and looked out the window, prepared for an awkward, silent ride.

But Alec had other ideas. As they drove along, leaving the village far behind them, he kept up a running monologue about winter sports in this part of central Vermont. The day was clear, with azure sky and puffy clouds. Britt gazed at the stark, beautiful landscape and tried to imagine it green, in summer. There were farms with rolling fields at the foot of the mountain, and then, as they ascended, dense forest with streams that ran through it. The road curved around sharp turns, and, as they rounded a particularly narrow bluff, a lake appeared below them, steam rising from its cobalt-blue surface. Britt gasped at the beauty of it.

"Spectacular, isn't it?" he said.

"Is it safe up here?" she said.

"As long as you pay attention. This is a logging road we're on now," he explained. "When we get up a little higher we'll leave the truck and take the machine. There's a trail along a ridge where you can see the whole valley."

"What sort of trail?" she asked.

"Oh there's a whole network of trails through these mountains, cut through the snow, by and for snowmobilers. The trails give you a chance to get into the back country and see what it really looks like. The touring skiers all bitch about snowmobiles, but they love our trails, all right. We do all the work for them. Without a trail, it's pretty difficult to negotiate up here. You have to be an expert, Nordic skier. Here, this is where we park."

The parking area was little more than a wide spot in the road. The pickup truck jerked to a halt and then Alec got out, and set up the ramp down which he was able to roll the snowmobile. While he readied the vehicle, Britt looked around. They were surrounded by evergreen woods, the tree limbs heavy with snow. Britt stamped her feet to keep her feet and legs warm, but her upper body was toasty in the parka.

"You need long johns," Alec observed as he wheeled the snowmobile over toward her.

"I wasn't exactly dressed for this," she said.

He handed her a set of goggles, and pointed into the woods. "We're going along that trail and we'll come out on a ridge. If you look to your left when we get there, you'll see quite an amazing sight. It's a steep drop down. About a thousand feet. You won't be able to miss it. Hop on," he said. He patted the back of the snowmobile.

Britt looked warily at the vehicle. "Don't I need a helmet?" she asked.

Alec frowned. "I never wear one. You'll be safe enough. I've driven these trails so many times . . ."

"I don't know," she said warily.

"Come on," he said impatiently. "We'll make it a short ride. We'll follow the trail winding down the mountain for a few miles. We'll go through the woods, past some streams and snowfields. And then back up to the truck. We'll even pass the spot I told you about. By the lake with the sugar shack. Where I'm going to bring Greta's . . ." He stopped and cleared his throat. "You know, the ashes," he said.

"Right," she said. "Okay. If you're sure . . ."

He climbed onto the snowmobile, and Britt got on gingerly behind him. The moment she was in place, he turned it on and revved up the engine. The noise was deafening and she grimaced. He shouted something to her, but she couldn't hear his voice over the roar of the engine. She shook her head, and then cried out as the snowmobile leaped forward, nearly toppling her.

She grabbed on to his bulky jacket and clung to it, as the vehicle took off through the trees moving at a smooth, roaring clip along the trail. Snow flew all around her, and bits of ice pelted her like pebbles. They burst forth into daylight, and mounted the ridge he had described. The vaulting sky was indeed magnificent, and for a moment, Britt was dazzled. Then, she looked to her left, and let out a cry as she saw the steep drop that fell off into the valley. On the right the wooded slope was also steep, and covered with snow. On either side it was a daunting prospect. She couldn't help wondering if these vehicles ever skidded out of control and lost their purchase on these trails, wiping out in a tangle of metal and human limbs.

She felt sweat trickle down underneath her shirt, and the wind whipped across her bare face, chapping her cheeks. She was uncomfortable and uneasy. She thought of tugging at his jacket, begging him to stop, but he seemed oblivious to her discomfort.

"How fast are we going?" she cried out, but her voice was only a squawk against the roar of the engine. She had the sinking certainty that he was not going to stop, no matter what she said or did. She told herself to calm down and try to enjoy the view. He wasn't about to wipe out while he was driving this thing. He knew what he was doing. She lifted her head to gaze at the picturesque, snow-covered world around her, and for a moment she reveled in the splendid isolation. But when she looked ahead, it seemed as if they were heading directly into a tree. "No!" she cried out, but Alec did not respond. He steered the vehicle on the narrow trail winding between the trees and, as they passed through a copse of evergreens, a snow-laden bough caught her on the side of her head, the snow landing in her hair, and under the neck of the jacket, the needles scratching her face.

She jerked back to get away from the bough, and the snowmobile teetered.

"Stop that," he shouted, and his voice carried back to her frozen ears.

You stop it, you bastard, she thought. *You did that deliberately. You're trying to knock me off this thing.* She grabbed a handful of his jacket and jerked on it as hard as she could. She could see his head snap back, and he brought the machine to an abrupt stop, throwing his feet out into the snow for balance as they came to a halt.

The minute the machine stopped, Britt threw her leg over it and slid off. "What do you think you're doing?" she demanded.

Alec glared at her. "Trying to give you a tour," he replied.

"You deliberately drove up against those trees so I'd get caught in the face. Why the hell don't you drive out there, where there are no trees?" she cried, pointing to the smooth, snow-covered hillside. "Isn't there a trail out there, or wouldn't it be any fun if I wasn't taking it in the face?"

Alec shook his head. "Yes, there's a trail out there, but there's also a lot of fresh snow. A steep slope like that with no trees is prone to avalanche, for your information."

Britt brushed herself off angrily. "The noise from this thing could cause an avalanche."

"All right," he said. "That was the rough part. Get back on. We're coming to some beautiful territory."

"No, thanks," said Britt, shaking her head. "You go ahead. I'll walk back to the truck." She turned around and started to march toward the trees.

"Get away from there," he cried. "Don't be an idiot."

Before she could take another step, he had grabbed her by the crook of the elbow and jerked her back.

"Let me go," she insisted.

"You're not even on the trail," he said.

"So, I'm in some snow. What difference does it make? I'm already sopping wet."

"You see those trees you're approaching?"

Britt did not reply but glanced in the direction he was pointing.

"The snow builds up under those trees, undisturbed, snowfall after snowfall. It makes wells. You fall into a tree well, and you probably won't be able to get out."

Britt did not reply, but she did return to the surface of the trail. "I want to go back. I've had enough of this. I can see why people hate these things," she said, looking in distaste at the snowmobile.

Alec glared at her. "You've had enough. Fine. I've had enough, too. But we've got to ride back to the truck, like it or not."

"Fine. And then I want to go back to town," said Britt. She suspected that he had wanted her to have a miserable, even a dangerous time today, but she didn't dare accuse him. Maybe this was nothing abnormal, she told herself. Maybe it was always like this on snowmobiles. She couldn't tell. She had nothing to compare it to. "I told you I wasn't very outdoorsy," she said, trying to be conciliatory.

Alec said nothing, but resumed his seat on the snowmobile and revved up the engine. As she climbed on behind him, she looked around regretfully. It was beautiful here. You'd have to be blind not to notice it. But being here with Alec made all the beauty of it seem oppressive. She just wanted to get away from this mountain.

* * *

"Thanks for letting me use your jacket," Britt said to Lauren, when they returned to the dealership. Without another word to her, Alec disappeared into one of the garage bays with the pickup truck and the snowmobile.

"Did you like the snowmobiling?" Lauren asked, gazing at her sympathetically. "It's not for everybody. I'll go get your coat and your boots."

"Thanks," said Britt. She sat down on a chair with a sigh, kicked off the oversize boots and socks and unzipped the raspberry parka. She put her hands in the pockets, and, when she pulled them out, a piece of paper came out in her hand. She unfolded it, and frowned. It was some kind of a gift card with a rose embossed on it. Under the rose were the words, "Love, Alec." Britt felt herself stiffen as she gazed at it.

"Here we go," said Lauren.

Britt shoved the card back into the pocket of the parka and shrugged the jacket off, handing it back to its owner. Lauren slipped it on and pulled her long, dark hair out of the hood so that it fanned over her shoulders.

"Alec asked me to give you a ride back to your car," she said. "Where did you leave it?"

Britt studied the pretty young woman intently.

"Britt?" Lauren said, frowning.

"Sorry," said Britt. "I left it on Main Street."

"Let's go then," said Lauren. "I don't want to leave the phones for too long."

Britt followed Lauren out to her car and they rode in silence up to Main Street. All the while, Britt had to fight the temptation to ask Lauren about the card in her coat pocket. It could be nothing, Britt thought. Some birthday or holiday gift. But then, Britt thought, why would she keep the card? And her thoughts circled back to Greta's letter from the detective agency. And most of all, to Alec, who was out riding around the countryside on a snowmobile the day after he learned his beloved wife had been murdered. She wanted to mention all these things to Lauren. But still, she kept silent. She directed Lauren to drop her off in front of the bookstore.

A bell tinkled as Britt opened the door to the bookstore. There was a calico cat asleep on a chair, and a pile of books on the front desk. Britt's insides were roiling. She began to walk the aisles, gazing blankly at the endless titles, hoping to distract her mind for a moment from her anxieties. Mozart was playing on the P.A. system and otherwise the bookstore was as quiet as a library. Eventually, soothed by the peaceful atmosphere, Britt began to browse through the shelves and pulled out a couple of timeless classics she had loved as a girl. *The Yearling, Little Women, Hans Brinker and the Silver Skates. Do girls still read books like these?* Britt wondered. *Or are these considered too old-fashioned these days?*

A young woman with glasses was shelving books in the next aisle over. Britt was just about to ask her opinion when she heard her cell phone ringing inside her bag. She reached in and pulled it out as the bookstore clerk glared at her with owlish disapproval.

"Yes?" said Britt. She could feel the glare of the clerk, boring into her.

"Is this Miss Andersen?"

"Yes," said Britt.

"This is the school nurse. You need to come and pick up your niece."

"Zoe? What happened?" Britt cried.

"She fainted in the classroom and hit her head."

"Is she all right?" Britt cried.

"Yes, but you need to come and get her. There's no answer at her father's place of business."

"I'm on my way," said Britt, realizing with relief that she had put the directions for the school into her bag before she left the house.

"Are you going to buy those?" the clerk asked accusingly, pointing to the books Britt was holding.

Britt looked uncertainly at the books. Anxiety about Zoe made her feel confused, and indecisive. "I don't know. It's my niece. She's sick. I need to go pick her up." Britt felt as if she was babbling. She took a deep breath. "It's just . . . I loved these books when I was her age. But kids are different these days."

"Not that different," said the clerk tartly. "A good story is a good story."

Britt nodded. *Why was she so full of doubts? She knew what was right. She just had to trust her instincts.* "That's true," said Britt. "I'll take them. Can you hurry?"

CHAPTER 12

Britt pushed open the door to the doctor's waiting room and nudged Zoe to enter. Near the door a young woman who was putting on her coat stopped to jingle her car keys at a squalling baby propped up in a plastic portable seat beside her. Once she was in her coat, she picked up the baby in its carrier and left. Otherwise the room was empty. There was no one visible at the receptionist's desk.

"I don't need a doctor," Zoe pleaded. "I just didn't eat breakfast. Can't we go home?"

"Have a seat," said Britt, ignoring her pleas. Zoe sank glumly into a chair. "If your mom was here, I'm sure she'd take you to the doctor. I have to do what I think she'd want me to do." Britt walked up to the receptionist's window and poked her head in. There was no one in the small office. She wrote down Zoe's name on a list of patients and appointment times and then went and sat down beside Zoe.

"My dad wouldn't make me go to the doctor," Zoe insisted.

"Look, we tried calling him. We couldn't reach him, so I'm in charge," said Britt. "How does your head feel?"

"Fine," Zoe replied irritably.

"Here," said Britt, rummaging in her shoulder bag. "I bought you something." She handed Zoe the shopping bag from the bookstore.

Zoe reached in and pulled out the books, frowning at the titles.

"These are some stories your mother and I both loved when we were girls. I thought you might like them," Britt said.

Zoe was clearly struggling not to appear ungrateful. "Thanks," she said uncertainly.

"I know they might look a little out-of-date to you, but give them a chance. I'll bet you'll enjoy them," said Britt.

"Zoe!"

The door to the offices opened and a stout woman dressed in a burgundy smock and white pants with a head full of black ringlets emerged. Zoe set the books aside and looked up. The woman, her dark eyes full of sympathy, came toward Zoe, arms outstretched. Britt recognized her from the funeral, remembered shaking her hand, although she didn't recall her name.

"Hi, Mrs. Hall," Zoe said shyly as the woman bent over and squeezed her.

"How are you doin', sweetie?" The woman did not wait for Zoe to reply. She turned to Britt. "I'm Emily Hall. We met at the funeral home."

Britt smiled gratefully and shook hands. "Nice to see you again," she said.

Emily Hall perched on the chair beside Zoe's and squeezed Zoe's hand. "What's the matter with our girl, here?"

"I fainted at school," said Zoe. "I hit my head on a desk."

Emily grimaced. "Well, Dr. Farrar will look you over real well in just a minute or two. Poor thing," she said, stroking Zoe's hair. "What were you doing there anyway? You just got out the hospital and had your mother's funeral. You should have been home resting. You didn't need to get back to school so quick."

"She insisted," said Britt, watching her niece. "I . . . I guess her father thought it might take her mind off things."

"Oh, I know," said Emily. "These kids. I got two of them in high school. They all know better than you, right? Well, I'll let Dr. Farrar know you're here. Actually, you're lucky. It's quiet today. We've been going crazy around here without Greta."

Zoe nodded, acknowledging the compliment to her mother. "I told my aunt we didn't need to bother you today."

"Oh no. You could never be a bother to us. Your aunt was right to bring you here." She winked at Britt and stood up. "Let me just try to speed things along."

Emily disappeared back through the door to the offices. Zoe rocked in the chair, tapping on the arms with tight fists. Britt noticed that Zoe left the new books lying where she had set them. She tried not to take offense.

Emily reappeared at the office door. "Zoe, honey. Come on back."

As Zoe stood up, Britt realized, with a panicky feeling, that she didn't know whether she was supposed to accompany the girl into the doctor's office or not. It would have been one thing if Zoe were a toddler but what did you do when a girl was eleven years old?

"Do you want me to come in with you?" Britt asked.

"No," said Zoe emphatically. Without a backward glance, Zoe approached the office door, pulled it open and disappeared behind it.

"Uh, Miss uh . . . Aunt Britt," said Emily apologetically.

Britt stood up and approached the window, leaning on the shelf there.

"Can you fill out these papers for me?" Emily asked.

"I'll try," said Britt, reaching for the pen and clipboard that Emily was holding.

"You can have a seat and do it," said Emily. "Just leave anything blank that you don't know."

Britt ignored the invitation to sit, and began to examine the form, leaning against the countertop. "I don't know what the insurance situation is now that Greta is . . . dead," she said.

"They're still covered," said Emily. "Dr. Farrar said we'll leave them on the plan for the foreseeable future."

"That's very nice," Britt said.

"I've got all Greta's information back here. Just fill out the stuff about today's visit."

"Okay," said Britt, quickly finishing the form and handing it back over the counter.

"That's fine," said Emily, giving it a glance. She opened a manila file on her desk and began to sort through it.

"So this is where Greta worked," said Britt.

Emily looked up, and gazed around the office. "Well, Greta worked in the back with the patients. But . . . yeah . . . this is where she worked."

"Just the two of you on staff here?" Britt asked.

"There's one other gal who's a nurse. She's a part-timer."

Britt nodded, wondering if perhaps this personable woman might have been someone whom Greta had confided in. Britt hesitated, and then decided to go ahead and ask. "Were you and my sister . . . good friends?"

Emily grimaced. "She was a very nice person to work with," she said.

"But you weren't that friendly," said Britt.

"We were friendly," Emily insisted. "But she was . . . quiet. She and her husband, they were kind of . . . not that sociable. You know what I mean?"

"I think so," said Britt.

"She just kept to herself. I mean, like, last summer when she had her vacation. She told us Zoe was going to a dude ranch, but she never even said what she and her husband were doing. I'd ask her and she'd say, 'We have plans,' and that was it."

"Unusual," Britt murmured.

"Exactly. I mean, usually you like to share your news . . ."

Britt nodded and was about to pursue the point when the phone on Emily's desk rang and the receptionist spoke into it briefly. Then she put the phone back on the hook. "Dr. Farrar would like you to come back so she can speak to you. Just go through that main door and down the hall. Last door on your left."

Britt followed the directions to the doctor's office, wondering what Greta's reticence meant. Was Greta keeping her distance from people to cover up for her husband somehow? She'd heard of marriages like that. Still ruminating, Britt tapped on Dr. Farrar's door. "Come in," said a low, clear voice. Britt opened the door and looked in. Olivia Farrar, wearing a lab coat, her silver hair coifed in a no-nonsense bun, sat behind an imposing cherry desk. The surface of the desk shone, at least the parts of the surface that were not covered by family photos in a vast assortment of silver frames.

In front of the desk, Zoe sat in a leather chair which was too large for her. Dr. Farrar smiled at Britt and indicated the chair beside Zoe's. Britt sat down and flashed Zoe a smile which the girl did not return.

"Thanks for seeing Zoe so quickly, Doctor," said Britt.

"I was happy to do it," said Dr. Farrar.

"Is she okay?"

"She'll be fine," said the doctor. "Her blood pressure is low. She appears to be a little anemic. I've taken a blood sample to check."

Britt felt her face redden, thinking she should have known, should have insisted she stay home today. "Is that serious? Do you think she should stay in bed for a while?" Britt asked.

Dr. Farrar pursed her thin lips which were painted a vibrant coral. "Not necessarily. Low blood pressure is not unusual at her age. And too much time on her hands isn't wise either. But Zoe needs to be especially careful to eat well, and to drink enough water, and take some vitamins. I've got a prescription here for some vitamins with extra iron that I want you to get for her. She also needs to take a rest when it all gets to be too much."

"What about the injury to her head?" said Britt.

"It's fine. I put a butterfly bandage on it. She'll have a nasty-looking bruise because of the spot where she hit it. There's a lot of blood in the scalp. And it may be a bit tender. She should probably avoid washing her hair for a few days."

"I'll make sure of that," Britt assured her.

Dr. Farrar frowned, and her dark eyebrows knitted together. "This was a warning to you, Zoe. It's not going to do to say you don't feel hungry. You've got to keep your strength up. A collapse like that can be dangerous. Do you understand me, dear?"

Zoe scowled. "I understand."

"I suggest you go home and put your feet up. You need time to rest and to get over your loss." Dr. Farrar stood up, and smoothed down the front of her lab coat.

Zoe nodded and got up from the chair. Without another word she walked toward the door, and then bolted out into the hallway. Britt stood up as well, but the doctor indicated that she should stay.

"Is there something else?" Britt asked.

Dr. Farrar turned and looked to make sure that Zoe was out of the room. Then she looked back at Britt. "You may as well know," she said. "I'm having Zoe's blood tested for more than just anemia."

Britt looked at her, puzzled. "I don't understand."

"I asked her point-blank if she had taken anything and she denied it."

"What do you mean? Taken what?" Britt said.

"If she has been taking drugs, it's going to show up in the tests."

"Drugs," Britt exclaimed. "You've got to be kidding."

"Do I look like I'm kidding?" asked the doctor.

"She's just a little girl . . . why would you think . . .?"

"Look, Miss Andersen. I attended Zoe at the hospital after the fire. I was suspicious about her appearance, about how she was acting, so I ordered a few tests of my own. She had a quantity of tranquilizers in her system. Out of respect for Greta's memory, I kept that information to myself."

Britt stared at her in disbelief. "Where would an eleven-year-old get tranquilizers?"

Dr. Farrar sat back down behind her desk tapping on the edge with her polished fingernails. "I suppose it doesn't matter if I tell you this now. Physically, Greta was fine. But she was very depressed. I wanted her to see someone about it, but she resisted. She didn't want to talk to a psychiatrist. I tried to explain to her that anything she said would be confidential, but it was no use. But it seemed to me that she was getting worse. Anyway, I gave her a prescription for these tranquilizers, just to help her with some of the symptoms. Nerves, sleeplessness."

"And you think Zoe might have taken some of Greta's medication."

"I think it's distinctly possible."

"Oh my God." Britt shook her head. And then suddenly, Britt had a realization. "Is that what you meant at the funeral, when you told me Greta was suffering?"

"Depression can be a severe form of suffering," said Dr. Farrar.

"Do you know why she was depressed?" Britt asked.

"I couldn't say," said Dr. Farrar coolly.

"Does that mean you don't know, or you won't tell?" Britt asked bluntly.

Dr. Farrar returned her gaze. "Your sister and I worked closely for many years, and I had great respect for her. But we weren't *girlfriends*. We didn't gossip."

"But she told you she was depressed . . ."

"It wasn't like that. She never complained. I simply noticed the symptoms in her, and she admitted it when I questioned her about it," said the doctor.

"Her husband said she was fine," Britt said, hoping to provoke a reaction.

She was instantly rewarded. Dr. Farrar scowled. "Fine? Alec Lynch thought she was fine? She could scarcely function." She shook her head. "That sounds like him. He probably didn't notice it. Who am I kidding? He probably caused it. She could have fallen dead at his feet and he would have stepped right over her."

"Is he that bad?" Britt asked.

"Look, I'm the wrong person to ask," said Dr. Farrar, struggling to regain her detached demeanor. "Alec Lynch and I do not see the world in the same way. But their marital problems were none of my business."

Britt nodded. "No, of course not. Okay. Well, I can't help but wonder."

"Will you be staying with Zoe awhile, Miss Andersen?" asked Dr. Farrar.

"A little while," said Britt.

"She needs your help right now," said Dr. Farrar. The woman doctor had a piercing gaze that made Britt feel pinned, like a prize butterfly. "You know what I'm saying. The child has lost her mother. Is she seeing a therapist?"

"Apparently, she's seeing a counselor at school," said Britt.

"She may need more than just a well-meaning guidance counselor," said Dr. Farrar.

"I thought the same thing, but her father seems satisfied with what the counselor is doing," said Britt.

Dr. Farrar snorted. "He probably doesn't want to have to pay for a professional's fees. You can tell him that the insurance will cover it. Maybe he'll be convinced to put Zoe's interests first," she said.

"I'll mention it to him again," said Britt.

"There's a police investigation going on," the doctor continued, "and I feel sure that it will be very hard on Zoe. She's at a very . . . precarious time in her life."

"I know," said Britt.

"You need to keep a close eye on her. If you see any indication that she's high or spaced out, I want you to call me."

"Believe me, I will," Britt said. "She's important to me."

"Don't desert her," said the doctor, picking up a folder and beginning to make notations in it, as if to indicate that it was time for Britt to leave. "She has no one else."

CHAPTER 13

After a stop to buy vitamins. Britt and Zoe returned to the house. All the way home, Britt was distracted, thinking about what she had learned. Zoe had taken her mother's drugs on the night of the fire. Greta was depressed. Greta had hired a private detective. Did she believe that her husband was having an affair? What could be more depressing than that? One thing seemed certain. This happy family image had been a facade.

Britt glanced at the clock. It was nearly three o'clock. She had missed lunch, and she was pretty sure that Zoe had also. "Are you hungry?" Britt asked as she and Zoe took off their coats and hung them up. "Did you eat lunch? I could make you a grilled cheese sandwich."

"No, I'm not hungry," said Zoe listlessly.

"Zoe, remember what the doctor said."

"Oh, all right," said Zoe. She trudged down the hall to the kitchen and flopped down in one of the kitchen chairs. Britt began hunting around for a frying pan. She had noticed bread and cheese in the refrigerator this morning.

"Are you a good cook?" Zoe asked, as Britt put the sandwich together and turned on the gas.

Britt grimaced and shook her head. "I'm terrible," she said. "But I do know how to make grilled cheese."

"Even *I* know how to make grilled cheese," said Zoe.

Britt shrugged, and found a plate for the sandwich. Zoe pulled off the crust and nibbled at the edges, but she did continue eating. "You feeling better?" Britt asked.

Zoe nodded. "I feel pretty good. Maybe Dad will let me go to Kayley's tonight after all. She invited me."

"I don't know about that," said Britt doubtfully.

"The Dietzs' house is my second home," Zoe informed her.

Britt nodded. As she studied Zoe she kept on thinking about her conversation with Dr. Farrar. Finally, she said, "Zoe, Dr. Farrar told me that your mom was depressed and she gave her some medication to help her feel better."

"My mom was okay," Zoe insisted.

"But she did take a prescription. A tranquilizer."

Zoe placed the sandwich down on the plate and looked up at Britt. "So?" she said. "Lots of grown-ups take those."

Britt gazed at her. "I was just wondering if you might have taken some of your mom's medication. Just to see what it felt like."

Zoe stared at her with a hurt, insulted expression in her eyes. "No," she said.

She seemed so genuinely affronted by the question that Britt was surprised to find herself wondering, for a moment, if the doctor had been mistaken. "It's just that Dr. Farrar said . . ." Britt tried to explain.

"How could I take my mom's medication? All my mom's stuff is gone. Burned up in the fire."

"That's true," Britt admitted, realizing that Zoe was right. She couldn't have taken anything of Greta's. Today's fainting was just what it looked like—the result of exhaustion and being run-down.

"And besides. I don't do drugs. Why do you both think I do drugs?" said Zoe, shoving the plate away.

"We don't," said Britt. "I don't. It's not that."

"Well, you just said that," Zoe muttered.

"Zoe, listen. . . ." Britt hesitated. "The very last thing in the world that I want to do is make you feel bad. I wouldn't hurt your feelings for the world. But Dr. Farrar told me that after the fire, when you were in the hospital, she found drugs in your system."

"Well, she's wrong."

"But why would she lie about that?" Britt asked.

"I don't know," Zoe cried. "How come you think I would lie about it? If you weren't going to believe me, why did you ask me?"

"You're right," said Britt softly, her cheeks hot with shame at being chastised by a child. "I'm sorry. I didn't mean to upset you, Zoe."

Zoe sat silently, avoiding her gaze.

Leave her alone, Britt thought. *Why try to force her to admit it?* Maybe the situation at home had been so intolerable that Zoe was just looking for something, anything to escape. Kids did crazy things when they were sad and upset. She recalled some reckless experimentation of her own in her teenage years, haunted as she was by her mothers desertion. She remembered, even now, how angry she'd always felt. *Zoe doesn't need you to lecture her*, Britt thought. *She needs to be able to trust you.* This was no way to go about it. "I shouldn't have repeated that, Zoe." Britt reached out, and put a hand gently over Zoe's fist, which was clenched on the tabletop. Britt's heart twisted inside her at the sight of Zoe's obvious distress.

Zoe jerked her fist away. "That's right," she said, but her voice quavered, and her eyes glistened.

"Maybe you should lie down," said Britt.

"I'm not tired," Zoe protested, pushing back from the table.

Following Zoe out of the kitchen, Britt noticed the shopping bag from the bookstore sitting on a table in the hall. "Hey, how about this?" said Britt. "Why don't I read to you from one of these new books?"

"Read to me? I know how to read, Aunt Britt. I'm eleven, remember?" said Zoe.

"I know," said Britt. "But sometimes, when you're not feeling well . . . I thought maybe you could stretch out on the sofa," she said.

Zoe was still glaring straight ahead, unwilling to forgive Britt so readily.

"Zoe, I know these books probably seem corny to you, but I thought you might find them kind of comforting in a way. And I'd really like to try to make you feel better. If I start reading and you get bored you can just say so. I won't be offended. I promise."

Zoe hesitated. "Well," she said with a frown, "okay. I guess that would be okay."

Britt felt triumphant. "Okay, great," she said. "Let's go in the living room."

They sat down side by side on the couch, and Britt put the Indian blanket over Zoe's legs. Then she rummaged in the bag and pulled out *Little Women.* "Let's try this one," she said.

As Britt opened the book, she gazed for a minute at Zoe, who looked like a little child sitting there, huddled under the blanket. But Zoe was old enough to have dipped into her mother's tranquilizers. Children could keep their secrets so carefully hidden. You would never know by looking at them. Britt opened the book and cleared her throat. "Of course, if you have homework to do, I don't want to keep you from it," she said.

"Just a little homework," said Zoe. "I can do it later."

"Okay," said Britt. "Then let's give this a try." She opened the book to the first page and began to read.

Zoe closed her eyes, and rested her head against the back of the sofa, and Britt wasn't sure if she was even listening, but when she finished chapter one, Zoe said, "Keep going."

Somewhere in the middle of chapter three Britt heard Alec Lynch's heavy tread on the front steps. Then the front door opened. Zoe interrupted Britt's reading in midsentence, jumping up from the couch and running to embrace her father as he came into view.

"Hey," he said. "What's going on?"

"Aunt Britt is reading to me. She bought me some books."

Alec stared at Britt. He was unsmiling, his skin liverish from the cold.

"The school nurse called me," Britt said. "I had to take Zoe to the doctor."

"Lauren just told me that she called the dealership. That's why I came home early. What's the matter?" he said, searching Zoe's pale face with a worried gaze.

"I fainted," Zoe said. "Hit my head. I'm a big klutz."

"I tried to reach you at the dealership," said Britt, "but one of your salesmen told me you were out."

Alec ignored Britt and searched his daughter's face. "Are you okay?"

"I'm fine. I'm okay," said Zoe.

Alec looked questioningly at Britt.

Britt sighed. "Dr. Farrar says she's fine. Just a little run-down."

"You should get in bed, honey, and rest."

"Everybody tells me to rest. I was resting," Zoe protested. "I had my eyes closed when Aunt Britt was reading."

Alec tossed off his leather jacket and loosened his tie. "All right, now," he said. "You get up there and take a real nap. I'll be right up to check on you."

"Oh, all right," said Zoe glumly. She turned back to Britt. "Will you read more later, Aunt Britt?"

"Sure," said Britt.

"Go on," Alec said. He watched Zoe shuffle toward the stairs.

Britt slammed the book shut and tossed it on the table. Then she stood up and began to refold the Indian blanket.

"Sorry I missed your call," he said in a clipped tone. "They must have thought I went out. I was in the back."

"Really?" Britt asked coldly. "Doing what?"

Alec looked at her through narrowed eyes. "Do you know a lot about the snowmobile business, Britt? If I told you, would you know what I was talking about?"

Britt stared back at him defiantly.

"I didn't think so," he said. He rolled up the sleeves on his shirt, and began to look through one of the shopping bags on the floor. His gold watch gleamed through the dark hair on his arm. "Look at all this crap," he said, shaking his head. "I've got to start cleaning up around here. I feel like I'm suffocating under all this junk." He disappeared down the hall. Britt stood uncertainly in the middle of the room, trying to decide how much she dared to say to him.

Alec reentered the room, carrying two black plastic garbage bags. "Here. You want to be helpful? Start throwing stuff out."

"Dr. Farrar said something else about Zoe today," she said.

Alec looked up at her, instantly concerned. "What? Is she all right?"

"Dr. Farrar said she had drugs in her system the night of the fire."

Alec shook his head in disgust. He dumped a shopping bag out on the couch and began to sort through the contents, tossing socks and underwear into the garbage bag.

"Alec?" Britt said.

"It's bullshit. She's lying," he said.

"She had Zoe's blood tested when she was in the hospital. She said it tested positive for tranquilizers. Why would she lie about it?" Britt cried.

"To get back at me," he snarled.

"I don't get it. How does that get back at you?"

"Zoe wouldn't take drugs," he said. "You couldn't cram them down her throat. They get so much antidrug propaganda in school, you can't get her to take a Tylenol."

"Well, if she didn't take them, then how could she have . . ."

Alec turned on her angrily. "Are you going to talk or are you going to help?"

Britt stared at him. Did he really believe the doctor would lie about such a thing? "Dr. Farrar thinks Zoe should be seeing a psychiatrist, or at least a psychologist. She agrees with me that Zoe needs more help than she's getting from the school counselor."

"Oh, she agrees with you, does she? Well, I've got news for you. Zoe is going to be fine. I talked to Mrs. Slavin at the school this morning. Zoe likes this woman. She feels comfortable with her."

"Don't you think that Dr. Farrar might know a little more about this than you do?"

"She doesn't know Zoe. Zoe is my child. I'll make the decisions about Zoe." He turned his back on Britt and surveyed the mess in the living room. "I should give all this crap to Goodwill," Alec sighed.

Why would he ignore this? Britt thought. *Why would any father ignore such information.* Unless he'd known it in the first place. Knew that Zoe was experimenting with drugs. . . .

The phone rang, and Britt jumped. Alec left the room to answer it.

Britt sat down heavily, the black garbage bag hanging forgotten from her hand. She didn't believe for a minute that Dr. Farrar was lying about the blood tests. So either Alec was in complete denial or he was covering for Zoe. But why would any parent do that? Turn a blind eye to behavior like that. Behavior that could be deadly if it continued. Unless all this parental concern that he made such a show of was just that . . . a show. Another part of the elaborate, happy family facade. . . .

Alec grabbed Britt by the wrist and jerked her to her feet. Britt let out a cry. She could feel her own pulse thudding in his grip.

"You are really a stupid woman," he said. "Stay out of this. You think you're helping your sister this way? Where were you when she needed your help?" His eyes were blazing. "Who asked you to come here?"

"What's the matter with you?" she cried. "Let go of me this instant."

"That was Chief Stern. He wanted to know why my wife hired a private detective. He says that you told him."

Britt stared at him, trying not to be intimidated. "I thought he should know," she said defiantly.

"Dad?"

Alec dropped Britt's arm. It was stinging but Britt refused to give him the satisfaction of rubbing it. They both turned and stared at Zoe, who was standing in the doorway in her stocking feet, clutching a stuffed dog to her narrow chest.

"What's going on?" Zoe asked.

"Nothing. What are you doing up? I thought you were resting," Alec demanded.

"I thought I heard somebody fighting," she said.

"No, no," said Britt bitterly. "We weren't fighting."

"That's right," said Alec. "We were just talking."

"What were you talking about?"

"Zoe," said Alec angrily. "If I wanted you to know, I'd tell you . . ."

Edging by Alec, Britt walked over to the closet and pulled out her coat.

"Where are you going, Aunt Britt?" Zoe asked.

Britt avoided meeting Alec's stony gaze. "I need to get some air," she said.

CHAPTER 14

Britt got in the car and started driving, not caring where. It was only five o'clock, but it was already getting dark. As she ascended the winding roads there was nothing but the glow from an occasional farmhouse or ski chalet to light her way. She crept along, determined to turn around in the next driveway to get herself away from the dangerous twists of the dark road. When the next driveway appeared, she turned in sharply, only to realize, too late, that it was unpaved and muddy, beneath a thin layer of ice. The engine roared, but the car was stuck. *Oh God*, Britt thought. *What am I going to do now? I should never have come this way*. Anxiously, she shifted gears, rocking the car back and forth and wondering who she could call for help, when the tires suddenly jerked out of the ruts and she was able to get back onto the blacktop.

Heaving a relieved sigh, she drove back the way she had come, this time heading for the lights of Main Street. She pulled into an empty parking space, sat back in the driver's seat and exhaled in relief. Couples came and went on the sidewalk beneath the fairy lights, their eyes shining, hands entwined. Britt felt her solitude like a weight. Stuck in the mud, she had wondered for a moment who she would call to come and help her. She knew she would not call Alec. The idea of being at his mercy on some lonely road seemed a little frightening to her now. And there was nobody else. *Don't dwell on it*, she thought. *Get out of the car.*

She looked up and down the street. There were restaurants and cafés all along the street but none of them looked inviting to her. *Just pick one*, she thought.

She walked into Mason's Bar and Grille. It was wood paneled and cozy, with a gas fire, a nicked and well-worn mahogany bar and a number of tables, about half of which were full. Even in the candlelight, Britt could distinguish glowing, pink faces, snowflake-patterned sweaters and, unlike any bar she'd ever been to, no obscuring haze of cigarette smoke. These were people who were saving all their lung power for moving fast at high altitudes. A hostess wearing braids and dressed in a turtleneck and a plaid, dirndl skirt that nearly grazed the floor, approached Britt. "Would you like a table?" she asked.

Britt frowned. "Do you serve food at the bar?" she asked.

"We have a bar menu," the hostess said.

"The bar will be fine," said Britt. She wanted to turn her back on this fun-loving crowd and just sip some wine.

The bartender approached her. "What can I get you?" he asked.

"Red wine. Cabernet, if you have it."

The bartender nodded and eased a glass out of the hanging rack on the ceiling. He filled it from a bottle below the counter and placed the glass in front of her.

Britt took a sip of the wine. The warmth of it sluiced down into her empty stomach, which was soothing. As she set the glass down on the bar, she noticed her wrist was still red where Alec had grabbed her. Threatened her. It gave her no pleasure to think that she was right about him.

"Excuse me, miss, but has anyone checked your I.D.?"

Britt turned sideways on the seat and scowled into the smiling face, and slightly glassy eyes, of Dean Webster. "Hardly," she said.

"No, really," he said. "You look like you need a booster seat there."

Britt rolled her eyes, although she felt the warmth of the wine in her cheeks. "Don't bother," she said with a wry smile.

Dean slid down on the stool beside her and placed his beer bottle carefully down in front of him. "You didn't call me," he said, wagging a finger at her.

"I've been busy," she said.

Dean drained his drink and then frowned at his empty bottle. Then he turned his high-wattage smile on her. "So, you're from Boston, eh?"

"Guilty," said Britt.

"I've got a good friend who lives in Boston. Peter Darien. He owns the Darien Gallery. On Newbury Street. Do you know it?"

Britt didn't know the gallery, but she knew the general reputation of the area. Rich, highbrow, and gay. She looked quizzically at Dean Webster. He seemed to ooze animal magnetism, but that didn't necessarily make him straight. And then she chided herself for even speculating about it. He wasn't trying to seduce her. He just wanted an interview and information. "I'm not much of a gallery-goer," said Britt.

"It's nice. Nice place. Very expensive."

"Well, Newbury Street," she said, as if he were stating the obvious. "Do you spend much time in Boston?"

Dean took a deep breath and frowned. "Not as much as I'd like," he said wistfully. Then he brightened. "Maybe I could come down and see you. You could do the town with me."

Britt had to smile at his cockiness. "I'm not sure we're ready for weekends together. What is it you wanted with me?"

"Okay," he said, clearly making an effort to marshal his fuzzy forces and switch into his reporter persona. "Let's get down to brass tacks. I want to know who you think might have wanted to kill your sister."

Britt started. "What makes you think . . ." she said.

"Don't pretend to be shocked," Dean said, gesturing for the bartender to send him another beer. The bartender frowned slightly, and then complied. "Everybody in town knows by now. They've been running my piece on the news all day. It was arson. Somebody had it in for your little sister."

"Older sister, actually. And it's hard to imagine anyone wanting to kill her," said Britt evasively. "She was a very gentle person."

"It must be frustrating to the whole family to have to rely on the Coleville police."

"The chief's been very nice," Britt said carefully.

Dean tapped his new, full bottle on the bar. "Well, Ray Stern is a very nice guy. But with all due respect, this department has no experience with this kind of a case. I don't think there's been a homicide here in years. They don't know what they're doing. They're clueless."

Britt took another sip of wine but it now felt sour in her stomach. "I don't know what you're talking about."

"Come on. You've been around. You know how it goes in a small town. Nobody wants to rat out their friends."

"They seem to be doing all they can," said Britt.

"You must have an idea about who killed her," said Dean resting his elbow on the bar and cupping his face in his hand.

"No," Britt said after a moment's hesitation.

"No offense," said Dean, "but in cases like this, the answer often lies . . . close to home, shall we say."

"I'm aware of that," she said.

"So, what was the relationship like between the snowmobile mogul and his wife?"

Britt reddened, and stared at her wineglass. "I wouldn't know," she said.

He looked at her skeptically. "You're awfully nice. There's such a thing as being too nice, you know."

Britt glanced over at him. He was practically a kid. But even with one drink too many in him, he was clever. His handsome face looked innocent in the candlelit bar, and the expression in his eyes was unreadable, as if he had no agenda of his own. She knew perfectly well what he was up to. And she knew also, that if her suspicions of Alec ended up on the late news, Zoe would never forgive her. "You're wasting your time with me," she said.

"Tell me, Britt," he said playfully. "Is that who you suspect?"

"I wouldn't tell you if I did," she said.

"Well, that's who I suspect," he said bluntly. "I'm doing some digging on this guy. Did you know that your sister had a life insurance policy worth $400,000?"

"He said that was her idea," said Britt, trying to conceal how startling she found the figure.

Dean smiled broadly. "Yeah, I'll bet it was. He bought it two months ago."

"Really?"

"Surprised you, huh?" he said, looking satisfied with himself.

Britt was jolted by the information, and tempted to order another glass of wine and stay. She was tempted to tell him about the private investigator, and the discord in the Lynch marriage. And the drugs in Zoe's system. But she knew she had to resist the urge. She knew she had to get away from him because if she stayed much longer she was going to want to confide in him. Confide in someone who shared her suspicions. She glanced at her watch. "Look," she said, "that's going to have to do it for now. I've got someone I need to see."

"Right now?" he said.

Britt nodded. "Right." She began to rummage in her purse for her wallet.

Dean took out some money and laid it on the bar. "This one's on me," he said.

"Thank you," she murmured. "But you don't have to . . ."

"Oh, no, I want to. And I'll tell you something else. There's a lot that hasn't come out yet. I'm sure of that. And I'm gonna nail this son of a bitch. Just for you."

"I feel like I'm in a Western," she said, smiling wryly. "What's in it for you?"

Dean shrugged and then grinned boyishly. "Oh, I don't know. Satisfaction. A great story. And . . . maybe the gratitude of a well-connected sister."

"Ah," she said. Britt nodded. Just as she suspected.

"What? Are you saying that if I got the goods on this guy you *wouldn't* put in a good word for me at the network?"

"I didn't say that," Britt said.

"Hey, you don't know what it's like out here in the boondocks. I'm like in exile here. I'm way too hot for this place. I'm ready to make the move to a bigger market."

"Modest, too," she said.

"Modesty's for suckers," he said.

Britt watched as he swilled down another large gulp of beer. He was young and brash and rough around the edges, but his winner-take-all attitude was exactly what was required in the network news world. He might just make it. "Well, now I know the price," she said.

Dean looked indignant. "Hey, it's not just that. I think he killed that woman. I don't feel like watching him walk away."

"You'll get no argument from me," said Britt. She slid off the bar stool and hurried toward the exit.

* * *

Where to now? Britt thought. She didn't want to go back to that house and see Alec, playing the concerned daddy with Zoe. And she didn't want to hazard another restaurant for Dean Webster would see her and realize that she'd really had nowhere else to go. There had to be a convenience store, she thought, somewhere in the midst of all this quaintness. She could pick up a sandwich and eat it in her car.

She knew she wouldn't find a place like that on Main Street, so she followed the signs that led toward the highway. Sure enough, half a mile out of town on her left she saw an all-night convenience store and a service station, side by side. She pulled in, parked and walked inside the store. A bored-looking clerk put her premade sandwich in a bag and rang it up, along with a bottle of water. Britt took her dinner outside, and sat back down in her car. She unwrapped the sandwich and began to eat, looking around all the while to be sure that there was no TV newsvan in sight, to catch her at her solitary meal in the car. So preoccupied was she in her lookout for the white van that it took her a few moments to realize that she was sitting directly across the street from Lynch Rides, Alec's vehicle dealership. The lights were on inside the showroom, and there were a couple of people in the parking lot. Britt put her half-eaten sandwich in the bag on the seat and wiped her mouth with a napkin.

She knew Alec was at home tonight. Perhaps Lauren was minding the store. Immediately, Britt thought of the rose-embossed card in Lauren's jacket pocket with "Love, Alec" scrawled across it. This might be a good opportunity to speak to Lauren alone. Britt doubted that Lauren would tell anything willingly, but it was worth a try. If her suspicions were correct, Lauren Rossi might be at the heart of the matter.

CHAPTER 15

A well-groomed young man in a tattersall shirt and tie approached Britt as she frowned at the glossy purple snowmobile on the showroom floor. "Can I help you?" he asked. Then, he seemed to recognize her from the morning's excursion with his boss. "Oh, hi," he said.

"Hi," said Britt. "Is Lauren here?"

"In the office," he said, gesturing to a corridor on the parking lot side.

"I'll find her," said Britt. "Thanks." She walked down the corridor, which had several offices. Most of them were dark, but in the last one, which guarded the doorway to an office labeled, "Mr. Lynch," Lauren Rossi sat at a desk, talking on the phone. She was wearing a turquoise-blue leotard and black stretch pants, and even in the ugly fluorescent lighting she looked voluptuous and pretty. She finished her phone call and looked up at the doorway. Her smile faded at the sight of Britt.

"Hello," she said flatly. "Are you looking for Alec? He's not here."

"Actually I'm looking for you," said Britt.

"Really?" Lauren asked warily. "What do you want with me?"

"Can I sit?" asked Britt, pointing to a chair.

"We're about to close," said Lauren.

Britt ignored the warning and sat down.

"Did you see the news?" said Lauren. "They said the fire was arson."

"I know," said Britt. "I already heard."

Lauren made a face, and picked up a pencil and turned it over in her manicured fingers. "It's unbelievable," she said, shaking her head. "It's really terrible. Poor Alec."

"And Zoe," said Britt.

"Oh yeah, of course. Zoe."

"Lauren, I wanted to ask you something."

Lauren looked up, her eyebrows raised.

"I've heard that my sister was very depressed about something," said Britt.

Lauren looked at her, wide-eyed. "Really?"

"Do you know why she was depressed?"

Lauren spread her hands and shook her head. "How would I know? I hardly knew her. She hardly ever came in here."

"I've been thinking about it and I have a theory. You want to hear it?"

Lauren looked at her watch, and then gave a shrug of indifference. "I don't care," she said. "I guess so."

Britt crossed her legs and gazed at the toes of her boots. "Okay. I think she suspected that her husband was having an affair."

"That's not true," said Lauren. "He was not."

"My sister hired a private detective to follow him, you know." She did not look up at Lauren who sat very still like a rabbit, sensing the proximity of a fox.

Britt kept her gaze trained on her boots. "I'm no one to pass judgment about something like that," she said. She hesitated, then decided to continue, hoping one confession might prompt another. "I was involved with a married man myself. A man I worked for. I'm not proud of it, but these things happen. No one knows better than me."

There was still no response from Lauren. She was silent, unmoving. Britt felt a little guilty. This girl was so young and transparent. It was almost too easy to manipulate her. But Britt wasn't about to give up the advantage. She frowned, and continued thoughtfully. "It's just that now it might seem as if Alec's . . . fooling around might have something to do with my sister's death. I imagine it won't be long before the police find that other woman and start asking questions. . . ."

Britt couldn't stand the silence anymore. She was confident that she had hit the nail on the head. She looked up at Lauren, expecting to see guilt written across the girl's face and saw instead, to her surprise, that there was shock and dismay in Lauren's eyes, and a tear, sliding down her creamy cheek.

"I'm sorry. What's the matter?" Britt asked.

Lauren shook her head and opened her desk drawer, pulling out a Kleenex. She dabbed at her eyes and shook her head. "Nothing," she said.

Britt leaned forward and looked closely at the girl. "Something's the matter."

Lauren shook her head, and sniffed, angrily wiping away more teas. Then she peered at Britt through teary eyes. "How do you know all this? I don't believe you."

"I saw the letter from the detective agency." *Technically true*, Britt thought.

Lauren turned her head and stared out the door of her office, where her own reflection wavered in the glass wall of the corridor. Then she shook her head. "It's time to go," she said abruptly. "You have to get out of here now. I'm going to lock up." She stood up and began aligning the papers, stapler and paper clip box on her desk.

"Do you know who it was?" Britt asked. "The other woman?"

"No," said Lauren. "How would I know?"

Britt hesitated. "It's just today, when I pulled that card out of your pocket that said 'Love, Alec' . . . Are you in love with Alec?" she asked bluntly.

"None of your fucking business," Lauren retorted, blushing beet red. She looked humiliated, like a nerdy schoolgirl caught doodling the name of the football hero.

It's a crush, Britt realized in that moment. *A one-sided fantasy*. "You're right," said Britt. "I'm sorry. I just thought . . ." So, she had been wrong about Lauren and Alec. She felt a little ashamed of her own arrogance. She had been so sure that she was right. Well, she was half right. Lauren wished she was the one whom Alec was fooling around with. But, if it wasn't Lauren, it had to be someone else . . .

Britt took a chance. "So, if you're not his lover, why did you lie for him?"

"Lie for him?" Lauren cried.

"What else can you call it," Britt asked. "You gave him an alibi. You said he was here on the night of the fire when you know he wasn't. He was probably with *her*. And sooner or later the police are going to start asking why you were covering for him."

"It's not an alibi. They will not," said Lauren without conviction.

"Yes, they will," said Britt. "We all heard him say that he was back here, doing his taxes. And you backed him up. But if it turns out that it wasn't true, and you knew about it, I think that could make you an accessory or something . . ."

"An accessory," she cried. "An accessory to what?"

"Murder, Lauren," said Britt. "My sister died in that fire. And if Alec was the one who set it . . . Well, you can understand that it would upset me. The idea that you'd be protecting the person who may have killed her . . ."

Lauren inhaled deeply and then shook her head at Britt. "If you think Alec set that fire . . . you can't be serious. He would never . . . Zoe was home."

"I know."

"He wouldn't do that," she said indignantly. "He loves Zoe."

Britt nodded. "He says he loved my sister."

"That's different. A child is different."

"And yet there are people who kill their children. You read about it in the paper all the time. People who look just like you and me, but are minus a conscience."

"Not Alec," Lauren insisted, but her eyes looked worried.

"Look, I don't know who set the fire," said Britt. "But right now the police are investigating my sister's murder with false information based on what you said."

"I didn't say I was here the whole time," Lauren protested. "I just said I saw him here, working on the taxes."

"And did you?" Britt asked.

"I'm sure Alec didn't have anything to do with it . . ." she said.

"But you don't know whether he was here or not, do you?" said Britt.

Lauren shook her head slowly. "I just wanted to help him. He looked so . . . lost. I knew he would never do anything like that . . ."

All right, Britt thought. *She did lie for him.*

"Afterward, when he walked me to my car, he was scolding me . . . He said I shouldn't have said anything."

"But you did," said Britt. "And if you don't tell the police the truth, it's going to look like you're trying to help him cover up something."

"I don't want to talk about this," said Lauren, summoning her determination. She jingled the office keys. "Come on. Let's go. You have to get out of here."

Britt stood up and leaned toward her, speaking in a low, urgent voice. "You could end up in trouble for lying to the police. And you're trying to protect someone who . . . I'm only saying, maybe you shouldn't be sticking your neck out for him. You know, considering he's involved with another woman."

Lauren's shoulders slumped, and her eyes welled up again.

"Would you come with me, Lauren? Would you tell Chief Stern that it was all a big mistake? Say you were thinking of the wrong night. We need to get some of these lies out of the way, so that we get to the truth."

"I can't believe he's having an affair," she wailed.

"Come on," said Britt. "We'll go right now." *Before you have time to change your mind*, she thought.

CHAPTER 16

Alec opened the door and looked from Britt to Ray Stern in obvious surprise.

"Alec," Ray said, almost apologetically. "I know it's late but I'm afraid I need to talk to you again."

The police chief's apologetic tone made Britt want to grind her teeth but she kept silent. *It's only nine o'clock*, she thought. *Not late for something so important.*

"Come in," Alec said.

Britt entered Alec's living room behind Chief Stern, avoiding her brother-in-law's narrow-eyed scrutiny. She moved a box of books off the seat and sat down in a straight-back wooden chair by the door. Chief Stern sat down in a chair across from Alec, who sat on the couch.

"Sorry about the hour, Alec," Ray said. "But something's just come up. Now apparently your employee, Lauren Rossi, uh, realized she'd been mistaken when she said she'd seen you at the dealership on the night of the fire. So now, I need to know if anyone else saw you there."

Alec rubbed his face with his large hands. Finally, he sighed. "All right. Look Ray, I don't know whether it matters," he said. "But I never asked her to lie for me. She did that all by herself."

"But you didn't stop her," Ray reminded him.

"Yes," said Alec nodding. "That's right. But it wasn't because . . ." His voice trailed off.

From her seat just inside the doorway, Britt watched quietly.

Ray looked at Alec, shaking his head. "Alec, I need you to level with me."

"Look," said Alec wearily. "Let me tell you what really happened. I didn't tell you before because I knew . . . it kind of makes me look bad."

"Please," said Chief Stern. "Go ahead."

"That night . . . the night of the fire . . . I went home to have dinner. Zoe wasn't home. She was at her friend Kayley's for supper." Alec reached into his pocket, took out a pack of cigarettes and shook one loose. He put it in his mouth.

"So, you were at home that night . . ." Chief Stern said.

Alec lit the cigarette and shook out the match. "Do I need a lawyer?" he asked, peering at the chief through a plume of smoke.

"You're entitled to a lawyer if you want one," Chief Stern said.

That figures, Britt fumed. *A lawyer who will advise him not to talk.*

Alec sighed. "No. That's all right. I'll tell you what happened. I got there . . ." His eyes narrowed as he haltingly gave his account of that night, "and Greta heated me up something for dinner, and I was eating, and we were talking . . . and we got into a little argument."

Ray Stern looked smugly over his shoulder at Britt, as if to say that he knew Alec would not try to hide the truth. Britt looked away from him, disgusted.

"We understood you were having an argument. What did you argue about?" asked Chief Stern.

Alec clenched his jaw and stared into the distance. "Just . . . you know, marital stuff."

"What kind of marital stuff?" Ray asked.

Alec looked over pointedly at Britt. He clenched his fist, and then covered it with his other hand, holding the burning cigarette loosely between his fingers.

Britt readied herself for another lie.

"My nosy sister-in-law told you that she was going through my mail and she found out that my wife hired a private investigator."

"Yes. And you said that she was trying to find out about the disposition of some stocks you had purchased years ago . . ." Ray began.

"Well, that wasn't true," said Alec.

"Surprise," said Britt.

"I knew what you thought. You thought I was cheating on my wife," Alec said bitterly, looking at Britt, who avoided his gaze. "I was *not* having an affair. My wife did not hire those people to check up on me. I'm sure she's told you that I was fooling around on my wife." He looked at Ray and then turned his head and gazed at Britt. "You'd like that wouldn't you?" he said.

Britt refused to meet his gaze. Her heart was pounding. *Liar*, she thought.

"Why did she hire them?" Ray asked.

Alec ground out the cigarette. "It had nothing to do with me," he said.

Ray put his hands on his knees as if he were about to get up. "Well, perhaps before you tell us another half-truth we should track down the detective."

"No, I want to hear this," said Britt. "His latest spin on the truth . . . He's had plenty of time to prepare it."

Alec shook his head. "Sure. I'll tell you. But you might regret it . . ."

"I want to hear it," said Britt.

Alec ignored her and looked at Ray. Ray resumed his seat.

Alec sighed. "My wife was depressed. I'm sure Miss Know-it-all told you that, too."

Ray nodded. "She mentioned it."

"She was very depressed because . . . she had been trying to find her mother."

Britt gasped and jumped to her feet. "No," she cried. "Wait a minute."

"Where was her mother?" Ray asked, confused.

"Whether you like it or not, that's the truth," Alec said to Britt. He turned back to Ray. "She left the family when these two were just children. The detective had tracked her down once. Then they lost her again. The detective told me himself, she didn't want to be found. Greta was very upset about that. Very ashamed of that. She couldn't accept it."

Britt was stunned. "No," she said. "You're lying . . ."

"Fine. I'm lying. Do you want to wait until Gardner gets back to you? Because I've really had enough of this for one night."

"Alec, take it easy," said Ray. "We're just here to straighten out this matter. You were the one who was less than honest . . ."

"Okay, okay. But look, Zoe could be home any minute and I don't want her to know anything about this," said Alec. "As far as she knows she doesn't have a grandmother. Greta wanted to keep it from her until she . . . found her mother. We never mentioned anything about it to her. Or to anybody else."

"That's convenient," Britt muttered.

"That's the truth," Alec insisted.

"This isn't right," Britt cried. "He's trying to make it seem like it's all Greta's fault. He's the one . . ." She was incoherent. She could hear herself babbling. Anything not to have to think about her mother, the ghost who, apparently, still walked.

"It makes sense to me," said Ray. "And I don't see any need for Zoe to know about it."

"Thanks, Ray."

"So, on the night of the fire . . ."

"Wait a minute," Britt demanded. "What happened the first time the detective found my mother? Where was she?"

"You want to know? You hire the detective," Alec snapped.

"You bastard," she said. "This is another lie."

"Miss Andersen," Ray said sharply. "I'm sure you have a lot of questions about this, but now is not the time. I'm going to ask you to leave if you don't . . ."

"Sorry," said Britt, sitting back down. She could feel her lip trembling and she was afraid she was going to cry.

"Now," said Ray calmly. "What was the argument about?"

"This," said Alec. "Their mother."

"Can you tell me about it?"

Alec nodded. "Greta was in the dumps, as usual. I was trying to convince her to forget about it, and get on with her life. She just blew up at me. It wasn't something she was reasonable about."

"So you two got into an argument and then what happened?"

Alec got up and walked over to the window, rubbing his palms together as he looked outside. "I know how this sounds . . ." he said.

"Did you threaten her?" Chief Stern asked.

"No," said Alec. "But I said I was sick of it . . ."

"How did the argument end?" asked the Chief.

"I left," said Alec.

"And went where?"

"Pardon me?"

"I need you to account for your time that night, Alec. Where did you go? What did you do? Did you see anyone?"

"All right. Well, I got into my car and I was . . . it was a mistake to get behind the wheel feeling the way I did. I know that now. But at the time I wasn't thinking straight. I just . . . did it. I pulled out of the driveway and tore off down the street and as I rounded the next corner . . . There was a guy . . . I didn't see him. He was halfway out in the road, hitchhiking. It all happened very fast. I didn't see him until he was in my headlights."

"You hit him?" Britt cried.

"I swerved when I saw him, but he was too close. I came around the corner too fast. So I . . . I clipped him. I felt the thud, and I saw him going down."

"God in heaven," Britt cried.

"Does she have to be here?" Alec demanded.

Chief Stern ignored his question. "What time was this?"

Alec frowned. "Eight o'clock, maybe. Eight-thirty."

"So, you hit this pedestrian, and then what happened?"

"Well, I pulled over right away and I jumped out of the car and I ran back to see if he was okay. And he was kind of . . . struggling to get up. I was so relieved to see that he was alive. I asked him if he was all right and he said that his leg hurt, but otherwise . . . Well, he was shaken up but basically he was all right."

"Did you think to call the police?"

"Yes, as a matter of fact I did. I said we should probably report it, but he said it wasn't necessary. That he was okay and not to bother."

Chief Stern looked at Alec in mild disbelief. "So let me see if I understand this. You hit a pedestrian with your car . . ."

"A hitchhiker," Alec said.

"An innocent pedestrian," Chief Stern said, "is hit by a car, injured, but doesn't want to report this accident or receive medical attention."

"I know it sounds crazy, but that's what happened," Alec insisted miserably. "He said he lived in Montpelier. That's where he was trying to go. I said that the least I could do was to drive him to his destination."

"I see," said Ray.

"That's where I was all that evening. I drove him to Montpelier and then I drove back home. It was late when I got back. I was almost home when I heard the sirens."

"I see. So, this fellow that you knocked down with your car. Presumably he could corroborate this story. Do we have a last name and an address for him?"

Alec shook his head. "No. I know it sounds weird but . . . no. He wasn't a very talkative guy. We didn't talk much on the ride. He said his name was Dave. That's all. I asked him a few things but he was keeping to himself."

"And the address?"

"I dropped him off. I can tell you the corner where I dropped him. He said he wanted to buy cigarettes so I left him near a convenience store. He said he lived nearby."

"We have no name, no address. Just Dave."

"I didn't think I'd need a name or address. I mean, why would I think of having to account for my whereabouts? There was no reason."

"Can you describe this fellow?"

"He was a young guy. Maybe twenty. It's hard to tell. He was kind of pudgy. And pale. One of those blond, scraggly beards. He was wearing an old army-green parka. It had these orange chevrons made out of reflector tape on the sleeves. I guess because he was hitchhiking."

"Didn't do him much good where you were concerned," Britt snapped.

Ray ignored her. "What about the name of the convenience store? They often have cameras that record the comings and goings of customers. Maybe we could locate Dave that way," said the chief helpfully.

"That I can tell you. It was a 7-11 store. It was at the north end of town, not three blocks from the highway. You could see the highway from the parking lot," Alec explained. "If you see him on the tape, he's probably limping a little bit from where he took the hit. He was limping when he got out of the car."

"Limping. That's a nice touch," said Britt.

"Although he didn't even ask you to help him with any medical bills he might have from damage to that leg," said Chief Stern.

"I know how it sounds," Alec said. "I mean at the time I thought I was lucky that he wasn't going to sue me or something. I admit, I was thinking about my insurance premiums going up . . . I gave him some cash I had on me but it wasn't all that much."

Chief Stern rose to his feet. "All right, then. We will pay a visit to the 7-11 and have a look at their tapes."

"Wait a minute," Britt cried indignantly. "You're buying this story?"

"I'm going to check out Mr. Lynch's alibi," said Chief Stern in a noncommittal tone. "We'll be in touch, Alec." The chief left the room, trailed by Britt, while Alec sat in the corner of the sofa, and deliberately lit another cigarette.

Britt intercepted the chief at the front door. "I don't get it," said Britt in a low voice. "He admitted he lied about where he was. He admitted that he lied about what the detective was hired for. He admitted that he was arguing with my sister. That he was furious with her. And now, this ridiculous lie . . ."

"Miss Andersen," the chief said patiently. "Britt. I realize you want action. You want an arrest. And I know you're upset with this news about your mother. But the detective agency will confirm or deny what he's told us. Meanwhile, we have to check out his alibi."

"This is not right," Britt protested. "I feel as if I'm doing your job for you. I've caught him in one lie after another. Do you know about the huge insurance policy . . .?"

"Yes, I do," said the chief.

"You really believe that was Greta's idea?"

"That's what he told the agent at the time," said Ray.

"Well, yeah. If he was planning to kill his wife, that is what he would say. I can't accept this laid-back attitude you're taking. You're not even treating him like a suspect and everything points to him."

"Not really," said Chief Stern stubbornly. "The fact that his child was at home . . . I'm sorry. I have a lot of questions."

"Not that again," said Britt. "Did you people ever hear of sociopaths?"

There was the sound of a car door slamming, and girlish voices bell-like in the cold, clear air outside. Then the sound of footsteps, thundering up to the front door.

"That must be Zoe and her friend," said Britt.

"Don't antagonize him, Britt," the chief warned her. "Let us do our job. I appreciate what you did to get Miss Rossi to come forward, but now, you stay out of it."

The front door banged open and Zoe stood in the doorway, her cheeks pink from the cold. She was flanked by Kayley Dietz and another young girl whom Britt did not recognize. The three girls were loaded down with bags of board games and stuffed animals. Zoe's smile faded when she saw Chief Stern.

"Hello, girls," the chief said kindly.

"What's going on?" Zoe asked.

"Routine business," said the chief as he passed them in the doorway. Zoe watched him go, frowning.

"What's all this stuff?" Britt asked.

"Aunt Britt. This is my friend, Sara, and you know Kayley."

"We figured Zoe needed some games and a few animals," said Kayley. "So we gave her some of ours."

"That's nice of you." Britt smiled at the two girls.

A horn sounded from outside. "We have to go. We still have to drop off Sara," said Kayley. "See you tomorrow, Zoe."

At that moment, Alec came out of the living room, and Zoe rushed to greet him.

"Dad," she cried, wrapping him in a hug. "Why was the chief here?"

Alec kissed the top of her head. "Never mind," he said. He looked at the bag of toys. "Is all this yours? Let me take it upstairs for you."

"You're not mad about more bags?" she asked.

Alec shook his head. "No. What's a few more bags?"

"You're the best, Dad," she cried.

Britt clenched her fists and turned away so that Zoe could not see her face.

CHAPTER 17

As Alec mounted the stairs with the bags of books and animals, Zoe followed Britt down the hall into the kitchen.

"Aunt Britt, is everything all right?" Zoe asked.

"Sure, fine," said Britt, distracted. "I thought you were going to stay home and eat pizza tonight."

Zoe shrugged. "Kayley called and Dad said I could go."

"Did you eat at Kayley's?"

"I didn't like what they had for dinner," said Zoe.

"Zoe." Britt gave her a warning glance.

"It was fish sticks. I'll have a snack now, though."

"What do you want?" Britt asked. "I'll get it."

"Peanut butter, I guess."

Zoe sat down at the table and watched as Britt searched the cabinet for a jar of peanut butter. Then Britt found a knife and slathered the peanut butter on some bread.

Britt's stomach was in knots. She set the sandwich on the table and sat down across from her niece. "What did you girls do tonight?"

"Nothing," said Zoe.

"Looks like you did your nails," Britt observed.

Zoe blushed and then extended one hand in Britt's direction.

"Blue fingernails. Very groovy," said Britt.

"Groovy?" said Zoe, rolling her eyes.

"And what else? Let's see," said Britt. "Did you call boys and hang up when they answered?"

Zoe's eyes widened and she laughed. "How did you know that?" she asked.

"I was a kid once," said Britt.

Zoe picked up the soft bread and balanced it on her fingertips as she took a bite. Then she set it back down on the plate and pushed the plate away. She folded her arms on the table and put her head down. Her shoulders shook, and Britt could hear gulping sobs.

"Oh Zoe, what is it? What's the matter?" Britt said.

Zoe's eyes spilled over with tears. "My mom," she wailed between sobs. "She always used to sit and talk to me about stuff when I got home from Kayley's." Then Zoe lowered her face against her arms again.

Britt rubbed Zoe's back and nodded, as if she understood, but she didn't really. It was Greta whom she used to talk to when she came home from a friend's house. Not Jean Andersen. Jean Andersen was long gone by then. "You know, your mother and I used to talk like that," she said. "I didn't have my own mother to talk to."

Zoe did not lift her head. "Now, I don't either."

"I know, sweetie. It must hurt something awful."

"You don't know," Zoe cried, between sobs. "You just said so."

"I know what it is to grieve," said Britt. "I do know that."

"I want my mom back," Zoe said, her voice squeaky and almost inaudible.

Britt felt heartbroken for her niece, who was crying with helpless abandon. Heartbroken and inadequate to the situation. Britt didn't know what to say to alleviate Zoe's misery. What could she say? A loss like Zoe's wasn't something you could gloss over with the right phrase.

"What am I gonna do? I need my mom," Zoe squeaked. "I need her to be here with me. How can we have Christmas without her?"

"I know, honey," said Britt. "It seems like more than you can bear. But you will survive this. I can promise you that. You'll be able to handle it. Your mom would want you to handle it. She'd want you to be okay. You know she would, right?"

Zoe nodded and sniffed, and wiped her eyes with the back of her hand.

"You want to try a little more of the sandwich?"

Zoe shook her head, staring at the bread on the plate. Then she did her best to draw in a deep breath. "Your mom ran away, didn't she?" Zoe asked, as if trying to prompt the retelling of an old, favorite ghost story.

"Yes, she did," said Britt.

"And she never came back. I know. My mom told me."

"No, she never came back," said Britt, thinking of Greta, and Alec's latest version of the private detective story. Was it possible? Had Greta initiated a search for their mother? Jean Andersen, who had dropped out of their lives without a tear or a word of regret? "In the beginning, after she left, we'd get a birthday card or a few bucks at Christmas. Always from a different place. Then that stopped. She could have come back, but she didn't."

Zoe pulled the sandwich plate toward her, and took a tiny bite.

"That's the difference with your mom," said Britt, looking squarely at her niece. "She didn't leave you by choice. You always have to remember that. She never would have left you by choice."

"I know," said Zoe solemnly.

Britt tipped her head back, resting it against the wall and stared blankly across the room. Despite her suspicions of Alec, he had to know that he couldn't get away with another lie about the reason for Greta's hiring the detective. And more than that, something inside her told her that it might well be true. There was never really a face or a voice attached to those cards in the mail for her from her mother. But she remembered that for Greta, every perfunctory dollar with a card was the subject of hours of speculation. Speculation

Britt found boring and annoying. Greta was always rueful that Britt didn't take much of an interest. Looking back on it now, Britt realized that those impersonal missives must have pierced Greta to the heart. Filled her with hope and then let her down again. Why else would she have tried to find that woman again? Britt never even thought of her. "I think that was the worst part for your mother, you know," said Britt. "The hope that our mother might come back."

"Didn't you hope for it?" Zoe asked. She sniffed again. Britt handed her a tissue, and tried to form an honest answer. Finally, she said, "I don't know. I guess so. I mean, I was so little when she left . . . I couldn't even figure out what was happening. And afterward, I didn't remember what life was like when she was there."

"Do you still think about her?" Zoe asked.

How can I think about her? Britt thought. *I can't even picture her.* She was just a face in a photo album. Not a mother. Britt was still so shocked by the idea that Greta had been searching for Jean Andersen. And was she going to let me know, Britt wondered? Was she hoping for some sort of surprise reunion? Or was she just going to pretend that I wasn't a part of it? That I didn't exist.

"Aunt Britt?"

"Some people just aren't cut out to be parents, Zoe," Britt said wearily.

"My mom still cried when she talked about her."

"Your mom was a lot closer to her than I was," said Britt. "I always favored my dad."

"I favor my mom *and* my dad," said Zoe.

Britt nodded noncommittally and then stood up and walked over to the cabinets. "Where did I put those vitamins?" she wondered aloud, opening the cabinet doors. "You should take one."

"I think you put them in the refrigerator," said Zoe.

"That's right. It said to refrigerate them. I don't know where my mind is," she said, although she did know. She just didn't want to tell Zoe. "Here we go," Britt said.

Zoe made a face, but took the proffered vitamin. "These are gross," she said.

"Down the hatch," said Britt.

Zoe swallowed the vitamin and then yawned.

"Zoe," Alec called out from down the hall. "Time for you to get in that shower and then to bed. Hurry up."

Zoe made a face. "I have to clean up the kitchen," she called out.

"I'll do it," said Britt. "You go on."

"Thanks, Aunt Britt." She gave her aunt a brief hug and before Britt could respond, Zoe was gone from the kitchen.

Slowly, Britt began to gather up the bread and the peanut butter and put it away. She replaced the milk in the refrigerator and rinsed off the plate and the glass before setting them in the dishwasher. She did not want to go back out into the living room. She did not want to see Alec. For a moment she thought about trying to slip upstairs without being seen, but then she chided herself. She wasn't going to hide from him. She hadn't done anything wrong.

After she had dawdled as long as possible, she walked down the hall to the living room. From upstairs she could hear the shower running in the bathroom, and the sound of Zoe, singing. Children were resilient, she thought. I was resilient. I didn't spend my life longing for my mother. Greta had always seemed strong, but here was a piece of the puzzle Britt would never have suspected. Clearly, Greta had never stopped hoping to find her mother.

Alec was sitting on the couch, staring at a basketball game on the television but he was not relaxed. His frame was tight as a bowstring.

Britt took a deep breath and walked into the room. He did not look up at her.

"Alec," Britt said. "I want to talk to you."

He kept his eyes trained on the television screen and did not reply.

"Is this really true?" she asked. "That Greta was trying to find our mother?"

"No, I'm lying," he said sarcastically. "You were right. She hired the detective to trail me."

"Look, maybe I shouldn't have jumped to that conclusion," she admitted.

He turned and glared at her. "No, you're sorry it's not true. You were hoping that's what it was. You've been such a busy lady since you got here."

"I know you're angry but . . . I just want to know. What happened when the detective tried to find my mother? What did they find out?"

Alec stood up and walked over to her. His gray eyes glittered under his black eyebrows. "I guess you weren't listening," he said. "If you want the information, you can hire them yourself. You can pay for it."

"Don't be obnoxious. She was my mother, too. Greta would want me to know."

"Did Greta ever call you and tell you?"

"No," Britt admitted.

"Then, I guess she didn't want you to know," he said. "And I don't owe you a thing. Except my thanks, of course, for trying to frame me for murdering my wife."

Britt glared back at him, refusing to back down. "I wonder what Zoe would think about you hoarding this information."

Alec blanched. He shook his head slowly. "Don't you dare," he said. "Don't you dare try to use my child against me."

"Or you'll do what?" Britt demanded.

Alec took a deep breath, and then turned away from her. He sat back down on the couch and stared at the basketball game.

"Look Alec, can't we . . ."

He turned up the volume on the remote so that it drowned out her voice. After she stopped speaking, he turned it back down again.

"I want you out of here," he said.

Britt was stunned, although, when she thought about it. . . . "What about Zoe?" she said.

"I think she'll live through it," he said.

In a way it was a shock, and in another way a relief. She didn't know where she was going to go, but the thought of spending another night here was impossible. She stalked out of the room toward the stairs. He came out and stood in the hallway.

"Didn't you hear me?" he said. "Leave. Now. No good-byes, please."

"I'm going to get my stuff," she said, through clenched teeth.

"Don't bother. It's all out on the porch," he said. "I packed for you while you were in the kitchen."

Britt stared at him, speechless.

He looked satisfied by her surprise. "Did you think I was kidding?" he said.

Part of Britt was humiliated. She'd never been kicked out of somebody's home before. Part of her was furious. But she wasn't intimidated. She hadn't worked her way up in the world by being timid. "Zoe wants me here," Britt said.

"It's not Zoe's house," he explained carefully, as if Britt were a small child. "It's my house. I decide who stays and who goes. Now, get out of my house."

"If anything happens to Zoe . . ."

Alec stalked toward her, his eyes ablaze. "You interfering witch," he cried. "I'll take care of my daughter."

"That's what I'm afraid of," said Britt.

Alec clenched his fist as if he was ready to strike her. Britt gazed back at him without flinching, although inside she was trying to steel herself for the blow.

His whole body was trembling, but when he spoke, it was in a low, menacing voice. "She'll do whatever I tell her. Do you think she'd take your part over mine? She adores me. I'm her father. You are nothing to her. Less than nothing. She never even set eyes on you before this week. Go back where you came from. She will never miss you. I promise you that."

He was so close to her that Britt could feel his warm breath, and smell tobacco and aftershave. She could see the creases that seemed to be sculpted into his face.

"You don't scare me," she said. "I'm not some schoolgirl you can push around."

"Leave or I'll call the cops myself. I believe I still have a right to kick you out of my house if I want to."

Britt hated to retreat, but she couldn't wait to get away from him. "You know what? You don't have to," she said calmly. "I'll get out of here. But I'm not leaving town. I'm going to stick around until I'm sure that Greta is going to get some justice."

Alec stared at her with an unreadable expression in his eyes. Then, he shook his head and gave a mirthless laugh. "Yeah. That's right," he said. "You do that, Britt. You come through for your sister. Way to go."

"Shut up," said Britt, suddenly furious at him, despite her intention to remain cool. She went out to the hall closet to collect her coat.

"Looking for your coat? That's out on the porch, too," he said, with a satisfied smirk.

"Go to hell," said Britt. She opened the front door and slammed it against him, before he had a chance to reply.

CHAPTER 18

Britt pulled into the driveway of the secluded white farmhouse and looked at the address on the slip of paper she was holding. This was it. A discreet scripted sign which hung beneath the lamppost near the driveway read Bayberry House, Bed-and-Breakfast, Letty and Michael Morrison, Proprietors.

Her first stop had been the Glace Mountain Lodge. The manager there had explained apologetically that the lodge was full for the weekend but he would have rooms available by Monday night, and offered her a list of the local B & Bs which might be able to accommodate her over the weekend. Bayberry House was at the top of the alphabetical list.

Britt sighed. Part of her was ready to call the airline and get a flight back to Boston. The humiliating sight of her belongings set outside the door on the porch as Alec locked the door behind her made her want to just leave this place in the rearview mirror. But if she did that, Alec would spin some lie about her for Zoe, and, more important, there would be nobody here to pressure the police on this investigation. Nobody but Dean Webster, she reminded herself. And he might give it up if he thought his network introduction was gone. Britt was certain that Chief Stern was dragging his feet because he sympathized with Alec. She had no such feelings. She was not going to give up on this. Not now.

Britt trudged up to the front door of the house and heard a dog barking inside as she rang the bell. A chubby woman with her shiny, brown hair twisted up in a silver clip answered the door, telling her dog to hush, a command that the golden lab cheerfully ignored. "Mrs. Morrison?" Britt asked.

"Call me Letty," she said pleasantly.

"I'm sorry to come by so late. I just um . . . got to town. My name is Britt Andersen. I need a place to stay for a couple of nights."

"Come on in," she said. "Get down, Ranger," she said as the dog, tail wagging, tried to position his head under Britt's hand for a pet.

Britt stepped into the house. It was fastidiously kept, and decorated with twig wreaths, birdhouses, braided rugs and comfortable-looking furniture with checked upholstery. "Where are you from?" Letty asked.

"Boston," said Britt.

"Are you here to ski?"

"No. Just visiting family," said Britt not wanting to offer details about her situation.

"Well, I have two rooms available upstairs. Although I should warn you I have a seventeen-year-old who likes to blast his music."

Britt smiled grimly as the dog let out another explosive series of barks.

"Or, the cottage out back is available. It's a little bit more expensive, but it has its own kitchen and a separate driveway."

"That sounds perfect," said Britt, relieved. She didn't much relish the idea of meeting the family, coming and going to the shower.

"Well, I'll tell you what. It's late and you're probably tired. How about I just give you the key and you can make yourself comfortable out there? We can settle up on the details tomorrow."

"Okay," said Britt, a little surprised by the casual arrangement. She was more accustomed to the suspicion of strangers in the city. "That's awfully kind of you. Do you want a deposit right now?"

"That's all right. You have family here. I'm not worried. Even though you're in the cottage, you can still have breakfast in the main house. My husband, Mike, bakes all the bread himself."

"Oh, thanks," said Britt. "I'm not much of a breakfast eater."

"Well, it's included, if you change your mind. I haven't met the first person who can resist Mike's baking," she said.

"I'll keep that in mind," said Britt, examining the key which was attached to a large, maple-leaf key chain.

"You can just see the cottage from our backyard, but you have to take your car around to the other driveway, and pull in there. Just back out, and make a left at the first corner, and then it's your first left," said Letty. "You have to look for it. It looks like a little gravel path between the trees."

"Okay, thanks," said Britt.

"You stop by in the morning or whenever it's convenient and we'll do all the official business."

"I will," said Britt. "Thanks."

She went out to her car and pulled out of the driveway and followed Letty's simple directions. She soon found herself facing a little one-story cottage with a peaked roof surrounded by bare trees. She unlocked the door, and went inside, turning on the overhead light.

The cottage consisted of one room with a double bed, a bathroom and a galley kitchen. This will do fine, Britt thought with relief. She threw her bag on a chair by the window, and lay down on the denim-quilted bedspread, covering her eyes with her hands. In a way, it felt good to finally be alone again, but when she closed her eyes, she pictured Zoe, and wondered how Alec would explain her absence when Zoe woke up in the morning.

Never mind that, she thought. *You can get in touch with Zoe tomorrow and explain it yourself. Meanwhile, you have a place to sleep.* She forced herself to get up, unpack her toiletry kit in the bathroom, and throw her few clothes into the dresser drawer. *There*, she thought. *Unpacked.*

The events of the last few days ran like a loop through her mind. She needed to talk to someone. Someone who would take her side. Someone who was not involved. A friend. She looked at her watch. Nancy would be at the studio. It wasn't even airtime yet. Britt rummaged in her pocketbook for her cell phone and dialed Nancy's extension at the studio. They'd spoken a few times since she got up here, but mostly just to touch base on business matters. Britt hadn't had time for a proper conversation with her friend since she arrived in Coleville. The phone rang three times and then a man answered.

"Donovan Smith."

"Donovan," she said, surprised and flustered to hear his voice.

"Britt." He sounded chipper.

"Where's Nancy?" she asked.

"Oh, some business about the grandchildren being in a play. She had to leave early. How are things on the slopes?"

"I'm not up here to ski, Donovan. I came for a funeral, remember?"

"Of course I remember," he said. His voice was warm, unguent-like. It had a hypnotic effect on women and he knew it. "How was the funeral?"

"As funerals go, not much fun," she said.

"They rarely are," he said. "At least it's over."

"It was yesterday."

"You all right?"

"Yes," she said uncertainly, glad to be asked.

"I recommend that you do something nice for yourself. Go rent some skis and get out there on the slopes. You should take advantage of being there."

"You know I don't ski," she said.

"I know, but you could take a lesson or two," he suggested. "It's not hard. Just a rhythm you've got to get into. It would clear your head. Make you feel better."

"Actually I have other things on my mind," she said. *Donovan*, she thought. *He was smart and analytical. He might be just the person she needed to talk to.* "Maybe you'd have some ideas."

"About what?" he asked.

"I told you my sister died in a fire . . ."

"Yes . . ."

"Let's just say it was a fire of suspicious origin."

There was a brief silence. His tone of voice sounded suddenly detached. "Really?"

Britt heard the riffling of papers in the background. "Are you reading something while we're talking?" she demanded. She'd seen him do it many times to other people.

"No, of course not," he said indignantly, but the rustling stopped. "What were you saying?"

Britt didn't know whether or not to continue, but she knew it would seem childish to clam up all of a sudden. "Unfortunately, I don't have a lot of confidence in the local police department. So I've been asking a few questions of my own."

"Doing a little Nancy Drewing?" he asked with a chuckle.

She had expected him to show some curiosity about the fire, but obviously that was the furthest thing from his mind. Britt wondered why she had thought she could talk to him. "I just have some questions that need answers," she concluded abruptly.

"And I . . ." he said, "have a program that needs a producer. When are you coming home?"

"I'll be back soon," she said.

"Britty, Britty, Britty," he cajoled. "My pretty Britt. I'm sure it's all very interesting, but your job is here. I need you. You know I need you."

Her body reacted to his seductive voice as if it had a mind of its own. As if she had no mind at all. And it was all so much bullshit. "You don't need me," she said bitterly.

Donovan cleared his throat impatiently. "All right, look," he said briskly. "You can have a day or two more, but that's it. Life goes on, Britt."

She knew she should ask how the show had gone in her absence but his attitude made her feel rebellious. "Is that a threat?" she asked.

"Of course not. I couldn't do without you," he said. "Now wrap things up and get your little butt back here ASAP. Between all these pretty little airheads around here we can barely manage. I'll tell Nancy you called. I've got to run. Take care now."

Britt pushed the off button on her phone and stared at the ceiling, hating herself, and Donovan Smith. She found herself thinking of Zoe, eating that peanut butter sandwich and questioning Britt about her feelings toward her mother. *I told that child more about my mother today than I told Donovan Smith in our two years of so-called intimacy.* She'd wanted to stop him. She'd wanted to say, "Stuff your job. I quit." But she hadn't had the nerve. And if she did it, what would she have left? She lay on the bed with her eyes closed, feeling more alone than ever.

Your life with men has been a complete and utter failure, she thought. Suddenly, beside her on the bed, the cell phone rang. Britt jumped, and thought immediately of Donovan. Then, she banished the thought and pushed the button.

"Yes," she said warily.

"Britt, it's Dean Webster," he said. His speech was slightly slurred, but his tone of voice was forceful.

Britt looked at her watch. "It's kind of late," she said.

"I hope I didn't wake up the household," he said.

"No," she said. "No danger of that. I'm at a hotel now. A B&B actually."

"Really?" he asked, and she could hear him virtually licking his chops. "What happened? Things get a little tense around the house?"

"It was tight quarters," she said, unwilling to be a part of his news reports. "I just wanted to spread out a little. I got the cottage at Bayberry House."

"Oh, right," he said. "Well, look, I just thought you might be interested in something I heard tonight after I saw you."

"Oh, and what was that?" she asked.

"Apparently Alec Lynch was planning on leaving our fair town of Coleville. Our fair state for that matter. He met with a business broker about selling his business, and buying a business in Virginia Beach. I believe they were talking about jet skis."

"You're kidding," said Britt.

"That's not all. He rented an apartment there. He took a lease that started two months ago."

"Oh my God." So, she thought, perhaps there *was* a girlfriend, after all. "That's amazing," she said. "Where did you hear that?"

"My sources have been calling in," he said. "I told you, I'm good."

Britt ignored his bravado. "Does Chief Stern know?" she asked.

"He'll know tomorrow," he said.

For a minute it was silent except for the hum of the cell as Britt thought about what Dean had just told her. "What will the police do?" she said at last.

"Well, unless they're completely incompetent, they're going to be all over Alec Lynch," said Dean.

Zoe, Britt thought, and her heart dropped. She'll be devastated.

"You're awfully quiet."

"I have a lot on my mind. But, I have to admit, you are good."

"You don't know the half of it, Britt," he said in an insinuating tone. "I've got a lot of talents I haven't even showed you yet."

Britt rolled her eyes. "You're quite a kid," she said.

"I'm a man," he said softly.

Britt felt an undeniable jolt, a sexual buzz. "Good night," she said firmly, glad he could not see her blush.

CHAPTER 19

The next morning, a pewter-gray day with snow flurries blowing, Britt entered a diner called Henry's, went up to the take-out counter, and ordered a cup of coffee to go. She had avoided the Bayberry House breakfast. Despite the promise of Mike's homemade bread, the last thing she felt like doing was talking to a bunch of strangers over breakfast about where she came from and why she was here. There was a television suspended near the low ceiling above the counter and it was tuned to a local morning show. Britt paid no attention to it until suddenly, a familiar voice caught her ear. She looked up and saw Dean Webster on camera. His gold-tipped hair was perfectly coifed, his blue eyes were sober and serious. Behind him was the grotesque frame of what had once been her sister's house.

Britt stared at the news broadcast, transfixed. "Yes, Bob," Dean was saying, "rumors are flying that an arrest may be imminent in the arson homicide of Greta Lynch. Sources close to the investigation in Coleville tell us that the police have found some new information which is leading them in the direction of a suspect. We talked to the district attorney this morning . . ." The picture on the screen then cut to a somber-looking middle-aged guy in a blue suit. "Dean, as you know," he was saying, "arson is a crime that leaves very little evidence behind. That's one reason it's so difficult to prosecute. Almost always, arson cases rely on circumstantial evidence. But we are hopeful that we will have that evidence."

"Does that mean you are going to make an arrest?"

"I can't say any more at this time," said the D.A., shaking his head. The camera cut back to Dean. "Speculation is rampant about the identity of the suspect, but for now, it's a waiting game. We'll be staying on top of this story. Now, back to you, Bob."

Dean's image melted away, as the host thanked him and the morning show resumed.

"Here's your coffee," said a waitress, pushing a paper bag toward Britt across the counter.

"Oh, sorry," said Britt, startled. She fumbled for her wallet, and peered at the cheek, but her heart was racing. She hoped Zoe wasn't watching the television. Then she remembered. Zoe wouldn't think they were talking about her father. She wouldn't be thinking of him as a possible suspect. No, if they arrested Alec Lynch, it was going to turn her little world upside down all over again.

* * *

Britt started to get into her car, which was parked outside the diner, and then she thought better of it. She decided to walk the length of Main Street instead, to get a little exercise. Besides, it was early and she had plenty of time. She had slept so poorly that she had decided to get up and stop trying. Still carrying her take-out coffee, Britt pushed open the door to the Coleville Police Station. The station house was humming, officers in blue coming and going through the double doors. Britt walked up to the sergeant at the desk, who was typing on her computer and talking on the phone at the same time. The woman frowned at her, and indicated a nearby bench where several people were already seated.

Britt sat down, as far as she could from the nearest person, and pulled the paper cup of coffee out of the bag. She was willing to wait as long as was necessary, to talk to Chief Stern. She took a sip of the steaming coffee and nearly burned her lip.

"Hey there, Britt," said a friendly voice.

Britt looked up in surprise and saw a ruddy-faced man in an elegant suit and silk tie, walking slowly toward her. It took her a few moments to recognize the man. When she'd met him he had been lying in bed in his pajamas.

"Mr. Carmichael," she said, starting to get up.

He motioned for her to sit down, and he gingerly lowered himself down onto the bench beside her. "Kevin," he said. "Please."

"What are you doing here?" she said. "I thought you were bedridden."

"Had a call from a client they locked up last night, so I came down. Gotta keep the wolf from the door, you know."

"It looks like you're still in a lot of pain," Britt said.

Kevin shrugged, and then winced. "I'm taped up. What are you doing here?"

"I want to talk to Chief Stern about . . . some developments . . ."

"You won't see Chief Stern. He's not here. I hear he went to Montpelier to do some checking on an alibi."

Part of Britt was disappointed. But there was definite comfort in knowing that he was checking out Alec's story. "My brother-in-law's alibi," said Britt grimly. "He claims he drove a hitchhiker to Montpelier on the night of the fire."

"Ah ha," said Kevin, nodding. "I've been watching the news. They're talking about a suspect. I couldn't help but wonder if it was Alec . . ."

"His story was a little hard to swallow," said Britt. "At least for me."

"Well, I've been a defense attorney for a long time," Kevin said. "Police tend to investigate a crime like this in concentric circles, starting with those who were closest to the victim. Especially the spouse. So, when they start talking about a suspect this quickly, it leads me to think they didn't have to go much beyond that first circle . . ."

"You're an expert in this kind of thing," said Britt. "What do you think? Do you think he did it?"

"I don't know," said Kevin. "He's an abrasive guy, but he always seemed to dote on them. Greta and Zoe. But you can never tell about a marriage. I've defended a number of people accused of killing their spouses. There are some terrible things that go on behind closed doors. I'll tell you that. Women who take all kinds of abuse until they just snap. And from the outside, everything looked perfectly normal. There are men who seem to be loving husbands who brutalize their wives.

"In some cases, the woman just couldn't see any other way out. And the abuse tapped into something from her childhood that sent her spinning helplessly out of control," he said earnestly, as if he were addressing the jury.

"But the abusive husband. How do you defend him? Especially if it leads to murder," said Britt.

Kevin frowned, as if she had interrupted his train of thought. "You're talking about Alec now, right?"

Britt nodded, wondering what he had been thinking about.

Kevin seemed to resume his lawyerly stride. "On the one hand, we don't have any knowledge that he was abusive. I'd focus on that. The fact that he loved his child and had no reason to hurt her."

"Maybe the new girlfriend didn't want a man encumbered with children," said Britt.

"Is there a new girlfriend?" Kevin raised his eyebrows.

"Don't know for sure. Apparently, there's some evidence he was planning to start his life over somewhere else."

"That doesn't mean he was planning to kill his wife. Maybe she was planning on going with him."

"Did Greta ever say anything like that to you or Caroline?" Britt asked.

"Well, I don't think so, but . . . that doesn't mean they weren't planning it together."

"He rented a one-bedroom apartment," said Britt. "Room enough for one. Or a very romantic couple."

Kevin shrugged. "I see your point. He may need my services," he said. "Well, I'd better be getting outside. I called Caroline to come and pick me up."

"I'm gonna go, too," said Britt. "I'll try later, see if I can catch the chief when he gets back. You need a hand up?"

Without waiting for his reply, Britt gently hooked her arm around Kevin and helped him to his feet. His face paled at the effort. "I guess you can't drive," she said.

"Not for a while yet," he said. "With a cracked rib, you run the risk of puncturing a lung. Or so they tell me."

They walked slowly out of the police station together, and Britt helped him down the steps one at a time. Just as they reached the bottom step, a brand new red Toyota with a ski rack on top, and the dealer's sticker still in the window, pulled up in front of them and squealed to a halt. The driver sounded the horn.

Kevin looked quizzically at Britt. "Anybody you know?" he asked.

Britt shook her head, and then saw Caroline, in the Carmichaels' Explorer, pull up and park behind the Toyota. Caroline jumped out of the driver's seat and walked toward them with an apologetic expression on her face, just as the driver of the Toyota managed to struggle out of the front seat. It was Vicki, her coat agape around her maternity top. She lumbered over to where Kevin was standing on the sidewalk. She threw an arm awkwardly around his shoulders and pressed her cheek to his.

"Mr. C. Thank you so much. You're fantastic. How can I ever thank you?"

"Vicki don't," Caroline scolded as she hurried over to Kevin. She stopped short when she saw Britt standing beside her husband. "Hello," she said.

"Hello," Britt replied, feeling slightly embarrassed.

"Darling, are you all right?" Caroline asked. "How did it go in there?"

Vicki, who had been figuratively pushed out of the way, did not seem especially troubled. She gazed at the pair of them curiously.

"Whose car is this?" Kevin asked, ignoring Caroline's solicitous questions.

Caroline glanced at Vicki with a warning look, but Vicki's large blue eyes were alight. "I just got it," she said in her babyish voice. "We went and picked it up. It's so beautiful," said Vicki. She looked at the Toyota lovingly.

Kevin frowned and looked from Vicki to Caroline. "What do you mean, you just got it?"

Caroline pressed her lips together grimly and frown lines formed on her forehead. Britt wished that she could disappear from the sidewalk. Obviously the purchase of the car was news to Kevin. There was a terrible tension in the air. "I'd promised Vicki that we would get her a car. She needs a car, Kevin."

A closed expression came over Kevin's face.

Vicki glanced from Caroline to Kevin, confused. "I really love it," she said, with a shade less confidence. "If you want, I can drive you home, Kevin."

Kevin did not reply. He was staring at Caroline, who was pretending she didn't notice his baleful gaze. Britt was trying to think of something to say, when suddenly her cell phone rang in her pocketbook.

"Excuse me," she said, relieved, and pressed the phone to her ear.

"Aunt Britt," a voice cried.

"Zoe," said Britt, startled. "Are you calling from school? What's the matter?"

"I felt sick this morning so I stayed home. Aunt Britt, there's police here," she wailed. "They want to come in to search our house and my dad's not here."

Britt's heart started to hammer. "Did you call him?"

"Yes, I called him but I had to leave a message . . . The police were at the dealership, too. I'm all alone here, Aunt Britt."

"All right, okay," said Britt. "Calm down, sweetie. Are they trying to come in?"

"They're waiting outside for my dad," Zoe said.

"Okay. I'll come right over there. Don't worry. Just sit tight."

She looked at the Carmichaels and Vicki. "That was Zoe. She's very upset. The police are at the house. I need to go over there right away," she said.

"I'll drive you," Vicki offered. "I wanted Zoe to see my new car anyway."

Britt's first impulse was to decline, but she could see that Vicki wanted to escape the Carmichaels. And Britt's car was parked all the way up Main Street. She didn't want to keep Zoe waiting a moment longer than was necessary.

"All right. Thanks," said Britt reluctantly. "Can we hurry?"

"Sure," said Vicki, trundling around to the driver's side.

"Drive carefully," Caroline said anxiously. She remained standing beside her husband, still avoiding his gaze. When she tried to reach for his arm, he snatched it away.

CHAPTER 20

"How do you move this seat back?" Vicki complained as she squeezed herself behind the wheel of the new car. "I'm squooshed."

"Try that lever at the bottom," said Britt, buckling up her seat belt.

"Ah, that's better," said Vicki. She wrinkled her nose and made a face. "You know everybody always raves about that new-car smell but I think it smells gross. I'm gonna get one of those little pine trees to hang off my mirror. I hate this smell."

Britt shrugged. She was not able to think about Vicki's new car. Vicki stuck the key in the ignition.

"Now, let me just push some of these buttons and make sure I know where everything is. I need the windshield wipers with these snow flurries."

"Okay, okay," said Britt, impatiently. "But I told her I'd be right there."

Vicki familiarized herself with the dashboard and then pronounced herself all set. She put the car into gear and stepped on the gas. The car lurched forward and Britt grabbed the dashboard.

"Sorry," said Vicki, giggling. She glanced at Britt and seemed to notice her frown. "Okay, okay, we're going." She looked in her mirror and pulled away from the curb. "I was used to driving my boyfriend's car which was an old wreck on its last legs. You'd press on the gas with all your might and the thing would barely move. It finally broke down completely."

Britt nodded, wondering if that boyfriend was the baby's father. And if he even knew that Vicki was expecting a baby. Trying to be considerate, despite her own anxiety, Britt said, "How are you feeling these days?"

Vicki shrugged, as she craned her neck, watching the road. "Like I swallowed a whale," she said. "I can't get any sleep. I get gas from everything I eat."

"Not much longer," said Britt.

"Thank God," said Vicki.

Britt looked back at the sidewalk in front of the police station. Kevin and Caroline were nowhere in sight. "How did you happen to pick the Carmichaels to be the parents?"

Vicki frowned, as if trying to remember. "Well, I liked their ad. And it was convenient with him being a lawyer. He can handle the whole legal thing. And they seemed to really want a baby . . . and they have that nice house. Of course, I found out she can really be hell on wheels. I hope she's not going to give the kid the same kind of hard time she gives me. The kid'll hate me forever."

"She's just nervous," said Britt absently. "I'm sure it will be fine."

"I hope so," said Vicki, shaking her head.

Britt had to force herself to keep quiet. She knew Vicki was driving as safely as possible, but it seemed too slow to suit her. *Leave her alone*, she thought. *She's doing the speed limit.* "What are you going to do after the baby's born," she asked, trying to be pleasant. "Where's home?"

Vicki hesitated. "I think I'm just going to take it easy for a while. I'm not sure what my plans are going to be," she said vaguely.

"Do you keep in touch with the baby's father?"

Vicki seemed startled by the question, and then irritated. "Look, I don't know who the baby's father is, okay? I wasn't too careful about that kind of thing. The guy I think it was is long gone. Went to Mexico right after he knocked me up. He probably wouldn't even remember being with me. I don't want to talk about this," she said. "You sure ask a lot of questions."

"Sorry," said Britt. "Didn't mean to pry."

"This is the street," said Vicki. "I think that's the house, right over there, where they're staying. Oh, there are the cop cars."

"That's the one," Britt said. Two black-and-whites were parked out in front, lights flashing. *God, Zoe must be terrified,* Britt thought. "Pull over," she said.

"All right. Keep your shirt on," said Vicki.

Britt frowned, wondering what kind of influence this girl might be on Zoe. Just as well that Vicki would soon be leaving town. Vicki had a very young, almost immature side, that seemed to appeal to Zoe, and, of course, the cat, Kirby, but Britt doubted the girls had much else in common.

Vicki pulled up behind the police car and Britt jumped out. "Hey," a cop called out to her, but she ignored him. She ran across the snow-covered front yard to the steps and began to bang on the door. The policeman followed her, walking slowly and deliberately up to where she stood.

"Zoe," Britt cried, knocking on the door. "Honey, it's me. Aunt Britt."

"We'd prefer you don't go in there, ma'am," said the policeman.

"I'm not trying to go in," said Britt. "My niece is in there. She's not feeling well and she's scared to death. I'm going to take her with me, all right? Then you guys can do whatever you have to do."

Zoe opened the door a crack and looked out fearfully. "Aunt Britt."

"Put your coat on, honey," said Britt. "You come with me. This is none of your concern."

"My dad finally called me back. . . . He's coming."

"Zoe, you just come along with me. Right now. I'll explain everything to your dad. Come on." The last thing this child needed, Britt thought, was to have the police come in and tear this already chaotic house apart in front of her. "Do as I tell you, now."

Zoe closed the door, and then opened it again a few moments later. She was wearing her pink parka, bare wrists dangling from the sleeves. Britt gently pulled the hood up over her hair.

"Come on," she said. "Look who's here."

Vicki rolled down the driver's side window and waved. "How do you like my new wheels?" Vicki cried out cheerfully.

"Nice," Zoe said listlessly. Britt opened the back door for her and Zoe slid in. Britt went around and got into the passenger seat.

"Let's go," said Britt.

"Go where?" Vicki asked.

"Anywhere," said Britt.

"Okay," said Vicki. As she began to pull out of the driveway, Alec's Mercedes roared up and wheeled to a halt.

"Aunt Britt," Zoe cried. "Dad's back."

"Hold it, Vicki," Britt said. "Zoe, you stay in the car. I'll talk to your dad."

Vicki stopped the car, and Britt opened the passenger door and walked toward the Mercedes. Alec was getting out of his car, stared at by the cops who were waiting for him. "Alec," she called out.

He turned and looked at her, his gray eyes like thunderclouds.

"Zoe called me. She was frightened. I thought I'd take her out of here," she said.

"This is your doing," he said. "If she's frightened, it's your fault. You and your friend, the TV reporter. You're trying to destroy me. And my family."

"Oh, you don't need me to do that," said Britt.

He started to stride toward the driveway. "Zoe," he cried, "get out of that car."

"Leave her alone, Alec. Haven't you done enough to her? She's scared. She doesn't need to be in the middle of this."

Zoe's white face appeared at the car window, looking out helplessly. Alec hesitated and then, before he had a chance to continue, one of the policemen approached him and demanded that he unlock the house.

"I'm going to take her," said Britt.

"You'll be sorry for this," said Alec, glowering.

"Don't threaten me," said Britt. She turned and walked back to Vicki's car, and settled into the passenger seat. She was shaking when she sat down. "Let's go, Vicki," she said.

"Aunt Britt, why are the police here?" Zoe asked. "What are they looking for?"

"I don't know, honey," said Britt.

Zoe was silent.

"Your dad told me to take care of you until they were gone," Britt said with her fingers crossed.

"Where are we going?" said Vicki.

"Why don't I take you girls out for some lunch or something," said Britt.

"Cool," said Vicki.

"Okay," said Zoe with a sigh.

"I want Burger King," said Vicki. "I'm so sick of health food."

"That's fine. Whatever," said Britt.

"Dad told me you went back to Boston," Zoe said to Britt.

He *would* say that, Britt thought furiously. She didn't want to contradict him to Zoe's face. "It was time for me to get out of the way. But I'm still here in town. I got a room. It's perfectly comfortable."

"Why didn't you stay with us?" Zoe asked.

"Your dad and I had a little bit of an argument, Zoe."

"Hey," Vicki interrupted. "What about my new car? You haven't even said one word, Zoe."

"It's nice," Zoe said. Then after a moment's silence she added, "I wonder how Kirby's gonna like it."

"He'll probably pee all over it," said Vicki, and Zoe smiled.

They arrived at the Burger King and parked the car. The three of them got out and walked slowly toward the restaurant, Vicki frowning and holding her belly with one hand. They selected a booth and Zoe slid into the seat.

Britt peered at Zoe. "How's your stomach? Is it okay?"

"It's okay," Zoe said impatiently.

Britt reached over and felt Zoe's forehead. It was cool, and a little clammy. "All right. I guess you'll be okay with some junk food here. The soda will probably settle your stomach. I'll go get it," said Britt. "Just tell me what you want."

They all decided on their order and Britt started toward the line at the counter.

"I have to go to the john," said Vicki and started to lumber in that direction.

Britt joined the line and waited, looking back at Zoe from time to time, who sat alone in the booth, resting her chin in her hand, staring glumly out at the gray sky. *The poor thing*, Britt thought. *How much does she have to endure?* Britt finally reached the head of the line, placed her order, dispensed the three sodas, and then paid the cashier. When she returned to the table with the loaded tray, Zoe was still alone in the booth.

"Vicki didn't come back yet?" Britt asked.

Zoe shook her head.

"Maybe I'd better go see if she's okay," Britt said. "Do you want to come with me?"

Zoe turned a little pale and shook her head. "I'll wait here with the food," she said.

"Okay," said Britt. "I'll be back in a minute."

She walked down to the door of the ladies' room and pushed it open. "Vicki?" she said. "Are you in here?"

"Over here," said Vicki weakly. "The wheelchair booth."

Britt walked over and gingerly pushed open the door of the booth. Vicki was seated, fully clothed on the toilet, her face dead white and sweaty. She looked up at Britt, her blue eyes wide with alarm. "I don't feel good," she said.

CHAPTER 21

With Britt at the wheel of Vicki's new car, they rushed to the hospital. Once Vicki was whisked inside the examining room, Britt called Caroline. Britt and Zoe were seated outside the emergency room when Caroline burst in, looking frantic.

"Where is she?" Caroline demanded. "Is the baby coming?"

"I don't know," said Britt honestly. "They took her in right away. We haven't seen her since."

"Oh my God," said Caroline. "I hope I'm not too late."

"Why don't you talk to the nurse at the desk," Britt suggested. "Maybe she can give you some more information." Muttering absently to herself, Caroline rushed up to the desk where the two people ahead of her looked coldly on her frantic pleas to let her go ahead of them.

Britt and Zoe sat back down. "Do you think the police are gone now?" Zoe asked.

Britt glanced at her watch. "I don't know. Maybe."

"What were they looking for?" Zoe asked.

"I'm not sure. I think it's about the fire."

"That doesn't make any sense. We didn't even move into that house until after the fire happened." Zoe cried.

"That's not even our stuff. Everything in there is stuff people gave us."

"I know," said Britt. "I don't know what they're looking for."

"They want to blame it on my dad, don't they?"

Britt stared at her. "Why do you say that?"

"I heard some kids at school saying it."

"I'm sorry, Zoe."

"Oh, don't be sorry," said Zoe. "That's just crazy and stupid. They can look all they want. They won't find any reason to blame it on my dad." She looked up at Britt. "Are you sure you can't change your mind and stay with us?"

"I don't think so," said Britt.

Zoe sighed. "I want to go home now. I want to see my dad."

"Are you sure?" Britt asked.

"Positive," said Zoe.

As they gathered up their coats and Britt slung her bag over her shoulder, Caroline came rushing up to them. "Vicki's blood pressure is spiking," she said. "They're going to admit her."

"Is Vicki having the baby?" Zoe asked.

"No, but they might have to do a caesarean," said Caroline. "They don't know yet."

"What's that?" said Zoe.

"That's when they do an operation on the mother to take the baby out," Britt explained.

"Gross," said Zoe. "Poor Vicki."

"Is there anything we can do for you?" Britt asked Caroline. "Where's Kevin?"

"I couldn't wait for him," said Caroline dismissively. "I've got to go to the baby. To Vicki."

"Hope everything works out," said Britt, but Caroline was already heading through the double doors to the treatment area.

As they came off the elevator into the lobby, they met Kevin entering the hospital. He was moving slowly, laboriously, and his face looked drained. "How's Vicki?" he asked.

"They're admitting her," said Britt. "I think she's going to be okay."

"Is Caro all right?"

"Seems to be," said Britt, watching him as he walked slowly into the elevator. *Are you all right?* she wondered.

Britt drove Zoe back to the borrowed house on Medford Road. Everything seemed quiet and she noted that Alec's car was parked outside. She got out of the car with Zoe and walked with her up to the front steps. She hung back as Zoe opened the door and rushed inside calling for her father. Zoe slammed the door shut behind her.

Britt stood alone in the driveway, feeling suddenly abandoned. She waited for a moment, wondering if Zoe would remember to say good-bye, and reemerge. But there was no indication that Zoe remembered her aunt was still outside. With a heavy heart, Britt returned to the car. She drove downtown and exchanged Vicki's Toyota for her car. Then she drove back to Bayberry House.

* * *

"Hello again," said Britt, smiling wanly at the acne-ridden teenager who opened the door of the bed-and-breakfast to her.

Without replying the boy turned around and brayed, "Ma . . ." toward the back of the house. "Come on in," he muttered to Britt.

Britt entered the house and stood just inside the door as he sat down in front of the TV and resumed the controls of a video game.

Letty came bustling in wearing an apron over her corduroy pants. "Hey, mister," she said to her son. "Upstairs and work on that project for school."

"Just let me finish this level," he protested.

"Now," Letty insisted.

With a noisy sigh, the boy turned off the game and unfolded himself from the chair.

"Come on in the kitchen," said Letty to Britt. "I've got my desk in there."

Britt followed her through the house to the large, well-appointed kitchen in back. Letty went over to a blond-wood computer desk tucked in a corner and stuffed with papers. She took out a book and opened it to the appropriate page. "Here you go," she said. "Just sign it here. Are you paying by credit card?"

"That would probably be easiest, if you take them," said Britt, removing the card from her wallet.

"Oh sure," said Letty. "Let me run it through my machine. This way you can stay as long as you need to and I'll just put it on the card. Have you got everything you need out there?"

"Yes," said Britt. "It's very comfortable."

"That's good," said Letty, handing her back the card. "By the way. Your brother-in-law was here earlier."

"My brother-in-law?" Britt asked.

"Handsome guy. Kind of tough looking. Dark hair."

Britt's heart was racing. "What did he want?"

"He wanted to know if you were staying here. I said you were but that you were out. I hope that's all right," Letty said, noticing the expression on Britt's face.

Britt thought about the isolated cottage, and didn't like the idea of Alec cornering her there. "Did you tell him I was staying at the cottage?" she said.

Letty nodded. "I did. I hope that's not a problem. You said you were visiting family so naturally I assumed it would be okay . . ."

Britt's eyes widened. "It's okay, it's okay," she said, trying to think. Then she said, "Look, I don't really want any visitors while I'm here," she said.

"Oh . . . kay," said Letty slowly.

Britt looked out the back window of the kitchen. The cottage was barely visible through the trees. Maybe she should move into the main house, she thought anxiously.

Letty put her hands on her ample hips. "Is there anything wrong, Miss Andersen? I mean, I don't want any trouble with anybody."

Britt shook her head. "No. No. Not really. We just had a little disagreement."

Letty frowned. "He's not one of those guys with a bad temper, is he?" Letty asked. "Because I don't need anything like that. I have children here."

Britt sighed. "I'm sure there's nothing to worry about. But, if you prefer that I go somewhere else . . ."

Letty glanced outside at the waning afternoon, the falling snow. "I guess it's all right," she said. Letty let her go out the back door and Britt picked her way across the backyard which was now covered with an inch of fresh snow. She put her face up to the sky, and stuck her tongue out to try to catch a few flakes. They landed lightly on her tongue, disappearing instantly. Britt looked around at everything now coated gently in pure, glistening white. It was pretty here, Britt thought, although she would be awfully glad to leave it behind.

Britt arrived at the copse of trees which surrounded the little cottage. Unlike the main house, which was cheerily lit, and had clouds of smoke drifting up from the chimney, the cottage looked lonely and deserted. As she walked up to the front door, and inserted her key in the lock, she felt a hand grasp her shoulder from behind.

Britt screamed and whirled, ready to strike. Dean Webster jumped back in alarm, letting her go. His eyes were bloodshot. His broad shoulders wore a dusting of snow.

"Goddammit," Britt cried. "Don't sneak up on me."

"Sorry," he said raising both hands, as if in surrender. "I was waiting for you. You're awful jumpy."

Britt exhaled and shook her head. "Sorry. Nothing personal. It's just . . . the woman who owns the place said Alec was here looking for me earlier. It's got me a little spooked."

"Why? What did he say?" Dean said, surprised. Despite the fact that Britt could smell alcohol on his breath, he seemed in control.

"The police searched his house and his business today. He says I'm trying to frame him. You and me. He thinks we're in it together."

"Paranoid," said Dean.

"I know. What are you doing here anyway?"

"I wondered if you knew about the search. Can I come in?"

Britt thought about the disorderly way she had left the room, and the bed unmade in the middle of it. This didn't look like the kind of place that had chambermaids to make up your bed. She knew, just by looking at him, that Dean would immediately sprawl out on the rumpled covers and suggest that she join him. "I'm really exhausted," she said apologetically.

"You sure?" he said.

"Well, have they got enough to arrest him yet?" Britt asked.

"No. They came up empty on the search. I know Ray Stern didn't find the so-called alibi witness. I've practically spoon-fed them everything they know. But they're so fucking incompetent," Dean complained.

"Hmmm . . ." said Britt, frowning.

"Hmmm what?"

Britt shook her head. "Nothing," she said.

"I feel like we're close," Dean said.

Britt sighed. "Not close enough."

"What did he say when he came looking for you?"

"I don't know," said Britt absently. "He hates me though. Hates me and would like to scare me away from this town and this investigation."

"Really," said Dean thoughtfully.

"It's just so maddening. I feel like he's making fools out of the cops, and out of us," she said.

"Not out of me," Dean protested. "I'm not done."

"I don't know," Britt said with a sigh. "Maybe I ought to get back to my real life. This could take a long time."

"It won't," Dean promised her. "Trust me. It's gonna happen."

"I hope you're right. You'll have to excuse me," she said. "I'm beat."

"You sure you don't want company?" he asked suggestively.

Britt shook her head, trying to suppress a smile. "I'm just gonna read, and turn in early."

"You can't blame a guy for trying." He gave her a brief wave as he backed away.

"Thanks for trying," she said. "Really."

Britt let herself in and locked the door behind her. She pulled the curtains shut, and turned on the lamp beside the bed, and the TV set which sat on the dresser, across from the foot of the bed. There wasn't really anything she wanted to watch. She thought about going out to eat, but she didn't want to see people. She just wanted to be distracted from everything that had happened. Britt began to yawn as she surfed the channels, and settled on an old Fred Astaire movie. When it was over she switched the TV off altogether. *I'll take a shower*, she thought, *and read*. She shed her clothes, and looked at herself critically in the bathroom mirror. There were circles under her eyes, and her hair looked greasy. *At least I can take as long as I want in the bathroom*, she thought. She had felt self-conscious at Alec's house about sharing the bathroom, and had showered as quickly and perfunctorily as she could manage. *Tonight*, she thought, *I'll take my time and wash my hair*.

But once she was in the shower, she was plagued by muffled sounds, which seemed to come from just outside the cottage. Three times she shut off the water and listened, but heard nothing. It had to have been her imagination. Finally, she gave her hair the quickest scrub she could manage and turned the shower off. She stepped out on the mat, dried herself, and pulled on her pajamas. Although it was warm in the bedroom, she found herself shivering, and pulled her sweatshirt on as well.

You're being paranoid, she thought. *It's perfectly quiet*. Still, just to be sure, she shut off the bedside light, and then pulled the curtain to one side and looked out. The lights from the main house were faintly visible, haloed through the falling snow. But the cottage itself was surrounded by darkness. There was nothing else visible but the trees. The driveway for the cottage was empty, and Britt had purposely left the outside light off. Except for the moonlight, the woods were in darkness. *No wonder you're paranoid,* she thought. *This is one hell of a lonely place. Beautiful, but lonely. Who wouldn't be paranoid?* Besides, Alec wasn't going to come looking for trouble. Even if he did decide to try the cabin door, she was locked in, and perfectly safe. And, if worse came to worst, and he started banging on the door, she had her cell phone. Britt turned on the lamp, then reached into her tote bag and set the phone on the bedside table. *There,* she thought. She climbed into bed, and picked up her book, but her eyelids were drooping before she had read even a page. "Forget it," she said aloud, switching off the bedside lamp.

The minute she shut off the light, her sleepiness seemed to vanish. She lay awake in the darkness as alert as could be. It wasn't that being awake in the night was so bad, in and of itself. It was the thoughts that plagued you when you lay awake. Britt tried to force herself to think about only good things—about being back in Boston, a guest she was particularly looking forward to for the show, a winter holiday she was planning for herself in the Caribbean. But it was no use trying to channel her thoughts. The minute she relaxed control, thoughts of Greta and Alec and Zoe filled her mind.

Stupid, stupid, she thought. *Don't think about it. It's up to the police to charge him now. You've done what you could.* Britt flopped over in the double bed and pulled the pillow down over her ears, as if she could drown out the internal voice of Alec Lynch, accusing her of trying to frame him. Thinking of her own shock when he'd said that Greta had hired the detective to find their mother, Jean Andersen. What had he found? *I have to know,* she thought, angrily recalling Alec's jeering advice that she hire her own detective. She wondered, not for the first time, what Greta had ever seen in him.

At least Greta had Zoe to show for her years of marriage. That was no small thing. Picturing Zoe, with her blond hair and braces, was soothing to Britt in a way. It made her smile to think of the girl, with her adolescent affectations and her good little heart. But in another way, it was even more disturbing. Because if they did arrest Alec for Greta's murder, what would become of Zoe? Lying there in the dark, there was no way for Britt to shut the question out of her mind.

All right, she thought, *why don't you just face it? She can't stay here alone. You are all the family she has left in the world. You're going to have to take her with you. Would that be so bad? Your apartment has two bedrooms. You can settle her into one of them, find out where a kid her age has to go to school. I'll ask Nancy,* she thought, and her heart lifted a little. Nancy would know all that stuff about kids.

Mentally, Britt began making lists. School, an orthodontist for those teeth. Stores that sold clothes for teenagers. Maybe she'd let her have a cat. What else?

Britt thought about Alec, and how he would probably want Zoe to stay nearby whatever prison he ended up in. *Well, too damn bad,* Britt thought. *Once Zoe finds out what you did to her mother,* she thought, imagining their confrontation in her mind, *she won't want any part of you anymore.*

Then Britt was plagued by a fresh set of anxieties. There were so many logistics to consider. They would probably have to make frequent trips back for a while. To testify. To settle legal matters. Her head spun and her stomach began to churn as she thought about it. *Goddammit, I'll never get to sleep,* she thought. She began to feel panicky. She needed sleep to face all of this. She couldn't stand it any longer.

Britt sat up abruptly in the dark room and sighed. She always felt like such a failure when she had to resort to sleeping pills. She thought about Greta, soothed by tranquilizers. And Zoe. Sneaking some from her mother. Seeking some peace of mind. *Runs in the family,* she thought. But sometimes there was just no choice. She padded into the bathroom and searched through her toiletries bag under the nightlight. She found the little amber plastic bottle and shook a sleeping pill out into her palm. Then, after a moment's hesitation, she shook out another. She swallowed the pills down with a glass of water and returned to the bed. She put a CD in her Discman and put on her headphones. In a few minutes, despite the anxiety that tingled all through her, she began to feel the leadenness in her thought processes that indicated the pills were doing their work. She wasn't aware of the moment when she fell asleep.

Sometime in the night, deep into a dream, she started to cough. She woke up coughing and found herself lying facedown on the mattress.

Britt's eyes stung, and began to tear. She sniffed, but her nose was stuffy. Then, she began to cough.

She wanted to raise her head from the pillow, but her mind was fuzzy and uncooperative. Even with her eyes closed, the room seemed bright, the light flickering. Her arm hung off the edge of the bed, her fingers trailing on the floor as if she were only a sack of cement lying there. Her eyes were watering freely now, and she let out a series of barking coughs. Even though her nose was stuffed up, she could smell something in the air. Something harsh and nauseating. She couldn't catch her breath. Clumsily, she pulled off her headset, and heard a whooshing, crackling sound. *What was that smell*, she wondered? Her brain responded, from a foggy distance.

Smoke.

It took a moment to register, and then Britt leaped up from the bed, as if an electric charge was surging through her. She understood what the crackling sound was now, and realized why, outside the curtained window, she saw a dance of light. She ripped the curtain back. Flames. The cottage was on fire. She tried to scream but she had no voice. Smoke was beginning to fill the room.

"Help," she whispered. *Oh my God.* For a moment she was paralyzed. Then she began to cough uncontrollably. Her frozen knees unlocked and she plunged through the billowing smoke in the direction of the door.

PART II

CHAPTER 22

"Walk, please," yelled Barbara Porter.

A frenzied rush of her students, returning from the art room, was taking place below Barbara's shoulder level. At the sound of her voice the rush slowed to merely rapid movement.

"Thank you, ladies and gentlemen," she said.

When the corridor was empty, she followed her students back into her classroom. The giggles and murmurs among those seated in the room began to diminish. "Okay," she said. "Everybody in your seats. Settle down. You're going to have to concentrate on this. We're working on decimals and fractions."

The students groaned and murmured again. Barbara stifled a smile and began to scratch out a series of equations on the board. There was a tap on her open door and she turned around to see Wilbur Thomas, the school principal, in the doorway.

"Hello, Mr. Thomas," Barbara said. The murmuring among the students began again as each one of them imagined themselves in some kind of trouble.

"Got a minute?" Wilbur asked.

"Sure," said Barbara, brushing the chalk off her hands. Immediately a buzz resumed in the classroom. Barbara turned to her students. "That's enough noise. Solve those problems. I'll be right back." She closed the door to her room behind her and went out into the hall. The principal was accompanied by a middle-aged woman with a short cap of graying hair and an unlined face. "Hey, Peg," said Barbara to her friend and colleague who was smiling at her. Barbara and Peg Slavin followed the principal across the hall to an empty classroom.

Wilbur leaned against the vacant teacher's desk crossing his arms over his worn, houndstooth blazer. Peg took a seat behind a desk, while Barbara hoisted herself onto one of the student desktops.

"What's up?" Barbara asked.

"Zoe Lynch," said Wilbur.

Barbara sighed and looked at Peg. "I thought maybe."

"We just got word in the office," said Wilbur. "Her father has been arrested."

Barbara, who was married to a Coleville police officer, Randy Porter, nodded and sighed.

"You're not surprised?" he asked.

"I heard about it from my husband at breakfast."

"Oh, right, of course."

"For both fires?" she asked.

"Yeah. The one the sister-in-law was in, too. That was my impression," said Wilbur.

Barbara glanced around as if she was concerned about being overheard. "Well, according to Randy, they did know for a fact, from the owner of the bed-and-breakfast, that he came looking for Zoe's aunt that day. Apparently, he'd threatened her . . ."

"God, what a tragedy. That poor kid," said Wilbur, shaking his gray head. "It's a lot for a child her age to have to cope with. First she loses her mother. Now this."

"I know," said Barbara. "My heart goes out to her. I just wish I could help her."

"Well, that's why I asked Peg to join us," said Wilbur. "I thought she could help us come up with a strategy. We've had other parents get themselves arrested, but we've never had a situation quite like this one before. So, I think we need to deal with this in a special way."

"How has she seemed to you in class?" Peg asked Barbara.

Barbara frowned. "She's . . . subdued. She tears up. She felt sick to her stomach one day. That seems only normal to me. You'd know a lot better about this than me, I'm sure. But, all in all, she seems to be coping. This arrest is going to make it much worse though."

"I'm afraid you're right," said Peg. "A parent's death at this age is a devastating loss. But even a young child can understand that death is part of the natural order of things. The idea of her father's involvement in the crime puts it on a whole other level."

"That's for sure," said Barbara. "I just don't want her to have to suffer any more than is necessary. She's not to blame for any of this."

"That's certainly true," said Wilbur.

"How have the other students been treating her?" Peg asked. "She told me that they don't mention her mother's death. I've explained to her that most kids this age are afraid to even bring up the subject. She says that everyone's been very kind to her, but I'm curious about your perspective."

"So far, I'd say the other kids have been pretty nice. They're awed by her loss. But that could turn in a minute. You know how they can be."

"All too well," said Peg grimly.

"Well, that's what we need to discuss," said Wilbur. "We've got to head off trouble before it starts. And it will start."

"I'd say to just be very aware of how they are treating her," said Peg. "It doesn't do any good to pretend this isn't happening and let the rumors fly. Mr. Thomas, I think that after they come and get her today it would helpful for you to come in and talk to Barbara's class. You know, level with them and appeal to their better nature. I think it's important that you, being the ultimate authority figure around here, impress on them that they have a responsibility to act decently and humanely."

"I'll be glad to if you think it would help," he said. Wilbur Thomas had been the principal of the school since Barbara was a student there. Despite his being virtually a relic from another era, he had a reputation for keeping current, and for not being easily fooled. The kids respected him for more than his title.

Barbara nodded agreement. Sixth graders had a tendency to keep their better nature well hidden, but as a teacher she knew that it lurked just below the surface bravado. "I think that's a good idea. I haven't known how much to say."

"It's all gonna be on TV anyway," said Peg. "They'll see it on the news tonight. Their parents are going to be questioning them about it. You might as well be frank with them. Answer their questions as honestly as possible. Try not to say too much about her father."

"That's right," said the principal. "We have to remind them that in our justice system, he is presumed innocent."

"Right," said Barbara. "Okay. That's what I think, too. I'll just follow your lead. *Is* somebody coming for her?"

Wilbur nodded. "Any minute now. I want to emphasize to both of you that we have to be careful about what we say. It's not our job to . . . make judgments on Alec Lynch. We don't want them going home and telling their parents that they heard in school that the verdict is in on him."

"No," Peg agreed somberly. "At least not from the faculty or the administration. What they say among themselves . . . well, I don't have to tell you. And I'm afraid there's no way that Zoe is going to escape the gossip and the cruelty."

Barbara shook her head. "It's such a shame. Zoe is a wonderful kid. Bright and nice. I hate that she has to go through this. I'm glad she has you to help her, Peg."

"It's going to be a challenging assignment to try to steer her through this," said Peg.

"We'll all try to make it easier on her," said Wilbur. "But you know as well as I do that somebody's going to act like a jerk."

"Without a doubt." Barbara smiled ruefully and the three of them exchanged knowing glances. "Well, I'd better get back in there," Barbara said. "God knows what might have happened by now." She thanked the principal and the guidance counselor again for coming by, and crossed the hall toward her classroom.

The din from inside the room ceased the moment she reentered. She quickly glanced at Zoe, wondering if the commotion had been at her expense, but Zoe was not crying. A good sign. *They aren't bad kids*, she thought.

"All right," she said, clapping her hands impatiently. "Let's see what you did. Martin, up to the board and show me what you got for the first problem. And . . ." she added in a warning tone, "how you arrived at your answer."

Martin Stinson went up to the board and began to laboriously scratch out his conclusions with the nub of a piece of chalk. Barbara nodded her approval and then glanced over at Zoe as Martin explained his answer. Zoe was sitting very straight in her seat, her blue eyes a blank. Her face betrayed no sign of distress, and Barbara wondered what that stoicism was costing her.

Why was it, she wondered, as she often did, that children were left to pay for the mistakes of their elders? They, who were blameless, had to take the brunt of the cruelty and misery in this world. Barbara sighed, and absentmindedly patted her own stomach. She was four months pregnant with her and Randy's first baby. She had seen enough in her three years as a teacher to know what she didn't want her child to endure. Her child wasn't going to suffer a broken home, or poverty, or the ignominy and woe of having a parent go to prison. Not while there was breath in her body. What people didn't understand these days was that misery was the norm. These kids knew more about the sleazy side of life than she had ever imagined when she was a child. It wasn't the good old days anymore. Not even here in picturesque Coleville, Vermont.

"Is that right?" Martin asked, and Barbara realized that he was talking to her. She gazed at the steps in his solution and nodded.

"That's it, Martin. Good work."

Martin grinned and resumed his seat, as the boy on his right side mimicked her enviously in a singsong voice. "Good work, Martin."

"All right, all right. Who's got the next one? Ashley?"

Ashley grimaced.

"I've got it," said Zoe.

Barbara looked at her, surprised. How could Zoe concentrate with all this whirling around her, she wondered? Much less get up in front of the class. *If it were me, I'd be home in a dark room with the phone off the hook*, she thought. "Okay, Zoe," she said. "Show us what you got. And how you got it."

Zoe walked up to the board and searched for a larger piece of chalk in the well below the blackboard. Then, slowly and deliberately, she began to write. The other kids in the class watched her intently, and Barbara wondered if they, too, were marveling at her self-possession. Zoe was wearing a pair of used, boy's jeans, which looked fine on her slim figure, and a stained sweater that didn't fit. *I'm going to take her shopping*, Barbara thought angrily. *She needs some proper clothes of her own*. All she'd worn, since the fire, were these mismatched hand-me-downs.

Just then, another knock on the door interrupted her train of thought. "Explain your answer, Zoe," said Barbara over her shoulder, as she got up and walked over to the door. Zoe began to loudly explicate the steps in her solution. Barbara opened the door, spoke to someone in the hallway, and then turned back to her classroom. Zoe's guileless blue eyes turned to her teacher expectantly, waiting for her judgment.

"Zoe," Barbara said gently. "There's somebody here for you."

Zoe pointed to her narrow chest, and then started to walk toward the door.

"Get your bookbag, honey," said Barbara. "You need to take your stuff with you."

"Am I leaving?" she asked.

"Yes," said Barbara.

"Aren't I coming back?"

"Of course, but maybe not today."

For once, the room was silent. No one said a word. Zoe walked back to her desk, not looking from side to side. She made a pile of her notebook and papers and tried to shove them into her backpack. A pink, plastic envelope with colorful erasers and iridescent pencils dropped out and fell on the floor.

Jared Morgan, the most physically mature boy in the class, the one that all the girls swooned over, quickly slid from his seat and picked up the envelope. He handed it back to Zoe without a word.

"Thanks," she whispered, avoiding his gaze.

With every eye glued to her fragile frame, Zoe hoisted her bookbag onto her back, and walked stiffly to the door. Barbara wanted to embrace her, or rub her shoulders as she passed by, but she knew that would only make it more difficult for the girl.

"You can use a homework pass tonight," she said. It was her way of trying to tell Zoe not to worry about her schoolwork.

"I don't need it," said Zoe irritably, as if shaking off the suggestion, and Barbara didn't know if Zoe was referring to the homework pass, or her teacher's sympathy.

CHAPTER 23

Britt studied the student artwork and hand-printed essays that were taped to the walls of the corridor. The theme of the artwork was obviously masks, for the beige walls were decorated with wildly colored, shield-shaped faces with strings hanging from the spot where ears might normally be. The essays were all entitled, "Things about myself that I hide from the world." Despite the provocative title, few of the essayists revealed any startling secrets. Britt searched for Zoe's name and read her offering. Like her classmates, Zoe admitted to minor transgressions, such as buying candy bars with her lunch money, and failing to study for spelling tests. But her last sentence pierced Britt to the heart. "I don't let people know it if I'm sad," Zoe wrote. *She must have written this before Greta's death*, Britt thought. *Before she found out what sadness really was.*

"Miss Andersen?"

Britt turned and met the worried, sympathetic gaze of Zoe's teacher, a pretty brunette wearing a shapeless jumper.

"Here she is."

Britt gazed at Zoe who emerged from her classroom dragging the pink parka and wearing her backpack. Mrs. Porter said, "If there's anything I can do . . ."

"Thanks," said Britt. "We'll be okay."

Barbara Porter nodded and ducked back into the classroom, closing the door behind her.

Zoe was staring at Britt's hands, which were wrapped in gauze. "Was that where you got burned?"

Britt glanced down at her hands and flexed them gingerly. "It's all right, Zoe. I'm all right."

"Does it hurt?" Zoe asked.

"Not too bad," Britt lied. She had a sudden, horrible recollection of the searing pain as her hand closed around the doorknob and she realized that the heat of the fire had traveled through the metal. She'd grasped it anyway, felt the skin of her palms adhering to the brass as she pulled on it, needing to free herself.

Zoe frowned. "I wanted to come and see you in the hospital but Dad said we'd see you when you got out. I can't believe you were in a fire, too."

"Yes, it's . . . crazy, isn't it?" said Britt. Although crazy was not exactly how she remembered it. The thick, acrid smoke choking her. The sound of sirens. Her memory of it was garbled. She remembered seeing the white newsvan, and hearing men shouting as fire engines and emergency vehicles arrived. Britt could recall standing barefoot in the snow in her pajamas, her teeth chattering uncontrollably. Someone draped a blanket around her and someone else rushed into Bayberry House to find something for her feet. The only familiar face looming out of the darkness was Dean Webster's, who jumped out of the white newsvan and came running up to her and threw his arms around her. She was lucky to be alive. Luckier than her sister had been.

Zoe looked up at her. "Why are you here? Why do I have to leave school?"

Britt reached an arm out and tried to slip it around Zoe's shoulders, but the girl backed away from her.

Britt sighed. All the way over here, she'd been trying to figure out the words to use. *How do I tell her this?* Britt thought. *How do I break the news that her whole world was destroyed by her own father?* One thing she'd decided was just to tell her, and make it quick. *It'll be like pulling off a bandage,* she thought. *Easier accomplished with one quick tear.* An instant of unbearable pain was preferable to long agony. Once Zoe had accepted this about her father, she and Britt could begin the next phase of life. Together.

But there was no minimizing how hard it was going to be on Zoe to learn this. Britt didn't know what to expect. She didn't know whether Zoe would weep or start screaming when she heard about the arrest. She didn't want Zoe to break down right here in the corridor outside her classroom. The teacher and her classmates might come running out, and that would only add humiliation to her misery.

"I'll tell you all about it, when we get in the car," Britt said firmly. "Put your jacket on."

"Tell me now," said Zoe. Her eyes were wide and her face pale with little pink spots in her cheeks.

"Zoe, let's just go outside and get in the car where we can talk in private."

"I'm not going until you tell me," said Zoe.

"Trust me. I'm saying this for your own good. Look, you're going to have to do what I tell you," said Britt.

"Why?" Zoe asked, her eyes flashing. "I don't have to listen to you. You're not my mother."

"Zoe," Britt said sharply.

"I don't want to leave school," Zoe insisted.

Britt wasn't used to seeing this side of her niece. Was this how it was going to be between them? *What am I supposed to do?* Britt thought. *She's not a baby. I can't pick her up and carry her out of the school.*

All of a sudden the door next to Zoe's classroom opened, and a middle-aged woman with glasses appeared in the hallway. "Excuse me," she said. "Can you keep it down out here? My class is taking a test and you're disturbing us."

"Sorry," Britt said. "Come on, Zoe."

Sticking out her chin defiantly, Zoe stalked down the corridor ahead of Britt. When she reached the front door,

Zoe put on her jacket, allowing Britt to catch up with her. Together they stepped out onto the broad, snow-covered lawn in front of the school. Britt got out her car keys and headed for her car but Zoe stopped short on the icy sidewalk.

"All right," she said. "We're outside. Now tell me."

Britt turned and looked from Zoe's angry face back to the facade of the old brick school building. She felt as if everyone in the building must be pressed up against the windows watching them. At least they were out of earshot.

"Zoe," she said, approaching the girl, reaching out for her arm. Zoe stepped away from her again.

"What?"

"Chief Stern told me I'd better come over here and get you. It's your father, Zoe."

Zoe's eyes widened. "Is Daddy okay?"

"He isn't hurt or anything," said Britt.

"Are you sure?" Zoe demanded.

"Yes, I'm sure. But . . . This is very hard to tell you, Zoe. Your dad . . . he's been arrested."

"Arrested? For what?" Zoe asked.

Britt took a deep breath. "He's been arrested for setting the fires." Britt steeled herself for the child's cries, readying herself to catch her if she should collapse.

Zoe stared back at her. "What?" she said, her voice registering utter disbelief.

"They arrested him about half an hour ago. He's going to be charged with arson and murder in your mother's death."

Zoe shook her head. "That's stupid," she said.

It wasn't exactly the response Britt had expected. *She's just shocked*, Britt thought. *She doesn't know what to say*. "I know this is hard for you to accept. I mean, I'm sure you never dreamed that your father would do anything like that."

Zoe reared back and looked at Britt as if she were speaking nonsense. "He wouldn't. He didn't."

"Well, I know that's what you think now . . ." said Britt.

Zoe glared at her. "That's not what I think. That's the truth. He would never do that. How did they get that idea?"

Britt reddened, thinking of her own role in the investigation. "Believe me, honey, it's not just an idea. They have certain . . . evidence . . . that your dad planned these fires."

"What evidence?" Zoe demanded.

"Honey, they have proof that he'd made certain plans . . . to start a different life."

"What does he say?"

"Well, he denies it, but he's refused to answer the questions the police have asked. The few answers he has given them have been . . . unsatisfactory. He can't account for where he was that night. He stood to gain . . . a lot of money. Look, I know it's hard for you to imagine, but sometimes . . . people do terrible things."

"Stop talking as if he did it," Zoe insisted.

"You're going to have to get used to the idea, Zoe," said Britt.

Zoe glowered at the ground. "Where is my dad now?" she asked.

"I guess he's at the jail, right now," said Britt gently. "He'll probably be arraigned later today."

"I want to go there," she said.

"That's not really any place for you, Zoe. I know this comes as a terrible shock to you. It's going to take some time to sink in. It must seem like your whole world is crumbling. But I want you to know that you're not alone in this. You can rely on me. I'll take care of you. I'll look after you. Nobody expects you to get used to this idea right away. But, in time . . ."

The child didn't say anything. Her backpack had slipped from her shoulders and hung from the crook of one elbow. Her narrow frame was shaking and she was staring fiercely at the sidewalk.

"Come on," said Britt, lifting the backpack from Zoe's arm with one bandaged hand. She slung it over her own shoulder, beside her own leather satchel, which still smelled of smoke. "Let's get in the car. You don't want people staring at you. You need a little privacy to digest this news. And Zoe,

I know you're trying to be brave, but sometimes it's best to just let it out. Go ahead and cry if you want. If anybody has a right to cry, it's you."

Zoe allowed Britt to steer her toward the car. She stood like a statue, eyes blank, as Britt opened the car door, tossed in the backpack, and then prodded Zoe to get in. Zoe slumped down in the seat and stared out the windshield.

Britt went around to the driver's side and got in. She sighed, and looked over at her niece. "Zoe, this is a terrible blow. Most adults wouldn't be able to absorb a blow like this, so don't think I don't understand. You take all the time you need. I know you're used to thinking of your dad in a certain way. This is going to require a terrible adjustment in your thinking. . . ."

Zoe shook her head. "Stop it, Aunt Britt. He didn't do it. He wouldn't have hurt us. He loved my mom. Why didn't they ask me? I could have told them that."

Britt sighed again, thinking of her own parents. They had always seemed fine to her, even up until the day her mother left. "Zoe, I'm sure they seemed fine to you . . ."

"They *were* fine," Zoe shrieked. "He did not kill my mom."

"Take it easy," said Britt.

"I'm not going to get used to the idea because it's not true," said Zoe.

Britt turned on the engine, and pushed the heat gauge to high. "It's freezing in here," she murmured.

"I want to see my dad right now," said Zoe.

"He's only going to tell you that he didn't do it," Britt said wearily.

"He doesn't have to tell me. I know he didn't do it," said Zoe. "I want to see him. Right now. Take me to see my dad, Aunt Britt. Or I'll jump out of this car."

"All right," Britt said. "Calm down. I'll take you."

What a tough kid, Britt thought. She had to admire Zoe's spirit in the face of this latest blow even though it seemed as if Zoe was just refusing to face the facts. The reality was too brutal for her to accept. Sooner or later, it was going to hit her. But for now, she was clinging to an image of her father. *He doesn't deserve to see you*, Britt thought. *Not after what he did.* But she could see that right now there was no use in saying that to Zoe.

CHAPTER 24

The county jail was located about ten miles from Coleville. Britt had to stop twice to ask directions, while Zoe waited, staring straight ahead. They hardly exchanged a word on the drive. Britt didn't press it. The child needed time to absorb this latest blow. Occasionally. Britt would sneak a glance at Zoe, who sat, dry-eyed, staring out the window, her hands resting limply in her lap. There was nothing tense or frantic in Zoe's demeanor. She seemed withdrawn and somehow . . . stoic. As if she was readying herself for whatever she had to cope with.

The jail, when they reached it, was housed in an ocher-colored building surrounded by a chain-link fence topped with barbed wire. Behind it, the rugged contours of a pine-forested mountain range were silhouetted against the leaden sky, emphasizing the isolation of the prison. Britt hated bringing Zoe to this grim place, but maybe seeing Alec behind bars would help Zoe come to grips with the reality of it.

Britt led the way into the building, holding the swinging doors for her niece. When they reached the locked doors, Britt explained their purpose to the guard on duty, who then conferred with someone on the phone.

"Okay," he said, pressing a buzzer. "The attorney will meet you in the holding area. Just go in and take a seat."

Britt and Zoe went in, and sat down on a wooden bench. There were other women there, some accompanied by children. They did not look up, or make eye contact as Zoe and Britt sat down. Britt and Zoe had been sitting for only a few minutes in the stark room when the locked doors were opened by another guard and Britt looked up to see Kevin Carmichael coming slowly through, wearing a charcoal-gray suit and carrying a briefcase.

"Kevin," Britt said.

Zoe stood up. "Mr. Carmichael. Are you here to help my dad?"

"I'm going to try to help him, Zoe," said Kevin.

Zoe threw her arms around him and pressed her cheek to his pinstriped suit jacket. Britt felt a little stab of envy for the attorney, whom Zoe clearly saw as a white knight, in contrast to her aunt, whom she now saw as the enemy.

"Why don't I escort you two back there. May I?" he asked the guard.

"They have to be searched," said the guard.

Zoe looked anxiously at Britt as the guard summoned a female counterpart.

"It's all right," Britt whispered. She obediently presented her bag, and allowed herself to be patted down. Zoe followed Britt's example. In a few moments, the guard nodded, and then led the three of them down the dim corridor to the visiting area. He indicated a molded plastic chair in front of a Plexiglas partition.

"You sit down, Zoe," said Kevin. "He'll be very glad to see you." He turned to the guard. "Can you bring my client back out?"

The guard nodded, and spoke into a small two-way radio which hung on his belt. Zoe sat down and tried to peer into the darkened area beyond the Plexiglas.

Britt sighed and turned her back on the cubicle, speaking in a low voice to Kevin. "What's he saying? He didn't do it, right?"

Kevin frowned. "He's not saying a whole lot. I'm trying to explain to him that I can't help him if he doesn't tell me the truth. I know he's concealing information, but I'm not sure why."

"Because he did it," Britt muttered.

"Here he comes," said Kevin in a warning voice.

"Dad!" Zoe leaped from the plastic chair and pressed her nose and her flattened palms against the barrier.

"Sit down, miss," said the guard, approaching Zoe.

Alec nodded and Zoe sat down in the chair. Alec, his gaze riveted on his daughter, settled himself in the matching chair opposite hers. His complexion was sallow, and the lines in his face seemed more sharply etched than ever. His gray eyes were sunken. His pale, muscular upper arms bulged from the short sleeves of the blue jumpsuit he was wearing.

"Hello, sweetheart," he said, and for a moment, his eyes glistened.

"Are you okay?" Zoe asked.

Alec shook his head. "I'm fine. Don't worry about me. I'll be out of here in no time. I promise."

Don't lie to her, Britt thought bitterly. But Zoe greeted this promise with complete faith. "Today?" she asked.

"Maybe not today," Alec admitted. "But soon. Are you okay, honey?"

"I'm all right," said Zoe. "Dad, why are you in here? You didn't set those fires."

"It's a mistake, honey. Soon, they'll realize that they made a big mistake."

"Mr. Carmichael's gonna help you," said Zoe.

"I'm sure he will," said Alec. "Meanwhile, you have to be brave. Okay? And do what your Aunt Britt tells you."

Britt stared at him in disbelief.

"I want to stay here with you," Zoe pleaded.

Alec smiled ruefully. "I don't think they'd let you do that."

Kevin leaned over and spoke into the wire mesh opening in the Plexiglas. "Alec, I'm gonna have to take off. I've got to get to the hospital to see what's happening with Vicki."

"We should go too, Zoe," said Britt, avoiding Alec's gaze which she could feel, scrutinizing her through the Plexiglas.

"Kevin," said Alec, "can you take Zoe with you?"

Kevin shrugged. "Sure. No problem."

Zoe began to weep. "I don't want to leave you here, Dad."

"Zoe," he said. "I need you to be brave. Do your homework. Get your rest. Please. I promise you everything will be okay. You'll see. Now, go along with Mr. Carmichael."

"But I came with Aunt Britt."

"I need to talk to Aunt Britt. You go see how your friend, Vicki, is doing."

Zoe sniffed and wiped her eyes. "Okay. I love you, Daddy."

"I love you, too. Now go on."

"I'll see you tomorrow," said Kevin. He put a hand on Zoe's shoulder. Reluctantly, Zoe rose from the seat, pressing her hand to the Plexiglas. Alec fitted his large hand to hers from behind the shield. Then Zoe turned away, and hid her face.

"I'll pick you up at the hospital," Britt whispered. Zoe did not look at her, but followed the guard, and Kevin Carmichael, out of the visitors' area. Britt turned and looked down at Alec Lynch, who was still in his seat, staring at her grimly. He indicated the chair and Britt sat down, holding her satchel on her lap in front of her with her bandaged hands and leaning away from the glass. She returned his gaze coldly.

"Disappointed?" she asked.

"About what?"

"That I'm still alive," she said.

"You can't really believe that I was responsible for that fire," he scoffed. "Why would I . . .?"

"You threatened me. You killed my sister."

Alec sighed and ignored her remark. "Britt," he said. "I haven't got much time. Let's not waste it on these empty accusations."

"Empty?" she cried. "Obviously the police don't think they're empty."

"Are you done?" he said. "I need to ask you a favor. I need you to stay with her. Stay with Zoe."

Britt shook her head in disgust. "Alec, how long are you going to keep this up?"

Alec's gray eyes reminded Britt of a malamute. They studied her with detachment, almost shaded from view by his black eyebrows. "Keep what up?" he asked.

"She's going to find out," said Britt. "Right now she believes in you but when this gets to trial, she's going to hear the truth and find out what you did. Meanwhile, she's going to be ostracized by everyone for defending you. Haven't you hurt her enough? Why don't you be a man and admit what you did? Instead, you're asking a child to have faith in you when you know you don't deserve it. It's despicable."

Alec glared at her. She could see the muscles in his jaw working. Finally, he said, "I am trying to protect her. Whether you believe it or not."

"Oh, right," said Britt. She pointed a finger at him. "Does it make you feel good to have your daughter sticking up for you, fighting your battles out here because she believes your excuses?"

Alec did not respond to the insult. "Look, they're going to take me back there in a minute. I need to settle this. Will you do it? Will you take care of her?"

Britt shook her head. She had no intention of abandoning Zoe, but she didn't want Alec to think, for one minute, that she was flattered by his ostensible trust in her. "I will stay with her. I will do it for the sake of my sister," she said. "I will do it because Zoe is my niece and I want to do all I can for her. I will do it for her sake, not for yours."

"I don't care why you do it," he said.

The guard approached Britt and said, "Time to go."

She got up from the chair. "Gladly," she said. She turned back to Alec, who was rising from his chair beyond the shield, with another guard at his side. "As long as it's clear," Britt said.

"Your opinion doesn't matter to me," he said. "Only Zoe matters."

Britt shouldered her satchel and snorted in disgust. "You should have thought of that before you ruined her life."

* * *

When Britt arrived at the hospital, she found Zoe, scratching answers in a grammar workbook and eating a bag of potato chips in the lounge just across from Vicki's room.

"How come you're out here?" she asked Zoe. "Is Vicki okay?"

"The doctor's in there with them," said Zoe.

Britt nodded, and glanced at her watch.

"What did my father say?" Zoe asked.

Britt hesitated. "He was just . . . worried about you. I told him I was going to be staying with you."

"You are?" said Zoe, surprised.

"Yes."

"What about your job and everything?" Zoe asked.

"Let me worry about that," said Britt.

Zoe sighed and nodded. "Okay."

At that moment a bespectacled Asian-featured woman wearing a lab coat with a stethoscope in the pocket emerged from Vicki's room.

"That's the doctor," Zoe whispered.

Britt nodded. "Oh. Okay. I guess she's finished in there. Let me just tell the Carmichaels we're leaving."

Zoe nodded glumly and began to gather up her books and papers. Britt crossed the hall and stuck her head into Vicki's room. Vicki was lying in the bed, attached to monitors, her huge stomach covered by a thin blue blanket. She was sipping from a plastic cup through a straw. In the dim room, at the foot of Vicki's bed, Kevin and Caroline stood, holding hands, watching her. They looked up at Britt when she stuck her head in the door. "How's everything going?" Britt asked. "I saw the doctor leaving."

Vicki sighed, and Caroline gave Britt a stricken look. "Touch and go," said Caroline.

Kevin released his wife's hand and walked over to where Britt hovered, in the doorway. "We just spoke to Dr. Yasushi. Vicki's got something called preeclampsia," he said. "Dr. Yasushi says it's common in pregnant women who are either very young or very old to be pregnant. The blood pressure gets out of control. Unless it subsides, it means they'll have to do a caesarean section soon. They're just trying to hold off as long as possible."

Britt winced. "That's tough," she said. "How's Vicki taking it?"

Kevin glanced back at the bed. "She's hanging in there."

"Well, we're going to go," she whispered. "Thanks for bringing Zoe back, Kevin."

"Glad to do it," he said. "What did Alec want to talk to you about?"

"Just wanted to be sure I would stay with Zoe."

"Doesn't sound like the request of a man who wanted to kill you," Kevin observed.

"Look, it's your job to think he's innocent. Personally, I'm not rooting for either of you. No offense."

Kevin nodded absently. "None taken. Look, I asked Zoe to go over to our house and feed Kirby. I don't know when we'll get home."

"Oh, sure," said Britt. "We'll take care of it. Don't worry about it. I hope everything is okay here." Britt waved to Caroline and Vicki, and squeezed Kevin's hand. Then she withdrew from the room. "Come on," she said to Zoe. "I hear you have a cat to feed."

Zoe nodded. "I hope they aren't mean to him in there," Zoe fretted.

At first Britt was confused, thinking Zoe was talking about the cat. Then she realized that she was referring to her father. Britt couldn't bring herself to agree. "We'd better be getting home," she said, although the word sounded fake and foreign to her ears. Zoe gathered up her coat and bookbag as if she hadn't noticed.

CHAPTER 25

Britt pulled into the Carmichaels' driveway behind Vicki's red Toyota. "I'll just wait here until you get the cat fed," said Britt.

Zoe, who already had the car door open, shook her head. "No, you can go home. I'll call you when I'm done."

"It's kind of isolated out here," said Britt, looking at the woods and fields which surrounded the Carmichael house. In the near distance, the low mountains surrounding Mt. Glace looked lavender in the gloom.

"It doesn't bother me. I used to live out here, remember?" said Zoe.

Britt frowned. "I can wait for you. It won't take that long."

"No. Go home. I have to find the cat first," said Zoe. "He might be out in the woods. You never know. And then I need to play with him for a while. In case he's nervous or lonely with Vicki being gone."

Britt hesitated. It was clear to her that Zoe wanted to be left on her own for a while. *Maybe she just needs time to think, and nuzzle the cat,* Britt thought. They say that petting animals is good for relieving stress. But she just wasn't comfortable leaving her alone out here. It was too desolate. Still, Zoe didn't need to know that. She could pretend to leave, and then wait right nearby.

"Okay," said Britt slowly. "Okay. I'll . . . go do some errands in town. Call me on my cell phone as soon as you're done. Do you have the key?"

Zoe rolled her eyes. "Yes. Of course."

"All right," said Britt. Zoe did not look back as she bolted from the car and walked up the porch steps to the Carmichaels' front door. Zoe unlocked the door and went inside, closing the door behind her without even glancing back at Britt.

Britt backed out of the driveway, and made a great show of zooming off, but she only went as far as Zoe's former home, where she parked out in front. She put the car in neutral and left the engine running so she could have heat. Though she tried to avoid looking at it, her gaze was drawn to the burnt-out shell of the house and she felt her spirits droop. When she had imagined Alec being arrested, and Zoe becoming her charge, she had just assumed that Zoe would be willing to leave this place and start her life over in Boston. She thought that Zoe would turn on her father once she learned what he had done. And surely a move to the big city would seem glamorous and exciting to a budding teenager.

But now Britt was faced with a different reality. At least for the moment, Zoe seemed determined to believe in her father and not to leave him. She was going to trust her father's word over any legal accusations. It shocked Britt that a child could be so implacable in the face of the police and the law. It took guts, and a willful blindness as far as Britt was concerned. She could only hope that this was a temporary reaction and that Zoe would come around before long. But she didn't feel optimistic about it. Zoe had rejected the possibility of Alec's guilt completely. And she resented Britt for accepting it so readily. The growing affection between them seemed to have vanished.

Meanwhile, time was getting away from her. Donovan had told her days ago that he expected her back at work. *I'd better let them know it's going to be a little longer*, she thought. She rummaged in her satchel, picked up the phone and punched in the number, asking for Nancy's extension when the operator answered.

"Hey," said Nancy, sounding delighted to hear from Britt.

"I have to stay," said Britt without preamble.

"You have to stay there? In Vermont?" Nancy asked.

Britt sighed and gazed out the car window at the blackened ruins of Greta's house. "My brother-in-law's been arrested."

"Oh my God," said Nancy.

"I have to stay with my niece," said Britt. "She's all alone here."

"Well, sure you do," said Nancy.

"Even though she hates me now," said Britt. "She shakes her head at everything I say."

"Kids that age do shake their heads at everything adults say. It's how they communicate."

"That's reassuring," said Britt.

"Besides, why would she hate you?" Nancy asked.

"Because she knows that I think her father is guilty."

"Do you really?" Nancy asked. "Do you think he did it?"

"Nancy, he tried to kill me," said Britt.

"What? What are you talking about?"

"It's a long story. He threw me out of their house, and then he set fire to the place I was staying."

"Oh my God, Britt. Are you okay?"

Britt winced as she flexed her bandaged hands. "I'll live. Luckily I woke up in time to get out of there."

"I can't believe it," said Nancy. "Is he insane? Why would he want to hurt you?"

"He knew I didn't believe him. I kept on bugging the police about him."

"Obviously you were right."

Britt sighed. "It would seem so."

"I hope for his sake he's got a good lawyer," said Nancy.

"Well, their former neighbor is a criminal attorney who used to practice in Boston. Apparently he was pretty high profile. He's agreed to defend him."

"In Boston. Really? What's his name? The lawyer." Nancy asked.

"Carmichael. Kevin Carmichael."

"Kevin Carmichael. That rings a bell for some reason."

"I guess he was involved in some big cases."

"Well, there are so many lawyers," said Nancy.

"Anyway, now I am stuck here," said Britt. "Will you tell Donovan for me? Or do you think I should call him? I know he won't be happy."

"What's he going to do about it?" said Nancy. "You have to stay with the child. She needs you right now, more than Donovan Smith does. You take all the time you need. That child has to come first and he will just have to understand. I'll make it clear to him," she promised.

"Yeah, I suppose. Thanks Nancy," said Britt. All of a sudden she heard a series of clicks in the receiver. "Nancy, there's another call coming through on call waiting. I told Zoe to call me . . ."

"Say no more. I'll break the news to Donovan. Let me know what's happening."

Nancy hung up, and Britt hit the flash button so that she could speak to the other caller.

"Hello," Britt said.

"Aunt Britt!" Zoe's voice was breathless.

Britt sat up straight in the car seat. "Zoe? What's the matter?"

"I don't know. There's some strange guy out here. He's lurking around in the trees behind the house. I'm scared."

Britt's heart started to pound. "Zoe. Listen to me. Don't be frightened," she said. "Lock the doors. Are all the doors locked?"

"Yes," said Zoe in a small voice.

"Can you see the man from where you are?"

"He's sort of hidden in the trees."

"Okay, don't panic. It's probably nothing. You stay right there. I'm right next door. I'm here by your old house. I'll be there in a minute. Don't let him in, no matter what. You hear me? Don't let anybody in but me."

"Okay," said Zoe.

"I'll be right there. You just stay put."

"Hurry. I'm scared," said Zoe.

Britt put the phone down, and jerked the car into gear.

* * *

Britt pulled into the Carmichaels' driveway and rushed up the steps to the front door. "Zoe," she called out, banging on the door. "It's me. It's Aunt Britt. You can open the door now."

There was silence inside the house for a moment and then she heard the lock on the front door turn, and the door opened a few inches. Zoe peered out at her aunt, her narrow face pale, her eyes wide.

"Are you okay?" Britt asked.

Zoe nodded.

"The guy didn't try to get into the house?" said Britt.

"I haven't seen him since I called you," said Zoe.

Perhaps, Britt thought wryly, it was scarier to be alone out here than Zoe had expected, and the mysterious man was only a figment of an overactive imagination. But Britt didn't say that. *I'm learning*, she thought. "Okay," she said. "That's good that you haven't seen him. Now, get your stuff and we'll go. Are you done with the eat?"

Zoe grimaced. "He ate and went outside again. He hasn't come back in yet. Will you go and get him for me?"

"He's probably fine out there," said Britt. "He's an outdoor cat."

"But it's cold. And he has no way to get back inside. What if it snows again?" Zoe cried. Tears stood in her eyes.

"All right," said Britt. "All right now. Don't get upset. I'll take a quick look around for him. You get your stuff together."

"Just be careful," said Zoe.

"I'll be careful," said Britt, grateful that her niece felt some concern for her. She went back down the steps and walked around the side of the house to the back. When she looked up at the house, she saw the little white triangle of Zoe's face behind a window, watching her gravely. Britt waved, and continued out back.

The farmhouse sat beside a field covered with brown grass and snow. At the end of the field, behind the house, masses of evergreens formed a natural fence, and beyond that, the terrain started to rise, toward the sloping hills. Britt trudged through the snow toward the trees. The wind was restless, rustling the branches. *That's probably what she saw*, Britt thought. *Why would anybody be standing out here in the cold in a copse of trees?*

But at the exact moment that she had that thought, a movement to her left caught her eye. *Could be an animal*, she thought. *A deer*. This looked like the kind of place you'd find a deer. Carefully, Britt walked into the grove. Her heart was thudding. *There's nobody here*, she chided herself. She peered through the trees and then back toward the house. As her gaze scanned the area she felt a sudden anxiety. At first she didn't know why. She couldn't see anyone. And then she realized she was being watched. She whirled around and saw yellow eyes studying her from the crotch of a tree. "Kirby," she said aloud. She wanted to laugh. The cat was huddled there, gray against the gray bark.

"All right, you," Britt said, walking over toward his perch in the tree. "It's cold out here. You've got to get back in the house. Your friend, Zoe, is worried about you." She picked the cat up, held him against her coat, and started to carry him back toward the house, smiling and shaking her head. The cat trembled and meowed in protest, but remained in her arms. Suddenly, as she retraced her steps through the grove of trees, she noticed something. Britt's smile faded as she studied the surface of the snow.

Zoe was not imagining things. Someone had been here, hidden by these trees. In addition to the dainty tracings of bird claws, and the cat's tiny pawprints, there were other prints, newly made. Someone wearing boots with deep treads had stood in these woods, and crushed their heavy imprint into the virgin snow. Stood here in those boots and smoked a cigarette. Several cigarettes actually. A tiny plume of smoke still rose from one of the butts which had been tossed down into the snow at the smoker's feet.

CHAPTER 26

Britt gasped, and a chill ran through her, unrelated to the temperature. She looked around warily but the gloomy woods were quiet. Zoe *had* seen someone in these woods. Someone had made those bootprints. And smoked those cigarettes. Britt's heart was hammering.

Stop it, she thought. *Just stop it.* Just because someone was here didn't mean they had any wicked intentions. Alec had told her that lots of people went snowmobiling, and hunting and cross-country skiing in this area. Maybe it was one of those. A hunter. This was the kind of place where people hunted. This area was surrounded by woods. Maybe he came walking through these trees and then realized how close he was to a house and retraced his steps. She walked slowly up to the footprints and forced herself to examine them.

They seemed to be coming from the woods that curved around the Carmichaels' property, and heading in the direction of Greta's old house. *All right,* she thought. *Don't be a coward. Check it out. It's probably nothing. A workman. Someone who got off track. Maybe even a cop, still searching the area after the fire at Greta's.* Britt glanced back at the house. Zoe was okay. The doors were locked. *Just find out,* she thought. She took a deep breath, and forced herself to follow the prints. She felt relieved when she came to the edge of the wooded area, and saw that the bootprints led out into the field headed toward the road, out of sight of the house. Whoever it was had gone, walking toward the road which led to the highway. Britt didn't want to cross the field. She knew there were swampy patches, thinly covered with ice, and the wet snow was already seeping through her leather boots. She looked as far as she could around the trees, but there was no sign of anyone.

Britt turned, and walked back toward the porch at the back of the house, stamped off her boots on the porch steps, then crossed to the back door of the house and turned the doorknob. The door was locked. Zoe had followed her instructions. She knocked, calling out for Zoe in a loud voice.

Warily, Zoe came to the door, pulled open the curtain and looked out at her.

"It's okay, Zoe. Let me in."

Zoe unlocked the door and opened it. Britt walked in, still holding the cat.

"Kirby," Zoe cried, burying her face in the cat's fur against the front of Britt's coat. Kirby tolerated the affection for a moment, and then leaped down from Britt's arms. Zoe also backed away.

"You know, you were right," Britt said. "There *was* someone back there."

Zoe's eyes widened. "How do you know?"

"Well, there were some fresh bootprints out in those trees. And cigarette butts. Apparently the guy was smoking. One of the butts was still smoldering."

Zoe shuddered. "Why would somebody be standing around out there?"

"I don't know, honey. Maybe a hunter, I thought."

"You can't hunt this close to people's houses," Zoe scoffed.

"Well, I don't know," said Britt. "All I'm saying is that you did see someone. It wasn't your imagination. And you were right to call me. Now, are you ready to go?"

Zoe nodded, gathering up her coat and gloves and followed Britt out to the car. Zoe had to go back once to make sure all the doors were locked and then she got into the front seat and buckled her seat belt. "All right," she said.

"Are you sure you've got everything?" said Britt.

Zoe shrugged. "I guess."

"Because you're not coming back here. Not by yourself anyway."

"I have to," Zoe protested. "Somebody has to feed Kirby."

"Well, it's not going to be you. Not with some strange guy lurking around out here. Besides, the Carmichaels will be back later."

"I promised I'd feed him," Zoe cried angrily.

"I'll come with you if they need you to feed him again," said Britt. "I don't want anything to happen to you."

Zoe nodded sullenly in agreement, but did not reply.

Britt pulled out of the driveway, and turned out onto the road. She looked up and down the country road, banked by trees, but there was no sign of anyone. *He's long gone by now*, she thought, although she realized she had not heard the sound of a car engine firing up from anywhere nearby. *Who goes around here on foot?* she thought. *You never see anybody walking along these roads*. And there was no way it was a bicyclist. You'd have to be young and fit to ride up and down these hills. This person in the woods was a smoker. It was doubtful that a smoker would have the wind to ride a bike around here. *Maybe it's somebody who lives nearby*, she thought. *Maybe he walked up one of these wooded driveways, set far apart, the houses screened from view*. The thought that it might be a neighbor gave her the creeps. At the first large intersection, she turned again onto a wider road, and noticed an ancient Volkswagen van pulled over to the side of the road which was the access road to the interstate. The van's blinker was flashing to indicate that it had just pulled over temporarily. "God, I didn't think any of those vans were still running," Britt said aloud. "That one probably just bit the dust."

"Actually, they're picking up that hitchhiker," said Zoe.

Britt glanced over just in time to see a young man in an olive-drab, hooded parka limping up the ramp toward the open side door of the van.

"Hardly anybody hitchhikes," Zoe observed.

Britt was about to agree when suddenly, as she watched the blond-haired hitchhiker climb into the van, she noticed the flash of orange chevrons on the sleeve of his coat. Britt gasped, recalling Alec telling Chief Stern about his whereabouts on the night of the fire. A hitchhiker. A limp. An olive-drab parka with orange reflector tape on the sleeves. "It couldn't be," she said aloud.

"What's the matter?" Zoe asked.

The van roared into gear, and rumbled up the ramp. Britt slowed down to a stop and watched as the van signaled and then turned onto the highway.

Zoe stared at her. "What are you doing?" she said.

"Nothing," said Britt.

"Why did you stop?" Zoe asked.

Britt stared after the van as it accelerated, and disappeared from view. "Nothing," she said. "I thought I recognized . . . someone. . . ."

"That hitchhiker?" Zoe asked.

Britt did not reply.

Zoe shrugged, uninterested in her aunt's acquaintances. "Let's stop at Kayley's," she said. "Can she come over?"

Britt frowned. Should she have tried to stop that van, she wondered? No, that was silly. There were lots of people who wore army-style parkas. This was Vermont, in the winter. It could have been anybody.

"Aunt Britt?" Zoe asked.

"What?" Britt turned and looked at her niece.

"Can I have Kayley over?" Zoe asked.

"Sure," Britt mumbled. "Why not. You need to show me where she lives."

"Okay," said Zoe. She began to give directions in an authoritative tone, and Britt followed them automatically.

All the while, a wave of guilt assailed her, which she tried her best to rationalize away.

The police had gone looking for Dave, Alec's ostensible alibi witness. They would have found him if he had been real. They had checked those tapes in the convenience store. There was no sign of him. The fact that this guy in the tape-decorated parka was hitchhiking, near Alec's house, was just a coincidence. The fact that he had a limp . . .

"Stop," cried Zoe.

Britt jammed on the brakes and the car skidded, and slid to one side of the road. Fortunately the street was deserted and they bumped harmlessly up against the sidewalk curb. "Dammit Zoe," Britt cried. "What's the matter?"

"You were passing her house," Zoe said meekly.

"Well, don't yell like that," said Britt, trembling. "My God. We could have been killed."

"Sorry," said Zoe. "I didn't know you were going to do that."

"Well, think next time. Think before you shout out." Britt took a deep breath, and tried to calm her racing heart.

"I'm sorry," Zoe repeated angrily.

"All right," said Britt, knowing she had been distracted, that she had not been paying attention. That it was partly her own fault. "Never mind. Which house?"

CHAPTER 27

Britt stopped in front of the neatly kept house that Zoe indicated. "You can go get her," said Britt. "Tell her mother I said it was all right."

Zoe eagerly jumped out of the car and ran up to the door. The front light had been turned on against the gathering twilight. The sky threatened another snowfall. Britt sank down in the driver's seat and tried to reassure herself. *Your imagination is just playing tricks on you*, she thought. *Just because you see a hitchhiker, it doesn't mean he is the missing alibi witness. Remember, Alec was planning on leaving his wife. Alec has been arrested for setting the fire. There is no "Dave."* But no matter how she tried to reason it away, she kept seeing, in her mind's eye, that pudgy, blond-haired guy in a parka, limping toward the door of the van.

The passenger door opened, and Zoe sank down into the seat, a tearful expression on her pale face.

"What's the matter?" Britt asked.

"She can't come," said Zoe.

"Too much homework?" Britt asked sympathetically.

Zoe shook her head.

Britt peered at her. It was hard to read the child's face in the gloom. "Why don't you ask if she can come tomorrow?"

"She can't come tomorrow," said Zoe. "She can't come at all."

Instantly, Britt understood. She understood, and felt indignant for her niece. Zoe was being made to pay for the shame Alec had brought on their family. Britt thought of Mrs. Dietz, speaking at Greta's funeral, saying how much she had admired Zoe's mother. So this was the way she treated Greta's bereaved child. Britt switched off the engine.

"I'll have a word with her mother," said Britt.

"No, it's not her mother. It's her dad," Zoe protested.

"Her dad, then," said Britt.

"No, don't," said Zoe.

"Wait right here. I'll be nice. Don't worry." Britt got out of the driver's side and slammed the door. She strode up the walk to the front door of the Dietz house and knocked. It was opened by a moon-faced man with a graying crew cut wearing a plaid flannel shirt. Britt remembered seeing him at Greta's funeral, and tried to remember his name. Her name was Joyce and his name . . .

"Yes," he said coldly.

Britt could see past him into the house. Kayley was in the living room, sitting on the sofa, her face buried in her hands. Her mother was rubbing her helplessly on the back. She looked up at Britt with a guilty expression in her eyes and then looked away.

"Mr. Dietz," said Britt. "My name is Britt Andersen. We met at my sister's funeral. I'm Zoe's aunt."

The man stared at her impassively. "Yeah."

Norman, she thought. That was it. Norman Dietz. "Zoe just told me that there is some problem with Kayley coming over. I wanted to reassure you that I am taking care of Zoe and there's absolutely nothing to worry about. Your daughter will be perfectly safe with me." Britt knew that this wasn't the reason Zoe had been denied, but she also knew better than to be confrontational. "Zoe has had a lot to cope with, and she's really suffering. I know having Kayley over would be a great comfort to her right now."

"I'm sorry about Zoe's parents, but I don't want my daughter involved in this," he replied.

You hypocrite, Britt thought, but she kept a pleasant smile on her face. "But all the girls want to do is play together. Do some homework . . ."

"Look, your niece just told my daughter that her father didn't do anything wrong. You and I both know that he did. I don't want Kayley's head filled with lies like that. I've brought my children up to respect the law. Now, I understand that none of this is Zoe's fault, but, if she's going to take that attitude, I see her as a bad influence on my daughter."

"A bad influence!" Britt exclaimed. "She's just a child."

"She's old enough to know right from wrong," he insisted, his voice rising. "Her father is a criminal and she's defending him. I don't know how you can justify that."

Britt blushed, knowing that she herself found it hard to accept Zoe's vehement belief in her father. But it wasn't defiance that fueled Zoe's belief. It was . . . trust. A history of trust. And love. "She can't just . . . accept it," Britt tried to explain.

"Why not? Time she faced facts," said Norman Dietz.

Britt peered at the man's stolid, bulldog expression. "Mr. Dietz, if you were arrested for a crime, would you expect your children to immediately believe you were guilty?"

"I wouldn't commit such a crime," he said.

"Dad, please let me go over," Kayley pleaded from the living room.

"Kayley, go to your room," he snapped. He turned back to Britt, "You're disturbing our household. Please, there's nothing to discuss, Miss . . ."

"Andersen," said Britt, trying to keep her voice from shaking. "I realize you have a right to decide about your own children, but I think you are being very cruel to a child, who has done nothing to deserve it. Except to be loyal to her father."

"That's your opinion," Norman Dietz said, and closed the door.

Britt stared at the door that had been shut in her face. *What a creep*, she thought. She wanted to tell him to pick on somebody his own size. As she started back toward the car, the front door of the house opened and Mrs. Dietz came out, and rushed down the walk to Britt. "Wait a minute," she said. She was wearing a thin blouse and she wrapped her arms around herself to keep warm. "I'm sorry to disappoint Zoe. I'll try to talk to my husband. Just give him a little while to get used to the idea. It's still such a shock."

"I don't see why you have to punish Zoe for what her father did."

"I know," said Joyce. "Let me just try to talk to him. You tell Zoe it will all work out."

Marriage, Britt thought. It turned you into somebody who had to compromise your values to please somebody else. Then she sighed, realizing that her affair with Donovan Smith fit that same definition. "I'll tell Zoe. Maybe that will make her feel a little better."

Mrs. Dietz hurried back up the walk and slid inside the front door to the house.

Britt got back into the car and Zoe looked at her hopefully. "Soon," she said. "Kayley can come over. Her mom says it will be okay."

"It will?" Zoe asked. "When?"

"I don't know exactly when," said Britt. She was still fuming at Kayley's father, but she figured she'd better not say anything negative about him to Zoe. "Look, honey, the less you talk about this whole business about your dad with Kayley the better, okay?"

"We talk about everything," Zoe insisted. "Besides, my father didn't do anything wrong."

"Zoe, that's not the way other people see it," Britt said.

"That's the way I see it," Zoe said stubbornly. "And that's the truth."

It's just as you told Kayley's father. She's used to trusting Alec, Britt thought, suppressing the urge to chastise her. "You don't know what the truth is," said Britt.

"I know more than you," said Zoe.

Britt stared through her windshield into the growing darkness and did not reply.

* * *

At the house on Medford Road, Zoe disappeared up to her room while Britt managed to put together a simple dinner for them. She called up the stairs to Zoe, who descended obediently, and together they ate in silence. After a mumbled request to be excused, Zoe bussed her dishes and then headed back upstairs toward her room. Britt followed her out into the hallway.

"What are you doing?" she called after her.

"Working on Vicki's present," said Zoe, without any rancor in her voice.

"What present is that?" she asked.

"I'm knitting her a scarf," said Zoe.

"I didn't know you could knit," said Britt.

Zoe nodded. "It started out to be a baby blanket but then I changed my mind 'cause she's not keeping the baby."

"That's true. A scarf is a good idea."

Britt sighed, relieved at the apparent truce between her and Zoe and returned to the kitchen to finish cleaning up. When she was done, she went out into the living room and looked around. *God, I hate this place*, she thought. *What a mess.* The trash bags that Alec had begun to fill lay discarded in the middle of the rug. She began to try to tidy up, sorting through the remaining boxes, and hauling the bags down the hall to a tiny utility room behind the kitchen. *At least there will be one room you can sit in*, she thought. She was returning to the living room for the last bag when there was a knock at the door.

Frowning, Britt thought about how grimy and disheveled she was, and then reminded herself that it didn't matter. There was nobody around here she was trying to impress. She opened the front door and saw Dean Webster, his blond hair glinting under the porch light, a bottle of champagne tucked under the arm of his unzipped parka. He leaned against the door frame and smiled boyishly.

The sight of him made her blush, remembering how she had clung to him the night of the fire. How he had pulled her up against him inside his coat. "Hi," she said shyly.

Dean grinned, and gazed at her bandaged hands. "You're looking a little better," he said.

Britt sighed. "I was kind of freaked out the other night."

"That's all right," Dean drawled. "You don't need any excuse to want to wrap your arms around me."

Britt shook her head and smiled. "Don't flatter yourself," she said. But she found his arrogance kind of amusing. And she couldn't help remembering, even though she'd been coughing, and her hands were experiencing a searing pain, how his body felt when she was pressed up against him.

"I just thought you might want to celebrate," he said.

Britt glanced up the stairs and then pushed her hair back off her forehead. "Celebrate?" she asked. "What's to celebrate?"

"Hey, we got our man," he said cheerfully. "He's right where you wanted him."

"Keep your voice down," she said. "My niece is upstairs."

He dangled the bottle by its neck. "Don't tell me you don't like champagne."

Britt sighed. "I guess I could use some company," she admitted. "Come on in." She turned to lead the way into the living room.

Dean started to slide by her in the doorway and then stopped, when they were face to face. He gazed down at her. His smooth young face had been tanned and creased by the sun and there was a wolfish gleam in his eye. Britt felt both uncomfortable at how close he was standing and how tempted she was to get even closer. *Oh no*, she thought. *Don't encourage him. He doesn't need much encouragement.* She started to edge away from him. His lips were close to her face, and she could smell alcohol on his breath.

"I see you started without me," she said wryly.

He peered at her as if he had no idea of what she meant. "What?"

Britt shook her head. *Don't be such a prude*, she thought. *He's a young guy who likes to have a drink. No big deal.* "Have a seat," she said. "I'll be right back."

She walked to the kitchen, stopping to glance critically at herself in the hall mirror, and then rummaged through the cabinets until she found a couple of dusty wineglasses. She carried them down the hall to the living room.

Dean, who was splayed out on the couch, looked up as she came in. Uneasily aware of his appraising glance, Britt set the glasses down on the coffee table. She was glad she had picked up the room a little. "There," she said. "You do the honors."

Dean wadded up the foil and then frowned as he untwisted the wire around the neck. He grimaced, and held the bottle away from him trying to displace the cork. When it didn't come out, he placed the bottle unsteadily between his knees. Britt watched him and wondered just how much he had already had to drink. He seemed to be having a very difficult time with the task.

Dean looked up at her suspiciously. "What are you looking at?" he said.

"Nothing," she said quickly. "I hate opening champagne."

"Nothing to it," he said, trying to tug the cork out. The bottle slipped out from between his knees and tumbled to the floor. "Oh shit," he said.

"No harm done," said Britt. "It landed on the rug. Maybe I can get it," said Britt. "Do you want me to try?"

He picked up the bottle and scowled at her. "Back off," he said. "I can do it."

Suddenly Britt had the familiar sinking feeling she had known on any number of bad dates. This was a mistake. She felt grateful to him for his help, and she was certainly lonely here, but not that lonely. Maybe she was too picky, but she didn't like sloppy drinkers. She'd crossed that category off her list a long time ago.

"Never mind," she said. "I'm not thirsty."

"Oh, come on now," he said, patting the seat beside him. "I'll get it open. Just keep your panties on."

"I mean it, Dean. Forget the champagne. I don't want any."

"You're not even going to sit down?"

Britt sat, but at a distance.

"So," he said. "If we don't open the champagne, how we gonna toast to success?"

"What do you mean, success?"

"I told you I'd get him for you."

"You might be exaggerating your importance just a little bit," she said.

"And you could show a little gratitude," he snapped.

"And you could show a little self-restraint. I told you to be quiet. My niece might hear you."

"Are you telling me she doesn't know about it?" he asked.

"She knows," said Britt grimly. "I just don't want to upset her."

"Hey, she better get used to it," said Dean. "Daddy's headed for the Big House."

Britt nodded, chewing the inside of her mouth.

"You don't look too happy about it," Dean observed. "What does it take to make you happy?"

"Believe me. I'm not feeling very happy," she said.

Dean nodded, and tried to look solemn. But a smile broke through. "Still, you have to admit. We're a good team, aren't we?"

Britt looked at him narrowly. "Now we're a team?" she said skeptically.

"We could be," he said in a teasing tone, leaning toward her on the couch. "If you were to give me a few introductions in the right places."

"Ahh," she said. "Of course. I almost forgot. The price tag."

"Are you saying you won't do it?" he demanded.

"Oh no. I'll do it."

"All right," he said, clenching his fist and pumping the air.

"When I get back to Boston," she said.

"What do you mean? What's keeping you?" he asked.

Britt inclined her head toward the staircase. "I'm staying here with Zoe."

Dean sat up straight on the couch. "Here, in Coleville? For how long?"

"For as long as I need to," she said.

"What about the network? And Donovan Smith?"

"Well, I'm hoping my job will still be there when I get back."

"Hoping?" he said.

"Don't worry. I can still give you references."

"They won't be much good to me if you're out of work," he said sarcastically.

"Look, Dean, I know a lot of people . . ."

"Yeah, and you're gonna be asking them to give *you* a job," he complained. "Never mind about me."

Britt felt suddenly weary of his presumptions. "Look. I'm sure you're good at what you do. But, I don't owe you anything, Dean. It's not as if you've actually done anything for me. You dug up information. You did your job. The police would have gotten the same information sooner or later."

Dean's face reddened. "That is such a lie. I spoon-fed them that information."

"Maybe you did," said Britt impatiently. "That doesn't mean you're ready for prime time, my friend. I'm not saying I won't introduce you around. But I have to tell you. You seem to be a little overly fond of the cocktails. You have to control that stuff in the big leagues, you know."

"Oh, I get it," he said. "You got what you wanted and now you're going to get high and mighty and give me advice. Treat me like a kid. I hate it when women are in charge. That's what they do. They have to lord it over you. I've got the power and you don't. Never mind that I put my butt on the line to help you. Never mind that that little fire put it right over the top for you . . ."

Britt's head jerked up and she stared at him. "What are you talking about?" she said. "What little fire?"

CHAPTER 28

Dean's expression was surly. "What's your problem?"

Britt stared at him. "What little fire?" she repeated.

"Let me think," he said sarcastically. "What could he possibly mean by that? Don't play dumb."

"I asked you a question," said Britt. "Are you referring to the little fire at the Bayberry cottage?"

"What about it?" he said.

"You said that I got what I wanted . . ." she said slowly.

"That's right," he said in a defiant tone. Then he shook his head. "And now you're not gonna help me, are you? You're going to pretend you didn't promise me anything. I can't believe you," he said. "I can't believe what a waste of time you've turned out to be."

Britt's heart was beating fast. "You set the fire? Why?"

Dean scowled at her. "Look Britt, I've been trying to help you," he reminded her. "You wanted Alec Lynch arrested. The cops were dragging their feet. You said everything was moving too slow. You were threatening to go back to Boston."

Britt stared at him in amazement. "So you decided to move things along by setting fire to the place where I was staying?"

Dean stood up unsteadily. "Oh, stop making it sound like it was a big deal. You wanted me to do it. You told me how Alec came to Bayberry House and made threats against you. You complained about the investigation and how it wasn't getting anywhere. You practically asked me to do it, and now you're all righteous." He made a face of outraged respectability. "'Oh Dean, how could you?' Come off it. It was no big deal. Nobody got hurt," he said.

"Nobody got hurt? How can you say that? Never mind these," she said, waving her bandaged hands, "or the fact that all those volunteer firefighters risked their own safety. Don't you care that Alec Lynch could be paying for your crime?"

Dean walked to the front door and pulled it open, with Britt trailing him. He opened the door and a blast of cold air hit the two of them. "Oh, you're defending him now? Excuse me. Isn't this the guy who killed your sister?" Dean asked. "Or did you forget about that?"

"Aunt Britt?"

Britt looked up the staircase and saw Zoe, leaning over, clutching her brightly colored knitting in one hand.

"I heard weird noises."

Dean looked up at Zoe and smiled. "Hi, sweetie," he said.

Oh no you don't, Britt thought. "Don't talk to her. Get out of this house," she said. Then she lowered her voice and said, "I'm going to call the police."

Dean inhaled a deep breath of the frigid night air and it seemed to steady him. "And tell them what? I don't know what you're talking about. I didn't say anything. Your imagination is running away with you," he said.

Britt shook her head. "You're going to get into big trouble."

Dean lifted up Britt's chin with one finger and gazed at her lips as if he were about to kiss her. Before Britt could jerk her face away from him he said, "No wonder you never got on camera."

"You're drunk. Give me your keys," said Britt.

"You know something? I'll tell you a secret. All this time, you thought I was interested in you. I wasn't interested in you. I wanted to get to Boston because there's someone there . . . I was just playing you . . ."

"The keys, Dean."

He dangled the keys in front of her face and then snatched them back when Britt reached for them. "I'll get to Boston on my own steam. I don't need you."

"I'm calling the cops," Britt warned him.

"See which one of us they'll listen to," he said. He walked down the steps and away from her without a backward glance.

Zoe, who was still watching from above, said, "Is that the guy on the news?"

Britt took a deep breath, slammed the door and locked it. "Yeah," she said.

"What was the matter with him?"

"He had too much to drink," said Britt.

Zoe nodded, as if this was something she could understand. "What was he doing here? Is this about my dad?"

"No. Nothing about that." She held up a hand. "Let me just . . ." She walked down the hall to the phone, and dialed the police.

"Yes," said the sergeant who answered.

"A man just left my house. I'm afraid he's . . . intoxicated. And he wouldn't give me the keys to his car."

"Can you describe the car and tell me where you're located ma'am," said the sergeant. As Britt gave the information, her mind was racing. Should she start to explain to this sergeant about Alec and Dean and the fire at Bayberry House? She went over the conversation in her mind, trying to remember if he had actually admitted to it. Maybe this was something she needed to discuss first with Kevin Carmichael. It wasn't as if this information would exonerate Alec Lynch in Greta's death.

"All right, ma'am," said the sergeant. "We'll keep an eye out for him."

"Thank you," said Britt.

She hung up the phone and turned around. Zoe was standing in the doorway, watching her. "What's going on?"

"Nothing, nothing. How are you coming on your scarf?" Britt asked, wanting to avoid the subject of her phone call.

Zoe looked at the wad of yarn in her hands. "I'm almost done," she said.

"Let me see," said Britt.

Zoe handed the knitting to her aunt.

"Let me look at it in the living room." Britt walked into the living room and sat down on the sofa, switching on a lamp to have a better look. The champagne bottle had rolled onto the floor. Britt shuddered at the thought of the ugly scene. She could not help wondering if what he had said was true. Did she, unwittingly, encourage him to set that fire? To cement the case against Alec Lynch. No, that was crazy. *The idea never crossed my mind*, she thought. She examined the knitting under the light. Her hands were trembling a little bit as she held it up. "How did you get all those colors in it?" she asked.

"The yarn came that way, see?" said Zoe, showing her the brightly variegated skein of turquoise, orange, yellow, white and green.

"That's great," said Britt.

Zoe cocked her head and examined the knitting. "I lost the first one in the fire. Frances at the Knit Kit replaced the wool for free."

"That was nice," Britt murmured.

"Since it started out as a baby blanket I thought these colors would be good for a boy or a girl," she said. "But now it's a scarf."

"And it will look great on Vicki. I'm sure she'll really appreciate it."

Zoe sighed. "I still have a lot to do though."

"You want me to read aloud for a while and you can knit down here?"

Zoe looked at her shyly. "Yeah. That would be fun."

"Okay," said Britt, "where did I leave that book?"

"Over there," said Zoe. "By the chair. I'll get it."

Britt watched as the girl hunted through a pile of books and came up with *Little Women*. "All right, great," she said.

Zoe brought the book over and flopped down on the sofa beside her. Britt could feel the warmth of her arm through the sleeve of her shirt, and she could smell the sweet scent of her hair. Zoe began to arrange the yarn and her knitting on her lap.

"Tomorrow," said Zoe, "I'm going to tell dad about my plan."

Britt frowned. "What's your plan?"

"I'm going to get my Girl Scout troop to have a bake sale for him. For his defense fund."

"Defense fund?" Britt said sharply.

"That's what you have to do," Zoe explained. "Mr. Carmichael told me about it. When he drove me back from the jail, I asked him what I could do to help my dad and he said that it would take a lot of money and you have to have a defense fund."

"Mr. Carmichael said you needed to start a defense fund?" Britt asked.

"Well, first he said I should just say my prayers and hope for the best but I told him that I wanted to actually *do* something for my dad. So, that's when he said I should save my money for the defense fund and he would do the rest."

Britt nodded, feeling a kind of grudging admiration for Kevin Carmichael. He had not just tried to placate Zoe, and brushed off her pleas as childish. He had actually tried to answer her. And also, protect his own interests.

"Plus, I figured my troop could write letters to our representatives in Congress and stuff. Or maybe to the judge."

Britt thought about Norman Dietz, who didn't even want his child to play with Zoe, and she had little doubt about how such a proposal would go over with the Girl Scout leaders. But despite the rebuff she had suffered today, despite *all* she had suffered, Zoe seemed to have no doubts about the potential success of her plan. In a way, Britt felt envious of her. Zoe was so sure in her belief. So certain that her prayers would be answered. Britt could not remember ever feeling that way.

"What do you think about my plan?" Zoe asked.

"That sounds great," said Britt.

Zoe settled in beside her, needles clicking. Britt opened the book. She tried to block the thought of Dean Webster, and that encounter between them, out of her mind. She tried not to think about a fire that might have been set to please her, by a guy whose ambition outweighed his common sense. Most of all, she tried not to think about Alec Lynch, who obviously had not tried to kill her. And how bitterly she had accused him.

Tonight, after Zoe went upstairs, she would call Kevin Carmichael and tell him. She wondered if she had brought this about with her quest for vengeance. Was it as much her fault as Dean's? Had she given him the idea that she would reward him for implicating Alec, whether it was true or not? She never thought of herself as that kind of person. Still, she had inspired Dean Webster to commit a crime on her behalf. *I'll get Dean to admit to it,* she thought. *I'll make it right.*

Britt took a deep breath. "All right," she said. "Where were we?"

CHAPTER 29

Dean turned out of Medford Road on two wheels and careened down the darkened, icy streets of Coleville in the direction of the log house that he rented in the woods. *That bitch*, he thought, as he drove along, ignoring his speedometer. She had as much as asked him to do it. Offered to bring him into the network if he only helped her to get what she wanted. And now. Now she was all indignant, pretending not to know anything about it. And of course she wouldn't help him. That was what happened when women got power. They held onto it and weren't about to share the wealth. Especially not with a man. Especially not with a man who was young and a stud. They were threatened by a guy like him. He reminded them of everything they were missing in life. The only fucking they wanted to do was to fuck their way to the top.

On the other hand, there were young women, who wanted him the minute they set eyes on him. There was no challenge to it. No thrill, no . . . mystery. He'd had so many of them, but it always left him feeling empty and sad. The fact was, and he had only lately been able to admit it to himself, that the only satisfying encounter he'd ever had was with a man. And not just any man. Most men did nothing for him. He didn't even notice them. But Peter was different. Peter messed with his mind.

I have to get to Boston, Dean thought. And, when he got there, he knew he had to *be* somebody. He had to arrive in glory, so that Peter Darien would be proud of him. Proud to introduce him to all his snooty, art-crowd friends. *And I was almost there,* Dean thought. *It seemed like it was so close.*

Dean rounded another curve with a screech and felt the tires start to lose purchase along the icy road. *Oh shit,* he thought, trying to remember how to pull out and keep from spinning. Somehow, miraculously, he managed to regain some traction and continue on his way. Every time he thought about the evening he wanted to kick himself for having blurted it out about the fire. What if Britt told the cops? What if they believed her? Not only would he never make the networks, he'd lose his gig at this rinky-dink station as well. And be disgraced in Peter's eyes. Everything he'd worked for would go down the drain.

He'd been dreaming of being somebody important since he was a kid, pushed around by a bullying father who mocked everything he tried to do. Now, he had a toehold on the good life, and nobody was gonna take it away from him, he vowed. If the cops asked about that fire, he didn't know anything about it. It wasn't like it was some big deal. He set it outside the cottage, in plain view of everybody who was in the main house. There was no chance Britt was going to be hurt in that fire. He had stayed nearby, calling Jeff to meet him there in the newsvan. Telling him he heard about it on the scanner. He'd taken every precaution, and it turned out exactly the way he planned. Alec Lynch, who'd been throwing threats around, had been blamed. And so what? He was guilty of worse than that. He had killed his own wife.

Still, Dean cursed himself for having mentioned it to Miss Network Television. She was gonna play the ethical journalist and turn him in. *Don't worry,* he thought. *All it's gonna be is her word against yours. That's all it's gonna be,* he told himself. *And you're the celebrity around here. She's nobody around here*. But he felt sick at his stomach, and it was hard to breathe when he thought about the questions and the accusations. *Calm down*, he told himself. *Get over it. She can't hurt you*. And just when he'd talked himself into feeling a little safer, and a tiny bit better, he heard the whine of the sirens, and, looking in his rearview mirror, saw the lights coming up on his rear end. *Shit*, he thought. *She did it. She called them*. They were coming after him. *That bitch*, he thought, stepping on the gas. *That fucking bitch*. He pressed down on the gas, wanting to shake them, wanting to get away. The car hit an icy patch and began to hydroplane on the lonely, tree-lined road. He could feel the wheel under his sweaty palms losing its authority as the car seemed to achieve a will of its own. Things started to spin around him and he glanced at the speedometer as the car went into its slow twirl on the patchy ice. *Too fast*, he thought. And then he saw the tree.

* * *

Britt went to bed early, but slept badly, plagued by guilty anxieties, and the wail of sirens on the night wind. She tried not to toss and turn too much, for fear of waking Zoe. But Zoe seemed to sleep peacefully, her own conscience utterly clear. The next morning, as Britt was in the kitchen putting breakfast on the table, there was a knocking at the front door.

"Zoe, get that will you?" she cried.

She heard Zoe run to open the door and then the murmur of voices. In a moment, Zoe appeared in the kitchen doorway. "Guess what?" she cried.

Britt turned and looked at her. Kevin Carmichael, the shoulders of his black cashmere topcoat dusted with snow, stood behind Zoe. In his right hand he held up a long, brown cylinder tied with a blue ribbon. "For you," he said, holding it out to her. Britt peered at it for a moment, and then recognized what it was.

"Vicki had her baby?" she asked, accepting the cigar from Kevin's outstretched hand.

"How'd you know?" Zoe said, disappointed that her newsflash had been scooped.

"It's a cigar," said Britt. "People give them out when babies are born. A boy, I take it."

Kevin nodded. "Kent Thompson Carmichael," he said proudly. "Born at five o'clock last night."

"Oh Kevin, that's great," said Britt. "I'm really happy for you. Everybody doing okay?"

"Yeah, everybody's fine. After all that worrying, Vicki actually went into labor yesterday afternoon so she delivered him the normal way. And he's fine. He's great!"

"How's Vicki?" asked Zoe.

"Vicki's doing fine," said Kevin. "It's a strange condition she had. Once the baby's born, the blood pressure returns to normal, right away. It's the oddest thing. Anyway, she's done her part, and I've got the papers." He patted the breast pocket of his coat. "It's all legal now. Signed, sealed and delivered. We brought our baby home this morning."

"Caroline must be thrilled," said Britt.

"She is. And she's utterly exhausted. I made her promise me she would get some rest today. When she gets tired she gets really stressed out."

"And what's happening with Vicki now?" Britt asked.

"Taking the money and splitting," Kevin said wryly.

"I've got to wrap up my scarf so I can give it to her," said Zoe, running from the room.

Kevin turned to Britt. "I got your message, but it was late when I got home last night. What's up?"

Britt grimaced. "I thought about calling the cops, but I figured I would talk to you first. It's about Dean Webster. You know, the TV reporter?"

"Oh yeah, I heard," he said.

Britt looked at him in surprise. "You heard?"

"About the accident," he said.

Britt shook her head. "What . . .?"

"You didn't know?" Kevin suddenly looked wary.

"Know what?" Britt asked, clammy with dread.

"There was a terrible accident last night, Britt. Dean Webster drove his car into a tree. They had to airlift him to the trauma center at Mid-State Medical."

"Oh my God," Britt cried.

"Oh yeah," said Kevin. "It's touch and go. He's critical."

CHAPTER 30

Britt's mouth fell open. "I can't believe it," she said.

"Yeah. Late last night. Didn't you hear the sirens?"

Britt was about to say no, and then she remembered. "Yes. Yes, I did."

"He was speeding out on the state highway. The cops were after him because they'd gotten a tip that he was drunk. Anyway, he lost control of the car and slammed into a tree."

"Oh my God," Britt said again. She saw spots in front of her eyes, and felt as if she was going to faint. She gripped the countertop.

Kevin shook his head. "Haven't you had your TV on? It's been all over the news."

Britt shook her head. "I didn't want Zoe to have to hear anything about Alec . . . I don't believe it. He was here last night."

It was Kevin's turn to be surprised. "Dean was?"

Britt nodded, reliving Dean's visit in her mind's eye. "He was drunk. I tried to take the keys but he wouldn't let me. So, I called the police."

"Oh," said Kevin, understanding. "Well, you were only trying to help. You did what you could."

"I can't believe it," said Britt, sitting down on one of the kitchen chairs. Her legs were weak beneath her.

"Does this have anything to do with what you wanted to talk to me about? You said in your message that you wanted to discuss something about Alec's case?" Kevin asked.

"Kevin, he admitted to me . . . Well, not in so many words, but . . . Dean as good as admitted to me . . . He set the fire at the Bayberry cottage."

"What?" said Kevin. "Why? Why would he do that?"

Britt shook her head.

Kevin walked over to the sink and ran a glass of water. He handed it to Britt. "Here, drink this. You look like you need it."

Britt sipped the water, holding the glass with an unsteady hand. "I'm afraid," she said. "I'm afraid he was trying to do what he thought I wanted."

"By burning down the place where you were staying?"

"By implicating Alec," she said. "He knew I thought that Alec was guilty of setting fire to the house. Killing Greta. He was hoping I would be grateful. That I would be his entree to the network news. I had no idea, really . . ."

"Wow," said Kevin.

"I know. I feel so guilty. Believe me, I never suggested any such thing. He got this into his head, and I had no idea . . ."

Kevin sat down opposite Britt, frowning. "Well, but, in a way, this is very good. For my client. I mean . . ."

"I don't know if he's going to admit it, Kevin. Even if he pulls through this."

Kevin chewed on his lip thoughtfully. "Is there anyone else he might have told? Anyone else who might know?"

"I have no idea," said Britt. "I don't know anything about him. I wasn't paying attention."

Kevin looked at his watch. "That's all right. Let me see . . . They helicoptered him last night to the trauma unit at the Mid-State Medical Center," said Kevin. "Maybe I'll drive down there. To the trauma unit. Maybe I can talk to him. Is that all right with you?"

"Sure," she said. "I guess so. I feel so guilty. I feel like I caused his accident."

"Nonsense," said Kevin briskly. "Now you listen. I'm going to get this straightened out. You just sit tight."

Britt, still somewhat numb from the news, walked him to the front door. "Thanks Kevin," she said. "It's awfully good of you to go down there, today of all days. And thanks for coming to tell us. About the baby."

"Happy to do it," he said. "Enjoy your cigar," he said with a wink.

Britt watched him as he walked jauntily toward his car. Once he was behind the wheel he honked the horn briefly. Both Britt and Zoe, who was descending the stairs toting a gift bag, waved at him. As the car disappeared into the whirling snow, Britt shook her head. She thought about Dean, who had seemed so cocky and at the same time so . . . clumsy. He had been willing to sacrifice her safety, her life even, to try to advance his career. And all the while she had trusted his information, believed he was trying to help her.

"Can I call my dad?" Zoe said.

Britt frowned, and looked at her niece. "No, Zoe, you're not allowed to call him at the jail."

"After school can I go see him?" Zoe asked.

"I think so. I'll have to check on the visiting hours," Britt said absently. "They have a very strict policy." *Now, what do I do when I see Alec?* Britt thought. *Do I have to apologize for blaming him? Apologize, when he is still charged with killing Greta*? Part of her wanted to avoid seeing him altogether. Maybe she could wait outside while Zoe went in to visit by herself.

The phone rang and Zoe cried, "I'll get it."

Zoe murmured into the phone, hung up and then turned to Britt. Her eyes looked tragic. "It was Vicki, calling from the hospital. She wanted to say good-bye. She's leaving today."

"Leaving the hospital?" Britt asked.

"Leaving the hospital and leaving town," Zoe cried.

"Wow, that was quick. How's she feeling?" Britt asked.

"She sounded kind of down."

I'll bet, Britt thought. *She's just given birth, and given away her baby.* "I guess that's to be expected," Britt said. "Well, I know you two are friends. I know you're going to miss her."

"I didn't even give her my present yet," said Zoe. "I wanted to bring her my present."

"I'm sure she's anxious to put this whole experience behind her," said Britt.

"She told me to mail it to her." Zoe, obviously still concerned about her present, looked mournfully at the address she had scribbled down on a piece of paper. "I won't even get to see her open it. Why does she have to leave so soon?"

"Well, it's a difficult time," said Britt. What she didn't say to Zoe was that now that they had the baby, the Carmichaels were no longer concerned about Vicki. It had to be an empty feeling, Britt thought, in more ways than one. "Tell you what. If you want, I'll stop up at the hospital and give her the scarf after I take you to school."

"I don't see why she couldn't wait for me," said Zoe.

"She probably just wants to get back to normal. To her old life. She was always saying that, you know." Britt stared outside at the falling snow. "So, do you want me to bring her the scarf?"

"I guess so. I wish I didn't have to go to school," said Zoe.

Britt understood that as much as Zoe wanted to give Vicki the scarf she had made, she also wanted to avoid going to school. And Britt was tempted to let her. It had to be difficult, facing all those kids. But running away from it was no solution. Zoe had to face her classmates, sooner or later. "You need to get back to school, Zoe," Britt murmured. "You'd better go get ready."

* * *

Zoe clutched the bag all the way to the school and stared anxiously out the window. When Britt pulled up in front of the school, Zoe turned to her with fear in her eyes. "Can't I come to the hospital with you, Aunt Britt? It won't matter if I miss one more day."

Britt felt sick at heart at the sight of Zoe's misery. She sighed, wavering in her resolve. *Why not let her skip it today?* she thought. What difference did it make if Zoe missed one more day of school? Suddenly there was a thud on the passenger-side window, and a face appeared there. A mittened hand wiped the snowflakes off the glass. Zoe started, and turned to look.

"Kayley!" Zoe cried, and quickly opened the door, abandoning the gift bag and clambering out of the car, delighted to be with her friend again. The two girls walked up the snow-covered path to the front door with their heads together, and Britt watched them go, her own heart considerably lightened by their rapprochement.

There was a powdery inch of new snow on the ground by the time Britt arrived at the hospital. She parked in the visitors' area which had already been cleared by snowplows. Obviously, Britt thought, this was a town that was always ready for a snowfall.

She picked up the gift bag containing the brightly colored scarf and walked into the wind, toward the hospital. She opened the front door and approached the information desk.

The white-haired woman at the desk smiled. "Who are you looking for?" she asked.

Britt hesitated, realizing that she didn't know Vicki's last name. She'd heard it, but had forgotten it. "Oh," she said, "this is embarrassing. I'm delivering a gift. Um, she just had a baby last night. Her first name is Victoria."

The woman consulted her computer. "Let me see. I'm checking maternity . . . Manfred, Victoria?"

"That's it," said Britt.

"Room 420," said the volunteer behind the desk.

Britt thanked her, walked down the hall to the elevator, got in, and pushed the button marked four.

She got off the elevator and looked up and down the cheerful hallways of the maternity floor. The nurses' station was in the center of two parallel hallways. Room 420, Britt thought, slightly disoriented. Would that be this way, or. . . .

Britt looked to her right, and then looked again. Her heart jumped as she recognized a pudgy young man with wispy, blond hair, wearing an olive-drab parka. He was stepping away from the nurses' station. Under his arm, he was holding a pale blue teddy bear. On the coat sleeve of that arm was an orange chevron, made out of reflector tape. He looked furtively up and down the hallway, and then limped down the corridor. Halfway down the hall he turned to his left and entered one of the rooms.

CHAPTER 31

Britt looked in the doorway of Room 420. Vicki was lying on her back in the elevated bed. The TV was blaring overhead, but Vicki's eyes were closed, her mouth hanging open. There were dark smudges that looked like bruises under her eyes. A pale blue teddy bear was tucked under one of her arms.

Sitting quietly next to the guardrail beside Vicki's bed was the young man Britt had seen in the hallway. He was watching Vicki sleep. When Britt entered the room, he looked up, startled, and then seemed to relax. Britt felt her heart pounding at the sight of him. It was the same guy they had seen hitchhiking out by the Carmichaels'. The very same guy.

Britt walked up to the guardrail on the other side of the bed, and found the remote control for the television. She switched it to off, and the abrupt silence awakened Vicki. Her hand flew to her belly, and then she winced, and slumped back against the pillow. She gazed, bleary-eyed, at her two visitors.

"Hi, Vicki. Sorry to have to wake you," said Britt.

Vicki frowned, and rubbed her eyes. She turned her head to gaze at the young man in the chair and smiled faintly. "Hi," she said.

"Brought you something," he said, pointing to the stuffed bear.

Vicki picked it up, looked at it and sighed, letting it tumble over her knees into the guardrail. Then, she peered up at Britt. She made no effort to introduce one of her guests to the other. "What do you want?" she asked.

Though her heart was thudding, Britt hoisted the bag. "Zoe wanted me to bring you her gift. It's a scarf. She made it for you."

Vicki took the gift bag, lifted the tissue paper and looked in. Her grumpy expression softened into a broad smile. "How cute. She's sweet." Vicki pulled the scarf out of the bag. "Dave, look," she said.

The blond-haired guy nodded. "Nice," he said.

"The little kid that lived next door made it for me. The one that was in the fire."

Dave, Britt thought. *This is Dave.*

Vicki looked up at Britt. "Tell her I said thanks. That was so cute of her."

"She wanted to give it to you herself, but when you said you were leaving . . ."

Vicki stuffed the scarf back into the bag and her frown returned. "Yeah. I'm leaving."

"Feeling all right?" Britt asked.

Vicki blinked and then sighed. "At least it's over." She squinted at Britt and then up at the television suspended above the foot of the bed. "Who turned the TV off?" she demanded, looking at Dave accusingly.

"I did," said Britt. "I need to talk to you."

Vicki shifted her bulk in the bed so that she was sitting up. "Put that pillow behind me, will you?" Vicki asked Dave in her babyish voice.

Dave jumped up and adjusted the pillow. "Okay?"

"I guess," said Vicki, sighing again. She turned to Britt. "What do you want? You want him to leave?" There was an edge to her little baby voice.

Britt looked over at Dave. "Actually, I need to talk to both of you."

Dave seemed surprised that she was addressing him.

"Are you a close friend of Vicki's?" said Britt.

Dave looked flummoxed by the question.

"What's it to you?" said Vicki.

Britt continued to look at the young man, who seemed very uneasy. "It's not a hard question," she said.

"Yeah, sure," he said.

"Have you ever hitchhiked, Dave? Out near where the Carmichaels live?"

Dave's eyes widened, and he looked helplessly at Vicki.

"That's none of your business," Vicki declared, glaring at Britt again. "There's no law against it. Look, I just had a baby. I feel lousy. Do you mind going?"

There was a tap on the door and Britt looked up to see the obstetrician, Dr. Yasushi, coming into the room. The doctor was petite and attractive, with glasses that had narrow black frames. She exuded energy, "Hello," she said cheerfully to all three of them. "How's my patient doing?"

Vicki turned around and looked at the doctor gratefully. "I'm tired," Vicki complained. "I need to rest."

"Let me have a look at you. Would you excuse us, please?" the doctor asked Britt and Dave. She indicated that they should step outside.

"Dave," Vicki warned. "Don't you say anything. She's a friend of Hawkeye's."

Britt edged past the doctor and went out into the hallway, and Dave limped out after her. There was an atmosphere of happy excitement on the maternity floor as men and children arrived with flowers and balloons. She could hear pleased murmurs and babies squalling from the open doorways on the corridor. Most of the nurses who came and went were smiling.

Dave leaned against the wall, avoiding Britt's gaze.

Britt hesitated, not sure how to begin. "Who's Hawkeye?" Britt asked. "Is that Caroline?"

Dave shrugged, studying the toes of his work boots.

"Dave, look," said Britt. "I'm not a friend of Caroline's. I hardly know the woman. And I don't care what's going on with you and Vicki. Believe me. But Alec Lynch says that he picked up a hitchhiker and drove him to Montpelier the night my sister was killed in a fire. That's all he could tell the police. A guy named Dave. My niece and I saw you out hitchhiking by the Carmichaels. And you fit the description to a T. Are you that man? Can you give my brother-in-law an alibi? Because he's in jail now, charged with setting that fire, and whatever your situation is with Vicki, it can't be more important than that."

Dave scuffed the heavy treads of one of his work boots against the wall and sighed. "No," he said miserably. "No. It's just that. . . ."

"Come on, Dave," said Britt. "You seem like a decent guy."

Britt could see the internal struggle he was having reflected in his face.

"You see, Vicki told them she was . . . unattached," he said. "I wasn't supposed to be coming around. I had to sneak around to see her. I'd meet her out in the back. Sometimes we'd meet in that barn there behind your . . . you know, next door."

"What do you mean, told *them*?" Britt asked.

"Them. You know, the Carmichaels. She knew they wouldn't like it if the baby's father was in the picture, you know what I mean?"

"That's you," said Britt, her suspicion confirmed. "You're the baby's father."

Dave shrugged and smiled bashfully.

"Well, look, that's your business. You and the Carmichaels. But you've got to understand. A man's life could depend on this. Did Alec Lynch pick you up that night? He drives a blue Merceedes. He said he sideswiped the hitchhiker as he was coming around the corner. When the hitchhiker got out of the car, he had a limp."

Dave nodded, and looked resigned. "Yeah. He drove me back to Montpelier."

"He did," said Britt. Britt felt as if her heart was going to fly out of her chest. *It was true. This was the guy. The one the police had not been able to find. He'd been under their noses the entire time. Vicki's constant, secret visitor.*

The doctor came out of Vicki's room, making notes on a chart. She gave Britt and Dave a brief smile.

"Doctor," said Dave. "How's she doing?"

"Doing great. You the father?"

Dave nodded.

"She's young. She'll bounce right back."

"That's good," said Dave.

"I signed her release forms. She's okay to leave. I told her to get dressed."

"Isn't that kind of quick?" Dave asked.

The doctor shrugged. "No insurance," she said, and Dave hung his head slightly. "But she'll be fine at home. No problem. Bring her back for a checkup in a month."

"Oh, okay," Dave said seriously, nodding.

The doctor started down the corridor. Dave limped back into the room, with Britt behind him.

"Do you mind?" Vicki cried. "I'm getting dressed." She was pulling up a pair of sweatpants around her still-ample belly.

"She said you could leave," said Dave.

Vicki rolled her eyes. "I know. The nurse told me this morning, when she took the I.V. out."

"Vicki, Dave and I had a talk out in the hall. I need for him to go to the police and tell them that he's the man that Alec picked up in his car on the night of the fire. Dave can give Zoe's dad an alibi," said Britt. "They'll have to let him out of jail."

"I should do it, babe," he said.

"Fine, do what you want," said Vicki.

"Hey, don't be mad, babe. I'm just helping the guy out."

Vicki shook her head. "And then you'll tell *them* . . ." she said.

Britt knew that Vicki was referring to the Carmichaels. "They're going to find out anyway," said Britt. "Kevin is Alec's attorney now."

"What about *her?* You can't tell Hawkeye," said Vicki.

"You're in no position to make conditions," said Britt.

"Oh shit," said Vicki, exhaling a gusty sigh. "They're gonna kill me," she said. "They think I was living on my own. That's what I told them."

"They've got the baby," said Britt. "That's all they want."

"I told them I didn't know who the father was. Or where he was," said Vicki.

"Well, things change," said Britt, spreading her hands wide. "And maybe it's for the best. I mean, they need the father's permission, too, to adopt the baby."

"They do?" said Dave. He looked at Vicki in surprise.

"Sure. That way they won't have to worry about the father showing up someday and claiming paternal rights," said Britt. "That happens sometimes, you know."

Dave nodded and was silent. Britt detected potential trouble for the Carmichaels in that silence. Was it possible that Dave would balk at signing away his paternal rights? Britt had no desire to screw up the Carmichaels' adoption. But, in a way, Britt thought, it wouldn't be all that surprising. Surely, Kevin Carmichael knew the risks with one of these private adoption deals. He was an attorney. He had to know how many times these kinds of arrangements fell through on the adoptive parents. Even Britt knew that, just from reading the newspapers. She often wondered why they had chosen this most hazardous of routes. Why hadn't they gone through the regular channels?

Vicki brushed her hair and put on some lipstick. "What a mess," she said. "Well, that's as good as its gonna get today."

"How are you two getting home?" Britt asked.

Dave and Vicki exchanged a glance.

"Won't Caroline come for you?"

"I'd never call her," said Vicki. "We'll get a cab, I guess. And go get my new car. Remember, I got that new Toyota out at the Carmichaels'. And my money."

Britt couldn't help noticing that Vicki said "my money" instead of "our money." "I'll drive you out there," said Britt. "I want to make sure you get that car so that Dave gets to the police station."

"I said I'll go, and I will," Dave protested.

"That's great," said Britt soothingly. "I'm not trying to pressure you. It's just that you have to realize how important this is."

"I realize it, okay?" said Dave.

"Okay, sorry. My car's down in the parking lot," said Britt. "Anything you want me to carry?"

Vicki looked around the room. There was an arrangement of flowers from Kevin on the windowsill and the blue bear, still upended on the bed. She reached across the bear, and picked up the bag with Zoe's scarf in it. She shook out the scarf and wound it around her neck. "Let's go," she said.

A nurse came padding into the room on squeaky white shoes. "Everything okay in here?" she asked.

Britt turned to the nurse. "Everything's fine," she said.

The nurse shrugged. "Okay." She bounced back out of the room.

"You're a real pain in the butt, you know that?" said Vicki to Britt. "You better not ruin everything for me."

Britt didn't flinch. "You ready?" she said.

"Ready," Vicki grumbled. She began to lumber toward the door. Dave reached across the bed, and picked up the blue bear, tucking it back under his arm. Britt followed them both out into the hall.

CHAPTER 32

Britt pulled into the Carmichaels' driveway behind the cherry-red Toyota. Vicki shook her head and looked around. "Man, I cannot wait to get away from this place. I hated it here. I just want my money, and the car, and to get out of here. Now Dave, you just keep quiet, and let me do the talking."

All three of them got out of the ear and climbed up on the front porch. Vicki looked around the snowy yard. "I wonder where Kirby is," she said. "I'm not leaving without him." She fiddled nervously with the end of the brightly colored scarf.

She'll leave without her baby, but not the cat. People are weird, Britt thought.

Summoned by the bell, Caroline opened the door. She looked pale and tired and when her gaze rested on Vicki there was an undisguised loathing in her expression. "Hello," she said.

"I came to get my stuff," said Vicki. "And the money. And the car."

"Everything's in your room," said Caroline. "Except the car. Obviously."

"What about Kirby?" Vicki asked, peering past Caroline into the living room.

"He's outside," said Caroline. "It's not safe for cats to be around little babies. If they scratch the baby it can be deadly. They can get some terrible disease from it."

Vicki rolled her eyes. "That's stupid," she said. "Lots of people have cats. Dave, you go look for him while I get my stuff."

Caroline peered at Dave as he obediently descended the porch steps and began to limp toward the back of the house. "Who's that?" she said.

"Friend of mine," said Vicki, sweeping past her into the house.

Caroline smiled thinly at Britt. "Do you want to come in?"

The tension between Caroline and Vicki was palpable, and Britt would rather have stayed outside, but she didn't want to appear unfriendly. She followed Vicki inside and sat down on the couch. Vicki started up the stairs.

"Don't wake him," said Caroline.

"I won't," said Vicki, although she seemed to be stomping up the steps as noisily as possible.

Caroline sat down opposite Britt, perching on the edge of the chair. She pushed a long lock of her shiny hair behind her ear and glanced anxiously up the stairs.

"How's he doing?" Britt asked.

Caroline's worried face broke into a tremulous smile. "My baby? He's great. He's perfect. He's the perfect child."

Britt nodded. "That's . . . that's wonderful. It must be tiring though. Taking care of a baby."

"I'm not tired," Caroline protested. "I can do it."

"I'm sure," said Britt. "I didn't mean . . ."

Caroline looked at Britt quizzically. "Why are you here?"

"Here? You mean here at your house?"

Caroline nodded.

"Well, they needed a ride from the hospital."

"She's leaving, isn't she?" Caroline asked.

"As far as I know," said Britt. "She seemed eager to be on her way."

"It's not like you're close to Vicki," Caroline said.

"No, not at all. I just happened to be there when she needed a ride. I came over to give Vicki a present from Zoe. Zoe wanted her to have it before she left town."

"Who is that boy?" Caroline asked suspiciously.

Britt didn't want to get into this discussion. "Just a friend, I guess. He was visiting when I arrived."

"What kind of a friend is he?" Caroline asked. "A boyfriend? She told me she didn't have a boyfriend."

This isn't my concern, Britt thought. *This is their business*. She stood up. "I don't know anything about that. Look, I've got some things to do. I guess I'll be going."

Caroline stood up and trailed her to the door. "How come he's here?"

"They didn't say. Moral support, maybe," said Britt. "As you said, I hardly know Vicki. Look, I'm going to take off. Good luck with the . . . with your new baby."

Caroline stood in the doorway watching Britt as she went down the stairs. Dave was standing out beside the red Toyota smoking a cigarette, and kicking a tire absently with one of his scuffed-up work boots. The cigarette, the boots. Britt had a sudden realization. She walked up to him. "Dave, were you out in the woods behind this house yesterday?"

Dave looked up at her blankly and then nodded. "Vicki was supposed to meet me. When she didn't come out, I didn't know what happened to her. This morning I just took a chance and called the hospital. They told me she had the baby. Why?"

"Nothing," said Britt. "My niece thought she saw someone back there when she was feeding the cat. It scared her a little bit."

"I didn't think anybody knew I was there," said Dave.

"No harm done," said Britt. "Look. I'm going to have to take off now. Can I tell the police chief you are coming in to corroborate Alec's story?"

Dave nodded absently.

"I know that Vicki is eager to be on her way, but there's a little girl who needs her father back. It all depends on you, Dave."

"I said I'll do it," he replied irritably.

"Could you give me your address and a phone number where I could reach you? I don't even know your last name."

Dave ground out his cigarette in the snow. "My name's Kronemayer. Dave Kronemayer. If you want me, you can always call Vicki. But I told you I'd go to the cops and I will."

"I don't have . . ." Vicki's number, Britt started to say. Then she remembered that Vicki had given it to Zoe. "All right," she said.

The squall of a crying baby was suddenly audible from the direction of the house. Dave and Britt looked up at the porch as Caroline rushed back inside the house.

"Is that him?" Dave asked. "Is that my son?"

Uh-oh, Britt thought. "Sounds like a baby all right. You know, I think your . . . son will be very happy here," she said. "The Carmichaels really want to give him a good home. It's a very generous thing to do. To give a baby up to people who really want to love him and take care of him. I really admire people who do that."

But Dave didn't answer. He was gazing up at the house with a wistful expression in his eyes.

* * *

Britt stopped at the police station, and learned that Ray, alerted by Kevin, had also journeyed to the trauma unit at the Mid-State Medical Center. She left Ray a brief message explaining that she had located Dave and confirmed Alec's alibi to her own satisfaction. *All right*, Britt thought, as the sergeant read back the message she had been given. *Now, Chief Stern, its up to you to question him and cross all the legal Ts, so to speak*. For her part, Britt was undeniably eager to deliver this news to the person to whom it mattered the most.

She drove above the speed limit, and tried to formulate in her mind the way she would break the news to him. As little as she liked Alec, she still could hardly wait to see the look on his face when she told him that she had stumbled across the keys to his freedom. It wasn't often in life that you had the opportunity to deliver such news. And, if she was going to stay close to Zoe, and she certainly planned to do that, it was important for her to get along with Alec somehow. She didn't want him to always think of her as the woman who'd done her level best to get him arrested. Not that she was doing it for that reason, she reminded herself. It was simply the right thing to do.

She arrived at the jail as several family members of prisoners were leaving, some tearful, some hard eyed. Britt locked her car and hurried inside, submitting her coat, her satchel and herself to a search. She signed all the paperwork that was required from a visitor and then a prison guard with a holstered gun and handcuffs hanging from his belt escorted her to the visitors' area. She sat down in front of the Plexiglas shield, waiting impatiently while the guard on the other side went to fetch Alec.

Britt took a deep breath and tried to compose herself. She couldn't help smiling when she thought of Alec's reaction to her news. She heard the door open on the other side of the shield and looked up. Alec was being led in by a guard. Unsmiling, he stared at her as the guard removed his handcuffs, his silver eyes wary beneath his dark eyebrows. He rubbed his wrists, but his gaze did not waver.

Britt returned his gaze and wished, not for the first time, that she had been able to perform this small miracle for someone she liked better than Alec Lynch. He took his seat and the guard stepped back.

"Where's Zoe?" he demanded, not bothering to greet her.

"At school," said Britt.

"Is she all right?" Alec asked.

"Zoe's fine," said Britt. "She asked me to tell you . . . She sends her love."

"Well, if you didn't bring Zoe, what are you doing back here?" he asked. He made it sound as if being removed from his cell to meet with her was an irritation to him.

Britt felt like telling him to go to hell, and walking out, but she resisted the impulse. She reminded herself that he was sitting in a jail cell, unfairly accused. And she was partly to blame. It would be enough to make anyone surly.

"I have some news for you," she said. "Good news. Great news, actually, where you're concerned."

Alec frowned and regarded her suspiciously. "What are you talking about?"

Britt took a deep breath. "Well, first of all, Dean Webster admitted to me that he started the fire at the Bayberry cottage."

"Dean Webster? The news guy?"

Britt nodded.

"I heard he was in an accident last night. That he's critical."

"It's true. They airlifted him to Boston. Kevin and Chief Stern have gone to see him, to try to obtain his confession."

"Jesus," said Alec. "I can't believe it. Why?"

Britt blushed, not wanting to admit to Alec that Dean had set the fire to try to satisfy her. *The less said the better*, she thought. She realized he wasn't expecting an answer from her. "Alec," she said. "That's not all. Remember, when Chief Stern asked you about your alibi the night of the fire, you told that story about the hitchhiker and how you were driving him home when the fire started?"

"Yeah . . ." he said cautiously.

"Well, at the time I was skeptical. Actually, I thought it was . . . a lie."

"I know," he said coldly.

"Well, the other day," said Britt. "I thought I saw the guy. I mean, I saw a guy who fit the description. He was hitchhiking out by your old house. By the time I realized who it was, he'd gotten away from me." Britt knew this was not precisely true. She'd hadn't tried to stop him the first time. But this time, she made up for it. Britt tried not to smile, but she couldn't help it. The grin spread across her face. "Today . . . I found him!"

Alec peered at her and shook his head slightly.

"I found him," Britt repeated. "I found Dave. The guy you picked up. It turns out that he was hanging around on

Brightwater Road because he's the father of Vicki's baby. You know Vicki? The girl who is giving her baby to the Carmichaels? He used to come and visit her in the evenings. They'd meet outside on the sly. Sometimes in the barn behind your house. That's why you saw him hitchhiking. And why I saw him. 'Cause he was out there as often as he could get there without a car. Anyway, I went to the hospital today to see Vicki, to bring her a scarf Zoe made for her, and he was there, visiting her. I recognized him from your description. So I questioned him. And . . . I learned that everything you said was true. I've just come from the police station. I told them that your witness is coming in. Your alibi is going to be corroborated. They're going to have to let you out of here."

Alec turned his face away from her, and Britt wondered if there might be tears in his eyes that he wanted to hide from her.

Britt leaned toward the mesh-covered hole in the Plexiglas. "This will prove it Alec," she said eagerly. "This will prove that you didn't kill Greta."

Alec began to shake his head. "Oh God," he said. Then he sighed. "Oh no."

CHAPTER 33

"Excuse me?" Britt demanded. She thought she must have heard him wrong. She could not believe her own ears.

Alec turned and looked at her as if he had forgotten she was there.

Britt felt the color rise to her cheeks. "This is what you have to say?" she demanded. "Oh . . . no . . .? I find the man who can free you and that's all you can say?"

Alec frowned. "Sorry," he said. "I should be thanking you."

"Don't bother," she said. She shouldered her satchel with her bandaged hand and stood up.

Alec looked up at her and his clouded gaze seemed to clear for a moment. "Britt, I'm really sorry. Sit down, please. I'm sorry. I am grateful."

Britt remained standing, glaring at Alec.

The guard behind Britt approached her. "You done here?" he asked.

"Please," Alec pleaded to the guard. "Just give us a few more minutes, okay? Britt, sit back down."

There was something absurdly familiar in the way her ordered her to sit that was almost amusing. Not quite. "Like hell," she replied.

"I need you to," he said simply. "Please."

Britt hesitated, tempted to ignore him, but finally she spoke to the guard. "I'll stay a minute more," she said, resuming her seat.

The guard shrugged, and stepped back.

Alec kneaded his hands together on the other side of the Plexiglas and then he looked her in the eye. "That is great," he said. "Really. I'm trying to take this all in. How did you find him?"

"I told you. It turns out he was Vicki's boyfriend," she said coolly.

"Vicki?" he repeated, frowning.

"The pregnant girl who lives at the Carmichaels'. Earth to Alec."

Alec shook his head. "Oh, right. I'm sorry."

"Apparently he came to visit Vicki from time to time, this Dave. Without the Carmichaels' knowledge. They'd meet out in the woods behind the house. Yesterday, Zoe saw him there, lurking in the yard while she was feeding Vicki's cat. She called me, and I . . ." Britt said, starting to explain again. Then she hesitated. She could see that he was following what she was saying with only half of his attention. "Suffice it to say, I found him," she said abruptly. "Don't let me interrupt your train of thought."

"Britt, I really am . . . I'm trying to think about . . . everything. What it means."

Britt rolled her eyes. "I saved your butt. That's what it means."

"You did," he murmured, nodding. "I don't know why, but you did."

"For Zoe's sake," she spat back at him.

He nodded again, compressing his lips. "That's the problem," he said. "Zoe."

"What are you talking about?" she demanded irritably. "She'll be thrilled. She . . . loves you. She believes in you."

"I know that," he said. "She'll always believe in me. Even if they sent me away for life, she would never believe I did it."

It was Britt's turn to shake her head. "Isn't that a little, oh, I don't know, egotistical, conceited? You pick the word. How can you be so sure of that?"

"That's the way it is," he said.

Britt sighed. "If you say so." But a little part of her thought that he might be right. Zoe's faith in her father did seem to be unwavering, even in the face of public scorn and disapproval.

Alec leaned forward and commanded Britt's gaze. "It's because I believe in her that I was able to stand it. I could do the time. For her sake. To spare her."

"To spare her? How does that spare her? Am I missing something here?" Britt demanded sarcastically.

"With what you've done, I'll be cleared, and they'll have to reexamine all the evidence. If they keep at it long enough, I'm just afraid . . ."

"Afraid of what? I should think you'd be afraid of the gas chamber."

"I'm afraid the truth will come out, and they will know who really set the fire. I wanted to spare Zoe from that if I could. If it meant jail, so be it."

Britt stared at him. "What do you mean, who really set the fire? Do you *know* who set the fire?"

"I'm pretty sure," he said, nodding.

Britt frowned. "Who?" she asked, genuinely mystified.

Alec hesitated, chewing his lip. "Can you keep this to yourself?" he said. "I mean it. To the grave."

Britt looked at him with narrowed eyes. "Why would you confide your secret in me?" she demanded. "You hardly know me."

"Because you probably have a right to know. She was your sister," he said.

"What?" Britt reacted as if he had slapped her.

"You heard me."

"Are you insinuating it was Greta! How dare you?"

"She was depressed. She was suicidal."

"You're trying to blame my sister for something that was your fault?" said Britt. "If she was depressed, it was because her marriage was on the rocks."

Alec shook his head. "Our marriage was not on the rocks. She was depressed about your mother . . ."

"Oh that's right. It was the fault of our long-lost mother. Look, I know all about you. I know you were planning to leave her. I know you talked to a business broker about selling your dealership. I know you rented an apartment in Virginia Beach. Behavior you still haven't accounted for to the police."

"That's right. The apartment was for your mother," he said.

Britt gaped at him.

Alec looked around, as if to be sure he would not be overheard. Then he leaned forward. Britt leaned toward him, transfixed in spite of herself. "When Gardner, the private detective, first located Jean," Alec said, "your mother was in jail in Virginia. An assortment of crimes. Fraud, forgery . . . Greta went down there to see her. She wrote to her. Sent her packages. Testified at her parole hearing. Greta promised to take care of her and Jean seemed to be really grateful and happy. We rented an apartment for her for when she got out on parole. A brand new complex. With a pool. Nothing but the best for Jean. By the conditions of her parole, Jean wasn't supposed to leave the state, so Greta wanted to move down there to be near her. She wanted Zoe to know her grandmother. We hadn't told Zoe about finding her. We thought we'd wait until Jean was out of jail. First impressions and all. It was too hard to explain to a child.

"Anyway, we went down to visit her while Zoe was at that sleep-away horse camp. That's when we contacted the business broker. Greta wanted to move there to be near her mother, to make up for lost time, and I agreed to it. Reluctantly, but it seemed as if it was the only thing that would make your sister happy."

"My mother is in Virginia Beach?" Britt asked weakly.

Alec snorted. "No. Not anymore. The minute they let her out of prison, she bolted."

"What do you mean, bolted?" Britt asked.

"Bolted. Ran away," he said abruptly. "Blew off her parole, the apartment, her long-lost daughter, everything. Left the county, the state. For all we know, she left the country. Greta hired Gardner to try to find her again but it was no use. Gardner told my wife that her mother didn't want to be found. Greta was devastated. That's when the depression set in."

"I don't believe you," said Britt. But she did. Though she didn't want to, she did.

"Gardner can tell you all about it."

It was difficult to take it in. Britt thought about her sister, searching for Jean Andersen, finding her. Thinking they would be reunited at last. And then, being betrayed again. And this time, Jean Andersen had not left any room for doubt or hope. After all those years of hoping. Britt thought about Dr. Farrar, telling her about Greta's deep depression. And then, of course, the inescapable conclusion. Depressed people did, sometimes, attempt suicide.

"At first, when I found out about the fire," Alec continued, "I assumed it was an accident. I mean, at first, just like everybody else," he said. "The curtains catching fire, the candles. That sounded right. Greta often used candles. And she was taking a lot of pills. She could have been too groggy to help herself. But then, when I heard about the paint thinner on the walls of the room where Greta was sleeping. That it was arson . . . I started to wonder. . . ."

Britt frowned, trying to absorb the idea. Trying to picture her sister, planning her own death. Tossing lighter fluid on the walls of the room where she was going to sleep. Despondent. Lighting the candle and setting it by the curtain. Awaiting her fate. "Wait a minute," Britt cried. "Wait a minute. It's impossible. Greta would never have set that fire. Zoe was home. Greta knew she was home."

Alec nodded and sighed. "Yes. And she loved Zoe so much. But she wasn't all that rational at the end. When I realized that Zoe was home, and that she'd been drugged . . . When you told me what Dr. Farrar said about her being drugged, that's when I started to think the worst. I knew Zoe didn't take those drugs on her own. She never would touch drugs. I told you that."

"What do you mean? You think Greta drugged her?"

Alec nodded. "Probably put it into her dinner that night."

"You're insane," said Britt.

Alec shook his head. "Greta talked about suicide a lot. She insisted that I increase the amount of our life insurance, even when I yelled at her that they didn't pay it out for suicides. That's why we had such a big policy on her life. She insisted."

"You were worried that they wouldn't pay," Britt said angrily.

"Oh please, Britt. Give me *some* credit. I would get frantic when she talked that way. It made me crazy. I would argue with her and plead with her. But to calm me down, she always said . . ." His voice cracked, and he stopped for a moment and Britt was shocked to see this break in his composure. Alec took a deep breath. Then he continued in a steady voice. "She always said that she would never leave Zoe alone, motherless, the way your mother had left her. She didn't want Zoe to suffer the same way she had."

Britt felt as if his words were bricks he was piling on top of her heart. She gasped from the weight of it. She had never understood how much her sister had suffered. Greta had always tried to be strong, for Britt's sake. But all the time, she had felt such despair it had made her think of suicide. And then Britt thought about Zoe. Greta's beloved daughter. Whom she would never leave behind.

Britt stared at Zoe's father. "Are you saying . . .?"

"I'm saying she decided to take Zoe with her. She didn't want her to suffer. So she made sure that Zoe would be unconscious when the fire happened. Even now, Zoe doesn't remember a thing about it."

"No," Britt insisted in a whisper. "It's too horrible."

"She always said that. She wouldn't leave Zoe. I was reassured by it. I didn't realize it was actually a threat," he said in a dull voice.

"No, I don't believe it. Greta wouldn't do that."

"You didn't know her," Alec said flatly.

Britt glared at him, but in her heart she knew he was right. She didn't know her sister. She'd seen Greta as calm and confident and able to deal with anything life threw her way. And all the time. . . . *No,* Britt was forced to admit to herself. *I didn't know her.*

"Britt, listen to me. I don't want Zoe to know that I suspect this," Alec insisted. "Ever. Not for any reason. I don't want her to ever think for a moment that her mother was willing to let her die in that inferno. Zoe could never be expected to understand it or forgive it. And she'd never get over it. No. Not if it means I have to spend my life in jail, I don't want her to know."

"But if you were convicted, she would think the same thing of you. Worse. That you'd killed her mother and tried to kill her."

"She'd never think that," said Alec. "Nothing in this world would ever convince her of that. Not as long as I have breath in my body to tell her the truth—that I didn't do it. She'll believe in me. She's my girl."

Britt looked at him and saw the implacability in his silver-gray eyes. "You would do that? Go to prison . . .?"

"I'd die for Zoe," he said sharply. "She's my only child."

His eyes were dry, and his gaze was steady. But Britt felt tears, rushing to her own eyes. She blinked them back. She could see that he meant it, and the realization was humbling. "She's lucky . . . to have you," Britt said sincerely.

"I don't want her to know," he repeated forcefully.

"I understand," said Britt. "She'll never hear it from me. I promise you."

Alec peered at her as if he was trying to see inside her soul. Then he said abruptly, "Okay."

"Okay," Britt whispered.

Alec sighed and leaned back in the chair. "I have to admit, it feels better just to say it out loud. It's been the most oppressive thought. You can't imagine . . ."

Britt shook her head. "I just can't believe it of Greta. She adored Zoe. I mean, from everything I've seen and heard . . ."

"I didn't want to believe it either. But the more I've thought about it . . ." he said.

"I understand," said Britt. She wished she could reach through the Plexiglas partition and cover his knotted hands with her fingers. "I understand. And I can see why you think that. But, maybe . . . Have you told Kevin about all this? I mean, he could have used it to defend you . . ."

Alec glared at her. "Haven't you understood a word I said?"

"No, of course . . . I'm sorry."

The guard stepped up behind her and clapped a hand on her shoulder. "All right," he said. "You're done. Let's go."

Britt looked frantically at Alec. "I have to go."

On Alec's side of the partition, the guard was likewise nudging him from his seat. "In my office desk at the dealership," Alec called to her. "There's a box in the bottom drawer with a VHS tape in it. Greta didn't want to keep it in the house, in case Zoe accidentally looked at it. But you should watch it."

"I will . . . I'm sorry," Britt called after him helplessly as the guard directed her toward the door. She didn't know what she was sorry for. *You've saved him from a life in prison*, she reminded herself. But as she watched him being handcuffed again and led away, she knew. She was sorry for how she had misjudged him. She was sorry she had not realized sooner who he really was.

CHAPTER 34

Britt opened the tinted glass door of the Lynch Rides showroom and stepped inside. She couldn't help remembering her first visit here, when Alec had taken her out to ride on the snowmobile. What should have been an enjoyable outing had been nightmarish, thanks to her suspicions. She had thought the worst of Alec, and of Lauren, that day. And she had pursued those suspicions. She had been so sure. And so wrong. There was one couple looking over snowmobiles but otherwise the place was quiet. Lauren Rossi was chatting and laughing with two of the salesmen. Britt felt a little surprised. She had not expected to see her here. All three looked up as Britt walked in, and abruptly they all fell silent. Lauren's eyes narrowed as she watched her approach.

"Lauren," said Britt, pretending not to notice their obvious hostility, "how are you?"

"What do you want?" Lauren said.

"Alec wanted me to get something out of his desk," said Britt.

The two salesmen exchanged a glance, and then drifted off to their offices. Lauren glared at Britt. "Oh, right," she said.

"He said there's a videotape in his desk drawer. He told me to pick it up."

"I don't believe you," said Lauren. "The police chief probably sent you. You're probably looking for evidence against Alec."

Britt sighed. "I don't blame you for thinking that. But actually, it's just the opposite. He's going to be getting out of jail. Very soon, I think. I kind of . . . accidentally . . . found his alibi witness."

"You did," Lauren said scornfully.

"I'm afraid I misjudged Alec," Britt admitted. "It seems that everything he said about . . . Everything he said was true. At any rate, he told me to come and get the tape, so here I am."

Lauren folded her arms across the tight pink sweater she was wearing. "If Alec's getting out of jail, why doesn't he get the tape for you himself?" Lauren countered.

"I guess he wanted me to see it right away. But I admire your loyalty," said Britt. "I do."

"I never should have listened to you," said Lauren angrily. "I betrayed him because of you."

Britt sighed. "Well, I see he didn't hold it against you. You're still here. Besides, all you did was tell the truth. That's nothing to be ashamed of."

Lauren sniffed. "That's what Alec said. But I'm still sorry I did it. And for your information, he's not having an affair."

"Look, I'm not trying to hurt him, no matter what you think. I was just over at the jail. Alec told me that the tape is in a box in the bottom drawer of his desk. Why don't you look there? If there's no tape, you can call me a liar."

Lauren tossed her hair. "All right," she said. "I'll look. But you stay here."

Britt felt awkward standing in the middle of the showroom, and she could sense that the salesmen were studying her from their glass cubicles, assessing her with dislike. Britt pretended to admire the snowmobiles that were on display. She circled around them, pretending to be curious about their unique features, but apparently the salesmen weren't fooled. No one came out, or offered to help her.

Britt was relieved to see Lauren round the corner formed by the glass wall and approach her. In her right hand Lauren held a black VHS tape in a cardboard sleeve. Britt thought about Alec's warning. Don't let Zoe see it. Britt had a good idea of what was on that tape. It had to be Jean Andersen. She felt her heart start to pound at the thought of seeing her mother's face again. A face she could scarcely remember. The thought of hearing her long-forgotten voice.

Lauren handed the tape to her. "All right, here," she said. "But if you try to use this against him, whatever it is . . ."

"Don't worry," said Britt, stuffing the tape into her satchel. "It's nothing like that. I'll bring it back. I promise."

* * *

The house was gloomy and unwelcoming when Britt returned. She pushed up the thermostat and turned on a couple of lights. She poured herself something to drink and checked her phone messages, all the while aware that she was putting off the inevitable. She looked at her watch, calculating how long she had before Zoe got out of school and she needed to go and pick her up. Finally, she turned on the television, pushed the tape into the VCR and sat down on the sofa.

The images on the tape began abruptly, a series of shoeboxlike brick buildings, shot, obviously from a moving car. "That's it," said a woman's voice, clearly the operator of the camera. Then the camera panned for a moment on a sign that was too blurred to read except for the words "For Women" at the bottom of it. Abruptly, the sign and buildings vanished, and were replaced by a plain, bisque-colored room furnished with molded plastic chairs and formica-topped tables. The camera panned around the room to reveal bookshelves at one end, a couple of sofas and a coffee table, and a woman in a police uniform, standing by the door of the room, a gun tucked into the leather holster at her waist. There were people milling about, greeting one another in unintelligible voices, and there was the sound of laughter and loud remarks in the background.

"Why don't you sit down, honey?" the camera operator, a male voice this time, asked.

A familiar-looking woman wearing a barn jacket moved hesitantly in front of the lens, and then looked back at the camera operator. "Here, do you think?" she asked.

Greta, thought Britt, and her heart flipped over at the sight of her sister. Greta's blond hair was arranged in a loose bun, but there were wisps that had come loose all around her face, forming a kind of halo. She was as pretty as she had ever been, although her face was thinner, and there were dark circles around her beautiful eyes.

"That's good," said the camera operator, and Britt realized at that moment that it was Alec making the video.

Greta sighed, massaging her hands, and sat down in a plastic chair. Nervously, she brushed her hair off her face and gave her husband a wan smile. "I'm nervous," she said to the camera. "I wish I still smoked."

Greta smoked? Britt thought. *For how long?* The thought was fleeting as she watched this stranger, her late sister, in fascination. Greta took a magazine off a pile on the shelf and flipped through it, crossing her legs and nervously bouncing one of her feet. She looked up again at the camera, a worried expression in her eyes.

"You're okay," said Alec from behind the camera.

The lens of the camera swung around to the door of the room, just as Britt heard a voice say, "Hi there," from near the door.

"Here she is," the cameraman said, his voice sounding loud to Britt's ears.

"Oh my God," said Greta. Alec jerked the camera back toward his wife, and then at the woman who was coming through the door. The woman had long, coarse brown hair pulled back into a severe graying ponytail. Her skin was pallid, and she was wearing glasses so that her eyes were difficult to see. She was pudgy in the face, and there was a roll around her middle which was plainly visible despite the loose-fitting sweat suit that she wore. The remains of a pretty face lurked somewhere in that murky visage, but any beauty was long gone.

"Oh my God," Greta cried again, in that tone people always used when they had won a big prize on a game show. "Mother."

Jean Andersen suddenly became aware of the camera and reared back, looking at it warily.

"It's just Alec," Greta explained. "My husband." Her voice broke, and tears were running down her cheeks. "Oh, Mom," she said.

The two women approached one another, Greta with her arms wide, while Jean kept her arms at her sides. Jean allowed Greta to embrace her and then mumbled something. "Sit down," she said.

Obediently, her face glowing, Greta did exactly that. She sat down and patted the seat of the chair beside her. Jean sat cautiously on that chair, her putty-colored skin a blank mask. *My mother*, Britt thought. *That's my mother*. She could feel herself perspiring in the cool room. She had vague memories of her mother, but in no way did they resemble this woman sitting in the molded plastic chair, her arms resolutely pinned to her sides.

Wiping her tears away, Greta reached for the woman's limp, puffy hand, and placed it gently between her own slim fingers. "We brought you all kinds of stuff but we had to leave the bag at the entrance for them to look through it."

Jean nodded, and began to cough. "That's what they always do," she said. "Did you bring the . . ." She turned her head and her voice was too muffled to be understood.

"I brought everything you asked for," Greta said kindly, and suddenly Britt could remember Greta saying those very words to her, when she would come home from a trip to the mall, around her birthday, or in the days before school started.

Jean nodded, and submitted herself to another of Greta's fierce hugs. Greta kept on touching the older woman, on her arm, her shoulder, her knee. As if she wanted to convince herself of the physical reality. Her mother, seated there beside her.

"This is a helluva place to meet after all these years," said Jean with a gravelly laugh, squirming slightly in the chair seat.

"It doesn't matter," said Greta, sniffing, and wiping her eyes again. Jean regarded her curiously, but did not seem to have any trouble holding her emotions in check. Britt thought about what Alec had said. How elated Greta was to track down their mother. How devastated she had been when Jean decided to disappear all over again.

Suddenly, Britt understood why Alec had wanted her to see this tape. Not simply to see her long-lost mother. But to see Greta. To imagine how this weeping woman—who was alternately embracing someone she thought to be gone forever, and thanking her lucky stars—how she would react when this, too, proved to be an illusion.

Britt stared at Jean Andersen and felt absolutely no desire to weep. This was the person who had changed their lives forever. Left Greta and Britt and their father behind, and never looked back. Made them, all three of them, feel expendable and unloved. And for what? To embark on a drifter's life of petty crime. Part of Britt wanted to know her story, wanted to know where she had been, and what she had done. But didn't this meeting place tell it all? Jean was incarcerated in a women's correctional facility. She was passing her time in prison where Greta had found her. Now, captured at last in this video, Jean was studying Greta, her older daughter who was overcome with emotion, with a kind of reptilian detachment. Greta, who had tried to live a good life, a useful life, and always hold out hope. "You didn't deserve her love," Britt said aloud to the image on the screen.

As if in answer to this, Jean turned and faced the camera. "Turn that damn thing off," she said. Alec kept the camera trained relentlessly on her ruined face.

"Aunt Britt?"

Britt jumped at the sound of Zoe's voice and pushed the off button. She stood up guiltily from her seat on the couch.

Zoe came into the room as the image faded from the screen. "What are you watching? Who were you talking to?" Zoe asked.

"Nobody," said Britt anxiously. "You're back. How'd you get home from school?"

Zoe shrugged. "I got a ride from Sara's mom."

"You and Kayley friends again?"

"I guess. How did Vicki like the scarf?"

Britt thought of Vicki's hospital room, and Dave, the alibi witness, sitting there right in front of her eyes. She wanted to tell Zoe everything, but she hesitated. Maybe she should wait until it was official. Until Alec was actually coming home to her.

"She liked it," said Britt. "She was really touched. Maybe you two can keep in touch, since you have her address."

Zoe chewed the inside of her mouth and didn't reply.

She seemed so downcast that Britt wanted to tell her about Dave, just to give her something to be happy about. It wasn't as if she was giving her false hope. This was the real thing. Dave was the key to Alec's freedom. "Zoe," she began. "Something did happen today that . . ."

But Zoe was preoccupied. "Homework," she murmured, and before Britt could halt her, the girl was already pounding up the stairs.

I'll tell her later, Britt thought. She sighed, but her stomach was fluttering. She wanted to see the rest of the tape. She went back into the living room and waited until she heard the door to Zoe's room close. Then she went back to the TV, and furtively turned on the VCR again, muting the sound.

Jean Andersen swam back into view, staring into the lens of the videocam, the light glinting off her glasses. Without the sound, Britt watched as Greta fussed over the older woman, smoothing her clothes and timidly caressing her, while Jean Andersen remained rigid in her chair, glaring occasionally at the videocam as if furious that her order to turn it off had been defied.

He knew it right away, Britt thought. He had seen, even in this first meeting, that no good would come of this, and, by refusing her command, he had let his newfound mother-in-law know that, unlike her vulnerable daughter, he was not duped by her. He was busy recording it for Greta, hoping someday he could make his wife understand that she wasn't to blame. How was he to know that she could never understand? That this longed-for encounter would finally destroy the woman he loved.

Britt felt her grudging respect for Alec grow as she watched the taped scene unfold through his unforgiving eyes. Jean Andersen was sitting beside her faithful, long-lost daughter, already planning her escape. You could see it in her eyes. And Alec knew it. And hated her for it. "Good for you, Alec," Britt said aloud, as angry tears made the scene swim before her eyes.

CHAPTER 35

All evening, Britt waited for the phone to ring. She was waiting for the call from Ray Stern saying that Alec was free. That they should come and get him. She put off telling Zoe any more about it as the hours ticked away. Her own agitation was making it difficult to wait. She thought about calling the Carmichaels to see if Kevin had heard anything, but she hated to interrupt their first night with the new baby. She didn't want to wake him up, or tear Caroline away from caring for him.

Finally, at nine o'clock while Zoe was glumly watching a sitcom on TV, Britt called the police station. Ray Stern was still there, and quickly got on the line.

"You're working late," said Britt, trying to sound confident and cheerful.

"Things piled up while I was at Mid-State Medical Center today," he said.

"What happened with Dean?" she asked.

"He admitted it," Ray said shortly. "He wanted to turn the screws on your brother-in-law."

Thank you, God, Britt said silently. "Well, we haven't heard from you. Did Dave Kronemayer come in?" Britt asked.

"The so-called alibi witness?" said Ray, and Britt's heart sank. "We haven't seen him. He hasn't been here."

"Dammit," said Britt.

"Nope. No sign of him."

"Dammit, he promised me," said Britt.

"Well, don't give up on him. Give him until tomorrow. If he doesn't come in by then, we'll go hunt him up. Maybe something came up this afternoon."

"Alec Lynch is in jail," said Britt, "and he doesn't belong there."

"He'll live until morning," said Ray. "I must say, you've changed your tune."

"I know what the truth is, now," said Britt.

Ray sighed. "Well, I'm happy for you. But I need to get home myself. Why don't you come by in the morning?"

Britt hung up the phone, and stood beside it for a moment thinking. Then she called to Zoe. "Have you got that phone number Vicki gave you?"

"I'm watching my show," Zoe grumbled.

Britt walked to the door of the living room. "This is a little more important than your TV show, okay?"

Zoe looked up at her, wide-eyed. "What is it?"

Britt was glad she had not told Zoe the whole story earlier. The girl had endured so much heartache and disappointment. This would only add to it. Dave, being a no-show. She shook her head. "Never mind. Just get me that number."

Zoe ran to get the piece of paper on which she had scribbled the address and phone number. Britt thanked her, and dialed the number, but there was no answer. A message machine picked up and Vicki's babyish voice said, "We're not here right now. Leave a message."

"Vicki," said Britt sharply. "If you're there, pick up." She waited a moment, but no one answered. "Look, this is Britt. Dave has got to come in to the Coleville Police Station. I know it's late now, but I want you to get him there in the morning. Please, for Zoe's sake." She sighed, and hung up.

She thought again about calling the Carmichaels, to find out what time Vicki and Dave had left, but the thought of the baby was daunting. Besides, Kevin had devoted the whole day to questioning Dean Webster. He needed a little peace and quiet with his wife, and the new baby. *In the morning*, Britt thought. *First thing.*

That night, Britt went to bed and endured one nightmare after another. In one of her dreams, she entered a hospital room and found Jean Andersen sitting up in the hospital bed, gazing at her with that cold, detached stare, and laughing her mirthless laugh that turned into a cough. "Leave me alone. I don't even know you," Jean said, in the dream. "Why are you following me?" By the time the morning came, tired as she was, Britt was glad to get out of bed.

* * *

Britt pulled into the Carmichaels' driveway and saw that the cherry-red Toyota was gone. Kevin and Caroline's cars were parked, one behind the other beside the house, and some smoke curled from the chimney making the air fragrant with the smell of wood smoke. For a moment, Britt envied the Carmichaels. Home together, with their new baby and a fire in the fireplace. It was the kind of contented image that she generally avoided thinking about. She'd never seen that kind of happiness up close in her life. She always wondered if it ever was real.

Britt climbed up the porch steps and knocked. After a few minutes the door opened. Kevin, wearing a bathrobe over pajama bottoms and a T-shirt, opened the door. His normally rosy complexion was gray and haggard, and his eyes were bleary. So much for the bliss of the new baby, Britt thought.

"Hi, Kevin," she said.

"Britt."

"I'm sorry to disturb you. You look a little beat."

"The baby was up," he muttered. "Pretty much all night."

Britt smiled. "It's bound to get better. Can I come in?"

Kevin shrugged, and opened the door. Britt walked into the living room. Kevin followed her. "Caroline and the baby are asleep. Finally."

"I'll be quiet," said Britt.

"Do you want to sit?" he asked in a tone that said, "Please don't."

Britt shook her head. "First, I wanted to thank you. For going to the trauma center yesterday. Getting Dean's confession about the Bayberry cottage fire."

Kevin stood in front of the fireplace and stared at the flames, rubbing his face with his hands. "Ray Stern was the one who questioned him," he said, not looking at Britt. "I was just there to represent Alec's interests."

"Well, all the same, I appreciate you making the trip."

"All in a day's work," he said dismissively.

"The reason I'm here," she said. "I'm looking for Vicki and her friend, Dave."

Kevin looked startled. But he recovered quickly. He turned his head and gazed at her coolly. "They left," he said. "They beat it out of here. Yesterday afternoon."

"Where were they going?" Britt asked.

"I don't know. What difference does it make?" he asked sharply.

Britt frowned at him. He must be one of those people who gets really irritable when he's tired. Surely, he's not having second thoughts about parenthood already. "Actually," she said, "it makes a great deal of difference. It turns out . . ." She hesitated. She didn't want to be the one to tell him about Dave's relationship to his new baby. "It turns out that Vicki's friend, Dave, is Alec's missing alibi witness."

"Really," said Kevin. "What makes you think that?"

"Well, it's a long story, but, believe me, it's true. And he promised me that he would go to the police and back up Alec's story. But he didn't show up . . ."

"Great," Kevin snorted. "That's just great."

"We have to get in touch with him and urge him to go to the police. Maybe if you were to try to talk to him . . ."

"I wouldn't know where to find him. From what Caroline told me, those two were getting set to burn through that money we gave Vicki."

"Is that what they told Caroline? Do you think I could talk to her?"

"I told you, she's asleep," he snapped. "I'm not going to wake her up for this."

Britt felt a little irritated by the tone of his voice, even if he was extremely tired. "Hey, Alec's your client, Kevin. He'll be a lot better able to pay your bill if you manage to get him released from jail. That's all I'm trying to do."

"You're right, you're right," said Kevin. "Sorry." He pressed his forehead against his forearm which was resting on the mantel. "I'm so tired. I've never been so tired in my life."

"I guess it's a pretty hard adjustment, having a new baby," said Britt.

Kevin managed a thin smile. "He's a good boy. It's not his fault."

"He's just doing what babies do," said Britt.

All of a sudden, the thin, wailing cry of a newborn drifted down from the second floor. Kevin flinched. "Look, Britt, I'm not myself today. Not thinking clearly. Maybe, I don't know . . . I don't know where they went. I'd try Vegas if I were you. Or Atlantic City."

Uh-oh, thought Britt. *You really aren't yourself.* "Well, I've bothered you enough. I'll see what I can do. I'll um . . . I'll be in touch."

"Kevin," called a frantic voice from upstairs.

"Is that Caroline? Is she up?" said Britt.

"Just leave her," said Kevin sharply.

Britt frowned. "I just want to ask her. . . ."

"I told you," said Kevin. "They left. Vicki was in it for the money, and once she got her money . . ." he said bitterly. "They could be halfway across the country by now. I don't want them dragged back into our lives."

"Kevin, we have to find them. Like it or not, they have to be dragged back. Look, I don't know how much you know. . . ."

Kevin peered at her. "About what?"

"Dave," said Britt.

"Kevin," Caroline cried out again.

"I can't discuss this now," said Kevin, shepherding Britt toward the door. "Maybe this Dave will have an attack of conscience and come back and do the right thing. I don't know. We can hope he does."

Britt could see that he didn't hope anything of the kind, that he couldn't care less, in fact. It was as if he didn't have a client in Alec. As if the only thing that existed in his world right now was his wife and the baby. Anything outside of that little circle just wasn't important to him right now.

I'll do it myself, Britt thought. *If you won't help me, I'll find them myself.*

CHAPTER 36

Britt returned to the house on Medford Road, thinking all the while about Vicki and Dave. Of course it was possible that they'd taken off for Las Vegas. But it was also possible that they just wanted to get home and curl up together and turn off the phone. They'd been separated for quite a while. Maybe they went out to celebrate last night, and this morning they would be back at home.

Home, Britt thought. *Where was that address that Vicki gave Zoe*? She'd called Vicki on the kitchen phone last night. Maybe the slip of paper was still in there. She went over to the phone, and looked on the counter beneath it, but didn't see the paper. There was a small bulletin board behind where the phone was, with a few snapshots of the home's owner and friends, and a couple of take-out menus. Stuffed into the corner of the bulletin board, and affixed with a red pushpin, she saw it. Vicki Manfred, and an address in Montpelier. *All right*, she thought, *it's worth a try*.

* * *

It was flurrying again by the time Britt got on the road to Montpelier. If they weren't there, at this address, maybe someone would be who would know where they went. She felt as if she was doing Ray Stern's job for him, and she told herself that it would all be worth it when Zoe had her father back. Besides, she was the only one who really knew about Dave.

Of course, if Ray Stern had been competent . . . Suddenly, she remembered Dean Webster warning her that the Coleville police were inept. She wondered how bad his injuries were, and what would happen to him once he got out of the hospital. Then, she willed the image of Dean out of her mind, and tried to concentrate on the task at hand. The fact was that Dean was right about the Coleville police. If Ray Stern had located Dave, the alibi witness, himself, Alec would never have gone to jail in the first place.

Glancing at the address on the seat beside her, and the printed directions she'd gotten off the Internet, Britt managed to locate the street where Vicki and Dave lived. It was a run-down street in a part of town that had a shuttered factory and a wealth of auto repair places. Britt recognized the convenience store Alec had mentioned on the corner, and rolled slowly down the block, passing a series of old houses which might have been charming at one time, but now looked sorrowfully neglected. Paint flaked from the clapboards and the white paint which covered a majority of the houses was gray with dirt. There were a couple of more recently built brick houses, which were dark with grime. Front porches were littered with broken toys and sofas with the stuffing coming out of the cushions. Many of the houses had more than one car in the driveway, although few of the cars appeared to be in working condition.

Britt pulled up in front of number 23 and got out of her car. The house in front of her was as dilapidated as its neighbors. The front windows had the shades pulled low and there were graying net curtains visible below the shades. Britt climbed the porch steps, avoiding a broken riser, and knocked on the door.

The door was opened, after a few minutes of shuffling sounds from inside, by a middle-aged woman in stretch pants and a sweatshirt. She peered suspiciously at Britt through thick glasses which were being held together at the bridge by first-aid tape. There were a couple of pink rollers stuck haphazardly in her hair. The sound of a television blared from the front room.

"Excuse me," said Britt. "I'm sorry to bother you. My name is Britt Andersen. I'm looking for Dave Kronemayer? And Vicki Manfred. Do I have the right house?"

The woman narrowed her eyes. "Who's askin"? Are you from the cops again?"

Britt was momentarily taken aback. "No," she said. "Why would you think . . .?" Then she realized that Ray or one of his men must have been here before, must have knocked on every door on this street looking for Dave. Instantly, Britt sensed that she shouldn't mention anything about witnesses, or the police, or court testimony to this woman. This was a person with a healthy mistrust of the police.

The woman in the doorway crossed her arms over her chest and glared at Britt.

"No," Britt continued. "I just really need to speak to Dave. It's really important."

"Are you from the welfare?" the woman asked suspiciously.

"No, no, I'm just a friend . . . of Vicki's."

"You don't look like any friend Vicki would have," the woman observed.

"Actually, I'm a . . . neighbor of the . . . uh . . . family where Vicki was staying."

Immediately the older woman looked curious. "You've seen Vicki?"

"I was going to ask you that question. She and Dave were together when I saw them yesterday, and I thought they were headed home, Mrs. . . ."

"Dot," said the woman. Apparently convinced by Britt's information, she relented. "Well, this is where they live," she said. "Their apartment's got its own entrance. Around the back."

"Oh, okay," said Britt. "I'll try back there. I'm sorry to bother you." Britt stepped away from the door and walked back toward the porch steps.

"They ain't home though," said the woman.

Britt turned and looked at her. "Are you sure?"

The woman nodded. "I don't miss much," she said.

I'll bet you don't, Britt thought. "Any idea when they'll be back?"

Dot shook her head. "Did she have that baby yet?"

Britt hesitated. "You know about the baby?"

"I ought to. She was showin' when she left here. Then she went off somewhere to have the baby. I think she's gonna give it away. It's a sin. He's broken up about it," Dot said in a confiding tone.

"Dave is?"

"Yeah, he's crazy about her. I mean, she's right they couldn't take care of the kid. She was on welfare. He works odd jobs, manages to scrape up the rent. Hell, they don't even have a car. Their car gave up the ghost months ago. He's been hitchhikin' off to see her, wherever she's at. He don't tell me anything. She was the one always told me what was goin' on."

Britt wanted to encourage the woman's garrulousness. She figured she'd better divulge a little information. "Vicki was staying in Coleville, actually."

"Oh, that's pretty fancy," said Dot. "They got a home there or something?"

"A home?" Britt asked.

"You know, for girls who get knocked up."

"Oh," said Britt. "No. Not exactly. She was staying with a family. Anyway, she did have the baby."

Dot's face lit up. "She did! What'd she have?"

"A little boy." Britt shivered. The temperature on the porch seemed to be dropping by the minute.

"What'd she name him?" the woman asked.

"Well, actually the people who adopted him named him Kent."

Dot snorted. "I don't get that. How can you give away your own flesh and blood?"

Britt shrugged, and rubbed her hands together. "It's a tough decision, I guess."

Dot suddenly seemed to notice that Britt was chilly. "Come on in. It's cold out there. What's your name again?"

"Britt."

"Well, you better get in the house," said Dot.

"Thanks," said Britt.

Dot led the way down a dingy, wallpapered hallway into the front room of the house. There was a movie running on the television. Dot sat down with her back to it, insensible to the volume. "Sit down," she said. "Maybe they'll be back soon."

Britt perched on the edge of an armchair covered in tufted velour and grimy at the arms from use. "What are you watching?" she asked.

Dot turned and looked at the TV. "Some picture I seen before," she said, and punched the mute button on the remote control, to Britt's relief.

Dot shook her head. "I feel sorry for the guy, you know. Dave's a good boy. He's not the smartest guy. She's the smart one. She's got it all over him for that."

Britt nodded sympathetically. "Well, a good heart counts for a lot," she said.

"Not to her. She's always naggin' at him 'cause he doesn't make good money. I think she's givin' that baby away just to punish him."

"It is hard to raise a child without money these days," said Britt. She glanced out the front window, wishing she would catch sight of the cherry-red car pulling up.

"You got that right," said Dot. "And Dave. He wouldn't know a chance to make money if it hit him on the head. It's a good thing Vicki doesn't know about the latest . . ."

"The latest?" Britt asked.

"This happened while she was gone. Don't you tell her this," the woman warned.

Britt shook her head. "I won't."

"Well . . . when was it? The other night. I don't know. A week or two ago. Dave comes in limpin'. I noticed it when he was goin' up the walk. Like I said, I don't miss much. So I asked him 'what happened to you?' He tells me he got knocked down by some guy in a Mercedes Benz."

Britt felt the hair stand up on the back of her neck. "Really?" she said faintly.

"Yup. The guy was racin' around a corner and he clipped him while he was hitchhikin'. So, the guy's all apologetic, and he offers to drive Dave back to town here."

"I should hope so," said Britt carefully.

"Yeah, I know. But listen to this. I says to Dave, you should sue him. Anybody that's got a Mercedes has got insurance. You know what I mean? I mean, you don't drive around in a car like that without insurance, right? Just for occasions like this."

"Right," breathed Britt. She wiped her damp palms off on the front of her pants.

"So, what does Dave do? He doesn't call the cops. He doesn't even get the guy's name. He lets him drive away. He could be sittin' pretty by now. That's what I mean about Dave." She tapped her index finger against her own wrinkled forehead. "No smarts."

"I see what you're saying," said Britt.

"You know when the cops came lookin' for him the other day, I figured maybe it was about that. But this cop says right away they're knockin' on every door around here. Lookin' for a witness in some police matter, so I kept quiet. I thought about it and I thought, you know this is not like the prize patrol arriving. The cops only come around when there's trouble. So, I kept my mouth shut. I pretended I didn't know anything. I figured if they wanted to find him they could go down the walk and knock on the door."

As if they'd have any way of knowing there was an apartment back there, Britt thought. This Dot was a cagey old girl. Britt suspected she may have had her own share of encounters with the law in her day.

"The way I see it," Dot continued, "the kid doesn't need any more trouble. But you know, this is why Vicki gets so fed up with him. He should have reported that guy in the Mercedes. He could have made a bundle. Instead, he's just a live-and-let-live kind of a kid. No ambition."

"That could be frustrating," said Britt.

"When you're trying to raise a kid of your own. You bet your bippy," Dot offered helpfully. She reached over and adjusted the framed photo of a young woman and a little girl that decorated her end table.

Britt nodded, wanting to speak carefully. She had realized, while Dot was talking, that her testimony alone would probably be enough to free Alec. If she could get her to cooperate. "You know, that story about the man in the Mercedes . . . I actually knew about that."

Dot studied her with narrowed eyes. "You did? How'd you know about it? Did Dave tell you?"

Britt folded her hands together and brought them up in front of her mouth. How to tell this story without scaring Dot off. She was tempted to softpedal it, but there was something about this woman that told Britt bluntness was the way to go. "Okay," she said. She licked her lips. "I'm going to tell you something . . . pretty terrible. My brother-in-law is in jail, for setting fire to his house and killing his wife, my sister."

"That bastard," Dot breathed with admiration at the magnitude of the calamity.

"That's what I thought," said Britt. "But here's the part that should interest you. When the cops questioned him, he told this story about how he'd knocked down a hitchhiker and then ended up giving him a lift to Montpelier."

"Just like what happened to Dave," Dot exclaimed.

Britt gazed steadily at Dot. "My brother-in-law drives a dark blue Mercedes."

Dot frowned, clearly confused. "So, he was the guy . . . I don't get it. What are you driving at . . .?"

"I'm saying that if what Dave said was true, my brother-in-law couldn't have set that fire because it occurred during the time he was driving here and back."

"Oh . . ." said Dot. Then she peered at Britt. "Is that what you want?"

"I want the truth," said Britt.

Dot nodded thoughtfully. "So you should get Dave to tell the police that."

"I asked him to," said Britt. "And he said he would. But he never showed up at the police station. That's why I came here. To try and find him."

"Oh, I get it," said Dot.

"But if you were to tell that story . . . the one you just told me. I think that would confirm what my brother-in-law said."

"Wait a minute," said Dot, holding up her hands. "I don't want to get involved with the cops."

"I know, I understand," said Britt. "It's just that . . ." She glanced at the display of framed photos. "There's this little girl. My niece. She's eleven years old. Her name is Zoe. She's lost her mother, and now her father is in jail. And from what I'm hearing, from you and from Dave, he doesn't belong there. But the only way to prove that. . . ."

Britt looked hopefully at Dot.

Dot sighed. "It's always a mistake to get involved with the cops." She glanced back at Britt who was gazing at her steadily. "And it usually is the husband who does these things. Are you sure that bastard didn't do it?"

Britt thought about it, and shook her head. "I'll be honest with you. At first I was sure he did. But now I think that it was all a mistake."

"And you came all this way just for him?" Dot asked.

"For Zoe," said Britt steadily. "For my niece. She's only eleven."

"Oh hell," said Dot.

CHAPTER 37

The phone rang and Britt jumped. She felt as if she had been waiting for days, though it had been only hours before that she escorted Dot to the Coleville Police Station and then, reluctantly, on the advice of Chief Stern, departed. "Don't worry," Dot had said, winking at Britt. "Leave it to me."

"Call me when you're done," Britt told her. "I'll drive you back."

Britt had gone and picked up Zoe after school, and brought her back to the house. Zoe had immediately vanished into her room and stayed there with the door closed. Britt had not tried to dislodge her. But now, she heard Zoe's door open at the sound of the phone's ring. Britt ran to the phone and picked it up.

"Britt?" said an unfamiliar voice.

"Yes," she said warily.

"They're springing me. Can you pick me up?"

"Alec?" Britt cried, and was surprised at the way her heart rose when she realized who it was. *Zoe will be so happy*, she thought.

"They're bringing me down to the police station. Meet me there. Hurry," he said.

"We're on our way." She hung up the phone and ran to the bottom of the stairs.

"Zoe," she screamed.

Zoe emerged from her room and frowned down the staircase at her aunt.

"That was your dad. Want to go get him?"

"What do you mean?"

"I mean, go get him. Bring him home," said Britt, grinning.

Zoe hesitated, looking warily at Britt. "Like, they're going to let him go?"

Britt nodded.

"Like when?"

"Like right now," said Britt.

Zoe stood very still for a minute, and then she began to shriek.

* * *

Zoe burst through the doors of the Coleville Police Station as Britt locked the car and hurried to keep up with her.

"Where's my dad?" Zoe cried, running up to the female sergeant at the desk.

"Who is your father?" the woman asked.

"Alec Lynch," said Zoe.

"I think he's still being processed out. You can wait over there," she said, pointing to the benches at the front of the station.

"Is Chief Stern here?" Britt asked.

"Who shall I say is here?" the sergeant asked.

"Britt Andersen."

The sergeant picked up the phone and spoke into it briefly. Then she looked up at Britt. "Wait over there," she said, pointing to the benches again.

But before Britt could sit down, the door to Ray Stern's office opened, and Ray emerged followed by Kevin

Carmichael. Kevin was dressed in one of his magnificent suits, but he still looked exhausted and strung out. Britt hurried over to them. "You're letting him go then," she said.

Ray smiled. "Your witness convinced me."

"Where is she?" Britt asked, looking around. "I have to drive her home."

"I had a patrolman drive her home," said Ray. "You've done enough for one day."

Britt blushed and glanced at Kevin, who nodded wearily. "That was some nice work," he said. "You managed without Dave."

"Luckily," said Britt.

"I can see you're the determined type," he said, forcing a thin smile.

Britt shrugged, ready to deny this description of her, not sure whether it was a compliment. Suddenly, the door to the holding cells and processing area of the station opened, and a fatigued-looking Alec emerged, wearing a rumpled striped shirt and gray slacks. His leather jacket was folded over his arm, and he was putting his expensive watch back onto his wrist. Zoe, who had been waiting patiently beside Britt, saw him and cried out.

"Daddy!" She pushed past Kevin Carmichael and rushed to Alec's arms.

He enfolded her in an embrace, his tired eyes closed tight. "How's my girl?" he whispered.

Kevin hefted his briefcase. "So, all's well that end's well. I've got to be going. I've got another long night ahead of me," he said.

"New babies are tough," said Ray sympathetically.

Zoe was reluctant to let him go but Alec finally extricated himself from her embrace. Ray Stern stepped up to him and held out his hand. "I'm sorry about this, Alec. I hope there will be no hard feelings."

Alec shook the chief's proffered hand. "I know you were trying to do your job," he said.

"Well, I'm not through," said Ray. "I promise you. We will find out who set that fire and killed your wife."

Alec glanced at Britt and there was a warning in his silver eyes. Britt gazed back at him solemnly. "Thanks," said Alec.

"I know I should take you guys out somewhere to celebrate," said Kevin apologetically.

Alec clapped him on the back. "You go on and see that new son of yours. And your wife. We'll be just fine. Thanks for everything, Kevin."

Kevin nodded, clearly relieved to be free to go. "I need to get back," he admitted.

"I understand," said Alec. "Zoe, Britt, what do you say we get out of here?"

Britt nodded, and Zoe cried, "Yes."

They all started for the door. Once they got outside, Alec pulled on his jacket and glanced up and down the chilly, fairy-lit street. "How about we go over to the Mountainview Café for dinner?" he suggested.

"Yeah, they have pinball," said Zoe.

Aren't they worried, Britt wondered, *about people seeing us, talking behind our backs about Alec being in jail? Apparently not*, she thought as Alec riffled Zoe's hair and smiled at her with loving eyes. Then he looked up at Britt. "Is that okay with you?" he asked.

Britt shrugged. "Sure."

"Good," he said. He reached out and took Zoe's hand, drawing it through one of his arms. Then, to her surprise, he reached for Britt's hand. Britt instinctively pulled it back, and then pointed at her bandage. "Hurts," she said.

Alec nodded and turned to his daughter. "Ready?" Arm in arm, Alec and Zoe crossed the street, with Britt trailing behind them. They walked briskly up the block to the Mountainview Café. Rather than the hostility she had expected, Britt noticed that the people who recognized him greeted Alec warmly. She realized that the news must have already been broadcast on the TV. When they reached the restaurant, a pretty blond hostess in ski clothes seated them at a quiet, candlelit table. "Your waitress will be right with you," she said, and patted Alec on the shoulder before leaving the table.

In a moment the waitress arrived, took their drink order and brought them menus. Zoe pulled her chair up close to Alec's chair, and looked at his menu, despite the fact that she had her own. Alec rubbed her back gently, and she pretended not to notice.

"I'm gonna have the hamburger. With fries," said Zoe. "What are you gonna have?" she asked her father.

Alec frowned. "I don't know. I haven't looked yet." He began to study the menu.

"Was the food bad in there?" Zoe asked.

"Horrible," said Alec, and they both laughed. Britt watched them uneasily. They were a part of one another and she did not belong in this circle. As if he had heard her thoughts, Alec looked up and smiled briefly at her. "I guess it's thanks to you I'm not dining there again tonight."

Britt blushed and shook her head.

"What do you mean, thanks to her?" Zoe asked, and Britt detected a hint of hostility when Zoe referred to her aunt as "her."

"Well, Aunt Britt found a way to prove my alibi."

"The hitchhiker? I saw him first," said Zoe, slurping a teaspoon of water from her water glass. Britt had told her all about Dave on the way to the police station.

"It's true," said Britt. "I might not have noticed him if Zoe hadn't pointed him out."

"That's right, Dad. I did," said Zoe, smiling with satisfaction, and clinking her spoon against the inside of the glass.

"Well, I'm grateful to you both," said Alec, giving Zoe a mildly reproving glance. "It's a relief to be out."

Zoe placed the teaspoon back on the table. "You know, Kayley's father wouldn't let her come over while you were in jail," said Zoe. She leaned back in her chair balancing it on two legs.

"Zoe, sit up. You're making me nervous," said Alec. Then he sighed, and stroked her hand. "I'm sorry about Kayley's dad, honey. People are like that sometimes."

"I didn't think we were gonna be best friends anymore," said Zoe, unfolding her napkin and then tying two of the corners together absentmindedly.

"Don't blame Kayley for what her father did. That would make you just like her dad. Besides, you and Kayley are buddies. A good buddy is hard to find."

Zoe nodded. "It's okay, now. She was sorry about it." Zoe tied the other two napkin corners together and turned it inside out.

"Here," Alec said, rummaging in his pocket and pulling out some quarters. "Why don't you go play some pinball till the dinner comes." There were a bank of pinball machines across the far wall of the restaurant.

"I want to stay with you," Zoe protested.

"Go ahead. You always get fidgety sitting in restaurants. You know you do," he said wryly. "Besides, I'm not going anywhere. I'll be right here."

Zoe took the quarters from his palm. "Okay," she said. "But call me when the food comes."

"We will," said Britt.

"And stay where we can see you," said Alec.

Zoe threaded her way across the room, and Alec took a sip of his drink. "Dinner out with the grown-ups makes her antsy," he said apologetically.

Britt shook her head as if to indicate that it didn't bother her, although she felt a little less tense without Zoe's fidgeting.

Alec glanced over to make sure that Zoe was still at the pinball machine. Then he said, "I mean it, Britt. I can't thank you enough. I owe you one."

Britt shook her head. "Nothing. Really."

They sat in uneasy silence for a moment. Then Alec said, "Did you look at the tape?"

Britt nodded, and drank some wine. "I did," she said.

"I thought it might help you. To understand about Greta," he said.

"It was hard to watch," said Britt. "I honestly don't remember my mother but . . . well, there was nothing familiar about her. A total stranger."

Alec raised his eyebrows and took another sip of his drink. "I have to admit, I took an instant dislike to her."

"Kind of like you did to me," Britt said.

Alec frowned and squirmed in his seat, but Britt shook her head. "It's all right," she said. "I could tell you didn't like her. The way you kept the camera on when she told you to turn it off."

He nodded, his gaze faraway. "Greta was trying so damn hard. It was so painful to watch. But I could tell it was hopeless. You could just see it in that woman's eyes. She was like a snake." Alec stopped himself and looked apologetically at Britt. "Sorry. I know she's your . . . mother."

"She's nothing to me," said Britt firmly. "All I could think about when I watched the tape was Greta. How she didn't deserve the sorrow and the disappointment."

Alec nodded. "Can you understand how I came to the conclusion about Greta setting the fire?"

Britt glanced across the room at Zoe, who was gripping the sides of a pinball machine with intense concentration. "I understand," she said. "But still . . . I just can't imagine her doing that to Zoe. . . ."

"Do you think I want to believe it? Of my own wife," he cried. Then he looked around the dining room and lowered his voice. "But I think when a person is that down, they're not in their right mind. At least, that's what I understand. In her right mind, no. Never. But, you didn't see her when she was depressed. Obviously, that tape was made when she was . . . full of hope. Imagine what it was like for her to find out that her dear mother had trashed her again." He sighed, and shook his head. "Jean Andersen is the one that ought to go to jail for the fire. Because she caused it, just as surely as if she lit the match herself. Anyway, you heard the chief. He's going to be pursuing this. I'm counting on you, Britt. You've got to take this one to the grave."

"Believe me, he won't hear from me," said Britt. Then she cleared her throat. "Anyway, I think tomorrow, if I can arrange a flight, I'll be heading back to Boston. So I'll be . . . out of the picture, so to speak."

Alec frowned. "Are you sure? I mean, we'd like you to stay . . ."

"I have a life to get back to," she said lightly.

"Of course. I know you do. I just . . . uh . . . I want to thank you again for staying. For being with Zoe. I know you didn't plan to stay away so long."

Britt looked around the cozy candlelit dining room. "You know, you seem to have a lot of friends. Why did you trust me? You don't even like me."

Alec smiled crookedly. "Well, that's a little harsh . . ."

"Whatever," said Britt. "I mean, you didn't know me . . ."

"Greta told me a lot about you over the years . . ."

"About how thoughtless and selfish I was," said Britt with a trace of bitterness.

Alec shook his head. "That was a misunderstanding between you two. It should never have happened. I told her again and again to call you, but she thought you would find her . . . find us . . . dull and uninteresting with your big career and all . . ."

Britt inhaled deeply and tried to prevent any tears from rising to her eyes. *All that time wasted*, she thought.

"Anyway," he said. "As soon as you arrived, I could see that Zoe felt an immediate connection to you. As if she had always known you."

Britt nodded. "I have to admit that it astonished me. I never expected her to accept me the way she did."

"And I could see how you treated Zoe," he said. "I could tell that you loved her."

Britt felt shocked by the word. The ease with which he said it. The fact that he had realized it before she did. She forced herself to smile, but she could not meet his eyes. She felt as if he had bestowed on her the ultimate compliment.

The waitress arrived at their table, and regarded them with a perky gaze. "So," she said pleasantly, "how are you folks tonight?"

CHAPTER 38

"There, that's all arranged," said Britt, coming into the cramped kitchen with her cell phone in hand. "My flight is this afternoon at three." She was feeling more like herself, more in control today than she had the night before. During and after dinner, she found herself feeling shaky and constantly fighting off tears. The aftershocks, she thought, of the whole ordeal. Last night she had slept soundly, without dreams.

Now, Zoe looked up from her seat at the breakfast table where she was sitting knee to knee with her father. "I wish you didn't have to go," she said.

Britt smiled. "I'll be back to visit before you know it."

Alec put down the newspaper, with his picture and that of Dean Webster on the front page, and looked up at Britt. "Hopefully, we'll be in more comfortable quarters."

"Are you going to look for another house?" Britt asked.

Alec shook his head. "I think maybe we'll rebuild on the old site. It's a great piece of land. And we'll need the space if Zoe's going to have a horse. I've already got the barn, so I'm ahead of the game."

"Where will you live while you're building?" Britt asked.

"We'll rent something," he said.

"Well, make sure it's got room for me to come visit," said Britt lightly, avoiding his gaze.

"We will," Zoe promised.

Britt poured herself a cup of coffee and leaned against the counter to drink it. There wasn't room at the table for three people.

"Take my seat," said Alec, starting to get up.

"No, never mind," said Britt. "I've got other calls to make."

"It's a long time until three o'clock," said Alec. "What are you going to do till then? How about if I take you out to lunch . . .?"

It seemed suddenly important to Britt not to spend any time alone with him. "Oh, no, you'll be busy getting things back to normal at the dealership. And I've got stuff to do. I need to get to the airport early and straighten everything out with the new ticket. And by the time I drop off the rental car . . ."

"You should have somebody look at that hand," said Alec.

Britt suddenly remembered the excuse she had made last night, not to let him take her hand. "Once I get back to Boston, I'll see somebody . . . Well, I'd better call the office and tell them I'll be in tonight." She took her coffee and the cell phone into the living room and sat down. She dialed the number and, as she waited while the phone rang, she looked around the room, thinking of all that had happened since she'd arrived here. It had been wrenching, grueling really. And yet, when she thought about the fact that she almost hadn't come, it was hard for her to believe that she had hesitated. She couldn't remember the last time she had felt so needed.

The receptionist answered.

"Donovan Smith, please. Tell him it's Britt Andersen."

The receptionist hesitated and then said, "One minute, please."

There was a moment's silence and then Donovan came on the line. "Britt," he said. "What a surprise."

Britt felt instantly wary at the tone of his voice. She decided she had better make it brief. "Donovan, I just wanted to tell you I'm coming back to town today. I've got a short flight so, weather permitting, I'll be back in Boston by four. If you like, I can try and make it in for tonight's show."

"Oh, I don't think that will be necessary," he said.

Britt felt a chill. "It's no problem," she said stiffly.

"Actually, I'm glad you called. There have been some changes you should know about."

"Changes? What sort of changes?"

"Well, it didn't seem . . . prudent anymore to try to carry on without a producer. And I had somebody I was interested in trying . . ."

"Trying for what?" said Britt, her voice rising.

"Your position, Britt. Don't pretend to be shocked. You know very well you can't just walk out and then expect to come back when you please. This is a high-pressure business. I need someone I can rely on. You can't just disappear every time there's a crisis in your personal life."

Britt couldn't believe what she was hearing. She hadn't even *had* a personal life since she went to work for Donovan. Except, of course, for their ill-fated affair. "You didn't feel that way when you and I were together . . ." she reminded him sharply.

"Well, since you bring it up, that's another thing," he said. "I don't think it was healthy for you, being here, any longer. It has to be difficult for you, day in, day out, dealing with all the . . . baggage, if you know what I mean . . ."

Baggage, she thought. *Our late love affair.* Britt's hands were trembling and she was having difficulty maintaining her composure. Part of her wanted to cry out in protest that he couldn't do this to her. Part of her wanted to argue with him and beg for her job back. It was her life. Her identity, almost. How could he just dump her like that? She blushed, remembering how he had dumped her before, with apparent ease, when he found a younger, prettier girl. But this was different. He had no complaints about her work. She was good at her job.

And it wasn't as if she'd gone off on a lark somewhere. *This was a matter of life and death*, she thought. He was acting as if she'd left on a whim. She knew she could say all those things, and maybe he would change his mind. She could launch into a tirade, and threaten him with a lawsuit. He kind of liked it when they used to argue. Maybe he just wanted to provoke an argument, to see how much she cared. All she had to do was say . . .

"Britt?" Donovan asked.

"Yes," she said.

"I'm sure this comes as a shock," he said.

She could picture his aging face with that perfect bone structure, his slicked-back salt-and-pepper hair, his fine, light eyes, probing for a weak spot like a laser.

"No," she said at last. "It's fine, actually. It's fine with me."

"Well, that's it, then," he said imperiously. "Speak to someone in accounting about your severance."

Britt punched the button to end the call without another word. There was some small satisfaction in imagining him, staring at the phone in disbelief. Expecting her to argue and plead for his indulgence.

"Britt? Everything okay?" Alec was standing in the doorway to the living room, looking at her with a frown.

She tried to hide her trembling hands in her lap. "Fine," she said. "No problem."

Alec frowned. "Are you sure? You seem a little upset."

"I'm sure," she said sharply.

"Well, we're leaving now," he said, apparently ignoring her testiness. "I'll drop Zoe at school."

Zoe rushed into the living room and threw her arms around Britt, nearly knocking her over. "Promise you'll come back," she said.

"I promise," Britt whispered, not trusting her voice. She stood up and walked with an arm around Zoe to the door.

"Love you," Zoe whispered, squeezing her.

Britt felt shocked by the child's sentiment. "You, too," she mumbled, caught off balance and unable to form the words.

Zoe didn't seem to mind. She stretched up on tiptoe and kissed Britt's cheek. Zoe smelled fresh, as if everything within her was blooming, and no decay had set in yet. Britt breathed in her scent as if she had been trapped underground and starved for air.

"Let's go, honey," said Alec, nudging Zoe.

Britt and Alec exchanged a glance. Britt extended her bandaged hand, but Alec did not shake it. Instead, he put his arm around her gently, lightly. "I'll never forget what you did for me. Have a safe trip," he said. He released her immediately, almost before she could stiffen. "And come back."

Britt nodded and avoided his glance. She murmured good-bye, and watched as they went down the walk to the car, waving as they looked back at her.

* * *

It only took her a few minutes to pack, and then it seemed as if the day loomed interminably ahead of her. She had imagined herself busy, catching up on phone calls, making notes in her filofax and scanning the papers for possible new guests. Instead, she was looking around her at the empty house which now seemed unbearably dreary. For a moment, she second-guessed her decision to come here. If none of this had happened, she would still have her job, still have her life.

But even as she thought it, she knew it was absurd. Donovan had seized the first chance to get rid of her. She had been fooling herself into thinking she was important to him. Three years of service—for that's what it was, she thought—dismissed out of hand. While here, in a week, she had made a difference. She had earned . . . love. She thought again of Zoe's simple declaration. Love you. How long had it been, she thought, since someone had said those words to her? *Donovan Smith had never said them*, she thought bitterly. They had been too sophisticated for messy emotions. Donovan always said that they "enjoyed" each other. And that had been enough for her. *That's what's embarrassing*, Britt thought. She'd thought it had been enough to be enjoyed. To be accorded the same amount of appreciation one might have for a good meal.

Stop beating yourself up, she thought. *You were in love. It was Donovan who had insisted on the distance. And as for the job . . . You'll find another job. There are lots of jobs for someone with your experience.*

For one reckless minute, she thought of the TV station, here in Coleville. They're missing a reporter, she thought wryly, thinking of Dean Webster. For a minute she indulged in the idea of living here, being Zoe's aunt, her surrogate mom, even. Being needed, every day. Getting to know Alec better, a man who clearly had hidden depths. But no. She shook her head. What a ridiculous thought. She was a single woman. She had to live somewhere with opportunities and culture. And eligible men.

Stop feeling sorry for yourself, she thought. *Get going*. She pulled her coat out of the closet and picked up her bag. She'd wait at the airport. Some place impersonal. Some place that reminded her of her own life. Cool, detached, all business. Britt closed the door behind her and didn't look back. She went down the path to her car, and got inside, shivering. She turned on the heater, and looked at the clock. There were still hours before her flight.

Maybe, she thought, *I'll make one more stop. There was one person she hadn't said good-bye to*. For a moment, she wasn't sure where to say those good-byes. There was no cemetery plot, no headstone. Greta's body hadn't even been returned for cremation yet. Britt thought about it, as she sat in the idling car. She could go to the funeral home. It had a generic little chapel where she could sit. But somehow, that didn't seem fitting for Greta. Greta's world had been about her home and her family and her garden.

And a life that had ended in despair and tragedy. Immediately, Britt understood where she needed to go to say good-bye.

CHAPTER 39

Yellow tape was still looped around the perimeter of the remains of Greta's house, but the fire investigators and the police were gone for now and the site looked derelict.

Britt got out of the car, and walked up to it, carrying a bouquet of flowers which she had stopped to buy from the local florist in Coleville. Even though she was jobless now, she had requested the most exquisite, expensive bouquet the florist had been able to create. There were roses and lilies, baby's breath and stephanotis in shades of salmon, white and cream. The flowers looked fresh and dazzling against the ferns and greens they were arranged with. The florist had tied them together with a white bow.

You'd like these, Britt thought, silently addressing her sister. *You always did love flowers.* For a moment she recalled the accusing look in Alec's eyes when he had said, "You didn't know her." He had been right, of course. Britt had preferred to see the polished surface rather than the complex soul of her sister. She had never understood the depths of Greta's suffering, and how hard she had tried to overcome it. Greta's wonderful daughter and her husband's devotion were a testament to how well she had succeeded, in spite of her overwhelming heartache.

Britt walked around the house, searching for the right place to lay the flowers. Somehow the front of the house didn't seem right. Zoe had described the house to her in great detail, sketching the rooms out on a pad, trying to re-create that image of home for Britt, so she would understand all that had been lost. The living room, the dining room, the formal, social part of the house was not the real Greta. Britt knew that Greta's kitchen had been part of a great room around the back. That was where she had cooked and sewed and arranged the flowers from her garden. That was the real Greta. Trying to make a cozy, indestructible home, a fortress against her own broken past.

Eventually, she had failed, given up. It was a house built on sand. Angry tears rose to Britt's eyes. *How cruel for you*, she thought, addressing her sister. "I'm sorry," Britt said aloud. "It was so unfair." She leaned across the sooty tiles of the floor and laid the flowers down at the foot of the cast-iron woodstove which was now freestanding in the space that had been Greta's kitchen. Britt looked around at the jagged, blackened struts that remained. *I still can't picture you doing this*, Britt thought. *Setting fire to it. I know you were depressed, but even so . . .*

Britt turned away from the sight, and looked at her watch. She still had hours to go before her flight home. She jammed her hands into her coat pockets, and felt her cell phone, resting in the bottom of the right-hand pocket. *Maybe I should call and see if they have any cancellations on the earlier flight.* There was no use in hanging around here any longer. *But then*, she reminded herself, *what's the hurry to get back. No job to go to. No one waiting to see you*. She stood in the driveway and looked back at the barn. Zoe's stable-to-be. It was a hundred yards behind the house, far enough away to have escaped destruction from the showers of sparks which had rained down during the fire. The roof of the barn was gray with ashes, although the stone walls had been gray to begin with and so, showed no evidence of the fire.

I'm glad they're going to rebuild here, Britt thought, gazing at the surrounding woods, and the jagged, mountainous horizon. *It's so beautiful here. And it will be so great for Zoe to have a horse to love and fuss over.* Britt had always dreamed of that herself when she was a child, although it had never been within the realm of possibility. But here, it really was. Zoe had explained to her how the land behind their house led to trails that crisscrossed Mt. Glace. The foothills were heavily forested and not suitable for downhill skiing, but there were riding trails and it was a favorite area of hunters and riders and cross-country skiers. It was somewhere up there that Alec had taken Britt out on the snowmobile. At the time, she had refused to see the beauty of the land. She had been so determined to condemn Alec and his choices.

But, now she had to admit that Alec and Greta had chosen this property well. It was surrounded by a splendid landscape and still accessible to town. Britt picked her way through the ruts and tire tracks filled with dirty snow in the direction of the old barn. Since she had time to kill, she figured she would take a look. That way, when Zoe called and told her about the horse and the barn he was stabled in, she'd have a mental picture of the whole thing. She knew where there was an equestrian store in Boston. Maybe she could buy Zoe some riding paraphernalia for Christmas this year. A check in the mail wouldn't do anymore. This Christmas might require wrapped presents, and a visit.

The thought made her heart feel lighter. They wouldn't be moved back to this property by Christmas. But there was no harm in planning for the future. She looked inside the darkened barn through the crack in the doors. Enough light filtered through the ash-covered windows so that she could make out the outline of piles of hay on the floor. She pushed the door open a little ways and, saw, to her surprise, that there was a furry creature sitting there, facing her. A gray cat. The cat stared at Britt with its yellow, glittering gaze.

"Kirby?" Britt said. She couldn't help feeling a little concerned. Vicki had seemed so determined to take the cat with her. She might have been cavalier about the baby, but she had seemed fiercely devoted to the cat. "What happened?"

Britt tugged at the barn door which opened about a foot, and then got caught in a rut. Britt gazed in at the dumb creature. "Did you get left behind? Were you hiding or something? Well, that's what you get for hiding from people." She expected the cat to bound out through the opening, but it sat still where it was. "Come on," said Britt, "get out of there. Come on, you dopey cat," she said. She tried to pull the barn door open wider but it was stuck in the frozen tire tracks. *I'll have to lift it*, she thought, and then, as she braced herself against the door to lift it free, something she had scarcely noticed before registered on her consciousness. *Tire tracks?* she thought.

And at the same moment, the door rode over the tracks, swung open, and flooded the shadowy barn with weak gray light. Britt saw that a car was parked inside. Even in the gloom, its cherry-red finish seemed to glow.

Britt stared at the car. There was no mistaking it. It was Vicki's Toyota.

Britt felt a strange unease looking at the car. *What was it doing here?* She thought Kevin said they'd left town. Britt could imagine Vicki leaving her baby, and even the cat. But the car? That car represented blood money to Vicki. There was no way she was going to leave without it. Besides, they had no other vehicle. No other way to leave.

Even as she thought all these things, she was advancing slowly on the car, and there was a sickening feeling in the pit of her stomach. *Why was it hidden here, in the Lynches' barn?* she thought. Her heart was beating a tattoo. She looked into the car, and though it was difficult to see inside, she could make out that it was empty. She walked around to the driver's side and opened the door. The overhead light went on and she could see clearly into the front and the back seats. There was no one in the car. It didn't appear to be packed with stuff. It was simply parked.

Britt straightened up and stared at the car. Perhaps she ought to go over to the Carmichaels' house to insist on an explanation. What possible explanation could there be for

Vicki's leaving the car here? Hadn't Kevin said that they took the car and the money and left town? When Dave didn't show up at the police station, that's what Kevin had said. She was sure of it. She looked at her watch, and thought about her own plans. *It's none of your business*, she thought. What difference did it make if Vicki and Dave had left town or not? Alec was free, and everything was all right. And she needed to get out of here. She had to get to the airport.

And then it occurred to her. Maybe the Carmichaels had taken Vicki and Dave to the airport. Maybe she'd misunderstood when Kevin said that they'd left town. Maybe Kevin and Caroline had financed some garden spot vacation, and Vicki and Dave were going to pick up the car, and the cat, when they returned.

That's probably it, Britt thought, relieved. Kevin might have been too embarrassed to admit to giving in to that kind of extortion. But it was exactly what Vicki might demand. Britt sighed, feeling better. That made sense. She almost felt sorry for the Carmichaels. All they wanted was a baby. Vicki had certainly made them jump through hoops to get it. Well, it was none of her concern anyway.

"Kirby," she said, "last chance to get out of here." She was anxious to go and she wanted to at least give him a chance to get out. If he needed to get out of the cold, he could go and wail at the Carmichaels' back door. Obviously, they knew he was still here. Waiting for Vicki to return.

Britt started to walk around the back of the car when something caught her eye. It was sticking out of the trunk on the driver's side. She stepped closer, and crouched down to look at it. At first, she couldn't discern what it was. She took off her glove and rubbed it between her fingers. It was soft and fuzzy—a little triangle of wool. The darkness of the barn had leeched the colors but up close Britt could still make them out. Turquoise and yellow, white, orange, and green. Clumsily finished. Zoe's scarf.

The last time Britt had seen it, it was wrapped around Vicki's neck.

Britt gasped, and stumbled back, away from the car, staring at the tiny bit of the scarf, which had obviously been caught in the trunk lid when it was closed.

No, no, she thought, shaking her head. *It doesn't mean anything. There must be some . . . reason*. Maybe . . . maybe Vicki was packing stuff in the trunk and . . . and she figured she wouldn't need that scarf on a vacation in some tropical place.

That was it, she thought. That made sense along with everything else. For a moment, Britt wished she had never entered the barn. *This is none of your concern*, she told herself. *Now, just get out of here.*

She turned to go and then she let out a strangled cry. Kevin Carmichael was blocking the doorway.

"Britt," he said dully. He was dressed, but not for work. He was wearing a ski jacket and jeans. He still looked disheveled. "What are you doing here?"

"What?" she asked, stalling.

"I thought you left town," he said.

It was as if he had opened a door for her. "I am leaving," she said. "Right now. I was just on my way to the airport."

He stared at her, his face gray.

"Just on my way," she repeated. "I've got to take the car back to the rental place." *Why mention the car?* she thought. *Why did you have to mention the car?*

"What are you looking for?" he said.

"Nothing!" Britt cried. "I came out here to pay my last respects . . . this is my sister's property, you know." She took a deep breath. "I see that Vicki left her new car here. Did Alec say it was all right for them to leave their car in here?"

"Leave their car?" he asked, looking confused.

Britt didn't want to think about his reactions. She forged ahead. "Well, they're obviously not here. You told me they left town. And the car is still here. So I figured they must be planning on coming back for it."

It was like trying to engage a sick child in a game. Kevin just stared at her, his eyes dull and rueful. He watched her busy movements, and remained blocking the doorway. Britt didn't want to think about the scarf in the trunk or why Kevin was staring at her in such ominous silence. "Well, I'm sure he won't mind them keeping it here. But that's between you and Alec." She looked at her watch with an exaggerated frown and approached him, murmuring, "I've really got to run. Will you excuse me?"

For a minute, she thought he would try to stop her, but he let her go without making any effort to restrain her. Britt's heart was pounding as she edged past him and out into the yard. She began to pick her way back across the snow toward her rental car. She could feel his gaze on her, from the distance. *Good*, she thought. *I'm going. This is none of my business.* If there was something wrong, she didn't want to know about it.

She didn't know and she didn't care, just as long as he let her get away from here. She stuffed her hands in her pockets and felt her keys and her cell phone resting there. *As soon as I get to the airport*, she thought, *I'm going to call Alec and tell him.* Because no matter how many possible explanations she could conjure, in her heart she knew that there was something very peculiar about that red car being parked in his barn. Maybe Alec should get the police out here. If there was something wrong, the police could figure it out. She didn't want to think too carefully about what it might be. She would just get in her car, and lock the doors and get out of here.

But first things first. First she had to get away from Kevin. Britt arrived at her rental car and pulled the keys out of her pocket. She reached out to grasp the door handle. She thought for a minute of turning and waving at him, but decided against it. *Just get out of here*, she told herself. She pulled the door open and sighed with relief. Suddenly, she heard something rushing up on her, like the beating of wings, and she could feel the danger of it, overtaking her. Before she could look or protest, she felt herself being struck in the head, and then, all was darkness as she slid down the side of the car and crumpled into the snow.

CHAPTER 40

Zoe flopped down on the visitor's chair in her father's office and watched with a critical eye as Lauren leaned over Alec's desk. Alec winked at Zoe, and dictated a few last notes to Lauren. Lauren straightened up, tugged her spandex top back down over the waistband of her pants and looked from Zoe to Alec brightly. "How about you two come over to my place for dinner tonight?" she asked.

Alec looked questioningly at Zoe.

"I made your favorite, Zoe. Brownies," Lauren cooed.

Zoe yawned and stretched. "I want to go home tonight. I'm really tired."

Alec smiled at Lauren. "Thanks, kid," he said. "Maybe another time."

Lauren shot a withering glance in Zoe's direction, picked up her papers and left the office. Zoe reached over and closed the door behind her.

"Now what's this all about? You're too tired to eat?" he asked.

Zoe gave him a sly smile. "Never. I'm starved."

Alec wagged a finger at her. "That wasn't very nice," he said. "Lauren's been a big help to me since Mom died and . . . everything."

"Why do people always think I want brownies? I don't even like them anymore."

"Since when?" Alec asked. "You used to love brownies."

Zoe shrugged. "Ugh. I ate some that Mrs. Carmichael brought us and I thought I was gonna hurl." Zoe made a gagging expression.

"People were just trying to be nice, Zoe. Bringing us things."

"Oh no. This was before. She brought them to me and Mom after Mom saved their house from the flood. Didn't you have any of those?"

"I don't know," said Alec absently. "I don't remember."

"You'd remember these. Oh no, you know why. She brought them the day of the fire. Mom and I ate a couple of them, to be polite. Then she threw them out."

"Mrs. Carmichael's not the baker your mom was, eh?" Alec asked.

"No," Zoe said. Then, she sighed. For a moment the two of them sat in silence, each with thoughts of Greta. Then Zoe got up from the chair and came over to lean on Alec's desk. "I kind of miss Aunt Britt."

Alec studied some papers on his desk without looking up. "Why don't you give her a call? She's probably home by now. Find out how her trip was. I'm sure she'd love to hear from you."

"Okay," said Zoe eagerly. "What's her number?"

Alec checked the rolodex on his desk and read the number out as Zoe dialed. He continued shuffling through sales reports while Zoe balanced on one foot and waited, receiver to her ear. Finally, she said, "Aunt Britt, it's me. Zoe. Just . . . wanted to say hi. Okay, well, I'll talk to you."

"Not there?" he asked.

Zoe shook her head. "There was about a million clicks on her message machine," she complained.

Alec frowned. "Really? Doesn't she have that service where she can check her messages, long distance?"

"I don't know," said Zoe. And then she brightened. "Yeah, wait. She does. That's right. She does. I've heard her call up to check."

"So, that's odd," he said.

"Why?" she asked.

Alec shrugged. "That so many messages would still be on the machine. I guess she hasn't got in yet. Try her at work. That's probably where she is."

"You have her number?"

Once again Alec read off a number and then resumed his figuring. Zoe waited until someone answered, and then she asked for Britt. After a moment, she hung up.

Alec looked at her with raised eyebrows.

"She doesn't work there anymore," said Zoe.

"What?"

"That's what the lady told me."

"Give me the phone," Alec said impatiently. He rolled up his sleeves and sighed as he dialed and waited. He took out a cigarette and tamped it on the desk, but didn't light it. Finally, he got through to the Donovan Smith show. "Yeah," he said. "I'm looking for Britt Andersen. This is her brother-in-law."

Nancy Lonergan, at the other end of the line, couldn't conceal her surprise. "Mr. Lynch?"

"Yeah," he said warily.

"I thought you were . . . When Britt called she told me . . ."

"That I was in jail? I was," he said. "That's all over. They dropped the charges."

"Congratulations," said Nancy. "Britt mentioned to me that you had Kevin Carmichael as your attorney. I guess he lived up to his reputation."

"You know Kevin?" Alec asked, surprised.

"When Britt mentioned his name I knew I'd heard of him, but it took me a while to remember why."

"I assume it was because he's good at his job," said Alec.

"Well, that," Nancy drawled, "and that he married one of his clients. A woman who was tried for murdering her husband. He got her off and then he married her. It made him somewhat notorious around here."

Alec couldn't conceal his shock. "Caroline?"

"Was that her name? I forget. Anyway, he got her an acquittal. I meant to tell Britt when I remembered it. One of those diminished capacity defenses. Post-traumatic stress disorder I think it was."

"Really," said Alec thoughtfully. "I've never heard anything about that."

"I'm not surprised," said Nancy. "I doubt they broadcast it. It's not the kind of thing you want your new neighbors to know about."

"No. I guess not," said Alec. He felt a little guilty listening to gossip about Kevin. He would be forever grateful to him. He didn't want to hear anything negative about him, although he couldn't deny that he found this information very interesting. "Well, he did a great job for me."

"So it seems," Nancy said.

"Not to mention that Kevin saved my daughter's life," he said. "He rescued her from the fire."

"How admirable," said Nancy. "I'm sure you feel indebted to him."

"I do," Alec said abruptly, curtailing the subject. "Now, what's this about Britt not working there anymore?"

"Oh, well, I didn't find out about it until I got in," said Nancy. "Apparently, Donovan fired her this morning for being away too long. He was just looking for an excuse. Didn't she tell you?"

Alec grimaced. "I thought something was up by the look on her face," he said. "But she insisted everything was okay."

"Oh no. I'm sure she didn't want you to worry."

"I feel like it's my fault. I asked her to stay here."

"She wanted to stay," said Nancy. "She told me so. I'd just like to know where she's gone," Nancy said. "I tried her cell phone but she hasn't got it turned on, apparently. I left a bunch of messages at her house, but so far, I haven't heard back."

"Hmmm . . ." said Alec. "Do you think she might have decided to take a trip somewhere else? Since she wasn't going back to work?"

"It's possible, I suppose," said Nancy. "Not really like her though."

"Well, let me just check the airport," said Alec.

"She won't like it if you check up on her," said Nancy. "She's very independent."

"She needs somebody to check up on her," he said firmly.

"You're right," said Nancy, smiling to herself. "Let me know what you find out."

Alec hung up and frowned at Zoe. "Did Aunt Britt say anything to you about going somewhere other than back home?"

Zoe shook her head.

"Let me try the car rental place. Can you wait, or do you need to eat right away?"

"I can wait," said Zoe. "I want you to find Aunt Britt."

Alec nodded, and began to work the phone. After several calls, his frown had only deepened. Zoe had moved around and was sitting on the edge of his desk, her feet dangling so that she was kicking the drawers absently with her heels.

"Zoe, stop kicking that," he said irritably. "I'm trying to think."

Zoe stopped. "What's the matter?" she asked.

Alec sighed, and frowned at the notes he had made. "She didn't turn the car in. And, she wasn't on her flight. And she didn't trade her ticket in for any other flight."

"What does that mean?" Zoe asked.

"I don't know," said Alec.

* * *

A sharp, thwacking sound penetrated the fog in her mind, and Britt came to with a blinding headache. She was bound hand and foot, her mouth covered with duct tape. The instant she realized this, her heart started to hammer and she felt as if she couldn't breathe. *Calm down,* she thought. *You'll suffocate. Breathe through your nose.* She tried to get her bearings in the darkness.

She could see lights, and a sign through the window above her. Mountain Lodge, she was able to read.

Suddenly, she felt herself begin to move and she realized that she was in a car, in the well behind the front passenger seat. The sound that had brought her to was the sound of the car door slamming as someone got in on the passenger side. Now the car was picking up speed and she could see stars out the window above her whizzing by. Her arms were aching, and she was at the mercy of every bounce the car took, because she could not steady herself with her hands.

She tried to pivot on her rear end, so that she could wedge herself against the door, to stop the jouncing. With every bump the pain in her head was intensified. She managed to shift herself by pulling her knees up to her chest as tightly as she could and wriggling until she was wedged against the door. As she did, she was able to see that there, on the backseat, was a baby carrier, belted in the legal fashion so that the child would be facing backward. In the moonlight that came through the rear window of the car, she saw the tiny, slumped-over profile of an infant in a snowsuit.

She heard low voices from the seat in front and she remembered. She had been getting in her car when she was struck with the first blow. She had awakened to find herself lying on a rug in a kitchen that looked vaguely familiar. She had tried to get up and had met the fierce gaze of Caroline Carmichael. Before she could ask what was going on, Caroline was upon her, wielding something heavy. The two of them had struggled in the kitchen, upending a plant on the counter. But Britt, still dazed from the previous blow, had been unable to fend her off. And now, here she was, traveling in a car. Caroline was driving. *What is happening? Why are they doing this?* And then, with a chill that coursed all through her veins, Britt recalled that tiny triangle of wool, sticking out of the trunk.

"Did anybody see you?" Caroline asked.

"If they did," Kevin said, sighing heavily, "all they saw was a man parking a rental car. There are about fifty cars just like it in the Lodge parking lot."

"No one will even notice it's there till spring," said Caroline.

Britt tried to think. *A rental car. Her car?*

"That's the road, I think. Look at the map," Caroline said. Britt strained to hear the reply, but Kevin's voice was muffled.

"Well, I say we keep going," Caroline said sharply.

Looking up, Britt could see the top of Caroline's head and her profile, as far down as the bridge of her nose. She had turned to glance at her husband.

Kevin murmured something in soothing tones, but Britt could not make out the words.

"I don't want to talk about that," Caroline insisted. "What's done is done."

"It's not too late," he said. "We can still go back."

Caroline stared through the windshield wearing a stony expression.

"The thing is, anyone could see how it happened," Kevin said adamantly. "Anyone—any judge would be able to understand it. I mean, what else could you do? They were trying to take your child from you. It was virtually like trying to prevent a kidnapping."

"That's right," she said. "I had no choice."

Kevin seemed to have turned away. Britt could hear him murmuring agreement, and for a moment there was silence. Then he turned back, leaning toward Caroline. "You nursed that girl through her pregnancy, dreaming about the baby she had promised you. After all the disappointments we endured. They'd already signed the papers. Well, Vicki had signed them. How were we to know about the father? And then he shows up and insists that he wants the baby and he's going to take it back. It all came crashing down on you. All the disappointment and the worry. And the fear that they were going to walk off with your child. Any mother would have done the same thing."

There was a brief silence. Then Caroline said, "They're not going to go for it again."

"You leave that to me. I can handle a jury. You, of all people, should know that. You were extremely stressed out. And they were in your house, threatening to take your child away from you. Any jury would be sympathetic to that."

"Not for a second time," she said.

"They won't be allowed to introduce the first time into evidence," he said. "You were acquitted, remember? The jury will never know about it."

Oh my God, Britt thought. *What had she been on trial for? What had Caroline done?*

"But we've got to let Greta's sister go. Because if something happens to her . . . She simply wouldn't fall into the same category," Kevin explained.

What? If what happens to me? Britt thought. *Oh, yes. Listen to him. Let me go. Please, God, make them let me go.*

"There's no way I can argue that it was impulsive, or reactive. It's going to look premeditated. That's first degree," Kevin continued.

Premeditated. First degree. Britt felt goose bumps running up and down her arms. There was no way to tell herself it was anything else. They were talking about murder.

"We'll make it look accidental," Caroline insisted.

"Darling, listen to yourself. You're talking about taking a human life. In cold blood," he added.

"It's too late to worry about that," Caroline said dully.

"What? Because of Vicki and that shiftless boyfriend? Honey, that's different. You were pushed to the breaking point. It was self-defense, pure and simple."

"Like when I shot Tim," she said.

Kevin's voice faltered slightly. "Well . . . sort of."

"But, if we let her go, she'll tell everything," Caroline protested.

"She doesn't know anything right now," said Kevin.

"She knows Vicki's in the trunk," said Caroline.

Kevin did not reply.

They rode in silence as the car bumped along. The road they were on was getting worse, dipping and rising, shaking the car with repeated jolts. Britt's heart was pounding and her stomach was doing flips. *Don't vomit*, she thought. *You'll choke. Try not to think about it.* But in her mind's eye she kept seeing that little woolen triangle, caught in the trunk lid. She tried to move her hands again, and again felt the rope, binding them. She wondered if anyone was looking for her, but realized how unlikely it was. No one was expecting her, at home or at work. And as far as Alec and Zoe were concerned, she had left for the airport and home this afternoon. *How long would it be*, she thought despairingly, *before anyone even knew she was missing?*

Finally, Kevin said, "Caroline, for pity's sake. What kind of a life can we have, always wondering if someone is going to find out? What kind of life can Kent have?"

Caroline turned her head sharply and stared at him. "We're not going to tell him about any of this. How will he ever know?"

"I'm talking about a level of tension," Kevin said. "I'm so afraid it will poison our . . . love. Our life. But if we go back and turn ourselves in and face the consequences. . . ."

"Turn me in, you mean," she corrected him. "It's my life we're talking about."

"Baby, I don't have a life without you," he said. "You know that. You are my life."

"Me and Kent, you mean," said Caroline.

Kevin was silent.

"Kevin," she demanded. "What about our baby? Isn't he your life, too?"

"Haven't I moved heaven and earth to get him for you?" Kevin asked dully.

Caroline was silent for a moment. Then she spoke. "Are you saying that you could get me acquitted? No jail time?" she asked.

"We have a very strong argument. The strongest. A mother trying to protect her baby. I'll have the jury cheering for you before I'm done. You know I'm good," he said. "No one knows that better than you."

"You are," she murmured. "I know you are."

"It might be like the last time," he admitted. "A treatment program."

"I'd have to stay in a hospital, you mean."

"Maybe, for a little while," he said.

Caroline's reply came in a small but firm voice. "I can't, Kevin. Not now. I have to think of the baby. My baby needs me. I can't be separated from him. These are the most significant months and years of his life. No. I can't."

Kevin turned to face straight ahead. "Then we're ruined," he muttered in a hopeless voice.

Britt, who knew her own fate was hanging in the balance of this argument, felt as if she was going to pass out. *Don't give in, Kevin,* she thought weakly.

"Honey, this will work, believe me," Caroline pleaded. "These logging roads are treacherous. You know they are. If anyone even finds them up here, it will just look like they got confused in the dark and went off the road and had an accident."

"You don't know what you're talking about," he cried. "They have forensic science these days. They can pinpoint these things."

"Somebody had to make a plan," said Caroline indignantly.

"Why couldn't you let me handle it?" he shouted. "Why did you have to kill them?"

"You just said I had no choice. You said it yourself. What else could I do?" Caroline cried, affronted by his criticism.

The baby in the car seat let out a thin wail. Britt started, and then hunched down in the back, closing her eyes.

"Now you've got the baby crying. Please Kevin, stop your shouting," said Caroline. "You know I don't do well with stress."

“Right,” said Kevin grimly. “Who would know that better than me?”

Caroline kept her eyes on the road, but turned her face slightly in the direction of the baby. “Don’t cry, sweetie,” she crooned. “We’re almost there.”

CHAPTER 41

Annabel Stern ladled some soup into a bowl and then sighed, as she heard knocking at the door. Without missing a beat, she picked up the bowl and poured the steaming soup back into the pot.

Ray rose from his seat at the kitchen table. "Won't be a minute," he said.

He tossed his napkin down on the table and walked through the house to the front door. He opened it, and saw Alec Lynch and his daughter, Zoe, standing on the front porch steps.

"Alec," he said. "What's up?"

"I'm sorry to bother you at home, Ray. I've got a problem," said Alec. "Can we come in?"

Ray knew perfectly well that Alec wasn't sorry. In fact, Alec felt as if the police chief owed him, and perhaps, Ray thought, he did. Ray shrugged, and stepped back so they could enter. "Can I take your coats?"

Alec shook his head, and remained standing, wearing his jacket. "Look. I'm here because I'm a little concerned about my sister-in-law."

"I thought you two had buried the hatchet," said Ray.

"No, no, it's nothing like that."

Annabel Stern came into the foyer and looked quizzically at her husband.

"Do you want to come into the kitchen? We were just about to eat," said Ray.

Alec shook his head, intent on his mission. "This won't take long. It seems that Britt didn't get on her flight to Boston today. And she didn't turn in her rental car."

Ray frowned at him. "Maybe she changed her mind about leaving."

"Well, it's possible," said Alec. "But I can't help worrying that something happened to her."

"I guess it's only natural for you to be a little jumpy. After all that's happened to your family. But I'm sure there's some perfectly reasonable explanation."

"Just to be on the safe side, I wanted to do some checking on her," Alec said stubbornly.

Ray assumed a more professional demeanor. "You mean, a search?"

"Just some checking," Alec said.

"Alec," said Ray, "your sister-in-law is an adult. She's allowed to do as she wants. An adult is not considered missing for at least seventy-two hours. I'm sure you'll hear from her in the next day or two. If you don't . . ."

"I'm not asking you to call her a missing person," said Alec.

"Well, what then?" Ray asked.

"What about credit cards? I know you can check pretty easily to find out where she has been using her credit cards. If you run a check on that for me, and it turns out she's used her cards somewhere within driving distance, then I'll know she's okay."

"People have a right to privacy, Alec," said Ray. "This is crossing the line. If she ever finds out . . ."

"I'll take responsibility," said Alec.

Ray shifted his weight uncomfortably from one leg to the other. "That sounds good in theory. But the fact is, if I do it, then I'm the one who's responsible. Have you tried her cell phone? Have you called her home, or her place of business?"

"Of course I have. Ray, do you think I'm out here dragging my daughter around in the cold just for my own amusement?"

"I don't like to abuse my authority," said Ray.

"And I would hate to have to sue the police department for false arrest," said Alec.

"No need for threats," said Ray coldly.

"I didn't think so," said Alec.

Ray hesitated. Then he turned and led the way down the hall. "Come on through."

Alec and Zoe followed the chief down the hall to the kitchen. Annabel looked sympathetically at Zoe. "How about some soup?" she asked.

"What kind?" said Zoe.

"Chicken noodle," said Annabel.

"Yes, please," said Zoe. She shrugged off her parka and sat down at the table.

Ray picked up the phone and called the station.

* * *

The car stopped with a jerk, and Kevin got out, slamming the door. Caroline got out on the driver's side. Britt closed her eyes and willed her body to go limp as she heard the back door open on the side where the baby seat was attached.

She heard someone rummaging around, and the baby wailing softly. She squinted up and saw the baby, still buckled into his seat, being lifted, seat and all, from the car. Then, the door opened behind her.

"Britt." Kevin shook her. Britt feigned unconsciousness, let her head loll as he tried to shake her awake. Britt could hear Caroline singing a lullaby, "Hush little baby," somewhere on the other side of the car.

Kevin let go of Britt's shoulder and she slumped back down into the well. She could hear him, still near the open door beside her, but she could hear little else except for his labored breathing. Her head felt as if her brain had been rattled inside her skull after he had shaken her. Even her hair seemed to hurt. All of a sudden, there was movement around her and then, with a shock, she felt something icy cold and wet against her face and neck.

Britt gasped, unable to control her response, and tried to cry out. The duet tape muffled the sound, but there was no use pretending she wasn't awake. She blinked and looked up at him balefully. Kevin was brushing the remaining snow off his ski-gloved hands. Britt felt the snow on her neck melt and trickle down beneath her turtleneck.

Kevin sighed and met her gaze. "Come on," he said. "Get out of there."

How am I supposed to do that, she thought. She tried to say "How?" but it came out sounding like a grunt.

Kevin reached down to pull her out of the car. Britt tried to resist his tugging. Kevin released her and rested his arms on the door frame of the car. "Look," he said. "Don't make this more difficult. If I have to jerk you out of here I will. That's only gonna hurt both of us more." He rubbed his down parka in the area of his ribs. "I want to help you, Britt," he whispered.

Britt stared back at him implacably. She wasn't about to help him.

Kevin leaned into the car, his reddish-blond crew cut glinting golden under the car's overhead light. He glanced up to see if Caroline was watching him, but she was in a kind of trance, walking the baby back and forth in the moonlight.

"Britt," he said, and she could see sweat trickling down the side of his face, "we're on a trail that runs along a mountain ridge. Now, this car is about to be sent over the edge of that ridge. It's a steep drop, a free fall to the bottom, and you'll have no chance to survive if you end up down there. So, do yourself a favor, and help get yourself out of the car."

Britt thought about what he was saying, and knew that he was not making it up. She understood what their plan was now. And he was right. She didn't want to go into the ravine with the car. They might not let her live much longer, but she had to at least try. She could tell that Kevin did not want to kill her. She had to make a decision and she decided that her best bet was to follow his advice.

With that, she wiggled around as best she could, and threw her bound ankles over the door frame. Then, using her elbows she managed to push herself up into a sitting position at the door. She looked up at Kevin, imploring him with her gaze to help her but he turned away.

She marshaled her strength, and forced herself to lunge forward. Her shoulder and upper arm cracked against the door frame, and she cried out behind the tape. She bounced against the door frame and forced herself to fall forward, out of the car, landing on the side of her face in the packed snow. Kevin stood immobile and did nothing to help her.

Britt's face was freezing. She managed to pull up her legs and her knees, and roll up off her side to where she was kneeling in the snow, her hands and feet still bound behind her.

"Get away from the car," Kevin barked from above her. "Get over there."

There was no use in cursing him with her gaze. She was intent on following his instructions, in the hope of saving her own life. She managed to shuffle on her knees, a short distance away from the car. In the dark, she could see that they were on a wide, packed trail, but not much else. She looked up at Kevin, who was staring at her from his position beside the open door of the car. He had an angry, tormented expression in his eyes, as if he were a fellow prisoner. He turned, and left her kneeling there.

Caroline came around the side of the car and glanced at her briefly. She had the baby in her arms and was calmly giving him a bottle. While Caroline crooned to the baby, bouncing him lightly in her arms, Kevin leaned up against the side of the car, and slowly began to unfasten the skis and poles which were secured in the rack atop the car. He carried them awkwardly in his arms and laid them down near his wife's feet. They landed with a clatter. "Careful, honey," Caroline said, as she placed the baby on her shoulder and burped him.

Skis, Britt thought. *What the hell were they doing?*

"This is never going to work," said Kevin angrily.

"Of course it will, darling," said Caroline. "That baby seat turns into a carrier. You can wear it on your back."

"Caroline, I can hardly breathe now."

"Well, on my back, then," she said. "I'm strong. And I'm every bit as good at cross-country as you are."

"I don't know if I can," he said, shaking his head. "My ribs."

"Come on now. We're almost done with this. It'll be fine. If anyone goes looking for them, or if anyone saw the car, it's just one car, one set of tire tracks that has gone seriously off that logging road in the dark, and accidentally driven over the edge of the ridge. The head injuries will be perfectly plausible. I tell you, it's a good plan. Now, look, I know your ribs hurt, but you've got to put mind over matter here, just until we can get them set up in the car. Come on now, honey."

Without another word, Kevin went around to the back of the car. Caroline cooed to the baby as her husband threw up the lid to the trunk and began to drag out the first body.

Dave was still wearing his army-drab parka, though now it was spattered with huge, dark spots. His pale complexion was striped, in the moonlight, with meandering dark streams of dried blood. Kevin pulled him out and dumped him on the ground. The body landed with a thud. Then, Kevin returned to the trunk and pulled out his next bundle. Vicki's eyes were open, but she could see nothing. She, too, had dark rivulets, like long locks of dark stringy hair, all over her face. Many of them terminated in the loops and folds of the scarf that she wore around her neck. The scarf Zoe had made. It was saturated, stained beyond repair. Kevin set her down beside Dave and stooped over, gasping and holding his ribs.

"I need a hand here, Caroline," he said grimly. "I can't do it."

"Oh, for goodness sakes," said Caroline. "Here, you hold your son."

She handed the baby to Kevin, who managed to stand up straight enough to cradle him in his arms. Caroline walked over to the bodies that were slumped beside one another in the snow. Closing her eyes against the unpleasantness of the task, Caroline reached under Vicki's armpits, and began to drag her, heels scraping the ground, and heave her through the open door into the driver's seat of the car.

Caroline grunted as Vicki landed with her face against the steering wheel. "She's still so heavy." She smacked her gloved hands together and then went back to where Dave was splayed out in the snow. "Kevin, you're going to have to help me. Set Kent down in the carrier for a minute. I can't pull this guy around the car by myself."

Britt looked at Kevin, who was standing, round-shouldered, over Dave's body, clutching the baby to his chest. The infant began to wail and flail his tiny fists.

"Don't cry," Kevin murmured, shaking his head as he stared at the sight of the baby's father, dead on the ground. "Please don't cry."

CHAPTER 42

Ray hung up the phone and turned to Alec. "The only charge she's made since she left your house this morning was at Lily's Day, the flower shop."

"The flower shop?" said Alec.

"I called Lily at home. She remembered perfectly. Your sister-in-law came in and said she wanted to buy a bouquet for your Greta. To say good-bye."

"Well, that's not much help," said Alec. "I was hoping there might be some charges that would tell us where she went."

"Well, the first thing you do is to find out where she went with the flowers. Trace her steps, so to speak. Maybe she told somebody where she was planning on going."

Alec frowned. "Did she take the flowers, or have them delivered somewhere?"

"No, she took them with her," Ray said.

"To the cemetery?" Annabel asked.

Ray shook his head. "The body just arrived back at the funeral home from the autopsy," he said in a low voice, glancing apologetically in Zoe's direction, but she was busily blowing on the soup in her spoon. "The body's going to be cremated."

"I wonder if she went to the funeral home," said Alec.

"I'll call," said Ray.

Alec sat down in a chair opposite Zoe to wait while Ray called.

"You sure you don't want a bowl?" Annabel asked him.

"It's good, Dad," said Zoe.

"No thanks," said Alec as Ray returned to the room. "Anything?" he asked.

Ray shook his head. "She didn't go there."

"She probably went out to some place where they had fond memories together," said Annabel.

Alec and Zoe exchanged a glance. "They didn't have any fond memories here," said Alec. "Britt had never been here before the funeral."

"Oh," said Annabel, seemingly chastened. "Is she religious? She might take them to the church."

"I guess we could try there," said Alec.

Zoe slurped down some more soup and then laid down her spoon. "I think she took them to our old house. I'll bet that's where she would have gone."

Alec studied his daughter with narrowed eyes. "You could be right. We can go out there and take a look."

"Maybe she stopped by the Carmichaels'," said Zoe.

"We'll go ask them," said Alec. "Come on, Zoe. Get your coat back on."

"Take these cookies," said Annabel, slipping a couple of cookies into a plastic bag.

Zoe took them and put them in her pocket. "Thanks."

"You know, she's probably going to turn up at some spa or something," said Ray. "I've seen this kind of thing happen many times."

"I hope you're right, Ray," said Alec. "Thanks for your help."

"Don't mention it." Ray and Annabel walked them to the front door and watched them go down the front walk to Alec's Mercedes.

"It does seem strange that she'd go off like that without telling anyone," said Annabel. "Do you really think she's gone on some impromptu vacation?"

Ray thought about Britt, with her no-nonsense clothes and the grave expression in her eyes. She, who had been so determined, first to label Alec a murderer, and then to set him free. She seemed like a woman who always had a goal in mind. "I can't really picture it," he said. "But then, I really didn't know her."

* * *

"Okay," said Caroline, huffing as she slammed shut the passenger door on the car. "Okay." She glanced at her husband. "Are you all right?"

Kevin nodded.

"Let's hope this thing can pick up enough momentum to get up and over the ridge. Kevin, can you put it in gear and let the brake off?

Kevin opened the driver's side door. "You and Kent get out of the way," he said. Obediently, Caroline picked up the baby and the carrier, and stepped back, far away from the cherry-red Toyota. She set the carrier down on the ground beside her, and folded her hands tightly, as if in prayer. Trembling, Kevin leaned in across Vicki and started the car, wedging himself in there, up against her lifeless body.

"All right," he cried out. "I'm going to let out the parking brake. Stand clear."

The car began to move, and Kevin backed away from it, closing the door on the driver's side. The car rolled a short distance, and then came up against a sapling and stalled out.

"Shit," said Kevin.

The baby, resting in the carrier on the ground, began to cry. "Kevin, you're going to have to steer it until it gets going," said Caroline.

Kevin shot her a filthy look and then trudged back toward the car with a sigh.

Britt closed her eyes. *No. I don't want to be a witness*, she thought. *If I am a witness, why would they leave me alive?* She knew full well that closing her eyes to the actual event was similar to an ostrich, sticking his head in the sand and calling himself hidden. She had heard everything. She knew now that Caroline had killed Vicki and Dave. *No, no,* she told herself. *They thought you were unconscious while they were talking in the car.* But even as she reminded herself of that, she knew it was some kind of sick game she was playing with herself. Telling herself that there was a chance she was going to live through this. She had been holding out some obscure hope that Kevin would prevail. That he would convince Caroline to spare her life. Now, she realized that he had conned her into getting out of the car only so he could avoid lifting her. His ribs still hurt him from the night of the fire, when he had rescued Zoe.

How could it be? she wondered. This was a man who had bravely entered a burning building, and risked his life to save a child. Now, he was covering up the killing of two people. Whatever reservations he expressed, he was still doing it. He hadn't killed them, she reminded herself. Maybe there was still hope. She worked her hands, bound by the rope, trying to free herself. There was no way she was going to count on Kevin's better nature. Obviously, he would do anything for this woman. And she . . .

Britt kept her eyes shut as she stretched her hands apart, trying to loosen the rope. In her mind's eye she saw Vicki and Dave, their bodies heaped like trash in the snow. She bared her teeth behind the duct tape and tried to chew through it. There was no one to find her. No one to save her. She had to get free.

The car's engine roared. "Stick her foot on the gas pedal," Caroline cried. "You need to weigh it down."

Britt was able to get her hands far enough apart that she could feel one end of the rope. She worked her gloved fingers up the rope and encountered a knot. Her gloves made the knot feel like a formless lump. Reluctantly, because of the cold, she tried to work off her right glove, so that she could feel the knot to undo it.

"That's better," Caroline cried. "Now you've got it."

Britt didn't want to look, but she couldn't help herself. She opened her eyes and saw Kevin, running alongside the moving car. Its taillights were visible as it began to disappear over the ridge.

"Kevin, get free," cried Caroline. "Jump free." Sitting in the carrier at her feet, the baby picked up on the panic in Caroline's voice and began to shriek. There was a crashing roar from the other side of the ridge.

"Kevin, where are you? Are you all right?" Caroline cried. The baby's wails almost drowned her out.

"Stop it," she commanded. "Stop crying." She gave the baby carrier a vicious kick with her ski boot and it tipped forward. The baby gasped, its face in the snow.

Trudging back from the top of the ridge, Kevin saw his wife kick the baby carrier.

Caroline, seeing the look in her husband's eyes, began to wail. "I'm sorry," she cried. She rushed to lift the carrier out of the snow, and unlatched its little seat belt. She picked up the baby and wiped the snow off its tiny, red face. She began to cuddle him against her chest. The baby was silent, his eyes open wide and wary.

Kevin stared at her.

Caroline began to cry. "Don't look at me like that, Kevin. I didn't mean to do it. I'm just frightened. I'm at the end of my rope."

Kevin stood there, immobile.

"I'm sorry," she cried. "He's okay. It didn't hurt him. I would never hurt him. He's my angel. I'd do anything for him. Stop staring at me."

Kevin walked slowly past her and picked up a set of skis. "We have to get out of here," he said.

Caroline brightened. "That's right," she said. "We have to go. We have to go, baby." She put Kent back into the carrier, and picked it up. "Here, Kev, you have to help me put this on my back."

She walked over to him and held the carrier up, like a gift. Kevin did not look at her or the baby. He took the carrier from her hands.

"Turn around," he said.

Caroline turned her back to him, so that he could affix the carrier, and as she did, she saw Britt, still bound and shivering, kneeling in the snow.

"What about her?" Caroline asked.

"What about her?" Kevin asked in a dull voice.

"We have to get rid of her."

Kevin didn't reply. "She didn't hurt us." He was busy fixing the straps on Caroline's back.

"She's a nosy snoop, just like her sister."

My sister? Britt thought. Her leaden heart began to hammer.

Kevin stopped. "What about her sister?" Kevin asked.

"Nothing," said Caroline irritably.

"Caroline," he demanded. "What did you mean by that?"

"Look, I know you thought Greta was a real saint, Kevin. But she wasn't. Okay? She snooped in our things. While she was supposedly cleaning up that flood in your study? She was going through all your papers. She read everything. She did."

Kevin kissed the baby's forehead, and checked to make sure the straps were snug. Then he came around to his wife's side. "How do you know that, Caro?" he asked.

"Because she told me," said Caroline indignantly. "She knew all about my case. She'd read every clipping and she knew all about it."

Kevin knelt down in front of Caroline with her skis. "We always knew there was a possibility people would find out."

Caroline nervously lifted up her boot. "She was planning on blackmailing us."

Kevin snapped the skis firmly onto his wife's boots. "Greta Lynch? Blackmail?" he said softly. "I'm sorry I can't picture that. Besides, we agreed that if people found out, we would live with it."

"This was different. She threatened me," Caroline complained, warming to her subject. "I never told you, but she did. She said that Vicki had a right to know who she was giving her baby to. She thought it was her duty to tell Vicki. She said I had a week to tell her or she would. Now, I call that blackmail. Don't you?"

"Not really," he said softly. "It was a kind of extortion, I suppose."

"Any court would say it was blackmail," said Caroline.

"Did she tell?" Kevin asked.

Caroline stuck her chin up in the air. "She didn't have a chance to," said Caroline. "The fire put an end to that."

"The fire."

"It was her bad luck," said Caroline.

"And her bad luck," Kevin said slowly. "That was your good luck, wasn't it?"

"Our good luck," Caroline reminded him.

He shook his head, and sighed, as if he finally understood. "I remember now," he said. "Something woke me up that night. I thought it was a bad dream. But it was you, wasn't it? Getting back into bed."

"Don't look at me like that, Kevin," Caroline pleaded. "Please, I had to act quickly."

Kevin shook his head. "Don't you understand. I can't just ignore it. Caro . . ."

Caroline glanced over at Britt again. "I don't want to talk about this. What are we going to do with her?"

"We'll leave her," he said.

"I don't think that's wise, Kevin," said Caroline. She picked up her poles and shook out each leg. "Someone might find her."

"No one knows she's here. It's frigid," said Kevin. "She won't last the night."

"She's all tied up like that. They're going to know it wasn't an accident when they do find her."

"What difference does it make?" he asked, hopelessness in his voice.

"It makes a lot of difference," said Caroline. "If you untie her, and throw her down into the ravine as well, if they ever find her, then it will seem like she fell, too . . . I mean, she saw you send the car down into the ravine. She knows what you did."

Kevin turned and stared at her. "What I did?" he said.

Caroline shrugged. "Well . . ."

"Yes," he said. "What I did. That's right. I sent the car into the ravine. But who killed them? How many people have you killed, Caroline?"

Caroline's mouth dropped open. "I can't believe that's coming from you. It wasn't my fault. You're the one who told me that. Now, you're trying to change your mind. You told me that when you became my attorney, when Tim died. It was post-traumatic stress disorder. I'd never even heard of such a thing until I met you. You said none of it was my fault. And then you went into court and you proved it."

"I know," he said.

"So," said Caroline. "It's too late to change your mind. You can't just turn around now and say you didn't mean it. You proved I was innocent."

"So I did," he said.

CHAPTER 43

Zoe clambered up through the blackened struts and reached for the bouquet of flowers resting on the tiles.

"Zoe, be careful. For God's sake," Alec scolded, coming around the side of the house, not quickly enough to prevent her sealing the cinder blocks of the basement.

"I was right," she crowed, holding up the bouquet and waving it aloft like a jockey in the winner's circle.

"Give me that. Come down from there," Alec insisted.

Zoe climbed down, her face, her jeans and her pink jacket smeared with soot. She handed the bouquet to her father, who held it, blooms down, like a club, and stared at the remains of his home.

"So, she was here," he said.

"Yeah," said Zoe.

Alec held up the flowers and frowned at them. The blooms were already stiff and lifeless from being left out in the cold. "Beautiful," he said. Then he tossed them gently back onto the rubble.

"Now what?" Zoe said.

Alec shook his head. "I have no idea." He studied the snow-covered field in the cold, bright moonlight. "I guess we could go over and ask the Carmichaels. Maybe she stopped to say good-bye."

Zoe shrugged. "Okay. You want to walk over?"

"No, take the car," he said. "I'm just gonna look in the barn."

"I'll beat you over there," she said. She began to run, her hair lifting off her shoulders, her jacket flapping around her.

Alec smiled at the sight of her. *You probably will*, he thought. He walked back through the trampled snow to the door of the barn. It seemed a little strange that there should be so many tire marks in the yard, but the workmen had been cleaning up the site for days. He hadn't paid much attention to what they were doing out here. In a way, he didn't want to know about it. He opened the door of the barn and looked in. Moonlight filtered in the windows, illuminating the empty space. "Britt," he called out. But there was no answer. *Not here*, he thought. Not that he expected her to be. Everything was gone.

Alec closed the barn door and walked back to his car, past the skeleton of his home. All that remained of the haven that he and Greta had made. Gone. Happy memories flooded his heart, with bitter ones hard on their heels. *Why did it matter so much about your mother?* he thought. *Why weren't Zoe and I enough?* He knew no answer would ever be forthcoming. That question would torment him to his grave. He sighed, and got into the Mercedes. By the time he drove the short distance down to the Carmichaels' driveway, and rolled up to the house, Zoe was already standing on the front steps.

"Nobody's home," she called out, as he got out of the car and started toward her.

"Both their cars are here," he said.

"I know," said Zoe. Alec walked up the steps and joined her. He pressed his face to the door lights and tried to look inside, but the house was dark and clearly empty.

"Well, she's not here," he said.

"What'll we do now?" said Zoe.

"I don't know," said Alec with a sigh. "I guess we'd better go back."

"Aww, Dad," Zoe pleaded.

"Honey, I don't know where else to look."

"You want to wait until they get home?" Zoe suggested.

"Are you kidding? It's freezing out here. We'll call them later. Ask them if they saw her."

"But Dad, we can't just stop looking."

"I'll try calling her apartment again," he said. He took out his cell phone and consulted the list of numbers. He dialed Britt's number, but all he heard was the voice on the machine and the click of messages. He signaled to Zoe that there was nothing new.

Sighing, Zoe began to descend the steps. She walked over to the car, starting to get inside, when suddenly, something caught her eye and she began to walk down the driveway.

"Zoe," Alec called as he punched in another number. "Don't go far. Yeah, can I speak to Mrs. Lonergan?" Alec waited while he was transferred to Nancy's extension.

"Nancy Lonergan."

"It's Alec Lynch. I just wondered if you'd heard anything from Britt?"

"No, I haven't," said Nancy. "I was hoping you might have some news."

"Nothing," said Alec.

"I'm really a little bit worried," said Nancy.

"It's probably nothing," said Alec, but the downturn in his voice belied his offhandedness.

"I'm going to keep calling her," said Nancy.

"Well, we're going to head home," said Alec. "If you hear anything . . ."

"I'll let you know."

Alec punched the off button and went down the steps to his car. "Zoe," he called out. He could see her down the driveway, her blond hair and pink parka visible even in the darkness.

Zoe stood and came walking toward him up the driveway.

"Come on, honey," he said. "Let's get you home."

Zoe's face was a pale triangle, with dark hollows around her eyes. "Dad," she said in a hushed voice. "Kirby's here."

"Who the hell is Kirby?" said Alec, opening the door to the Mercedes. "Go on. Get in, Zoe. I'm freezing out here."

"Vicki's cat," Zoe said, glued to the spot where she stood.

"Is that the cat you were minding when they went away?"

Zoe nodded.

Alec sighed. "Look honey, when we get someplace permanent to live, you can have a cat of your own. But until then . . ."

"Dad," Zoe wailed, amazed at his obtuseness.

"What?"

"Vicki wouldn't leave him behind."

"Maybe she's still here," said Alec absently.

"Mr. Carmichael said she left."

"Well, honey, any woman who would leave her baby behind probably wouldn't have too much trouble leaving a cat."

"No," said Zoe, stamping her foot. "She wouldn't leave him. She wouldn't."

Alec stared at her, exasperated. "All right. All right. Whatever you say. Let's just chalk it up to inexplicable things in the universe, and go home."

"Is that what we're doing about Aunt Britt, too?" Zoe demanded ruefully.

Alec shook his head, and climbed into the front seat of the car. Zoe remained standing outside the car on the passenger side. Alec tapped on the horn. "Zoe," he said in a stern voice.

Zoe bent down and stuck her head into the car. "Dad, look." She pointed through the windshield.

Alec looked to see where she was pointing. At first, he didn't see it. Then, as he squinted, he saw movement in the trees behind the house, and two bulky figures, bundled up and wearing skis, gliding slowly out of the woods and into the backyard. One of the skiers was bending low, as if winded, and moving with obvious difficulty. Alec got out of the car.

The two figures halted at the sight of Alec and Zoe. Then Alec heard the pitiful squall of an infant and realized that one of the skiers was carrying a pack on her back from where the sound was emanating.

"Kevin?" he called out. "Caroline?"

Kevin and Caroline stood still in the yard.

He began to walk toward them. They looked at one another. Then Kevin called out, in a weak voice, "Alec."

"What the hell are you two doing," said Alec. "You went skiing?"

"Cross-country skiing. Just to get out of the house. Get a little exercise," said Kevin, trying to sound cheerful. But there was an unmistakable feebleness in his voice.

Alec approached the spot where they stood. "In the dark?"

"It's a beautiful night," said Caroline.

"Kevin, are you supposed to be doing that?" Alec asked. "With those ribs of yours?" He didn't mention how bizarre a decision it seemed to him to take a newborn out on a night this cold. These exercise nuts were all alike. They always overdid it.

"I'm okay," said Kevin dismissively. "What brings you here?"

"Do you want to talk inside?" asked Alec. "You look beat."

"No, no. I'm fine. But if you just came for a visit, maybe tomorrow would be better. Caro's got to get the baby down . . ."

"Oh, no. It's not . . . this isn't a visit. Uh, we were looking for my sister-in-law. Britt. She didn't get on her flight home today. Apparently, she came over to uh . . . our old place . . . to leave some flowers for Greta and . . . that's the last anybody's seen of her."

Kevin and Caroline stared at him.

"We wondered if she stopped by here maybe."

"Why would she stop by here?" said Caroline.

"Oh, I don't know. To say good-bye. I'm guessing."

"No," said Caroline. "She wasn't here. Was she, Kevin?"

Kevin held his side, and shook his head. "No, haven't seen her."

"Okay," said Alec. "Well, thanks."

"Why is Kirby here?" Zoe demanded.

"Don't speak to me in that tone," said Caroline angrily.

"Caro, please," Kevin whispered.

"She just left him behind," said Caroline, recovering her composure.

"She wouldn't," Zoe protested.

The baby began to wail again. "Well, she did. I have to go in," said Caroline. "You can take the cat if you want him, Zoe."

"Maybe when we get settled somewhere," said Alec. "We can barely manage ourselves right now. Look, we need to go. Come on, Zoe."

Caroline glided to the back steps and freed the skis from her boots. She started up the steps. "Kevin, come on. You have to help me with this baby carrier."

Kevin turned to Alec. "Sorry we couldn't help you."

Even in the moonlight, Alec could see the beads of sweat on Kevin's forehead. "Kevin, let me help Caroline with the baby carrier. You look like you're hurting," said Alec.

"I'm fine," Kevin snapped. He began to make his way slowly toward the door.

"Kevin, the baby," Caroline called from inside the house.

"I'll do it," said Alec, clapping Kevin gently on the shoulder and walking past him to the porch steps. "That's the least I can do. Come on. You saved my little girl."

"Leave it," Kevin cried, forcing himself to go faster.

"We won't stay," said Alec.

"NO," Kevin cried.

But Alec, trailed by Zoe, had already entered the house.

CHAPTER 44

"Let's just leave her here," Kevin had said to his wife. "She'll die of exposure. She'll never last the night."

"We can't take that chance," Caroline replied. "She knows everything. I'll do it if you want."

"No," said Kevin. "My God."

"Kevin, if she lives through this, she can . . ."

"She's a human being. Our son is right here with us. Do you want him to be a witness to a killing, his first days on earth?" He hesitated, as if realizing it was too late for that particular concern. "We can't just murder her in cold blood." And then he was quiet for a moment, obviously thinking of all he now knew about his wife. "I can't," he said.

"I know," said Caroline grimly. "You're not being much help."

"Stop it," said Kevin, grabbing her by the shoulders. "Don't do this. I can't stand much more of this. There's so little left as it is."

"So little of what?" said Caroline. Kevin let her go, and turned away.

"Never mind," he said.

"All right," Caroline said. "All right. But if we leave her like this, tied up and gagged, they'll know when they find her that it was no accident."

"Then let's untie her," he said.

"Are you kidding? All she has to do is make her way back along this trail to the logging road and somebody could see her and pick her up," Caroline protested.

"Who'd be driving up here at this time of night?" he cried.

Caroline shook her head. "Oh no. She might last till morning. By then there will be skiers and snowmobilers up here. Too risky."

Kevin shook his head in despair.

Caroline looked around and then began to nod. "I know," she said.

"What?" Kevin asked.

"How about a compromise? We untie her, but we roll her down the slope. She won't stop rolling until she hits a tree, and then she'll land in the tree well," she said.

Tree well, Britt thought. Alec had said something about tree wells when they were out on the snowmobile. Some danger . . .

"She'll never be able to climb out of it and get back up the hill," said Caroline cheerfully.

"She's not gonna roll down the hill in that long woolen coat. She'd go about two feet," Kevin scoffed.

"Ah," said Caroline. "Here's the good part. We take off her coat, and any sweater she's wearing. Plus her gloves. Her boots."

"Right," said Kevin sarcastically. "That won't look suspicious when they find her. I mean, doesn't everybody take their clothes off in twenty-degree weather?"

"Actually," said Caroline. "The answer to that is yes."

Kevin frowned at her, curious in spite of himself.

"It's well documented. When they find the bodies of hikers who have died of hypothermia, they are often mostly undressed. I read about it somewhere. The experts think that when a person is freezing to death, there's some kind of burst of heat in the body, just before death. And, of course, people are delirious by that time. They tear off their clothes."

"Really?" said Kevin.

Caroline nodded. "Shall we? I'm sure she'll roll just fine without her clothes. And she'll never last the night that way."

Britt stared at Caroline, who was deciding her fate with all the emotion one might accord to a potted plant. Caroline turned her back to Kevin. "Get the carrier off me," she said. "I can't do it with this on me."

As if he were dragging chains, Kevin trudged over to her and removed the carrier from Caroline's back. He placed it on the ground. Caroline crouched down beside Britt who was still kneeling on the packed snow. "Okay," she said. "First gloves, and then we'll get the boots off."

Caroline shoved Britt over on her side, and yanked her gloves down from her wrists. Britt clenched her fists, trying to resist, but Caroline stomped on her fingers, and Britt released her fists in agony. Then, Caroline crouched down and unzipped the leather boots Britt was wearing. One after the other, she tossed them down the slope. "Now the socks," she said.

Britt curled her toes against the assault, but Caroline pulled off her heavy socks with a couple of tugs, and tossed those away also. Britt's bare feet sank into the snow, and the cold shot up through her, making her head ache.

"Now," said Caroline, pushing the tweed coat down off Britt's shoulders. "I'm going to pull this down. When we cut her hands loose, yank it off her and toss it away. Kevin, you've got to help me. She's probably going to fight like a little demon."

Kevin walked over and squatted down, groaning.

"Have you got your knife?" Caroline asked.

"Yes," Kevin said.

Britt knew she was helpless, but she stared at Kevin. If he was going to kill her, she was not going to make it easier for him by closing her eyes. He was going to have to look in her eyes and acknowledge what he was doing. And then, when he cut her loose, she was going to claw those eyes out of his head if she could.

"When I say three," Caroline ordered, "cut the hands, but keep the feet bound. She can't get away with her feet bound. Leave the duet tape for last. Ready? One, two, three."

Britt felt a tugging at her wrists. In the next moment, her arms were free and she felt relief mixed with agony as they were released and separated. In the next instant, her coat was ripped from her back. She thrashed wildly, trying to punch and claw at them, but Kevin and Caroline had redoubled their grasp on her. Britt fought back, but the two of them struggled to hold her down. Caroline was trying to force her turtleneck up and over her head but Britt twisted away from her.

"That's it," said Kevin. "Let her go. That's all we can do."

"Oh, all right," said Caroline. "Cut her feet and roll her." She let go of the sweater and grabbed the corner of the duct tape on Britt's mouth. She ripped it off in one searing tear, and Kevin cut Britt's bare feet free.

Britt cursed, and kicked out, landing a blow on Kevin, who fell back on his heels. She tried to scramble away, but they were on her in an instant. Awkwardly lifting her thrashing, protesting body by the upper arms and ankles, they dragged her to the edge of the trail.

"Now," Caroline cried. "Lift her up and then we'll drop her." They swung and released her, and Britt felt herself sailing a short way down through the air, and then bouncing on the icy slope and starting to roll. She clawed at the snow with her bare hands and feet, rolling helplessly until she suddenly landed against a tree with a jarring thud that reverberated through her frame. *I'm safe*, she thought. *I'm free*. And for a moment her heart lifted. Then she tried to get up. The snow beneath the tree was soft and light and deep. She struggled, but could not get to her feet. Instead, she sank farther.

She kicked and clawed at it frantically, but it was like sinking into a pool of mercury. The tree well. Banked by the tree's trunk, and untrodden by any vehicles or creatures, the snow of a dozen snowfalls had accumulated in a hill of snow. Panic gripped Britt, making it hard for her to breathe.

"Let's go," said Caroline.

By the moonlight, at the top of the slope, Britt could see Kevin reattaching the baby carrier to Caroline's back. He stuffed the pieces of rope into the carrier, under the baby's blanket. Caroline stuck the toes of her touring boots into the pinholes of the lightweight skis and began to glide off on one of the cross-country trails through the woods.

"Come on," she called out to Kevin.

Kevin sighed heavily and turned around. He looked down the hill and met Britt's gaze.

Britt gasped for breath. "Help me, Kevin," she pleaded. "Don't leave me here."

He shook his head. "I can't," he said. He hesitated as if he wanted to say more but then he averted his eyes.

"Don't leave me here. Please. Help me."

He looked around the clearing, and found a tree limb on the ground. Walking over to the edge of the packed snow, he tossed it down to her. "I have to go," he said.

"How can you do this . . .?" Britt pleaded. "You're not evil."

Kevin laughed, but his eyes were tragic. He rose up to his feet, and pushed his boots into the skis. "Yes, I am," he said. "I just didn't know it." Then, he turned, and, stabbing the snow with his poles, glided off into the dark woods.

She watched him leave with disbelief, despair. How could he leave her here like that? It was inhuman. The quiet of the night was absolute, except for the whistle of the wind. Her feet were already numb. Her fingers were dead. She could no longer feel them. Her face was numb. Her upper arms ached from being pulled back so far, for so long. At least there was still sensation in them. She knew the night had not reached its coldest temperature yet. How long could a person survive in these conditions?

She'd heard of hypothermia. She'd just never imagined that that was how she was going to die. Hypothermia was for people who liked to go spelunking or mountain climbing for amusement. She'd never attempted any of those activities. She didn't even have a hobby. She liked going to Cape Cod in the summer, and swimming in the ocean, in August, when it warmed up a little bit. She liked sitting home, and reading. She started to imagine herself on a porch glider, on a warm day, drowsy over a book, and before she knew it, her eyelids were drooping, and the torpor of sleep was overtaking her.

Then, just before she fell into the insensible, deadly bliss of sleep in the freezing cold and the snow, she became vaguely aware of what was happening to her. *Wake up*, she thought. *Because if you fall asleep here, you may never wake up. It won't do you a damn bit of good to have been left alive.*

She thought about the last exchange between Caroline and Kevin. Obviously he had known she was a killer when he married her. All that talk of the first time she had been on trial. But now. Not only had she murdered Vicki and Dave. But Greta. The fire. She had set the fire to kill Greta and keep her secret from Vicki. In a way, that knowledge made Britt feel a small bit better. Just to know that Greta had not set the fire to kill herself. That she had not made any such decision to take Zoe with her.

But what, she thought, trying to rouse herself from the stupor which threatened her, *what did it matter anyway?* She had to stop thinking. Her only thought now had to be how to stay alive. That was all that should matter to her now. If she could make it back alive, she could tell Alec that it hadn't been Greta. She could imagine his relief when he learned how wrong he had been. *Stop it*, she thought. *Get out. Nothing else matters.*

Britt reached out across the fluffy snow, feeling herself sink down with every movement. She remembered reading once that if you were in quicksand, you should try to lie out lengthwise, like a swimmer. *Maybe it would work for snow as well*, she thought. She stopped trying to stand up but simply tried to lie flat and wriggle over the snow's surface, as if she were in the water. *Last chance*, she kept saying to herself. *Only hope.* Weakened by pain, it seemed as if she couldn't force herself to continue, and a despairing thought swept over her. *What kind of life is this that you have made? No one cares if you live or die*, she thought. *No one is waiting for you, wondering what became of you. What does it matter to anyone? Who would mourn you?*

And then she thought of Zoe. You love her, Alec had said. And Zoe, in parting, had said, "Love you." Hating herself now for her own weakness Britt tried to snuff out the flicker of that memory. *Zoe hardly knows you. She won't miss you. She won't even think of you.* But, Zoe's little flame would not be stamped out so easily. *How do you know that?* Britt thought. *How do you know she won't miss you?* The memory of Zoe's good, little face spurred her on, despite the threatening tide of cynicism in her heart.

After what seemed like an hour of inching along, nearly paralyzed by the cold, she managed to get far enough from the tree to touch the ground when she lowered her numbed foot into the snow. Now she grabbed the tree branch that Kevin had thrown her, and used it like a walking stick, jamming it into the snow ahead of her and trudging up toward the trail, her lungs burning in her chest. Finally, when she felt as if her legs could push her no farther, she groped out and felt the slick, hard surface of the groomed trail down which Kevin and Caroline had disappeared. *Oh, thank you God*, Britt thought. *Thank you.* With one last, massive effort, Britt crawled onto the trail like it was the deck of a ship in the midst of the ocean and collapsed, hugging the ground. After a few minutes she dragged herself up into a sitting position, and folded her arms over her waist. She bent down over them, embracing herself, and tears came to her eyes. She rocked for a moment, enjoying the blessed warmth of her forearms over her stomach. *I'm going to live*, she thought, and realized that she had never, until that very moment, really appreciated the simple fact of being alive.

Okay, okay. She couldn't afford to exult. She was still in the middle of nowhere in the depths of a snowy woods. And the pain in her head, which seemed to be increasing by the minute, was making it difficult to think. *What now*, she thought. *What do I do now?* She put her hands to her head and pressed down, as if that would somehow stop the pain. *Think. Think*. And then, soothing and uplifting, the realization came to her. *Ah*, she thought. *I may be in the middle of nowhere, but I am not helpless. My phone*. And then she realized. It had been in her coat pocket. And her coat was somewhere on that mountain slope in the dark. She couldn't risk going backward. Easier to get up, even in bare feet, and follow the trail back to the road they took up here. To try to find her way out. For a moment, despair threatened to overcome her again, but she fended it off. No time for that.

She had to find her way out of here. While she rubbed her numbed extremities, she looked around the desolate spot where she had been dumped, and tried to think how she was going to get to her feet. Her eyes were blurry, and she had only the moonlight to see by. A movement caught her attention out of the corner of her eye, but when she turned to look, her head began to pound unmercifully, and she saw nothing there. The sleepiness was coming over her again, like a soft voice urging her to take a little nap before she tried to go any farther.

No, she warned herself. *You'll die out here. You have to get back*. She didn't know how far they had traveled to get up here. But she was on a trail which meant that people would come through these woods during the day. And if they had managed to find a way for the car to get to this spot, it couldn't be far to the road. *All she needed to do*, she told herself, *was follow the tire tracks in the snow, and they would lead her back*.

Okay, she thought. *Steady now. Stand up*. Using her branch as a kind of crutch, she forced herself up onto her feet. Although she was finally upright, her aching head began to spin and, for a moment, she thought she might pass out again. She waited out the dizziness.

All right, she thought. *Keep your wits. The worst is over. You're going to be safe now. Push off and get moving.* She placed one wobbly leg out in front of her, and then followed it with the other. She took two steps and her knees gave way. She fell down into the snow again, landing on the ground on all fours. *Like an animal,* she thought. *Maybe I can crawl.* Slowly, she began to move her hands and knees.

You'll be sorry, she thought, picturing Kevin and Caroline in her mind. *You'll be sorry you didn't kill me.* In the moonlight, the snow sparkled and beckoned. *I'm coming,* she thought. Her head was throbbing and she closed her eyes telling herself that she didn't need to see to crawl. *You'll be sorry. You'll pay for what you've done.*

And at that moment, she heard, through the whistling of the night wind, a voice she knew calling her name. She could see the face in her mind's eye, coldly critical of this situation she was in. Britt lifted her head and looked around. "Mother?" she said aloud in confusion. There was something wrong with her vision. She looked down and saw black pools widening on the trail.

* * *

The kitchen was lit by only the light over the stove and a lamp which was affixed to the breakfast counter. Caroline was standing in the kitchen, her back to Alec as he came through the door. The room was in disarray. The hooked rug under the table was bunched up and an address book lay open on the floor, its assortment of business cards scattered about. A plant in a terra-cotta flowerpot had tumbled to the ground off the counter and broken as well. There was dirt scattered about on the normally pristine floor.

"Get him off me, Kevin," Caroline said.

Alec walked up to her and began to unhook the baby carrier from her back, surprised that she had not remarked on the mess. "What happened in here?" he said.

"What are you doing here?" Caroline cried. "I thought you left."

Alec lifted the carrier off her back. He looked at the baby facing him, bundled in a little snowsuit, his face red and wizened. There was a patch of white on the baby's nose. "Jesus, Caroline, I think this kid has frostbite. What were you thinking?"

Hurriedly, without turning to face him, Caroline slipped out of her parka and turned it inside out, dropping it on one of the chairs around the antique oak kitchen table. The jacket immediately slid off the chair to the floor.

"Zoe, get that for Mrs. Carmichael," said Alec. "I've got my hands full here." He set the baby carrier on the counter, while Zoe walked over to the chair and stooped down to pick up the coat on the floor.

"Just leave it," Caroline cried, and Zoe, startled, dropped the coat as if it were hot.

"But there's a . . ."

"I said leave it,'" Caroline insisted.

Alec looked at her with narrowed eyes. "I told her to pick it up. She was just trying to help," he said.

"We don't need any help," said Caroline. "Give me my baby."

"Fine," said Alec. He stepped back from the carrier as Caroline lifted the infant out of the seat. As the baby came out the seat, there was a rope dangling from his bootied foot. Alec reached out and pulled the rope away from the baby's foot. "What's this?"

At that moment Kevin, who had shed his parka on the porch, appeared in the doorway of the kitchen. His face was pale and strained, but he attempted to smile.

"What happened in your kitchen?" Alec asked.

"I'm taking him upstairs," Caroline said to her husband.

"Okay, hon." He turned to their visitors. "Sorry. It was that damn cat of Vicki's. Got into the house and started knocking things over before we left."

"And you just left it like this?" Alec asked.

"Caroline's distracted with the new baby and all. And I'm not much help with these ribs." Kevin rubbed his side and grimaced.

"I still don't understand what sent you out skiing in the pitch darkness. Is everything all right with you, Kevin?"

"I'm exhausted. We both are. Little Kent hasn't been sleeping. We thought the fresh air would help," said Kevin apologetically.

"I think you overdid it," said Alec. "All right, well. I'd offer to help but . . . obviously . . . Zoe, come on."

Kevin looked relieved. "Thanks Alec, really."

At that moment, they all heard the distinctive ringing of a cell phone. Caroline turned around in the doorway and looked back with wide eyes at Kevin.

"Must be mine," said Kevin anxiously. "Maybe I left it in my coat. Oh well, they'll call back."

"No," said Zoe, stooping down again. "It's here, under the table. I just saw it when I went to pick up the parka. That's what I was trying to tell you. Here." She straightened up and held up the phone. Kevin and Caroline both looked at it as if it were a ticking bomb. Zoe pushed the button and held the phone to her ear. "Carmichael residence," she said politely.

"Britt?" said a confused-sounding voice. "Is that you?"

CHAPTER 45

Zoe held the phone out to her father. "It's somebody calling Aunt Britt," she said.

Alec looked from Kevin to Caroline. Kevin averted his eyes. Alec took the phone and put it to his ear. "This is Alec Lynch. Who is this?" he demanded.

"Oh, Alec," said a voice in surprise. "This is Nancy . . . Lonergan again. You've found Britt, I take it."

"What?" he asked.

"Well, this is her number. Or did you just find the phone? Did she leave it at your house?"

Alec held the phone away from his ear and looked at it. Then he held it to his ear and said, "Nancy, I have to call you back." He punched the off button and looked up at the Carmichaels.

"I thought you said that my sister-in-law wasn't here today. Do you want to tell me why you have her cell phone under your kitchen table?"

"Well . . ." said Kevin.

"You said she wasn't here. But she was here, wasn't she? Something happened here."

"It was nothing," said Caroline.

"What was nothing?" said Alec.

Caroline looked to her husband. "Kevin . . .?"

"I don't know," said Kevin. "She was here yesterday. She must have dropped it while she was visiting."

"She had it this morning," said Zoe.

Kevin scratched his head in an exaggerated effort to look perplexed. "Maybe she came in here to leave a note or something and while she was bending over the table . . ."

Alec raised the phone and brandished it. "I don't believe you. Something happened here. Now are you going to tell me, or do I have to call the police?"

"Stop him, Kevin," Caroline cried.

"Alec, put the phone down," said Kevin. "This is just a misunderstanding."

Alec was fingering the buttons on the phone.

"Kevin, don't let him do this," Caroline cried.

"For God's sake," said Kevin. "Can't we talk about this? Can't you give us the benefit of the doubt?"

Alec stared into Kevin's feverish gaze. "I'm never giving anyone the benefit of the doubt. Not anymore." He punched in a number and held the phone to his ear. "Yes, can you connect me with the Coleville police?"

Caroline set the baby down in the carrier, walked over to the knife block on the counter, and pulled out a carving knife. In two steps, she was behind Zoe. She grabbed her roughly and held the knife to her neck. "Put that phone down," she said.

Zoe let out a cry, but stopped abruptly as she felt the point of the knife at her throat.

Alec pressed the off button and lowered the phone. "Let go of her," he said.

"Caro, for God's sake," Kevin cried.

"Don't you start," she said to Kevin. "I'm not listening to you. You were supposed to protect us."

"All right," said Alec, holding up his hands as if to show her they were empty. "All right. Just calm down and let go of Zoe. I promise you. I'll leave here and I won't ask any more questions."

"I don't believe you," said Caroline. "You've already called the cops. They can trace those 911 calls to the address."

"Caro, it's a cell phone," said Kevin. "They can't trace that. Think. Stop being hysterical."

"They can't?" she said.

"No," said Kevin. "They have no idea . . ."

"Yes, but if I let her go," she said, pointing at Zoe with the tip of the blade, "then he'll call them and it'll all start."

"What will all start?" asked Alec. He was studying her, taking her measure with his steely gray eyes. Thinking about what he knew from Nancy Lonergan. Caroline had killed a man. She had everything to lose. This was no idle threat.

"They're never going to leave us alone," Caroline cried. "Just like it was before . . . in Boston. You know. They'll start asking all kinds of questions."

Alec hesitated, and then the expression on his face relaxed. "Hey," said Alec. "You know what? I don't blame you for not wanting to be pestered. The cops can be a nuisance. Who knows that better than me? You let Zoe go and I promise you, that's the last you'll hear about it. If you and my sister-in-law had a little tussle over something, it doesn't matter to me. Really. She did her best to send me to prison while she was here. I'm glad she's gone. I was only looking for her because Zoe wanted me to. Britt is nothing to me. The only thing I care about is Zoe. You can understand that, Caroline. You have a child now. You know what it's like. Nothing else matters but that child."

"That's right," said Caroline, in a shaky voice.

"Here," said Alec. He tossed Britt's cell phone down on the kitchen floor. It skittered along until it collided with a chair leg and then the cap of the battery case flew off and the battery bounced out. "I don't care how it got here. Just give me Zoe back and we'll leave you in peace."

Caroline shifted her stance behind Zoe, but kept the knife at her throat. "How do I know you mean it?" she asked, uncertain.

"Look, you don't know what it's been like for me, having to put up with my sister-in-law. She was a pain in the ass from the minute she got here. You know about that, right?"

Caroline nodded uncertainly. "I know she had it in for you."

"Right," said Alec. "So, whatever arguments you may have with her are all perfectly understandable to me. And, they're none of my business. Zoe wanted me to try and find her, so we came looking. That's all. Now listen, I'm not going to risk one minute of my child's life for her sake. She was a nosy, pushy woman."

"That's what I told Kevin. It wasn't our fault that she came butting into our business," said Caroline.

"Exactly," said Alec.

"Nothing really happened," said Caroline. "She's fine, you know."

Alec shrugged. "Screw her. I don't really care. Just let go of my baby. Caroline, I will not pursue this. You have my word. Just give me Zoe back."

"She is fine. Britt. She's perfectly fine. Right, Kevin? There was nothing wrong with her when we left her," said Caroline.

Alec shook his head. "Hey, it's none of my concern. Zoe, this will teach you not to meddle in other people's business."

Zoe stared at him in horror and disbelief.

Caroline gazed at him with narrowed eyes. "That's fine for you to say that you'll leave us alone. What about Zoe? The minute I let her go she's gonna want to go running to some policeman."

"Zoe," Alec barked. "Tell Mrs. Carmichael you're sorry."

"No," Zoe retorted. She closed her eyes and raised her chin, as if to say that she wanted nothing further to do with him. She was rigid in Caroline's deadly embrace.

"Now you listen to me, little lady," said Alec through clenched teeth. "You will not defy my orders. When I tell you to do something, I expect you to do it. Now tell Mrs. Carmichael you're sorry, and that you will keep your mouth shut. Do it this minute."

Zoe opened her eyes and glared at her father. Alec returned her gaze without a hint of sympathy or complicity.

"Did you hear me?" he demanded.

"Yes," she muttered bitterly.

"Well, do it then. Tell her you're sorry. And that you won't bother her anymore."

After a long minute, Zoe looked at the ground. "Sorry . . ." she spat out.

Caroline tightened her hold. "You're just saying that because he told you to . . ."

"That's right. And she knows better than to disobey me," said Alec.

Caroline looked questioningly at Kevin. His face was pasty, his eyes frantic as he met her gaze. "Kevin, what do you think?" she asked.

Kevin swallowed hard. His fists were clenched, and there was sweat on his forehead. He stared at his wife with longing, as if she were on a boat, sailing away from him. As if he wanted to cry out, "Don't leave me. Don't go."

"Kevin?"

"Let her go, darling. It'll be all right. You . . . you haven't done anything wrong."

"I haven't, have I?" she said.

Kevin shook his head, and there were tears in his eyes. "No."

Caroline hesitated for a moment, and then heaved a sigh. Reluctantly, she released Zoe. Zoe did not run to her father, but stood there staring at Alec as if he were a stranger.

Alec did not move toward Zoe, but stayed where he was. Caroline sighed again, and then walked over to the counter and replaced the knife in the block.

The infant in the carrier began to cry. Caroline went to him and picked him up, rubbing his back and trying to soothe him.

Alec looked at Kevin. "May we go?" he asked politely.

Kevin's gaze was tragic. He nodded without speaking. Then, silently, he went to his wife and baby and put his arms around them. "We have to put our son to bed," he said.

Alec turned to his daughter. "Zoe. Come on. We're leaving."

Without a word, Zoe turned her back on him and stormed out the back door.

Alec looked at Kevin. "Thank you, Kevin," he said.

Kevin put a finger to his lips as if to say, hush.

Alec headed for the door, forcing himself not to run.

CHAPTER 46

He heard the car door slam in the cold night air. By the time he reached the Mercedes, Zoe was already sitting in the front seat, her arms folded over her chest. She kept her face turned away from him as he got into the driver's seat, and looked at her own reflection in the side window with a stony gaze.

Alec turned on the engine, and started to back out of the driveway. "Zoe," he said. "Use the cell phone. Dial 911."

Zoe turned from the window and stared at her father.

"Do it," he said. "Hurry. There's no time to lose."

"I thought . . ." she said.

"We may already be too late," he said.

Zoe's eyes widened. "You didn't mean it?" she said. "About Aunt Britt?"

"Zoe, I said hurry. And hand me the phone."

Zoe picked up the phone and punched in the number with trembling fingers.

Alec made a gimme gesture by wiggling his fingers. Zoe handed him the phone, and looked out the window again as the night sped by. She could hear him talking to the police, telling them what had happened, and how they needed to send someone out to the Carmichaels, and start a search for Aunt Britt. Her heart, so battered lately, lifted at the steady murmur of his voice. She was still fearful, but now her dad was in charge. She had faith in him, like in nobody else in the world. Even when she was so mad at him, she still believed. He would always protect her. No matter what, it would be all right.

"Okay," he was saying. "I've got a fleet of them we can use. I'm on my way to the dealership. Right. I'll meet you there." Alec frowned and handed the phone to Zoe. "Hang this up, honey," he said.

Zoe took the phone and replaced it in its cradle. "What's happened to Aunt Britt?" she asked.

"I don't know," he said. "There was some kind of a struggle. I'm afraid she may be hurt. They took her somewhere up on the mountain. Probably in her car and left it up there. That's what I figure. Then they must have come back cross-country on those skis."

"Why Dad?" Zoe cried. "Why would they want to hurt Aunt Britt?"

"I don't know why. There's a lot I don't know right now. Something bad has happened in that household. We'll worry about that later. Right now, we just have to find her."

"You mean the police?"

"The police are gonna start a search. The chief is getting some people together. We'll take the snowmobiles out. I think Mr. Carmichael will be willing to tell the police exactly where to look. To save time. To save himself," he added.

"I wish we could find her," said Zoe wistfully.

Alec did not respond.

"How come you said all those things about Aunt Britt, Dad?" she asked. "I believed you in there."

"You were supposed to," he said. "I was making a sale. I needed your help."

"I don't get it. What were you selling?"

"I was selling Mrs. Carmichael on the idea that I didn't care what happened to Aunt Britt. She had to believe that, so she would let you go."

"I almost ruined it," she said.

"Oh no," he said, shaking his head. "You did exactly the right thing. I knew I could count on you."

Zoe frowned, but she felt a little thrill of pride at his confidence in her. "Where are we going now?" she asked.

"To the dealership," he said. "To get a machine."

"Is Aunt Britt gonna die?" Zoe asked.

"No," he said.

* * *

Sprawled facedown in the snow, the front of her body unaccountably warm, Britt was watching her mother. Jean Andersen was standing at the edge of the ravine where Vicki's car had tumbled. And she was holding something in her arms. Britt strained to see what it was. It was difficult to tell in the moonlight. Jean was wearing the same clothes she wore in the video, and Britt was worried about her, being out here without a coat on. She could die of the cold. She tried to call out to warn her, but her mother ignored her. She seemed oblivious to the cold. She held the bundle in her arms and gazed over the edge of the ravine, straining her neck to look.

Don't get so close to that, Britt wanted to say. *If you fall in there, you'll disappear and I'll never see you again.* As if she had heard Britt's voice, Jean turned around and looked at her. Her eyes were invisible. Britt could only see the glitter of her glasses. After a moment, Jean looked down at the bundle in her arms again, and Britt imagined that her gaze was tender. And then Britt heard it. It was a faint, pitiful whine, that sounded like a feeble protest. Britt's heart leaped. *My God, it's a child in there. Mother,* she tried to call out. *There's a child in that bundle. Listen.*

The whine continued, high-pitched and growing louder. Jean began to seem agitated by it. She walked back and forth across the ridge, shaking the bundle impatiently. Nothing she did was any use. The child continued to cry, its wails growing louder. Britt saw a stillness come over her mother and she knew that her mother was about to do something. Something wrong. *No,* Britt called out to her. *Don't do it.* But it was no use. Her mother could not even hear her now. With one last look at the child inside, she tossed the bundle over the edge of the ravine and watched it fall.

"NO," Britt shouted, and suddenly she was awake, and in the real world, her face in the snow, her body splayed out, her head pounding. *Oh my God,* she thought. *How long have I been here?* And then she realized that loud, wailing sound from the child in her hallucination was still sounding in her ears. She dragged herself up to her knees, and saw something bright, glowing in the trees and getting closer with every moment. And, as she looked, she could see other lights flashing on the slope of the hill, winking as they wove in and out of the trees. *Here I am,* she thought. She licked her lips and tried to find her voice.

One light was nearer than all the others. It was zigzagging through the trees, and the sound was getting louder now. Coming toward her. She didn't know what it was, but it was a roaring engine and it was nearby. Like someone stranded on a desert island, she used all the strength she had left to force herself up to her feet and begin to wave her arms.

"Help me," she cried, although she feared she could not be heard over the sound of the engine. But she could be seen. The lamp turned and barreled toward her, accompanied by a deafening roar. She was about to leap, afraid to be in its path, when the snowmobile veered around, sending up a shower of snow, and came to a halt. The rider cut off the engine and the sound dimmed, but did not die. There were other, similar engines, their muffled roars still audible on the wooded slope.

Thank God, she thought. Overcome by relief, Britt swayed, and sank down again onto her knees. She looked toward the snowmobile, blinked and thought fearfully that she might still be hallucinating. A man in a dark jacket and a helmeted child in a pink parka were climbing off the vehicle, coming toward her. The girl was running.

"Here! Up here!" Alec turned and called out, waving a flashlight which he snapped on and off in a signal through the trees. "She's up here. Hurry. We found her."

"Aunt Britt," cried Zoe, flopping down onto the snow beside her. Zoe gazed gently at her aunt, and put out a tentative hand to touch Britt's icy cheek. "You're alive. Where's your coat? And your shoes?"

Britt felt Zoe's touch, and knew it was no fantasy, no delusion. *You're here*, Britt thought. *I'm alive.*

CHAPTER 47

"You've got mail! Britt opened the E-mails on her computer and checked the latest email to arrive. It was addressed to her, via the station. "Dear Miss Andersen," it began.

I recently ran into Donovan Smith at an affiliates meeting, and learned from him that you are no longer in his employ. I had a chance to watch his show on a number of occasions while I was in Boston, and I very much admired the work you did when you were producing for him. When I heard this, I checked up on you and found out about the award you received for your coverage of the Carmichael arson and murder investigation and trial up there in Vermont. While Mrs. Carmichael is clearly a very disturbed woman, and your own sister was one of the victims of her madness, you were admirably evenhanded in your reporting. I thought you placed a much-needed focus on the problems involved in private adoptions. A job well done.

As you know, the Denver market is large, and getting larger all the time. And all our research tells us that our show is likely to go national in a very short time. I would very much like to get together and talk to you about a future for you at our show. I plan to be in your area in the next few weeks. Any possibility we could meet to talk?

Britt recognized the name of the Denver talk show host. She was a woman whom Britt admired. *It probably would be fun to work for her.* Britt thought.

"Britt," said Jeff Herrick. "We done?"

"Done," said Britt.

"All right then. I'm going to go. You've got my pager if you need me."

Britt logged off her computer, checked her tapes for tonight's newscast to make sure everything was in order, and then gathered up her things to leave. As she passed through the small, quiet WGLC newsroom, everyone she met stopped to wish her a pleasant evening. She stepped outside and immediately was greeted with the riot of color that was the fall foliage in Vermont. The sunny sky was cobalt, and the mountain air was almost dizzying in its clarity. After nearly a year in Coleville, Britt had come to love the beauty of this place with its distinct, almost excessive grandeur of mountains and trees and sky. She had never realized how much she could enjoy living in a place so dominated by nature.

The air in Denver is probably pretty good, too, she mused, as she got into her car. That's the Rockies out there. The pay would probably be great, and it was undeniably flattering to be sought out like that. The pressure would be greater, and the hours longer. She wouldn't be able to knock off early to attend junior high school hockey games. Of course, she wouldn't need to, out in Denver. Britt drove to the playing field behind the junior high school, parked the car, and walked around the bleachers.

Alec was already in place, and he caught sight of her as soon as she rounded the bleachers. "Britt!"

She looked up and waved. He patted the seat beside him and she smiled, and began the climb. She was wearing a tailored jacket on top, to look businesslike for the camera, but jeans on the bottom, and suede, tread-soled boots. Climbing was easy in that outfit. She arrived at Alec's row and sat down beside him.

"Did I miss anything?" she said.

He shook his head. "Coach is just giving them the last-minute instructions. There she is."

Britt peered out over the athletic field and saw Zoe, hair pulled back in a French braid, dressed in her field hockey uniform, warming up on the sidelines. She craned her neck and caught Zoe's eye. Zoe saw her aunt and broke into a smile. She waved. Zoe had decided to join the team once she got to junior high, and she was good enough to immediately start playing in games.

Britt settled back on the wooden bleacher and looked around. "Pretty good crowd today," she said.

"Well, Rutland is a pretty ferocious rival," said Alec. "Here, want some?"

He held out a bag of yogurt-covered pretzels and Britt raised her eyebrows. "My favorite! How did you know?" She took a pretzel and had a bite.

"How did I know?" he said, and shook his head.

"How's your day been?" she asked.

"Good," he said. "Gearing up for the season. By the way, I got a line on a horse that might do from one of my customers today."

"Wow," said Britt. "Did you tell her?"

"Not yet. We just moved into the new house. I need a minute to breathe."

"Yeah," she agreed. "But she'll be tickled."

"I thought maybe we'd drive over and take a look at it anyway. Saturday. How's that sound?"

"Good," she said. "Sounds like fun."

They sat in companionable silence for a few minutes, enjoying the air, and the fading light of the brilliant day. Finally, Britt took a deep breath. "I got a line on something today myself."

"Oh?" he said. "What's that?"

Britt looked out at the field. The game had begun and Zoe was in the thick of it. "Alec, look," she said.

"I see," he said. "So what was this 'line' on . . .?" She heard a diffident note in his voice.

"A job offer, actually. For a talk show host out in Denver. She's very good. I've seen her work. They're thinking of taking the show national and she wants to talk to me about getting on board with it."

Alec nodded, his gaze riveted to Zoe. "Are you going to talk to her?"

Britt hesitated. *Am I going to talk to her?* she wondered. *Should I consider it?* Britt looked at him. The lines in his craggy face were even deeper than they had been when she first met him. They had all been through a lot this past year. Alec and Zoe had babied her while she recovered from frostbite and head injuries, and urged her to stay on in Vermont, where they could keep an eye on her. Dean Webster had recovered also, but was fired by WGLC. The television station had been glad to hire someone with Britt's experience to replace him. Together Alec, Britt and Zoe had gone through the ordeal of the Carmichaels' trial and conviction. Caroline was sent away for life. Kevin, who testified against his wife, got only four years. The baby was adopted by another family.

They'd also weathered holidays and birthdays, Zoe's first without her mother. Alec's first, in many years, without his wife. It had seemed perfectly normal for Britt to stay. Important even. They rented adjoining houses, while Alec hired a contractor and rebuilt, consulting with Britt about many of his decisions. Their lives had fallen into a comfortable routine of togetherness. Zoe, not long ago, after a trip to the county fair, had declared herself happy. Alec and Britt had looked at each other with full hearts, recognizing a milestone.

Britt gazed out at the field. Zoe had assisted in a goal, and was jumping up and down with glee. Britt smiled broadly at the sight of her and gave her a thumbs up. Zoe's smile was radiant in the fading light of the autumn afternoon.

It had just seemed necessary to be here at first. To huddle together in a family circle, like covered wagons, in the aftermath of Greta's death and all the horror they had endured. But was it necessary anymore? Was she necessary anymore? "I don't know," she said.

Alec frowned. "Are you missing the excitement? The challenge?" he asked.

"I haven't had time to miss it," she said honestly. "There's been so much . . . This job has been perfect, because it was all I could manage to do with everything else that was going on."

"Right," he said.

"But things are settling down now," she said. "We're past the worst of it. You two are in the new house. Putting everything behind you. Zoe's adjusting to life without her mother. Luckily, she has a wonderful father. So, I guess you two can manage without me now," she said, trying to sound airy.

"We're kind of like a job you've finished doing . . ." he said with a shade of bitterness in his voice.

"No," said Britt, recoiling at the sound of it. "That's not true. I just meant . . ."

"Sorry," he said. "I didn't mean that. Look, if you want to leave, I don't blame you. Life here probably seems pretty dull to you. You could go anywhere. Do something glamorous. Not spend Saturdays assessing second-rate horseflesh with your . . . with us," he said.

"Oh, Alec, come on," she protested. "You know I look forward to our outings." She said it in a teasing way, but she had known, for a long time now, that the time she spent with them, with him, was the highlight of her week. The minute he had suggested that she join them on the trip to look over the horse, she had felt her heart lift. She would have been hurt and disappointed if they had decided to go without her. She did look forward to being with them, no matter how mundane the errand. That was the truth of it. "Maybe you two are getting tired of having me tag along everywhere. You shouldn't have to feel obligated to include me."

"Obligated?" he said incredulously.

"I mean it. We were kind of . . . thrown together. But you two have your own lives. Maybe it's time I moved on."

He held up a hand to silence her. "That's not the way it is," he said.

Britt remained quiet. *What was he supposed to say, after all?*

"Look, Britt. I guess I've been dreading this for a while. Knowing it might come up. And I understand why you would want to go. I do. But I have to tell you . . . we don't want you to go. We want you to stay here . . . with us. Zoe will always need you . . ."

"And she'll always have me," said Britt, faintly disappointed in his response.

There was a silence between them for a minute. They both looked at the field, but neither one of them knew what plays were being made. Finally, Alec cleared his throat.

"*I* need you," he said. "And I don't mean thousands of miles away. I need you here. I . . . rely on you now."

"Well, I've tried to help out," she said. "But you don't need me for that. You have the best instincts in the world. I know Zoe's coming into those difficult, teenage years, and you think she needs a woman's touch, but really, you'll know what to do. I've seen you in action. You're a whiz at this parenting thing."

"That's not it," he said.

"Look, Alec, I think this was good for all of us. This year together. We both know that Zoe needed all the attention and the . . . the love that we could give her. But, maybe it's time for you and I to think about . . . our own lives. You know."

"Right," he said. "We're holding you back."

"I don't mean that," she said. "It's just . . . well, suppose you meet someone, it's kind of like . . . I don't know. I'm in the way. I'm always around. Zoe's attached to me. It just makes everything more difficult."

Alec shook his head and sighed.

"What?" Britt asked.

"Don't lay this on me," he said. "I'm not the one who wants to leave town."

"I'm not laying anything on you," she protested. "I'm trying to think of what's best . . . for everybody. Look, this is an opportunity for me, and, well, the longer I stay here the harder it's going to be for me to go."

"Why?" he said.

"Why?" She felt suddenly flustered. "I don't know why. Because, I'll get settled, because it'll be difficult to say goodbye. . . ."

"Because you're happy?" he said.

"I like it here," she said defensively. "Vermont is beautiful . . ."

"Screw Vermont," he said impatiently. "Look, Britt. Let's stop playing games about this."

"I'm not playing games," she said indignantly.

He scowled, and shook his head. He hesitated, and then, he looked as if he had made up his mind. "I don't mean you," he said. "I'm talking about myself. Look, I know this isn't the time or place. And I don't want to embarrass you. Or myself." He cleared his throat. "But if you are really thinking of going, then this can't wait. I can't wait until it's too late. I remember what you said at Greta's funeral. Don't wait until it's too late to tell the people you love how you feel."

He turned to look at her, and she blushed at the intensity she saw in his gray eyes, even in the gathering twilight. "You said that," he reminded her. "Do you remember?"

Britt felt her heart beating in her throat. "I remember," she whispered.

"So, this is clumsy and stupid . . . We're sitting here eating pretzels and getting splinters in our butts . . ."

Britt smiled, as she often did, now that she knew him well, at his blunt manner.

"The point is, I love you, Britt. That's what it comes down to. You can tell me I'm horrible and out of line, but you better know that before you make up your mind to leave. Because I don't want you to go. Not now. Not ever."

Britt felt as if her whole body was vibrating. She was blushing at the surprise of it. She *was* embarrassed. And stunned. She'd never really allowed herself to think about it. Every smile, every glance, every kind gesture he had made toward her this last year . . . She'd told herself that it was all about Zoe. And of course it was. At first, that was all that either one of them had cared about. But somewhere along the line, her heart had changed. And now, he was telling her that his heart had changed, too. She looked across the field at Zoe who was loping along, confident that they were still there, urging her on, while she was at one with the game. Britt could feel Alec's silvery gaze upon her, wondering what she was going to say, asking for a decision, ready or not.

You'll never be ready, she thought. *Because no one can guarantee that you will never suffer. Never be hurt. Just the opposite. Loving someone guaranteed that somehow, some way, you* would *be hurt. But you could live your life with your heart open or closed. Time to choose.* His hand was clenched around the edge of the bleacher, his knuckles white. She felt young, and awkward and tongue-tied. Britt reached down and folded her hand over his. "Then we're agreed," she said. It was all she said, but when she met his gaze, her eyes told him the rest.

THE END

THE JOFFE BOOKS STORY

We began in 2014 when Jasper agreed to publish his mum's much-rejected romance novel and it became a bestseller.

Since then we've grown into the largest independent publisher in the UK. We're extremely proud to publish some of the very best writers in the world, including Joy Ellis, Faith Martin, Caro Ramsay, Helen Forrester, Simon Brett and Robert Goddard. Everyone at Joffe Books loves reading and we never forget that it all begins with the magic of an author telling a story.

We are proud to publish talented first-time authors, as well as established writers whose books we love introducing to a new generation of readers.

We have been shortlisted for Independent Publisher of the Year at the British Book Awards three times, in 2020, 2021 and 2022, and for the Diversity and Inclusivity Award at the Independent Publishing Awards in 2022.

We built this company with your help, and we love to hear from you, so please email us about absolutely anything bookish at feedback@joffebooks.com

If you want to receive free books every Friday and hear about all our new releases, join our mailing list: www.joffebooks.com/contact

And when you tell your friends about us, just remember: it's pronounced Joffe as in coffee or toffee!

ALSO BY PATRICIA MACDONALD

FROM CRADLE TO GRAVE
SISTERS
MISSING CHILD
I SEE YOU
CAST INTO DOUBT
DON'T BELIEVE A WORD
THE GIRL IN THE WOODS
SAFE HAVEN
MOTHER'S DAY
SECRET ADMIRER
LOST INNOCENTS
LITTLE SISTER
MARRIED TO A STRANGER
STOLEN IN THE NIGHT
NOT GUILTY
SUSPICIOUS ORIGIN

Printed in Great Britain
by Amazon

19225813R00212